Penge Library
020 3915 7066
www.capitadiscovery.co.uk/
bromley/login

Renewals
0333 370 4700
www.bromley.gov.uk/libraries

9/17

THE LONDON BOROUGH
www.bromley.gov.uk

Please return/renew this item
by the last date shown.
Books may also be renewed by
phone and internet

First Published in Great Britain 2017
By Mills & Boon, an imprint of HarperCollins*Publishers*
1 London Bridge Street, London, SE1 9GF

BIG LITTLE SECRETS © 2017 Harlequin Books S. A.

Heiress On The Run, *The Ranger's Secret* and *The Billionaire In Disguise* were first published in Great Britain by Harlequin (UK) Limited.

Heiress On The Run © 2014 Sophie Pembroke
The Ranger's Secret © 2009 Rebecca Winters
The Billionaire In Disguise © 2014 Soraya Lane

ISBN: 978-0-263-92980-5

05-0917

HEIRESS ON THE RUN

BY
SOPHIE PEMBROKE

Sophie Pembroke has been dreaming, reading and writing romance for years—ever since she first read *The Far Pavilions* under her desk in Chemistry class. She later stayed up all night devouring Mills & Boon books as part of her English degree at Lancaster University, and promptly gave up any pretext of enjoying tragic novels. After all, what's the point of a book without a happy ending?

She loves to set her novels in the places where she has lived—from the wilds of the Welsh mountains to the genteel humour of an English country village, or the heat and tension of a London summer. She also has a tendency to make her characters kiss in castles.

Currently Sophie makes her home in Hertfordshire, with her scientist husband (who still shakes his head at the reading-in-Chemistry thing) and their four-year-old *Alice-in-Wonderland*-obsessed daughter. She writes her love stories in the study she begrudgingly shares with her husband, while drinking too much tea and eating home-made cakes. Or, when things are looking very bad for her heroes and heroines, white wine and dark chocolate.

Sophie keeps a blog at www.SophiePembroke.com, which should be about romance and writing but is usually about cake and castles instead.

For Mum & Dad
for always believing I could

CHAPTER ONE

'I DON'T UNDERSTAND,' Faith said, fingers gripping the fabric of her uniform too tightly. The body-hugging grey pencil skirt didn't have a lot of give, but she needed something solid and real in her hands. Something that definitely existed. Unlike the plane that was supposed to be taking her and her latest tour group back to London. 'How can there not be a plane?'

The airport official had the air of a man who'd had this conversation far more times than he'd like today, and in more languages than he was really comfortable with. It was in no way reassuring. 'There is no plane, *signorina*, because there is no company any longer. It's been declared bankrupt. All customers of the Roman Holiday Tour Company are being asked to contact their insurance companies and—'

'But I'm not a customer!' Faith interrupted, her patience exhausted. She'd been in the airport for three hours now, and she really needed a cup of coffee. Or an explanation for what the hell had happened to trash her immediate future overnight. 'I'm an employee. I'm the tour guide.'

The official's gaze turned pitying. Faith guessed that meant she wasn't likely to get paid this month. Or ever. Great. Just when her bank account could really have done with the help. 'Then I suggest you call your employer. If you are able to find him.'

Oh, that really didn't sound good.

Turning away, Faith gave what she hoped was a reassuring smile in the direction of the huddle of tourists waiting for her to report back on their journey home. Holding up her index finger in the universal 'just one minute' gesture, she fished in her capacious bag for her phone. Time to find out what the hell was going on.

'Marco?' she asked, the moment the phone stopped ringing. 'What the hell—'

There was a click on the other end of the line. *Thank you for calling the Roman Holiday Tour Company! There is no one available to take your call right now...*

Her own voice on the voicemail message.

Faith hung up.

Around her, Leonardo da Vinci Airport buzzed with life. The sounds of crackly announcements and suitcase wheels on smooth flooring. The chatter of excited holiday-goers. The smell of fast food and strong coffee. The twelve British tourists standing around their suitcases, looking at her hopefully.

Faith took a deep breath, and approached. 'Okay, guys, here's the situation. I'll be honest, it's not great, but I'm still here and I will help you sort everything out, okay?' Maybe she wasn't getting paid any more, and maybe her boss had disappeared off the face of the earth, but she'd spent the last two weeks showing these people the sights and sounds of Italy. They trusted her. She owed it to them to at least make sure they got home safely. Maybe, that way, their memories of this holiday wouldn't just be of a total disaster.

No one actually relaxed at her words, but at least they looked slightly less terrified, which Faith figured was the best she could hope for, given the circumstances. *Now for the hard bit.*

'So, let's start at the top. Does everybody have travel insurance?'

It took a full two and a half hours, four cups of coffee, twenty phone calls, and plenty of sweet-talking, but eventually Faith had everyone either rebooked on other flights or safely ensconced in a hotel room until their insurance could organise their return home.

Everyone, that was, except for her.

Dropping down to sit on one of the airport benches, ignoring the guy asleep with his head on his backpack next to her, Faith pulled out her phone and tried Marco's number again.

Thank you for calling the Roman Holiday Tour Company! There is no one available to take your call right now...

She jabbed the end call button, dropped her phone into her lap, and closed her eyes. Okay, so, time to review the situation. Where was she?

She was in Rome! Centre of history, romance and really great pizza. She knew her way around, she had, ooh, twenty euros in her purse, she...was unemployed, homeless and stuck.

Faith sighed, and opened her eyes again, looking around the busy terminal. Everybody there seemed to know exactly where they were going, and how they were going to get there. She didn't even know where she was going to sleep tonight.

She could call Antonio, she supposed. Except for the part where she really, really couldn't. Ex-boyfriends weren't generally inclined to be hugely helpful when her life fell apart, she'd learnt the hard way, and the one she'd left in a fit of anger only two weeks earlier would probably throw her out on her ear. Or worse.

And since everyone else she knew in Rome was either part of Antonio's ridiculously extended family or related to her missing employer, or both, that pretty much exhausted the local options.

Which left her with…home. She should be back in London by now, ready to pick up her next group and embark on a tour of the Italian lakes. She guessed that was off, too. She'd barely seen more of the homeland than the cheapest airport hotel at Heathrow since she left Britain a year and a half ago, and even if she hadn't cut all ties with the friends she'd had before that, how could she just call up and say, *Hey, I'm kinda stranded. Want to buy me a plane ticket?*

No, the only people anyone could do that to were family. And she really didn't want to have to call them, either.

She had no doubt that dear old Mum and Dad, the Lord and Lady Fowlmere, would welcome her back into the bosom of the family in no time. After all, the publicity of the wild child heiress returned to the Fowlmere estate would make great copy, and her father always loved anything that made him look good in the press.

Faith had left home three years ago, ready to be herself for once, not an aristocratic relic to be trotted out for charity galas and other occasions, or a standing joke in the society pages. Going home now would undo all that hard work. Not to mention bring up the reasons she'd had to leave in the first place.

But it didn't look like she had an awful lot of choice.

Rubbing a hand across her forehead, Faith straightened her white blouse, then ripped off the hideous orange and red necktie that Marco insisted on his guides wearing and shoved it in her bag. It meant that the neckline of her blouse was a little more revealing than was entirely appropriate, but she didn't care. If she was going to have to call her family, she needed a drink first. And perhaps flashing a little cleavage as she walked into the airport bar would mean that she didn't have to waste any of her precious twenty euros buying it herself.

'Explain to me again how this happened.' Lord Dominic Beresford looked at the icy-cold bottle of Italian beer sitting on the bar in front of him with longing. He'd spent all day in meetings, worked in the cab all the way to the airport, and was just ready to switch off and relax before his late-night flight back to London, when Kevin, the Temp from Hell, called.

Dominic's beer would have to wait until he'd fixed whatever Kevin had screwed up now.

On the other end of the phone line, he could hear Kevin frantically turning pages in one of the many files Dominic was sure he had stacked on his desk. Stupid Shelley and her stupid maternity leave anyway. Wasn't keeping him sane a higher calling than a baby?

Dominic swept a finger down the beads of water on the neck of his beer bottle. Even he had to admit, probably not.

'Um, best I can tell, sir, your secretary booked in the tour guide with your usual company some months ago. And then...' Kevin trailed off nervously.

And then, Dominic filled in mentally, the owner of that usual company, Lady Katarina Forrester, also known at the time as his fiancée, had been caught on camera in a rather compromising position, leading to a media storm that had threatened his family's reputation.

So he'd called off the engagement. And in retaliation she'd cancelled their professional relationship, too.

Which left him with six American businessmen and -women flying into London tonight, expecting entertainment and tourism to go with their meetings. And probably, now he thought about it, hotel rooms, too. Kat had always taken care of the accommodation for his business guests.

The fact that this was almost entirely his own fault for getting involved with a business contact in the first place didn't make Dominic want that beer any less. He should have known better.

'I think I can remember what happened next,' he told Kevin drily. 'But I'm more interested in what happens now. Here's what I need you to do. First—'

'Um…' Kevin said, the way he always did when he was about to ruin Dominic's day. Surely Shelley didn't need a full year off with the baby. What if she didn't come back at all?

'What?' Dominic bit out.

'The thing is, it's nearly eight o'clock, sir. I'm supposed to finish work at five-thirty.' Kevin sounded more whiny than apologetic about the fact. How had Shelley ever thought he'd be a fitting replacement for her? Unless her mothering instinct had kicked in early. Kevin certainly needed taking care of.

'Add the hours onto your time sheet,' Dominic said, attempting reason. 'I'll make sure you're compensated for your time.'

'Thank you, sir. Only it's not just that. I've got a… commitment tonight I can't break.'

'A date?' Dominic tried to imagine the lanky, spotty Kevin with an actual woman, and failed.

'No!' The squeak in Kevin's voice suggested he had similar problems with the idea. 'Just a group I belong to. It's an important meeting.'

The thing with temps, Dominic had found, was you couldn't just threaten them with the sack. They always had something new to move onto, and no incentive to stay.

And, it was worth remembering, Kevin had screwed up almost every simple job Dominic had asked him to do in the last week. Sometimes, if you wanted a job done properly...

'Fine. Go. I'll fix it.'

The scrambling on the other end of the line suggested Kevin was already halfway out of the door. 'Yes, sir. Thank you.' He hung up.

Dominic gave the beer another wistful look. And then he called Shelley.

The wailing child in the background wasn't a good sign. 'Dominic, I am on maternity leave. I do not work for you right now.'

'I know that. But—'

'Are you sure? Because this is the fifth time you've called me this week.'

'In my defence, you weren't supposed to go on maternity leave for another two weeks.'

'I am very sorry that my son arrived early and disrupted your busy schedule.' She didn't sound very sorry, Dominic thought. She sounded sarcastic. 'Now, what do you want? And quickly.'

'The Americans. Kat cancelled all our bookings and—'

'Told you not to sleep with her.'

'And I need to find them somewhere to stay and someone to look after them while they're in London.'

'Yes,' Shelley said. 'You do.'

'Can you help?' He hated begging. Hated admitting he needed the assistance. But Shelley had been with him for five years. She knew how he worked, what he needed. She was part of the company.

Or she had been, until she left him.

She obviously still had more loyalty than Kevin, though. Sighing, she said, 'I'll check my contacts and text you some hotel names and tour companies you can try. But you'll have to wait until I've got Micah back off to sleep.'

'Thank you.'

'And this is the last time, Dominic. You're going to have to learn to work with Kevin.'

'I could just hire someone else,' Dominic mused. The thought of a whole year with Kevin was untenable.

'Fine. Whatever. I don't care. Just stop calling me!' Shelley hung up.

Placing his phone on the bar, Dominic looked at the bottle of beer. How long did it take to get a child off to sleep, anyway? He might as well have a drink while he was waiting. But, as he reached for the bottle, a woman boosted herself up onto the stool next to him and smiled.

Raising the bottle to his lips, Dominic took in the low-cut blouse, too-tight skirt and wild dark hair framing large hazel eyes. The smile on her wide lips was knowing, and he wondered if she'd recognised him. What she wanted from him. A drink. A night. A story to sell. She wouldn't be the first, whatever it was.

And whatever it was, she wouldn't get it. He'd made a mistake, letting Kat close enough to damage his reputation. It wasn't one he intended to make again—certainly not for one night with a pretty girl with an agenda.

But, to his surprise, the first words she said were, 'Sounds like you have a problem, my friend. And I think I can help you out.'

It wasn't the way she normally got work, but there was a lot to be said for serendipity, Faith decided. Walking into an airport bar, jobless and broke, and hearing a guy talk about how he needed a London tour guide and hotel rooms? That was an opportunity that was meant to be.

'And how, exactly, do you intend to do that?' the guy asked. He didn't look quite as convinced by coincidence as she was.

Faith held out a hand. 'I'm Faith. I'm a tour guide. I know London even better than I know Italy and Rome, and I've been running tours here for a year and a half. And it just so happens that I've finished one tour today, and I have a break before my next one.' She didn't mention the slight hiccup in her heartbeat at the idea of going home to London. Probably it would be fine. She could be in and out in a week or so, heading off on a plane to sunnier, less panic-inducing climes.

Besides, at this point, it wasn't as if she had a lot of other options.

'Dominic,' the guy said, taking her hand. He looked familiar, she realised. But then, after a while, all men in grey suits looked the same, didn't they? Maybe not quite as attractive as this one, though. His gaze was cool and evaluating. The high-end suit said 'successful businessman', the loosened tie said 'workaholic' and the beer said 'long day'. She could work with all of those. 'And how, exactly, do you know I need a tour guide?'

'I eavesdropped.' Faith shrugged, then realised the move strained her struggling blouse a little more than was wise in a professional environment. Maybe she should have left the necktie on.

'Not exactly the key quality I look for in an employee.' He frowned down at her cleavage with more distaste than she was used to seeing in a man.

'Really?' Faith asked. 'Someone who listens even when they're not required to and anticipates your needs? I've always found that rather useful.'

It was funny, Faith thought, the way you could watch someone re-evaluate you, and see the change in their attitude as a result. When she'd first sat down, she'd known all he saw was boobs and hair. Then she'd offered to help him, and his expression had changed from dismissive to interested. And now...now he was really intrigued.

'Okay, so, we've established I need a tour guide. I also need seven luxury hotel rooms in a central London five-star hotel.'

Thank goodness for airport Wi-Fi.

Logging into her browser from her smartphone, Faith scrolled through to the late booking accommodation site Marco always used, and set her search parameters. 'For tomorrow?'

Dominic nodded. 'Staying six nights.'

There weren't a lot of options, so Faith just presented him with the best one. 'How about the Greyfriars?' She turned the screen for him to see the eye-watering price, next to the photo of a hotel suite larger than the flat she'd shared with Antonio in Rome.

A slight widening of the eyes, a tight smile, and Faith knew he was re-evaluating her again. Good. She could be useful to him, and he could be even more useful to her. Time he realised that.

'The Greyfriars should work.'

Faith tapped a few more buttons on her tiny screen. 'I've reserved the rooms. Do you want to trust me with your credit card information, or call and speak with them directly?'

He raised his eyebrows, even as he pulled his wallet from his jacket pocket. For a moment, Faith thought he might actually hand it over, but then he picked up his phone, too. 'Give me the number.'

Grabbing her well used red notebook from her bag, Faith scribbled down both the phone number of the hotel and the reservation reference, and pushed the page across to him.

While he spoke with the receptionist, Faith ordered herself a glass of wine, hoping that Dominic would be impressed enough by her efficiency that she wouldn't have to rely on her last twenty euros for much longer.

So. She'd got the man his hotel rooms; surely he had to offer her the tour guide job now, right? Which meant his next question would be 'What do you want?' She needed to formulate an answer—one that didn't let on exactly how much more she needed his help than he needed hers.

What did she want? For Antonio never to have found out who she really was. For Marco not to have done a bunk. For her parents to be normal middle-class people. Teachers, perhaps. People who fitted in, which her parents certainly did not. She wanted to not have to worry that every camera or phone she saw might be about to send her picture soaring around the realms of social media, ready to be identified as Lady Faith, the Missing Heiress.

She wanted to have never been caught on camera leaving that hotel room, three years ago. That was a big one.

But right now, she'd settle for a ride back to London, a hotel room for the week, meals and drinks included, and maybe a small salary at the end of the job. Enough to tide her over until she found her next gig. It wouldn't take long; she was good at her job, she enjoyed it, and people liked her. That was important in the events and tourism industry.

'Thank you for your assistance,' Dominic said, and put down his phone. Faith looked up with a bright smile. Okay, she didn't really know who this guy was, or what business he was in, but he could afford seven rooms at the Greyfriars, so he could get her out of Rome without having to call her family, which was the most important thing.

'Let me tell you a little bit more about what I need,' he said, and Faith nodded, her best attentive face on. 'My name is Lord Dominic Beresford, and I run a number of businesses from my family's estates.' Faith's stomach clenched at the name. Of course he looked familiar. She'd probably seen him on the society pages a dozen times when she lived in London, usually next to photos of her mother looking tipsy behind her fake smile, or her father charming another man's wife. Or even of Faith herself, leaving the current London hotspot on the arm of someone very unsuitable. Lord Beresford, on the other hand, was always immaculately dressed and frowning.

'I have six American businessmen and -women arriving in London tomorrow morning,' Dominic went on, oblivious to the way her stomach was rolling. 'I need you to meet and greet them, plan entertainment for the hours they're not going to be in meetings, and accompany them on tours, the theatre, whatever you come up with.' He gave her a sharp look. 'Can you do it?'

Spend a week in the company of a man who could at any moment realise exactly who she was and expose her, all while avoiding anyone she knew in London, and working at the same time?

'Of course I can.'

Dominic nodded. 'Then we'll talk salary on the plane. Finish your drink; we'll go get you a ticket. But first…' He picked up his phone again, tapped a speed-dial number, and waited.

Was that crying Faith could hear in the background?

'Shelley?' Dominic said, almost shouting to be heard. 'Don't worry. I've fixed it.'

CHAPTER TWO

HE'D ASKED THE wrong question, Dominic realised, later that evening. He shouldn't have asked Faith if she could do the job. He should have asked her if she knew how to be quiet.

The answer was now startlingly obvious: no.

She'd chattered through the ticket line. All through security. Yammered on in the first-class lounge. And kept talking all the way to the gate and onto the plane.

And now they were cruising at thirty-two thousand feet, the cabin lights were dimmed, and she was still asking questions.

'Have you taken clients on the London Eye before? What about up the Shard? I haven't done that yet, but I've read reports…'

Grabbing another file from his briefcase, in the vain hope that the growing stack of them on the table in front of him might suddenly make her realise he was trying to work here, Dominic tried to tune out the chatter from the seat beside him. It wasn't as if she took a breath long enough for him to answer anyway.

Why did she have to sit next to him? First class was practically empty. There were plenty of places for her to stretch out, watch a movie, sleep. Not talk.

'Do you know if they're theatre buffs? I can do some

research on what's the hottest show in town when we land. Or maybe the opera?'

Of course, there were plenty of other questions he should have asked, too. Like why she was so eager to come work for a total stranger for over a week. Did she need to get out of Rome? Or was she just homesick? Jobless? He should have asked for credentials, for references, for anything that proved who she was. He hadn't even managed a glimpse of her passport as she handed it over to the ticket clerk.

It wasn't like him to be so impulsive. Yes, he'd been in a corner and needed a quick fix. And okay, he'd wanted to prove to Shelley and Kevin that he could manage quite well without them, thank you. He was still the boss, after all.

But if he was honest with himself, he knew the real reason he'd hired Faith was because of her attitude. It took guts to walk up to a stranger in an airport and tell them to give you a job. Guts and desperation, probably. But if she had a reason for needing this job, she hadn't let on. She'd focused entirely on what she could do for him, and it had worked.

Coupled with her curvaceous, striking appearance, that courage and determination meant she'd probably go far, in whatever she decided to do—if her blunt, frank manner didn't get her into trouble first. She was the exact opposite of anything he'd look for in a woman normally, but Faith wasn't a woman. Not to him, anyway. She was an employee, and that was a completely different thing.

Of course, she wasn't exactly like his other employees, either. Shelley, outspoken as she could be now, hadn't started that way. For the first year she hadn't questioned anything, hadn't complained, hadn't offered an opinion. And she'd still never be seen dead in a skirt as tight as Faith's. No, Shelley was beige suits and pastel blouses, where Faith was red lipstick and high heels.

Dominic didn't even waste time on a mental comparison between Faith and Kevin.

'And, uh, actually…I should have asked…'

Good grief, was there a question she hadn't blurted out already?

With a sigh, Dominic looked up at her, only to find her plump lower lip caught between white teeth, and an uncertainty in her eyes for the first time since they met.

'Yes?' he asked, surprised by her sudden change in demeanour.

'Will you want me to stay at the hotel with your guests?'

He blinked. 'Well, yes. That would be easiest.' He'd need to get an extra room, he realised. Efficient as she seemed to be, he could hardly leave his most important clients with a stranger for the next week. No, he'd need to stay there too, that much was obvious. But if Faith was staying in the hotel, at least he could delegate their more mundane requirements to her. 'Unless you have a pressing need to stay somewhere else?'

'No, no, it's not that.' She gave him a smile, an understated, nothing to worry about here smile. One he didn't entirely trust. His mother had smiled like that, in the weeks before she left. 'It's just that I've been living in Rome for the last year and a half. I don't actually *have* anywhere to stay in London.'

It was only when the muscles in his shoulders relaxed that Dominic realised they'd tensed at all. Of course she didn't have anywhere to stay. That made perfect sense.

It didn't entirely explain why she'd been so eager to leave Rome on a moment's notice, with only a pull-along suitcase for company, but Dominic was sure he could persuade her to tell him that story, in time. He was a very persuasive man when he put his mind to it. And he *really* wanted to know what Faith was running away from. Just in case it was something he needed to defend his reputation against.

'You'll have a room at the hotel,' he promised, before realising something else. 'But we'll need to see if we can get one for tonight, too.'

Faith glanced down at her watch, and he knew what she was thinking. By the time they got into London it would be the early hours. Anyone checking in last minute to a hotel at that kind of time wasn't usually there on business. Not the legitimate sort, anyway.

'Maybe it would be best if I checked into one of the airport hotels?' she suggested. 'That way, I'll be on hand ready to meet your clients there in the morning.'

It made perfect sense. And suddenly Dominic couldn't face the drive into London, all the way to his penthouse apartment, just in time to wake up and pack ready to move into a hotel for the week. 'Good plan,' he said. 'As soon as we land you can book us both in.'

She flashed him a smile, this one more confident, more teasing. 'Does that mean you're trusting me with your credit card at last?'

He'd have to, he realised. She'd need a method of payment for all the things he'd asked her to do, to set up. Even if it was just having some petty cash to make sure she could buy the Americans a coffee if they needed it.

'I'll call the bank in the morning, get you set up with a card linked to my expenses account.' The bank knew him well, and he certainly gave them enough business to request a favour. They could monitor the activity on that card. 'In the meantime, I'll provide you with some petty cash. A thousand should do it.'

'Right.' Her eyes were wide, he realised. She hadn't expected him to actually hand over his money. She had to realise, from the way he'd casually paid for her incredibly expensive last-minute seat in first class, that money wasn't much of an object to him these days. But it obviously was to her.

As was trust. Interesting.

Dominic had a feeling he had a lot still to learn about his latest employee.

But that could wait until London. 'And now, if you don't mind, I've got some work I'd like to finish before we land.'

She nodded, silent, and he turned back to his file, enjoying the peace and quiet. Who knew that all he had to do to stop Faith talking was offer her money and trust? If he'd have guessed, he would have tried it hours ago.

She couldn't just sit there. Apart from anything else, it was boring. What was in those files that Dominic found so fascinating?

Faith wasn't a sitting still and waiting kind of girl. She got fidgety.

Besides, the longer she sat there, staring out of the aeroplane window at the night skies, the more she imagined, in detail, every possible way this whole plan could go wrong. It wasn't a pretty list.

He wanted to get her a credit card. Which meant he'd need her full name. She'd managed to avoid him seeing her passport information, just, but he'd have to have it for the bank. What did she do? If she gave him a fake name, the bank might not authorise the card and she'd have to explain everything anyway. No, the only option was to give him her real name, minus the assorted titles, and hope he didn't recognise it.

At least Dominic didn't seem like the sort to spend his mornings reading the society pages, however often he appeared in them.

She needed to know more about him, Faith decided. If she knew who he was, what mattered to him, she might be able to predict his response if he figured out who she was. Would he drag her back to her parents by her hair, as her great-uncle had threatened? Or would he out her to the media, like Antonio had said he would? Or would he let her slip back out of the country, quiet and safe, to carry on living her own life?

If only she could be sure.

Faith sighed and, beside her, Dominic made a small irritated sound. One thing was clear: she wasn't going to find out all about her new employer by asking him questions when he was trying to work. No, she'd have to do this the modern way—Internet stalking. Surely the airport hotel would have free Wi-Fi?

'Do you have to think so loudly?' Dominic asked, reordering his papers again so half of them crept over the edge of the table, almost onto her lap.

'I'm pretty sure thinking is, by definition, a fairly quiet activity,' Faith said, shoving the papers back up onto the table.

'Not the way you do it.'

Right. Well, if she couldn't talk *or* think, maybe it was time to go and find something more interesting to do. Somewhere Dominic wasn't.

'Okay, let me out.' She nudged her elbow against his side, and he looked up in surprise.

'Where are you going?' he asked.

'Somewhere I can think without disturbing your hypersensitive hearing.' Yes, he was difficult and crazy, but he was at least paying for her to get back home. Best not to totally annoy him this early in the game.

Shuffling his papers back into a neat stack, Dominic slid out of his seat, into the wide, wide aisle. God, she'd missed first class.

'Don't get into any trouble,' he said, looking disturbingly like Great-Uncle Nigel.

Faith gave him her most winning, most innocent smile. 'Me? I never get into trouble.'

And then, leaving him looking utterly unconvinced, she sashayed through towards business class to find some more interesting people to annoy with her questions and her thinking.

He was being ridiculous. How could it be harder to concentrate without Faith beside him, fidgeting, talking and *thinking*, than it was when she was there?

But somehow, it was.

Pushing his files across the table, since he clearly wasn't going to be able to concentrate on them tonight, Dominic leant back in his seat and considered. Where would she have gone? They were on a plane, for heaven's sake. It wasn't as if she could have run away. If they'd been sitting in any other area of the aircraft, he'd have suspected her of running off to first class to try and win over the affections of a wealthy businessman.

He glanced around the small section of seats on his side of the curtain. No sign of her. The only other occupants—an elderly gentleman in a suit and a woman with a pashmina wrapped around her, almost covering her face—were both asleep.

Maybe she'd gone back to business class to find a new friend there. Maybe the promise of a job with him wasn't enough. Maybe she just needed him for the flight home, and now she'd moved onto looking for her next opportunity...

Dominic forced himself to stop that line of thought. Just because certain women behaved that way, taking what they wanted then running, leaving destruction in their path, didn't mean that Faith would. He should give her the benefit of the doubt. Hadn't he just told her he trusted her enough to hand over a significant amount of money? Of course, money came easy to him, these days. Reputation was much harder won.

On the other hand, she was his employee. His responsibility.

The only responsible thing to do, really, was go find her.

To Dominic's surprise, there was no sign of Faith in business class. He got some funny looks as he peered across darkened seats, trying to spot a dark, curly head, but he ignored them. Maybe she'd found a steward or something to talk to? At least she hadn't been heading the right way to try and bother the pilot...

Pushing through the curtain, business class gave way to economy, where the occasional empty seats ended, replaced by cramped and crowded rows of people. Many were sleeping—it was the middle of the night, after all—but there were more screens and lights on than in either of the other sections. Dominic supposed it was harder to get some shut-eye when you were crammed in like cattle.

Faith must have disappeared into the bathroom, he decided. He just hoped that she was alone—the last thing his reputation needed was an article in the press about him and his employee being banned from an airline for joining the mile-high club. It wouldn't matter to a reporter that Dominic hadn't been the man with Faith at the time. Those sort of details never did, he'd found.

But then, as he turned back to try and get some more work done before landing, he spotted her and stopped, just to watch.

She was crouched down at the front of the economy section, just beside the seats with the space for a baby's bassinet against the wall; he must have walked right past her on his way through. Her dark head was bent over a bundle in her arms, and when she looked up at the parents of the child she was holding, her face glowed. Smiling, she whispered away in rapid Italian, all while tucking in blankets and stroking the baby's fine, downy hair.

This wasn't what he'd expected. In fact, this wasn't even recognisable as the woman he'd hired. Except... As he got closer, he caught a few English words scattered in her conversation. Big Ben. Madame Tussauds. The Tube.

A smile tugged at the corner of Dominic's mouth. She was offering them tourist advice. Planning their trip to London with them.

Without drawing attention to himself, Dominic slipped past, back through the curtain to where his files were waiting.

Perhaps he had hired the right woman, after all.

CHAPTER THREE

IT TOOK FAITH a moment to remember where she was when she woke up the next morning. Smooth white cotton sheets, rain battering the window, the glow of a reading lamp she obviously hadn't managed to turn off before she passed out the night before. Definitely not the flat she'd shared with Antonio and, given the rain, probably not even Rome.

No, Faith knew that rain. Knew that cold splatter and relentless fall.

She was in England. London.

Exactly where she shouldn't be, ever again.

Faith buried her head deeper into the pillow, as if she could block out the grey and the rain and the sheer London-ness of it all. She hadn't had a choice, she reminded herself. She'd made the best decision she could in a difficult situation.

But she couldn't help but wonder about all the people she'd left behind when she ditched the city she loved the first time. Were they still there? What would she do if she saw one of them on the street? Turn and walk the other way, or brazen it out?

She guessed she wouldn't know unless it happened.

Hopefully it wouldn't. In and out, that was the key. Do the job, take the money and run.

So, back to the job. And her employer.

Dominic had chosen the most expensive of the air-port hotels once they'd landed in Heathrow, which hadn't really surprised her at that point. To be honest, she could have slept in a chair in the terminal, she was so tired. But the blissfully soft pillows and firm mattress of the hotel room were a definite improvement.

Reluctantly pushing herself up into a seated position, shoulders resting against the headboard, she tried to wake up enough to get a handle on the day ahead. Dominic had said the Americans were arriving around eleven, and it was only eight-thirty. So she had plenty of time to shower, dress…wait. What was she going to wear? She had her uniforms from the Roman Holiday Tour Company, she had her going-out-for-dinner dress and she had some jeans and plain T-shirts. She hadn't exactly packed for corporate events when she'd left Rome. She'd packed for an overnight in London and then another tour.

It would have to be the uniforms, she supposed, for now at least. Maybe she could ask Dominic about an advance on her wages, or even a clothing allowance. Given the disapproving look he'd given her outfit in the bar the night before, she suspected he might be amenable.

A knock on the door dragged her thoughts away from her wardrobe and onto her growling stomach. Was that room service? Had she remembered to leave the breakfast card out the night before? She really hoped so. She was useless without a decent meal in the morning.

Swinging her legs out of bed, she glanced down at her rather skimpy red nightgown—a present from Antonio, of course. He never did have any concept of subtle. Still, she supposed that room service had probably seen much worse.

Except, when she yanked open the door with a smile, it wasn't room service.

Dominic's eyes travelled down over her body at an offensively quick speed. Any other man, Faith knew, would have lingered over her curves, outlined in red silk. Any other man would have enjoyed the view of her bare legs.

Her new employer, however, merely catalogued her attire and raised an eyebrow at her. 'Do you always open your door dressed like a lingerie model?'

Faith felt the heat flush to her face. 'I thought you were room service with breakfast.'

'I'm afraid if you want breakfast you'll have to get dressed. Assuming you have something more suitable to wear...' His eyes flicked over her shoulder to where her skirt and blouse from the day before lay draped over a chair. Faith winced when she noticed the pale pink lace bra lying on top of them.

'Actually, that was something I wanted to talk to you about...'

Dominic glanced at his watch. 'No time. Get dressed and we'll talk over coffee, before we head over to arrivals.'

'I thought your clients didn't get in until eleven?' Faith asked, confused.

'They don't.' Dominic was already walking away down the corridor. 'But you need a briefing before they arrive.'

He turned a corner and was gone. Apparently busy executives didn't have time to finish conversations properly. Or tell people where to meet them when they were decently dressed.

An elderly couple appeared at the end of the corridor and Faith realised, a little belatedly, that she was standing in the open in her really inappropriate nightie. Stepping back inside her room, she shut the door firmly behind her and headed for the shower.

Time to prove to Lord Dominic Beresford that she was capable of doing any job he needed doing, whatever she was wearing.

Good God, did she sleep in that every night? Even when she was alone and exhausted and straight off a plane, Faith managed to slip into a sexy little number for bed. Dominic shook his head. What kind of a devil temptress had he hired?

Unless, of course, she'd put it on especially for him that morning. Unless she planned to seduce and ruin him, just like Katarina had tried to do. Just like his mother had done to his father.

It was all still a little too neat. Dominic didn't believe in coincidences, or serendipity, or any of the other things Faith had chattered about on the plane, her smile too wide, her lips too tempting. She'd been in exactly the right place at exactly the right time and, in his experience, that sort of thing didn't happen without some forward planning.

Still, he did need a tour guide, and she seemed to be an adequate one. All he had to do was stay out of her way while she worked, and she'd never get the chance to put any sort of plans into action. It would be fine.

As soon as he could erase that image of her in fiery red silk from his brain.

Figuring she'd take an insane amount of time to shower and dress, Dominic headed down to the restaurant and ordered coffee while he perused the papers. He wasn't much for breakfast, but he'd grab a piece of toast or some fruit when Faith joined him. They had too much to discuss to waste time on food.

However she'd come into his life, and whatever she hoped to get out of it, the only thing that mattered to Dominic was that she did the job he hired her to do: take care of his clients. He knew his strengths weren't always in the socialising side of things—he'd generally rather be in his office. That was why his arrangement with Katarina had worked so well. She'd taken care of the smiling, small talk and looking interested side of things. He took care of the business.

Bloody Katarina. She was right up there with Shelley on his list of women determined to thwart him right now. He just hoped that Faith wouldn't be added to it before she and the Americans left at the end of next week.

Sooner than he'd expected, Faith appeared at the entrance to the hotel restaurant. She waved a hand in his direction but, instead of heading for his table, she made for the breakfast buffet.

Holding in a sigh, Dominic watched as she bypassed the platters of fruit and the glass containers full of cereal. Instead, she loaded up her plate with eggs, bacon, sausage, beans, fried bread…and grabbed a side plate for a couple of mini pastries, too.

Apparently those curves were made entirely of breakfast.

'Hungry?' he asked, eyebrow raised, as she finally made it to the table.

Depositing her plates, Faith ripped off a bite of *pain au chocolat* as she dropped into her seat. 'Starving. Do you think they'll bring me some tea?'

His mother's lessons in etiquette and good manners towards women were deeply ingrained, and Dominic found himself motioning over a waiter to request a pot of tea and more coffee for himself before he even realised he was doing it.

'You've eaten already?' Faith asked, after swallowing an enormous forkful of eggs and toast.

'I don't usually eat breakfast,' he replied, folding his paper neatly across the middle and placing it on the empty table beside them. 'Especially when I've an important day ahead.'

'That's just when you need it,' Faith said, sounding eerily like a nanny he'd had when he was eight.

'I've made it this far. I think I'll survive. Now. To business.' Casting his gaze over her outfit, he was relieved to find it less revealing than the day before, and certainly less fantasy-inducing than the silk concoction she'd had on first thing. The skirt, he realised, was the same as yesterday, but paired with a plain white T-shirt. Still, while the higher neckline hid the very tempting cleavage the blouse had displayed, it emphasised her curves even more.

I'm not thinking about this. I am not *thinking about this.*

Of any man alive, surely he knew better than most the perils of giving in to temptation and forgetting obligations. Faith was here to work, and that was all. He had to remember that.

'Yes. Work,' Faith said, bringing his attention back to the topic at hand. 'I wanted to run through a few things with you, actually.' To his surprise, she whipped a small notebook from her bag, uncapped a pen and sat poised to write down his answers. 'First, can your office send me an itinerary for the week so I know exactly what you've got planned for your guests, and I can work around it? Also, it means I can make myself available if anyone has any questions between meetings.'

'I'll ask Kevin to fax one over,' he said, trying to remember if Kevin even knew how to work the fax machine.

'Great. Once I have that, I'll put together a tentative itinerary and email it to you for your approval.'

'You'll need a laptop,' Dominic realised, belatedly.

'No need.' Pulling a tablet computer from her bag, she waved it at him. 'I use this.'

He blinked at her. 'Well, great. Okay then.'

'Next, do you have any background details on the clients themselves? Their lives, their families, their businesses, anything that I can use to get to know them?'

'You do realise you're a tour guide, not a dating service, right? You don't need to find them their perfect match.'

Her face turned stony, and he regretted the joke. She was trying to do a good job, after all. He should be encouraging her, not ridiculing her.

'These people are a long way from home for almost two whole weeks. It's my job to make sure they enjoy themselves and feel comfortable here. Knowing a little about them makes that easier. I'll talk to them myself when they arrive, of course, but a little forward knowledge would mean I can get going sooner.'

'Of course,' Dominic said contritely. 'Well, their businesses I can tell you about. But, as for the rest of it…' He spread his hands out. 'Katarina used to handle that sort of thing, I'm afraid.'

Faith paused with her mini cinnamon swirl halfway to her mouth. Katarina. That was a new name. 'Is Katarina your secretary?' If so, she could call and ask her for all the gossip.

'No. Not my secretary.' Dominic shifted in his chair,

looking sorry he'd ever mentioned the woman. Not a
secretary. Then...

'Your wife?'

He sighed, and reached for the coffee. 'My ex-fiancée,
actually. But, more pertinently, she runs the company
we usually use for this sort of thing.'

'But not this time,' Faith said.

'No. Not this time.'

'Because you split up.'

Dominic gave her an exasperated look. 'Can't you
ever take a hint to stop asking questions?'

Faith shrugged unapologetically. 'I like to know exactly where I stand with things. Makes life a lot less
complicated.'

'Well, she doesn't matter any more. She's gone.
You're here now to take her place,' Dominic said, entirely matter-of-fact.

Faith felt a peculiar squirming feeling in her stomach. 'As a tour guide. Not as your fiancée.'

Dominic looked up, appalled. 'That goes without
saying!'

Faith flushed. 'You don't have to be quite so horrified at the prospect,' she muttered.

'Right. No. I just meant...' He sighed. 'This is a business arrangement, for both of us. Katarina...she's out
of the picture now, and I'm afraid you can't really call
her for insights on our guests.'

Now, that was interesting. Surely the woman would
have an assistant or something that Faith could call for
some notes. For Dominic to be so certain she wouldn't
help, something pretty dramatic had to have happened
between them.

'Bad break up?' she asked.

'The worst,' Dominic groaned, and for the first

time since she'd met him in that airport bar he seemed human. Normal. As if he had actual emotions and feelings, rather than a sensor that told him when to be disapproving of something.

'Want to talk about it?' she asked.

'Not even a little bit.' He didn't leave any room for discussion.

Oh well. Human moment over.

'Okay, well, if you can't tell me about them as people, you must be able to tell me why they're here. What's the very important business you have with them?'

Dominic leaned back in his chair. 'I'm looking to expand the activities and operations we have running on the Beresford estate. We're considering buying up some neighbouring land to build on, as well as utilising the Beresford family's London properties.'

In which case, Faith thought, they'd be one of the only aristocratic families to actually *increase* their family estates in generations. 'So these guys are your investors?'

Dominic nodded. 'Potential investors. But also potential clients. They want to see what we have on offer, and possibly use Beresford Hall in the future for international corporate retreats.'

'Okay, that helps. Now, they've visited London before, right? I don't suppose you've got a record of what they've seen and done…?' Dominic winced. 'No. Of course not.'

Faith sighed. Looked as if she was doing this the hard way. In which case, she really needed a kick-ass outfit to give her confidence.

'Okay, since you can't actually give me any practical help to do my job—'

'I gave you the job itself, didn't I?' Dominic's words

came out almost as a growl, and Faith decided to change tack.

'And in order that I can do it to the best of my ability and present the right impression of your company to your clients...I was wondering if there might be some sort of clothing allowance involved...'

His eyes did that quick flash over her body again, and Faith gave thanks she hadn't put the other, scoop neck, T-shirt on that morning. Not that he'd have noticed, of course. All he seemed to care about was that she wasn't wearing some boring suit.

'You're right,' Dominic said. 'I do need you to make the right impression.'

Faith perked up a bit. 'So you'll give me money to go shopping?'

Dominic shook his head, and the smile that spread across his face was positively devilish. 'No. I'll take you shopping to find something suitable.'

Something suitable. Faith slumped down into her chair a little.

Why did she suspect that Dominic's idea of 'suitable' would translate into something she'd never usually wear in a million years?

CHAPTER FOUR

'I'M NOT WEARING THAT.'

Dominic sighed and turned towards his newest employee with his best 'I'm the boss' face in place. Faith stared back at him, unaffected.

He hadn't expected the airport to be a shopping Mecca—he was normally more concerned with finding a quiet spot in the first-class lounge to work when he passed through. Still, he knew that there were plenty of shops, and that people enjoyed taking advantage of them.

Sadly, it hadn't occurred to him that most of them would be selling holiday apparel, especially at this time of year. Options for professional attire were somewhat limited.

'It's a suit, Faith. An inoffensive grey suit. It's perfectly respectable. What's wrong with it?'

'What's wrong with it?' Eyebrows raised, she parroted his words back at him. 'It's a suit. A perfectly respectable, inoffensive suit. Do I look like the sort of woman who likes to appear respectable and inoffensive?'

'Well, you don't look like a Beresford employee yet, if that's what you mean.' Hooking the clothes hanger back onto the rail, he smiled apologetically at the shop assistant and followed Faith back out of the shop, into

the crowded terminal. A large clock, hanging somewhere overhead like a countdown, told him his clients
would be arriving in less than an hour, and Faith still
looked like a waitress in a university bar.

'Look, here's the deal,' he said, waiting until she
stopped walking and turned to face him before con-
tinuing. 'If you want to work for me, you have to look
like a professional, grown-up woman.'

'As opposed to?' Faith asked, eyebrows raised.

How to put it… In the end, Dominic decided to err
on the side of caution. 'This is a bigger, more important
job. You can't just look like a tour guide.'

Faith's mouth tightened, and Dominic prepared himself for an onslaught of objections. But instead, eyes
narrowed, she held out a hand. 'Give me the money.'

'What?'

She rubbed her fingers together. 'Hand over the cash
you would have spent on that hideous suit. Then go and
get yourself a coffee.'

'And what are you going to do?' Against his better
judgement, Dominic was already pulling the notes from
his wallet. It hadn't been a cheap suit.

'I'm going to show you that you don't have to spend
a fortune on something that looks the same as what everyone else is wearing to look professional.' She took
the money and tucked it into her bag. 'I'll meet you over
there in forty-five minutes.' Then, waving her hand in the
direction of a coffee shop, she walked off, leaving him
a few hundred pounds lighter, and minus one employee.

Apparently, she'd taken the trust he'd promised her,
and run with it.

If there was one thing Faith knew, it was how to shop
for clothes. Growing up, her mother had instilled in

her the need to look polished, appropriate and, above all, expensive. In the years when her father had spent most of the estate income on a horse that didn't come in or a woman who visited far too frequently, wearing something new and fabulous to every occasion could be something of a problem. And once her parents had finally admitted that the money was gone, and Faith said goodbye to her boarding school blazer, trying to fit in at the local secondary school, even in the same polyester skirt as everyone else, had been a whole new challenge.

There, clothes had been the least of her worries. There, she'd been the rich kid with no money, the posh kid who swore like a sailor, the girl who thought she was too good for them, even if she didn't. There'd been no place for her at all, no little corner to fit in, and the loneliness of it still burned if she thought about it too much. She'd spent lessons daydreaming about being someone else. About leaving home, her parents and her title behind her. Of being Just Faith, instead of Lady Faith.

She'd thought she'd managed it, once she left school and moved to London. Thought she was her own person for once. Except it was so easy to fall in with people who she realised, too late, only wanted her for her title. Women who had closets of spare outfits to dress her up in, dresses and skirts that cost a fortune but barely had the structural integrity to survive a night of dancing and drinking at whatever club they used her name to get into.

They definitely weren't the sort of clothes Dominic wanted her wearing on this job.

Later, living abroad, alone and with only her seasonal tour earnings to keep her, clothing hadn't been a priority. She'd been her own person for the first time ever, and she hadn't had to dress a certain way to prove it.

The sense of freedom, of relief, was enough. So she had uniforms for work and a small, flexible, casual wardrobe for the rest of the time.

Dominic had been right about one thing—not that she'd admit it to him—this new job required new clothes.

But she'd be damned if she was spending the next week and a half in one plain, boring suit.

She didn't have long, so she worked a strike attack formula, identifying the three closest mid-range high street stores most likely to stock the sort of thing she needed. In the first, she picked up two skirts—one grey, one black—and a couple of bright cardigans. In the next, a jacket, three blouses and a lightweight scarf. The last shop took the largest chunk of her money, but in return provided her with a pair of low heels that looked professional, but that she could walk miles in. When she mixed in the plain T-shirts, underwear, bag, dress, make-up and jewellery she'd brought with her from Rome, she thought she was pretty much prepared for anything Lord Dominic Beresford could throw at her that week.

Stepping out of the last shop, laden with bags, she checked her watch. Five minutes left. Just enough time to change.

It was strangely gratifying to walk into the coffee shop and realise that Dominic hadn't even recognised her. He glanced up when she walked in, but his gaze flicked quickly away from her and back to the clock on the wall. He expected her to be late.

Dumping her bags on an empty chair, she dropped into the seat opposite him and grinned as his eyes widened. This time, he studied her carefully, taking in the jacket and blouse—worn over her white T-shirt to en-

sure maximum modesty in the cleavage department—
and the way she'd pinned her hair back from her face.

She gave him a minute to appreciate the transformation, then said, 'This works for you?'

Dominic nodded.

'Great.' Grabbing his coffee from in front of him,
she drained the last inch of caffeine. 'Then let's go meet
your clients.'

He had to stop looking at her. What kind of a professional impression did it make if he couldn't stop staring
at his employee? It was just…a transformation. Faith
looked respectable, efficient, and yet still utterly herself. And he still didn't quite understand how she'd managed to make his money stretch to the bags and bags of
shopping he'd had to send back to the hotel before they
headed to arrivals.

Now, while his driver loaded up their suitcases and
Faith's shopping at the hotel, they were waiting in the
arrivals hall for the next flight in from JFK. He could
have sent a driver to meet them, Dominic supposed, but
Kat had always hammered home the importance of the
personal touch. And since she wasn't here to be personal
any longer, that just left him. And Faith.

His gaze slid left again, taking in the way she gripped
her fingers tightly in her other hand. Was she nervous?
Did Faith really get nervous? It seemed unlikely.

'They're a nice bunch,' he said awkwardly, in an attempt to set her mind at ease.

'I'm sure.'

'They'll like you.'

She rolled her eyes at him. 'Of course they will.
Being likeable is part of my job description.'

'Really?' Dominic glanced at her again. 'You don't seem to be trying that hard with me.'

Faith flapped a hand at him. 'Don't lie, you adore me. Besides, you matter less.'

'I am the boss,' he reminded her. Just in case she'd forgotten. He was starting to wonder...

'Yeah. So you'll be taking care of them in meetings and things, right? I'll be with them the rest of the time. When they're having fun. So it's important they think I'm a fun person to be around. You'll probably be back in the office by then anyway, so what do you care?'

It should set his mind at ease, Dominic thought, knowing that she wasn't expecting him to be around all the time, holding her hand through this job. She obviously believed she was capable enough to get on with it alone. And, against the odds, he was starting to believe that too.

So why was he mentally reshuffling his calendar to figure out which evenings he could join them on their tours and outings?

'You're right,' he said, shaking away the uncomfortable thought. 'As long as you keep them entertained and happy, that's all that matters.'

'Good.' Faith nodded, then sucked in a breath as the words and numbers on the display board changed again. 'Because they're here.'

She was not afraid. She *was* not afraid. She was *not* afraid.

She'd done this a million times before. The meet and greet was the most important part, sure—people tended to stick with their first impressions, even when they claimed not to. But she was good at this. Good at smiling and welcoming and helping and making people feel at home.

So why were her hands clammy?

Maybe it was the clothes. Maybe she should have gone with the stupid suit…

'That's them,' Dominic said, and then it was too late to worry about any of it anyway, because they were surging forward into handshakes and smiles and polite greetings. Faith beckoned over the driver who'd met them in the arrivals hall to start collecting bags onto a trolley, glad of something real and useful to do. Something she knew and understood. How could she have thought that looking after a group of high-powered businesspeople in London would be the same as shepherding holidaying Brits around Italy? They were already launching into conversations with Dominic that she couldn't even begin to follow. The three letter acronyms alone were baffling.

The drive into London, in a spacious limo complete with high-end coffee machine, at least gave her a chance to get her latest charges straight in her head. There was Henry, large and jocular—easy to remember, as long as she kept picturing Henry VIII when she looked at him. Next was Bud, skinnier in the face but a little rotund around the middle. Like a bottle of beer. Perfect.

The first two names fixed, she turned to the next pair. Both in navy suits, both dark-haired, both serious-looking. Thank God one of them wore glasses or she'd be getting them confused all week. Their names, however, were even easier—an improbable ice cream concoction of Ben and Jerry. As long as she remembered that Jerry had the glasses, she was golden.

The last two of Dominic's clients were easy, too. The blonde woman in the fantastic red suit was Marie, which made Faith think of Marilyn, which made her think of Monroe. And the brunette in the more severe black trouser suit with spectacular heels was Terri, who could just be the one she couldn't think of a great mnemonic for. Five out of six wasn't bad.

With everyone straight in her head, Faith settled back in her seat to nurse her espresso, and try to make some sort of sense of the conversation. She followed the discussion about land purchase and architects all right, until they started throwing out figures and referencing forms. She sighed to herself and decided she needed to have attended at least six months of previous meetings to even begin to understand.

'I'm guessing this is kinda dull for you,' Ben—no, glasses! Jerry—said, leaning in to whisper close to her ear.

'Not dull,' Faith objected. 'Just…not my area of expertise.'

Jerry's eyes flashed down to her blouse. 'And what exactly is that? Dominic didn't say.'

'Faith is your tour guide for the week,' Dominic said sharply, from the other end of the car. Faith looked up in surprise; she hadn't realised he was paying any attention to her. And how had he even heard Jerry from there?

Suddenly all attention was on her. Plastering on her best social smile, Faith said, 'That's right. So if you've any thoughts on places you'd like to go, things you'd like to see, just let me know!'

'Oh, I can think of a couple,' Jerry murmured, still looking at her breasts. Faith shuffled a little further away, until her leg pressed up against the car door.

Looking up, she saw Dominic glaring at her. He couldn't have heard Jerry's latest comment, but surely he had to know this wasn't her idea?

Or not. Turning his attention back to his clients, Dominic launched into another highly dense and baffling business conversation. Faith listened for a moment until she spotted Marie giving her a sympathetic smile. Then, tuning out the figures and the jargon, she pulled her tablet from her bag and started planning the week ahead.

She might not understand Dominic's job, but she was damn good at her own, thank you.

Dominic needed to get out of cars and hotels and into the office. How was he expected to concentrate on the finer details of the outstanding contract when one of his clients was hitting on Faith?

She'd handled it well, professionally even, but he was under no illusions that she wouldn't let rip if the guy pushed his luck. And quite rightly, too. Perhaps he should have a little word with Jerry...

The Greyfriars Hotel was a hit with his guests, proving Faith's knowledge of the luxury hotel market spot on. Procuring an extra room for himself wasn't difficult—although booking the penthouse suite seemed a little excessive even to him, given he had his own apartment just across town. Still, it looked as if it would be a long week. He'd probably need a luxurious space to relax at night.

'So,' Faith said as she handed out keycards, 'I know you've got meetings planned this afternoon, but what would you like to do this evening? Sleep off your jet lag, or go out and party?'

Dominic was secretly hoping for the sleeping option, but the Americans all seemed to be up for a party.

Faith clapped her hands together. 'Great! I'll make sure to come up with something really special.'

Maybe he didn't have to go. After all the meetings in Rome, plus this afternoon to get through, he could really use the time in the office. Surely Faith would be okay without him?

But then he saw Jerry sidling up to Faith with his spare keycard in hand.

Stepping closer, he heard her say, 'Oh, I wouldn't worry. If you lose it, the hotel can make you another one.' She pushed the card back into Jerry's hand, and Dominic gave a mental cheer.

As Jerry stalked off towards his room, not looking particularly beaten, Dominic leant in towards Faith. 'Count me in for whatever tonight's activity is.'

She turned to him and scowled. 'Don't think I can handle it by myself?'

He grinned. 'Oh, I'm certain that you can. I just want to watch the show.'

The smile she gave him in return was positively devilish, and he didn't even try not to watch as she walked towards the lifts, hips swinging.

Maybe he wouldn't have that word with Jerry. It might be far more satisfying to watch Faith cut him down herself.

He'd just make sure he was on hand in case she needed any assistance.

CHAPTER FIVE

HER HOTEL ROOM was bigger than most of the apartments she'd lived in since leaving home, but somehow Faith still found herself down in the hotel coffee bar, just off the lobby, as she planned out the week's entertainment. She told herself it was because the Wi-Fi connection was faster, or because she'd be able to see the clients and Dominic arriving back at the hotel after their meetings. But actually, it was just a whole lot less lonely than sitting upstairs on her own.

She missed Antonio. Well, actually, that wasn't true. She didn't miss *him* exactly. More the idea of him. What she'd thought he was. A future, a family, a proper place in the world. A life that revolved around who she really was, who she wanted to be—not what other people expected of her.

Well, now she'd just have to find her own new place to belong. Wasn't as if she hadn't done it before. Maybe, if she did a good enough job, Dominic would take her on full-time, replacing the infamous Katarina on a more long-term basis.

Except that would put her closer to her old life than she was comfortable with. No, better to get the job done then move on. Again.

Faith's finger hovered over the touch screen of her

tablet, ready to type in her search for availability at London tourist hot spots that evening. But instead she found herself typing in the name Dominic Beresford.

She shouldn't feel guilty about this, she told herself, as page after page of results scrolled up. She was researching a new employer—standard procedure. Dominic would probably have done the same to her, although hopefully using the name Faith Fowler, one she'd made her own on the Continent. The only stories of interest about her were tall tales of the Italian landscape, and reviews of popular tourist destinations. Nothing to alarm him, and absolutely no photos.

There were lots of photos of Dominic, though. Photos of him glowering at the camera, as flashbulbs went off around him. Photos of him with an icy-cool blonde on his arm, almost as tall as he was, perfect pout in place for the paparazzi. That must be Katarina, she supposed.

Lady Katarina Forrester, in fact, according to the caption. Faith didn't know her, she didn't think, but that wasn't hugely surprising. She'd never been particularly enthusiastic about socialising with the aristocratic set—at least, not the respectable ones—whatever her mother's dreams of her finding a perfect, financially supportive match amongst them. There hadn't been a space for her there. Her place at boarding school hadn't been the only thing she lost when the money was gone.

Her finger paused over another link. This one was harder to justify. This one, if she was honest, was just Faith being incurably nosy. As usual. It really wasn't any of her business what Katarina Forrester got up to, or why she'd split up with Dominic.

Of course, she pressed it anyway.

And was instantly glad that she'd turned off the sound on the tablet. The video that sprang to life was really not one to be watching in public. Eyes wide, she paused it, then stared for a moment longer before closing the window down. That had to be Katarina, with that long blonde hair let loose from the chignon it had been contained by in every other photo. But the naked guy there with her? Definitely not Dominic.

Well, she supposed that answered the question of why they'd broken up. And it kind of made her wonder exactly what she'd find if she Googled her own name. Possibly best not to know.

Except…she was back in Britain, working the kind of job that might get her spotted at any minute. Wasn't it better to know what was out there waiting for her if she was recognised?

Before she could change her mind, Faith tapped out her real name in the search bar and waited to see what popped up, apprehension stirring in her chest.

At the top of the page, a row of photos loaded. Two of her looking bleary-eyed in a too-short dress, blinking at the camera as she left some nightclub. The rest…all from that night. Or, rather, the morning after.

God, was it really even her? She barely recognised the woman she was now in the girl on the screen. She'd thrown away the clothes she wore in the photos—the tight black jeans and the corset top, moulding her curves and pushing up her breasts. Her hair was shorter than it was now, just curling around her jawbone. The hotel name, high end and far more expensive than she'd have been able to afford on her own, was clearly visible in the back of the shots.

And on her arm, Jared Hawkes, a little too pale and scowling, but otherwise giving no indication of the hellish night before. Or that he was about to go home and beg his wife for another chance.

No, the photo looked exactly like what everyone had believed it was—a money-grabbing girl stealing a famous, and famously troubled, rock star away from his patient, wonderful wife and adoring kids.

The guilt had faded over the years. She'd made a lot of mistakes when she was younger, sure, but who hadn't? And this one, that one time, she really hadn't done anything wrong, as much as the world's media had tried to convince her—and everyone else—otherwise. It had taken her a while to accept that and forgive herself, after she dropped out of the public eye. But she was done with guilt. All she had left now was the resentment, and the pain of the injustice.

Faith clicked the browser closed. She didn't need to see any more.

She took a large gulp of coffee and tried to clear her head. Time to get back to the matter at hand—finding somewhere to take the Americans that evening.

She took her time perusing the usual websites, and also reading the best London blogs, to get some more unusual ideas. She'd forgotten how much there was to do and see in London, how much she loved being there. Sure, Rome was romantic as hell and had plenty to offer, but London…it was more of a patchwork. More bits and pieces and scraps from all across history, and across humanity. She liked that in a city.

By the time the hotel lobby doors opened to reveal chattering Americans, she'd worked up a decent plan for the week and got some provisional bookings in place. The name 'Lord Beresford' had opened plenty of doors she suspected might have stayed closed to Faith Fowler, Event Planner and Tour Guide, and while she'd vowed not to use her own title for the purpose of getting ahead, she had no qualms about using Dominic's.

Pushing aside her empty coffee cup—the third of the afternoon—she packed up her notes and tablet and headed out to greet the Americans before they disappeared up to their rooms to change.

'How did the meetings go?' she asked Dominic as his clients got in the lift on the other side of the lobby.

He shrugged. 'As well as I could hope, I suppose.'

Which sounded rather Eeyore-ish to her. Maybe he was depressed. After all, he'd just lost his fiancée to a muscly premiership footballer in a YouTube video. Hardly surprising if he felt a bit down about things. 'Well, I'm sure they'll all be on board with anything you propose after the evening I've got in store for them.'

He raised his eyebrows at her, and his forehead crinkled up. 'Really? Do I get to know the plan in advance?'

'You kinda have to,' Faith replied. 'I need you to pay for it. They're holding the reservation for another hour.'

Dominic fished in his jacket pocket and pulled out his wallet. Opening it, he pulled out a shiny silver card with the name 'Beresford Estate Expense Account' emblazoned on it, and handed it to her.

Faith stared at the card, even as she noticed the slip of paper with it. 'Memorise the PIN and destroy that paper,' he said. Then, when she just kept looking at it, he added, 'Go on. Don't you have a reservation to confirm?'

Faith swallowed. 'Don't you want to know what I've got planned for the evening?'

Dominic's smile was wicked. 'I trust you. Surprise me.'

Later that evening, as Dominic stared at the limited wardrobe he'd brought to the hotel, he regretted not asking Faith to share the plan for the evening. At least then he'd know if he needed the dinner jacket or if an ordinary suit would suffice. Or if whatever she had arranged would be more comfortable in jeans… Surely she'd have mentioned if they needed any sort of special outfits, though. Right?

Why hadn't he let her tell him?

Sighing, Dominic dropped to sit on the edge of the bed, tie in hand. The reason, if he was honest with himself, was simply that she'd looked so excited about her plans. Standing there in her bright red blouse, with her hair tied back, she'd bobbed excitedly up and down on her toes. And just the idea that she was trying so hard to get this right, to do a good job…he wanted her to have a moment of glory when she pulled it off.

If she pulled it off.

He should have checked. He should be approving all the plans for the week. He would with any other new supplier or contractor. So why was it different with Faith?

Because Faith was different, he answered himself. Faith was so many worlds away from Kat and the way she worked. Faith, for whatever reason, needed this job, and needed to do it well. And he was going to trust her and let her get on with it.

Even if she could be using his credit card for anything right now. She could be on her way to the airport and back to Italy. Or anywhere.

No. Faith wanted this job; that much he was sure of. Still, they'd only talked vaguely about budgets on the plane, and Faith didn't seem the sort to be constrained by vague limits when the perfect opportunity for fun showed up. Although she'd been pretty canny with his money when she went clothes shopping.

He should have more faith.

Groaning at the unintentional mental pun, Dominic lay back on the bed and wished it was eight o'clock and time to meet in the lobby already.

In the end, he was twenty minutes early, dressed in a suit and clean shirt, no tie—although he had one in his pocket in case of emergency. Compromise, he'd decided, was the name of the game. Something the Americans could stand to learn at the negotiating table, actually.

He was early, but Faith was earlier, already standing in the lobby, dressed in a black dress that skimmed her knees, and with a red cardigan over it that hid the neckline. Respectable, but not too formal. Maybe he could ditch the tie at reception...

'You're early,' she said, smiling at him as he approached. 'Too impatient to wait any longer?'

'Something like that,' Dominic admitted. Up close, he could see the red lipstick that made her mouth even wider and more tempting than normal. And he was studiously ignoring the way her black heels made her legs look endless.

Rifling through her oversized handbag, Faith said, 'I've got receipts and confirmations here—printed them out at the business centre. Do you want them as we go along, or shall I put them together in a full report at the end of the week?'

Dominic let his shoulders relax. 'It can wait. Just give me the full accounting when we're done. Including your hours and salary.'

Her eyes widened again as she looked at him. 'Okay. Will do.'

What was it that made it so hard for her to let people trust her? he wondered. Was it just that the scope of this job was a little outside her normal remit? Or was it something more?

Maybe he'd ask her, one day. If he got the chance.

'So, is it time for me to know where we're going yet?'

Faith gave him a mysterious smile. 'Soon,' she promised.

The Americans obviously hadn't been given any hints, either. They arrived in the lobby in dribs and drabs, dressed in the same cautious smart/casual attire Dominic had opted for. As soon as they were all assembled, Faith clapped her hands to get everyone's attention and said, 'Okay, ladies and gentlemen. Time for your first, proper London experience of the trip.'

Leading them out of the lobby, she kept talking. 'I know you've all been to London before, and I know that you've probably experienced a lot of the standard tourist attractions. But there are some things that are so quintessentially London, it would be wrong to miss them out this week. I promise there'll be some more unusual outings in your future but, just for tonight, I went for the classics.'

She certainly had. Dominic blinked at the sight of an old-fashioned Routemaster double-decker bus parked outside the Greyfriars Hotel. It looked utterly incongruous, like a penguin in the desert. Glancing over at Faith, he saw she was biting her lip, nervously awaiting his reaction. The Americans were already jostling to get on board, chattering and joking excitedly. But she was waiting to see what *he* thought. His opinion mattered to her. He liked that.

'Can't wait to see where it's taking us,' he said, and offered her his arm.

Grinning, she took it, tucking her hand into the crook of his elbow, and he realised that it must be the first time they'd touched. Because if he'd felt that electric shock at contact before, he'd have remembered. The touch, the scent, the closeness of her filled his senses, and he had to concentrate on putting one foot in front of the other to reach the bus and help her up the steps.

Note to self, he thought as he followed her. *Do not touch Faith Fowler again. That way lies madness.*

Faith held her breath as she stepped onto the bus, praying it was everything Julian had promised. She'd called in favours from every person she knew in the tourist trade in London to find the best options for the week ahead, and sent up thankful prayers when Julian told her that his latest venture, Big Red Tours, had a last-minute cancellation for that night. The photos and testimonials had been great, but you never knew for sure until you were there…

With the last step, she looked around and let out a relieved sigh. It was perfect.

Ben and Jerry were already seated at the table at the back, and a waiter in black tie dress was offering them a drink. The original bus seats had been torn out, replaced by wooden tables for two and four, bolted to the ground, as were the mismatched chairs around them. Red, white and blue cotton bunting hung from the ceiling, and the adverts were all replaced by vintage wartime posters.

Terri and Marie ventured upstairs and Faith followed, wondering at the sight of more bunting and an honest-to-God rooftop garden, with more seating areas dotted about.

'This is incredible, Faith!' Marie said, beaming as she took a glass of champagne from the upstairs waiter. 'Where on earth did you find such a thing?'

Faith smiled. 'Trade secret.'

She waited until everyone had explored the bus and chosen a seat before instructing the driver to start the tour. Period music, the sort that would have played on the American bases during the war, sang out from the speakers as they drove along the river, through the heart of London. The waiters served canapés and topped up champagne flutes as they went, the lights of the city sparkling outside the windows.

And all Faith could focus on was the fact that Dominic was sitting opposite her, smiling.

'Do I want to know how much this is costing me?' he asked, holding out his glass for a refill.

Faith shrugged. 'They had a last-minute cancellation, so I got a good deal.'

'I had no idea you could do this sort of thing. I mean, in general, not you personally.'

Quite honestly, Faith hadn't been sure of either. But, since everything seemed to be going okay, she decided not to mention it.

'The guy who started up the business—Julian—used to work with me last time I was doing tours in London. I thought it might be a fun start to the trip.'

'It is,' Dominic said, and he sounded as if he meant it. Faith felt something inside her start to relax and she reached for a glass of champagne.

'I just hope the next part of the evening is as big a success.'

'What is next?' Dominic asked.

Faith smiled. 'Dinner.'

Dinner, it turned out, was a bit of an understatement. Dominic hadn't known you could have canapés and champagne and roof gardens on buses, but he also hadn't realised you could actually eat dinner on Tower Bridge. Or, rather, inside it.

'Has this always been here?' he asked, staring out over the River Thames.

'They opened it for catering years ago,' Faith told him. 'We got lucky with a spare table tonight.'

They'd been getting lucky a lot, it seemed to Dominic. 'Another last-minute cancellation?'

Faith squirmed a little. 'Not exactly.'

Dominic raised an eyebrow. 'Let me guess; you used my name?'

'Wouldn't you?' Faith asked. 'To get a table at a restaurant, or a better seat on a flight, or tickets to some play?'

He wouldn't, but he couldn't deny that Shelley sometimes did. It just made him feel a little uncomfortable. 'I suppose. So, what happens to the poor saps we kicked out of this place tonight?'

Faith shook her head. 'I wouldn't do that. I just... persuaded them to rearrange things a little. That's all.'

'Can you talk anyone into anything?' he asked. After all, she'd done all this over the phone in the course of an afternoon. He couldn't even blame the mind-boggling effects of touching her, or even just looking at her, for the world falling at her feet. Or was that just him? Was everyone else immune, and it was just Dominic Beresford who found himself handing over jobs, money, credit cards and trust to this woman without a second thought?

Faith gave him a rueful smile. 'I wish I could. Do you know how many places I had to call, how many people I had to talk to, and how much research I put in to pulling all this together? A lot of places just said no upfront. Some I'm still in negotiations with to fit us in later in the week. I lucked out tonight, but I've still got a lot of hard work to put in to pull off the rest of the trip.'

She stopped, as if she hadn't meant to say so much.

'I'm sorry,' he said. 'I didn't mean to suggest you hadn't been working hard.'

'That's okay.' Faith's gaze darted away, out of the window. 'I mean, it's supposed to look effortless, isn't it? That old swan metaphor. Swimming smoothly along, paddling like mad underneath.'

Ridiculously, all he could think of at her words was Faith in a bikini. He cleared his throat, buying time for the image to dissipate. 'Well, it all seems like, uh, very smooth swimming so far.'

She gave him a curious look. 'Good. I'm glad you're enjoying it.' She glanced over his shoulder. 'Looks like our table's ready. I'd better gather the others from the bar.'

She strode off towards the Americans, who were all ordering cocktails. Apparently the champagne had put them in an excellent mood. If only he could get them to sign the contracts now…except that would be unethical. And his lawyers would kill him.

Sighing, Dominic headed for the large round table directly overlooking the river. Usually this sort of an evening was nothing but a chore, time away from the office he could ill afford. But Faith had managed to make it fun, different.

He couldn't wait to see what she had planned for the rest of the week.

CHAPTER SIX

IT WAS NEARLY midnight by the time the group climbed onto the Routemaster bus again and headed back to the hotel. And as they pulled up outside the Greyfriars, Faith silently thanked Dominic for quashing Henry's suggestion that they carry on to a club after dinner. She needed sleep and, before that, she needed to check her emails and reply to any confirming spaces for events over the next few days. And, as Dominic had pointed out, the Americans had a lot of meetings to fit in before their trip to the Beresford country estate later in the week. He needed them alert in the morning.

Fortunately, everyone except Henry had agreed. And when she'd promised to take him dancing another night—something else to add to her never-ending list of requests—even he'd been mostly appeased.

As the others headed for the lifts, waving tiredly behind them, Faith hung back with Dominic.

'Bed?' he asked, and for one moment, before she remembered that this was Dominic Beresford, more automaton than man, she thought he meant together and her eyes widened.

He noticed. Damned observant man. 'Are you going to yours now, I meant,' he said, not looking at all flustered at the misunderstanding. 'Rather than any sort of inappropriate proposition.'

'I knew that,' Faith said quickly. 'And yes. Bed. After I finish up some emails and such.'

Dominic nodded. 'Come on. We can work in the office of my suite. Keep each other awake while we finish up for the day. I've got some things I need to go over with you, anyway.'

She shouldn't. All she really wanted to do was take off her make-up, curl up in her bed with the late-night TV on low, and answer her emails until she passed out from exhaustion. Working in Dominic's room meant keeping on her high heels and actually making coherent conversation, both of which seemed like they might be beyond her until she'd got some sleep.

And yet…

'We can have a nightcap,' he said, striding off in the direction of the lift. 'Come on.'

She followed. He was her boss, after all, and she was obliged to bow to his requests. At least, that was what she was telling herself. She was too tired to think about the part of her that wasn't ready to say goodnight to him just yet.

Dominic's suite was twice the size of her, already impressive, accommodation. It had a kitchen area, a full dining table, a lounge filled with an oversized corner sofa and a glass coffee table and, tucked away in a corner by the bedroom door, the office.

There was only one desk, but two chairs, and another low table between them. Dominic took the desk chair, flipping open his laptop as he sat, so Faith settled into the visitor's chair—lower, more comfortable, and far too likely to send her to sleep.

Wearily, she reached into her bag for her tablet, contemplating just kicking her shoes off regardless. It was late. He'd understand. And her feet couldn't smell that much, could they?

Hmm. Maybe better not to risk it.

'Drink?' Dominic asked, and when she looked up she saw that he'd taken off his jacket, his shirt collar lying open beneath it. Her gaze fixed on the hollow at his neck, just above his collarbone, and she wondered, in what could only be a sleep-deprived daze, what it would be like to kiss him there. How his skin would feel under her lips, under her fingertips. 'I've got brandy, whisky, probably some rum…'

Faith blinked, and brought her attention back to the real world. 'Um, a whisky would be great. Thanks.'

Work. She was here to work. She really had to remember that.

She swiped a finger across the screen to bring it to life, and brought up her email program. Thirty-seven new emails. And since this was a new account Dominic had set up for her to do the job at hand, chances were that very few of them were spam. She suppressed a groan. She was never going to get to sleep tonight.

Dominic returned from the bar in the kitchen area with two tumblers, filled with ice and topped with what she imagined would probably be the finest whisky. Did she even remember what that tasted like? she wondered. Her father had only ever drunk the best, most expensive Scotch whiskies, and he'd tried to ensure that she grew up with a taste for the finer things, too.

'Here.' Dominic bent down to hand her the glass, and Faith's mouth moistened as that hollow at his neck grew closer.

This was ridiculous. She needed to go to bed.

As soon as she'd finished work.

Leaning back in the swivel chair at the desk, Dominic stretched his legs out in front of him, arms folded across his chest, and studied her.

'What?' Faith asked after a few long moments of scrutiny.

'You did a really great job tonight,' he said.

A warm glow flushed across her skin. 'Thank you. I knew it was important to you that your clients start the trip off with a bang.'

'And you certainly did that. The bus was a masterstroke.' And yet still he kept staring at her.

'Is there a *But*... here?' Faith didn't care if she was being blunt. It was far too late at night for subtle.

Dominic shook his head, unfolding his arms to push himself up into a straighter seated position. 'No buts. Just a few questions.'

Questions. Possibly her least favourite things. 'Such as?'

'Well, I never got to see your full résumé. We didn't even have a proper interview.'

'And you want to do that now?' Was the man crazy? 'You realise I'm already doing the job, right? And doing it well, according to you.'

'I know.' Dominic sounded completely unruffled. 'Like I say, I just want to know a little bit about your background.'

Her work background, Faith reminded herself, as her heart started to beat double time. All Dominic cared about was the job he'd hired her to do. Even if he did start developing suspicions about who she really was, he probably wouldn't care unless it interfered with one of his meetings. All she needed to do was keep things professional. How hard could that be?

'Well, I started working in events in London,' she

said, carefully editing out that part about how, as Lady Faith Fowlmere, she'd mostly been attending the events. Or, at most, throwing epic parties at her famous friends' houses. 'Then moved more into the tour guide side of things for a while.' After she ran away from home and became Faith Fowler. 'That's where I met my previous employer, who hired me to run his tours in Italy, where I've been for the last year and a half.' After Great-Uncle Nigel spotted her at an event in London and almost dragged her home and she realised that another country would be much easier to hide in. 'That's about it,' she finished with a shrug.

Dominic gazed at her, his eyes still assessing. But finally he nodded. 'Well, you obviously learned a lot in your time. Like I said, you're doing a great job. I trust you'll find more wonderful experiences to entertain us over the next few days. And you're coming to Beresford Hall with us later in the week, of course?'

Faith froze, the pleased smile she'd had at his words fixing into place as she realised what he was asking. Beresford Hall. Family seat. Full of people who knew the aristocracy, knew the families, kept up with the news.

Full of people who might recognise her.

'Actually, I was thinking that perhaps I should stay here and get the last couple of nights' entertainment sorted out?'

Dominic raised his eyebrows. 'We have Wi-Fi at the Hall these days, you know. You can work there.'

'Right. Of course.' Maybe she could hide on the bus. Or in a deserted corner bedroom. Or a cupboard. Anywhere. 'Only, I was thinking—' she started, but Dominic spoke over her.

'Then that's settled.' He tilted his head as he studied her. 'I'll be interested to see what you make of the old place.'

'Oh?' What did it matter what she thought? She was only the hired help.

But Dominic nodded. 'I want Beresford Hall to be an all-inclusive events location. It's more than a piece of history now, more than heritage. There are a lot of opportunities there—at our conference facility for a start. If you wanted me to introduce you to the head of events there...'

'No,' Faith said, too loudly. 'I mean, thank you. But really, this job is just a one-off. In between tours, like I said. I'm not looking for a permanent conference and events job here in the UK.' Especially not at Beresford Hall, where someone was bound to recognise her on her first day. No, thank you.

'So you'll be going back to Italy, after this week?' Dominic's gaze was sharp, and Faith got the impression that this was the real question he'd wanted to ask all along.

'Um, probably not Italy, no,' she admitted.

'So, you don't actually have another job lined up there?'

'Not exactly.' Faith plastered on a sparkling smile. 'I like to keep moving, you see. Don't want to be tied down to just one country.'

'I see.' Dominic leant back in his chair again. 'You never did tell me exactly why you had to leave Italy.'

Because my ex-boyfriend was threatening to bring the international media down on me, and the company I was working for went bust.

Neither of those facts were really going to put Dominic's mind at rest, were they? When in doubt, lie and run.

Faith gave a high, tinkling laugh. 'Well, you know,

after a while even pizza gets a bit boring. Besides, I wasn't sure my hips could take any more pasta!'

Before he had a chance to respond, Faith gathered up her tablet and notebook and shoved them into her bag.

'And I know how lucky I am to have this great job,' she added, getting to her feet. 'Which is why I need to get some sleep, ready to do my best work again tomorrow. Goodnight!'

She kept smiling until the door closed behind her, well aware that Dominic was still staring after her. But her heart didn't stop racing until she was back in her room.

She needed to make sure that Dominic didn't have any more chances to ask her questions about her previous life. It was far too tempting to tell him the truth.

She was lying to him, Dominic thought for the hundredth time as he took his seat on the executive coach taking the group to Beresford Hall three days later. Faith had been the perfect employee so far, arranging dinners and tours with such finesse that Dominic would have felt entirely comfortable letting her take charge of everything alone, except for one thing: he knew she was lying to him.

He had absolutely no idea why, but Dominic hadn't got where he was without developing the ability to spot when he was being lied to. The only question was, what on earth could Faith Fowler have to lie about?

Even if her career history had been embellished—although, given how little she'd actually told him, it seemed unlikely—she was doing a good enough job that he wouldn't care. She clearly didn't want to visit Beresford Hall—she'd come up with half a dozen excuses over the past few days to try and get out of it. But he'd stayed firm. He wanted her there, if only to find out why she didn't want to go. But it still didn't seem like something to lie about. Which meant it had to be something to do with why she was in such a hurry to leave Italy.

The last of his clients climbed aboard and took their seats, followed by Faith, in full professional mode. Shading her eyes from the sun streaming in through the coach window, she did a quick head count and nodded to the driver, barely sparing a glance and a tight smile for Dominic as she chose her own seat—as far away from his as was possible in the circumstances.

He'd lain awake for far too long after she'd left the other night, dreaming up elaborate falsehoods and scandalous pasts she could be hiding. Associations with the Mafia, drug trafficking, murder. Just the fact he was having to think about these things meant he should probably fire her and minimise whatever risk her lies represented.

But he didn't. Partly because he couldn't believe it was actually that bad. But mostly because she was Faith, and he wanted to give her a chance. He wanted her to stick around.

Which didn't mean he was going to stop trying to find out what she was hiding.

Beresford Hall lay less than two hours' drive outside London. Dominic spent the journey catching up on some reading, chatting with Ben, Henry and Marie about his next trip over to the States, and trying not to stare at the back of Faith's seat.

It was just the mystery, he told himself. Strange woman walks into his life, just when he needs her, and proceeds to do a perfectly good job while lying to him the whole time. Of course he was intrigued. Of course he'd been thinking about her. He needed to know the truth to protect himself, even if he suspected it would turn out to be nothing. A row with a boyfriend, perhaps. Nothing more.

And, whatever her reasons for leaving Italy, she didn't want to come to Beresford Hall either, that much was clear. But maybe she'd open up to him there. Maybe he could get her to talk.

Seeing the estate he'd saved from ruin and built up into a multi-million-pound business often made women feel fondly towards him. No reason to suppose a little imposing grandeur wouldn't do the same for Faith.

The coach pulled up the long driveway, curving through the landscaped gardens, past the fountains and up to the front of the Hall. In the past, all you'd have seen from the road was woodlands and immaculately trimmed hedges. These days, Dominic got a thrill from spotting a gang of archers heading off to the archery range, and a group of men in suits making their way towards the conference facilities. No weddings today, he supposed, with it being a Wednesday, but there were at least two stag dos booked in for the weekend, taking over the rally track and go-carting on the outer edges of the estate.

Dominic didn't try to dampen down the surge of pride he always felt when he saw the Hall, and especially when he saw the reaction of his clients to the magnificent building. Yes, he'd been born into a privileged family. But it had taken every ounce of his own determination and ability to make his family name, and estate, what it was today.

Maybe the people looking on only saw the money made, the clever business decisions he'd taken. But he, at least, knew that it was more than that. He'd done his time feeling ashamed as a boy—of his mother, his name, his life. But he'd grown up since then. He'd taken on the challenge and surpassed it. He'd reclaimed his heritage, his self-respect, his future.

And he had every right to be proud of that.

But when he finally caught Faith's eye, as she stood to guide everyone back off the bus, he didn't see the expected awe or appreciation in her gaze. Instead, she was frowning at the Hall as if it personally offended her.

His most likely reason for her reluctance to come with them that day rose up in the back of his mind again. Perhaps she just resented the aristocracy, and perceived privilege. Hadn't she been happy enough to use his name to get what she wanted from their suppliers that week, though? If there was one thing he couldn't stand, it was a hypocrite.

Dominic clenched a fist against the back of the seat beside him as he stood. He'd make sure Faith Fowler got a full tour of Beresford Hall. He wanted her to understand exactly what he'd achieved here, although he couldn't have said why it mattered to him so much.

Beresford Hall was beautiful, magnificent, a shining example of some sort of architecture or another, and everything else the guidebook said it would be. But all Faith could see was the shadow of Fowlmere Manor hanging over it, reminding her how hard she'd worked to get away from places like this. People like this.

Sure, Fowlmere was maybe half the size of Beresford Hall, and there were far fewer people hanging around it these days, but the similarities caught her everywhere she turned, and she couldn't shake the shiver that crept over her shoulders when she thought how close she'd come to being trapped somewhere like this her whole life.

Dominic led them up the stone steps to the imposing front doors, hauling them open and holding one to let them pass into the main hall. It was early on a weekday, but there had been several coaches parked in the car park when they arrived and the hall already boasted three lines for tickets. This, Faith supposed, was where Fowlmere really differed. Even if her father had let them, what tourists would want to pay to visit a crumbling manor that had sold most of its heirlooms to pay gambling debts?

Beresford Hall was often held up as an example of heritage done right. Open most days to the public, save one wing that was kept as family quarters, Dominic had put history on display for all to share and he'd done it in style.

'Come on through, guys,' he said, lifting a red tasselled rope to let them skip the queue. 'I'll give you the house tour myself, before we get a better look at the newer additions to the property.'

Faith followed, remembering the horrible attempts to open Fowlmere to the public when she was a child. Only two days a year, her father had decreed, and he'd give the tours himself. Except, when it came down to it, it turned out he didn't know much about the history of the house, or the family. And when her mother had stepped in to take over, Faith had realised she was already slurring her words at ten in the morning.

Faith had learned everything she could about the Manor and her ancestry, to be ready for the next open day. But, in the end, her father had declared it a waste of time and shut the gates again.

Not so at Beresford Hall.

'This is the chamber prepared for Queen Victoria, when she visited the Hall.' Dominic waited as they all took in the room, with its rich red walls and imposing four-poster bed. Gold accents glittered on everything, adding a shine to the faded history. 'Beresford Hall has been host to five British monarchs, and we have memorabilia from each of their visits.'

He was obviously proud of his family and his history, Faith thought. She wondered what that would be like. Whether she'd have stayed if her own family hadn't been such a shambles. Who would she be if she'd grown up somewhere like Beresford, where her future was neatly mapped out for success, rather than finding buckets to catch drips from leaking roofs, or hiding bottles from her mother and lying to debt-collectors when they came looking for her father?

But she wasn't that girl. She was Faith Fowler now, and that was all she ever intended to be.

With a sigh for things lost, Faith followed Dominic through the next doorway to a magnificent dining room, staring out of the window instead of listening to him talk. She was his employee, not his girlfriend. She didn't have to hang on his every word. She didn't have to care about this house, or its history. She didn't have to learn which king stayed when.

Because this wasn't her world any more. And it never would be again.

CHAPTER SEVEN

'WHAT ARE YOU frowning at?' Sylvia asked.

Dominic looked down at his sister, taking in her wrinkled up nose and exasperated eyes, and tried very hard to shake his bad mood. 'Nothing. It's all perfect. Thanks for setting this up for me.'

Sylvia shrugged. 'Just an ordinary day's work. You do realise I do this for paying customers every day.'

It showed, Dominic thought. When they'd first opened the tea rooms in the old stables, he'd been doubtful. They already had the restaurant, over in the Orangery, offering fine dining to the visitors, and the café over on the other side of the yard, serving sandwiches and drinks. A third eating area seemed like overkill.

But Sylvia had wanted it. Sylvia, who never really asked for anything, only went along with his plans and said, 'If that's what we need to do.' So when she'd said, 'No, Dominic. You're wrong. This will be a really good thing,' he'd listened.

He was glad he had, now. Sylvia had taken on all the planning and running of the tea rooms, picking out the perfect curtains and matching tablecloths, light and airy without being too chintzy. She'd tasted every baker's cakes from Beresford to London, and finally hired a young man called Russell to bake the scones, cakes and biscuits for the afternoon teas. People flocked to them—not just the senior citizens on their day trips, which he'd sort of expected, but everyone. Hard-nosed businessmen on a break from their conference sched-ule over at the events suite. Lovers checking out the Hall as a possible wedding venue. Hungover stag par-ties. Everyone.

For once, Dominic was actually pleased to be proved wrong.

The Americans certainly seemed to be enjoying it, too. He'd originally asked Sylvia to find them a pri-vate room somewhere, but she'd refused, saying half the charm of the tea rooms was the atmosphere. And she'd been right again. They were chatting away with the tourists on the next table, exclaiming over the scones and clotted cream and the cucumber sandwiches.

Even Faith looked as if she might be enjoying her-self for the first time that day.

'You're staring at her again,' Sylvia commented, and he could hear the smirk in her voice.

Diverting his gaze towards the tower of cakes on the counter, Dominic said, 'Staring at whom?'

'Your event planner. Tour guide. Kat's replacement. Whoever she is.'

'Merely a last-minute employee for the week,' Domi-nic said, ignoring the tiny part of his brain that screamed at him that she should be more. 'Kat cancelled on us.'

'Understandably.' She gave him a sideways look. 'After that video.'

Just hearing the words made the shame rise up again, stinging in his throat. The memory of the moment he'd first seen it sharp and constant in his brain. And the swift realisation that what hurt most wasn't the personal betrayal, wasn't the fact that Kat had slept with another man. It was the humiliation. The way it sent him right back to his childhood, and those unbearable days after his mother left, when all anybody seemed able to talk or write or think about was his family's shame.

He'd promised himself he'd never be in that position again, and Kat had made him break that promise. Maybe he couldn't have changed what happened with his mother, but he should have been able to control Kat. And he could sure as hell make sure it never happened again. Which meant finding out what Faith was hiding.

Sylvia was still watching him carefully, as if waiting to see if he might explode at the very mention of the video. Dominic closed his eyes and wished very hard he'd never heard of YouTube. 'Just tell me you haven't watched it.'

'I don't think there's a person we know that hasn't seen at least a glimpse of it.' Sylvia shook her head. 'You think you know a person.'

'It's wildly unsuitable and inappropriate for you to even mention it.'

'I don't know why you're so bothered. It's not like you're in it.' Dominic looked at her, and she winced. 'Of course, I suppose that might not actually make things any better.'

'I'd like to stop talking about this now, please.'

Sylvia gave a quick nod. 'Absolutely. Good idea. You can tell me about your latest employee instead.'

As if that was any safer a topic. 'What do you want to know?'

'Her name would be a good start. Where you met. What she's like. That kind of thing.'

'You realise you'll probably never see her again after today, right?'

'Oh, I don't know,' Sylvia said airily. 'At the very

least, there's the theatre trip you promised faithfully to let me come along on…'

Damn it. He'd forgotten that. He'd have to ask Faith to try and score an extra ticket.

'You forgot. Didn't you?'

'Of course not,' Dominic lied. 'I just need to ask Faith something…'

'Aha! So her name is Faith. We're getting somewhere.'

Dominic rolled his eyes. Apparently she wasn't giving up on this one any time soon. 'Her name is Faith Fowler, she's a tour guide I met in Italy and hired to come over and run this tour, and she doesn't like stately homes. That's about all I know.'

Sylvia's brow furrowed. 'Except this one. She likes this stately home. Don't you, Faith?'

Glancing up, Dominic saw Faith approaching, too late to steer her away from his sister's insatiable curiosity.

'I love these tea rooms,' Faith said, not really answering the question. 'And the scones are to die for.'

'I'll introduce you to Russell before you go,' Sylvia replied, suitably distracted. 'He's a marvel in the kitchen.'

'Faith, we're going to need an extra ticket for the theatre tomorrow,' Dominic said. For some reason, the idea of Faith and Sylvia getting chummy made him nervous.

'Not a problem.' Faith whipped out her tablet and made a note. 'We're in the box anyway, and I think there are a couple of extra seats at the very back. Or I can always just skip it.'

'No. I need you there.' The words came out too firm, even to Dominic's ears, and both women looked at him in surprise.

'I'll still be around to get you all there and home again,' Faith said.

'Still, you don't want to miss the play,' Sylvia said, but she was looking at Dominic. He tried to keep his face blank. The last thing he needed was his little sister questioning his motives for hiring Faith. And he didn't want to explain that he needed to keep Faith close until he discovered what secrets she was keeping.

'I'm not much of a theatre person,' Faith said with a tight smile.

She was lying again, Dominic thought, wondering when he'd got so adept at spotting even her little fibs. But why? Why wouldn't she want to go to the opening night of the play she'd been so excited to score them tickets for?

'Is this another wardrobe issue?' he guessed, and Sylvia started staring at him again.

Faith flushed, the pink colour clashing with her scarlet cardigan. 'Not entirely. I could always wear my black dress again.'

'You've worn that dress every evening this week,' he pointed out. 'It's going to fall apart if you dry clean it once more.'

Faith blinked at him. 'I didn't think you'd notice.'

'I didn't think he could tell one dress from another,' Sylvia added, glancing between them. 'It must be a very special dress.'

'It's really not,' Faith told her.

'So go buy a new one,' Dominic said. 'You can go shopping while we're in meetings tomorrow. Just put it on the card.'

'I really don't need—'

'I'll come with you!' Sylvia clapped her hands together with excitement. 'It'll be great! I'm in town any-way for that evening, and I love a good shopping trip…'

Faith glanced between them, and suddenly Dominic felt just a little sorry for her. Not enough to get her out of a shopping trip with his sister, though.

'Well, that would be…' Faith started.

'Expensive,' Dominic finished for her. 'That's the word you're looking for. Expensive and exhausting.'

'Oh, shush,' Sylvia said. 'You want her to look her best, don't you?'

He didn't care, Dominic realised. He didn't care what she wore, what she looked like. He just wanted her there with him. And not just so he could uncover her lies.

He was in trouble.

Faith spent the coach ride back to the hotel sulking. Not that anyone could tell; she was cheery and chatty enough to the clients. Maybe Dominic might have no-ticed but, since it was his fault anyway, she didn't care.

How had this happened? She'd known all along the theatre trip was a risk, but not much more than anything else she'd agreed to that week. The theatre was one of her mother's passions; her circle of friends liked to pa-tronise up-and-coming directors, playwrights, actors. Tomorrow, the opening night of a well-hyped show, di-rected by London's next big thing…no way they'd miss it. Maybe her mum wouldn't be there, but someone who would know Faith on sight would be, she had no doubt.

She'd planned on hiding out in the coach. She could get them all in and settled easy enough, then slip out and hide. Mum's gang were bound to be the last in so, as long as she got the rest of them there early, she'd be fine. When Dominic had said about needing a seat for

Sylvia, things got even easier. They'd never even notice she'd gone.

But now, suddenly, not only was she attending the bloody thing, she was buying a new frock, just for the occasion.

And the absolute worst thing was, she didn't even mind. Because it meant an evening with Dominic, dressed up and looking her best, and as close to off-duty as she could get this week.

Faith sighed, and slouched down in her seat. Falling for her employer. How cliché. And just the sort of man her mother would love her to marry, too. Perfect.

After the long day trip, Faith had planned a quiet dinner at a restaurant not far from the hotel. With only an hour to answer emails, catch up on work and get changed for dinner, she didn't have much choice but to pull on the hated black dress again. She'd thought it was versatile enough to see her through the week, but then she hadn't fully anticipated having to accompany the group on every single one of their evenings out. And she hadn't counted on Dominic being there, watching her, either.

Taking in her reflection in the hotel room mirror, she pulled a face. And then she grabbed her red shoes, red cardigan and brightest red lipstick. Worn right, he might not even notice the dress underneath.

'Nice dress,' Dominic said ten minutes later when they met in the lobby. Faith pulled a face at him, and he laughed.

Dinner, Faith thought, would have been more or less perfect if it wasn't for two things. One, the heel of her shoe breaking as she returned from the bathrooms after dessert. And two, Jerry insisting on accompanying her back to the hotel when she decided to leave while the others had coffee. After four days of fending off his advances, she was running out of excuses.

Even then, it might have been salvaged if Jerry hadn't followed her up to her room, staring intently down her cleavage as she rooted through her bag for her keycard.

'Thanks for helping me home,' she said, smiling falsely up at him. 'I think I can manage from here.' She waved her keycard, just to prove the point.

'What kind of a gentleman would I be if I didn't see you safely into your room?' He gave her a smile that made her want to shudder. 'I can check for monsters under your bed, if you like.'

I'm much more concerned about what you want to do in *my bed.* 'I'm a big girl now, Jerry. I think I can manage.'

His gaze dropped down to her breasts again. 'You certainly are.'

Okay, that was enough. 'Jerry, I'm tired. I'm going to bed. I suggest you do the same.' How much wine had he drunk with dinner? His eyes weren't entirely focused when he finally managed to look up at her face.

'Aw, come on. Just a quick nightcap. After all, we missed out on after-dinner drinks.'

'I really don't think that's a good idea,' Faith said, slipping her keycard into the door. 'Early start and all tomorrow. Goodnight, Jerry.'

A hand appeared above hers on the door, pushing it open, and the first pangs of panic stabbed in Faith's chest. Focusing on her breathing, she grabbed the handle and yanked it closed again, almost catching Jerry's fingers in the door as she did so.

'I said goodnight, Jerry.' The words came out much

calmer than she felt. Her heart pounded against her rib-cage and she wanted to kick out, stamp on his feet in her one remaining red heel, the way the self-defence classes had taught her.

But he was Dominic's client. And he hadn't actually done anything yet, except make her feel desperately uncomfortable.

Of course, if his hands moved from the door to her body, she was taking him down.

Fingers, hot and sweaty, landed on her hip and Faith didn't waste time thinking any more. Stamping down with her right foot, she tried not to smile in satisfaction as Jerry let go and howled.

'Oh, I'm so sorry. Was that your foot?' she asked, her voice syrupy sweet.

'You bitch! You wait until I tell your boss about this.' Jerry was practically curled up over his foot, his face shining red, his eyes furious.

Faith managed one moment of relief before a figure appeared at the edge of her vision, coming around the corridor from the lift. And, before she could even look, she heard Dominic say, 'Tell her boss about what?' and her heart plummeted.

CHAPTER EIGHT

JERRY HAD SCAMPERED back to his room before Dominic could get any coherent account of what had happened, which he supposed meant he'd have to trust Faith's version of the story to be fully accurate. Normally, he hated only hearing one side. But on this occasion…he trusted Faith a hell of a lot more than the man he'd been doing business with for nearly three years.

'Tell me what happened,' he said as Faith let them both into her room, kicked off her ruined shoes and headed straight for the minibar.

'Pretty much exactly what you think happened.' She pulled out a small bottle of Scotch and reached for the glasses on the counter above.

'I don't know what happened,' he said reasonably as he took a seat in the armchair. 'All I saw was my client on the floor, practically crying in pain.'

Faith shrugged. 'I stood on his foot.'

Dominic's gaze dropped to the ridiculously high heels she'd discarded in the corner. The one with the intact heel certainly looked as if it could do some damage. 'Why?'

'Would you believe me if I said it was an accident?' Faith poured the whisky evenly between the two glasses and handed one to him.

'No,' he said, taking a sip. Not as good as his, but not bad.

With a sigh, Faith dropped onto the sofa, curling her legs up under her. 'He was drunk. He got…ideas. And he didn't appear able to comprehend the word *no*.'

Dominic stopped, stared, his blood heating up. He'd kill him. How could he even think for a moment that Faith—Faith!—would want to…?

'You don't believe me.' Glancing over, he saw Faith's wide eyes looking at him with disappointment.

'Oh I believe you,' he said, the words scratchy in his throat. 'And that bastard is on the next flight home.' Pushing himself to his feet, he let his anger carry him towards the door, but Faith stopped him before he got there, her small hand on his arm, a touch he hadn't expected.

'He was drunk,' she repeated. 'And stupid. Very, very stupid. But I took care of it.'

'You shouldn't have had to.'

'No, I shouldn't. But, trust me, it's not the first time it's happened. Guys get ideas in hotels, for some reason. But I learnt to look after myself, and no one has ever got any further than a hand on my waist unless I wanted them to, I promise.'

She sounded so calm, so certain, that Dominic's blood started to cool, just a little. 'I still want to punish him.'

'Oh, by all means,' Faith said, giving him a lopsided smile. 'Just find something more subtle than getting yourself arrested for grievous bodily harm, yeah?'

Dropping back down onto the couch, Dominic realised that he would have done. He'd have gone to that bastard's room and pounded him to a pulp, without caring what the police would do, or what the press would say, what damage it would do to the business, to these negotiations. Three years of strategising down the drain, and the Beresford name on the front of every paper for all the wrong reasons again.

He couldn't risk that.

He wanted to believe that he'd have done it anyway because he was a noble man who knew right from wrong. But, as Faith sat down beside him, her thigh close enough to touch his, he knew that gentlemanly behaviour had nothing to do with it.

He'd have hurt that man for touching Faith. Any other woman…he'd have reported it to Jerry's superiors, to the police if it had gone far enough. But Faith… was different.

'You okay?' she asked, bumping her arm against his.

He gave a humourless laugh. 'Shouldn't I be asking you that?'

'Probably. But I'm clearly fine.'

Dominic studied her, taking in her pale skin, and the spots of pink on her cheeks that were probably the fault of the whisky. 'Are you?'

She gave a half-shrug, and took another sip. 'Just a little shaken. I should have known better than to let him walk me back, really.'

'This is in no way your fault,' Dominic said firmly.

'Oh, I know that. Trust me, I blame him entirely.'

'Good.' Leaning back against the sofa, Dominic began to imagine ways of making Jerry pay. At the very least, he was going to get every meeting request for every video conference until the end of time, whether he needed to be there or not.

'You're thinking of torture techniques, aren't you?' Faith curled her feet up under her again, twisting to face him on the sofa, and he couldn't help but notice the way the skirt of that bloody black dress rode up her thighs. God, he was as bad as Jerry.

'Corporate torture,' he promised. 'Entirely legal.'

'Well, that's okay then. Wouldn't want my boss getting into trouble.'

Her boss. Of course that was all he was to her. And he wouldn't even be that much longer. Once the Americans were on the plane home, she'd be gone. Onto the next job, the next adventure. He couldn't even plan on calling her back next time he had guests in town; God only knew where she'd be by then.

Unless…

'I meant to talk to you about that, actually.' Or he would have, if he'd thought of it before now.

Faith's eyebrows drew together. 'About what?'

Dominic took a deep breath, and made his play. 'About whether you'd like to make the boss thing a more permanent arrangement.'

Faith stared at him long enough that he started to go out of focus, then snapped her gaze away. Of course he was so impressed by her professional abilities that he wanted to keep her around. Nothing to do with her more personal attributes. She had to remember that.

But still…he did want to keep her around. Just the idea gave her a warm glow greater than anything she'd got from the alcohol in her glass.

Except, she couldn't stay. The realisation made her wince into her whisky as she looked down so she didn't have to see his face as she answered.

'That's…very kind…' She scouted around her poor scrambled brain to find the right words, but Dominic was already talking again before she got to them.

'It makes sense, right? I mean, I need a new tour

company, one way or another, and I got to thinking that it would be easier if I just had someone on staff to take care of these things. Obviously we'd need to come to a more formal arrangement—you'd need an office in my building, and we'd have to discuss salary, relocation expenses and all of that.'

She wanted to say yes. It was a fantastic offer, something that would really let her build up her life as Faith Fowler. But how could she do it in the shadow of her family name? How could she risk living in London again, knowing that any moment they could find her and thrust her back into the limelight?

Dominic gave her an encouraging smile and she tried to return it.

Would it really be so bad, even if they did find her? She was a grown woman. They couldn't make her go home. And with a stable job with Dominic, she'd never be reliant on them for money, or anything else again. This could be her chance at true independence.

Until Dominic found out the truth. No way he'd hang onto an employee who brought the paparazzi down on him for harbouring a missing heiress. And once they'd found her, all the stories would start up again, and the pictures of her leaving that damn hotel room would be back in circulation, and the rumours about her relationship with a married drug addict rock star…no. Dominic wouldn't stand for any of that. Even if she could make him believe that the papers had it all wrong.

No. She couldn't stay. There was no place for her in Dominic's world any more, if there ever really had been. Getting close to Dominic…it was a mistake. One she was very afraid she might have already made. But there had to be a line, a point she couldn't cross. She couldn't fall in love. And so she couldn't risk staying.

Besides, she told herself, she didn't want to stay in London anyway. She wanted to see more of the world, more than just Italy.

Even if she'd rather see more of Dominic.

'You're going to say no, aren't you?'

Faith gave him an apologetic smile, and he shook his head.

'Is this because of the Lord thing?'

She blinked. 'The Lord thing?'

Shifting to face her, Dominic's expression was serious. 'Yeah. I saw the way you were at Beresford Hall today. You hated every minute of it. So, what's the problem? You hate the aristocracy?'

I was the aristocracy. 'Of course not.'

'So, what, then? Trust me, whatever it is, I've heard it before. That I'm an over-privileged, spoilt brat who only got where I am because of my family. That I'm stealing from the mouths of others by having so much. That—'

'Dominic.' Faith spoke as calmly as she could, placing her hand against his arm again. 'I didn't say any of those things.'

He sighed. 'But you did hate being there today.'

No point lying about that one. 'Yeah.'

'So, why?'

Faith drew in a deep breath while she considered her answer. Obviously she couldn't tell him the truth— that it reminded her too much of her own home. But he clearly wasn't going to be fobbed off with a blatant lie, either. Besides, even if she couldn't stay, she wanted him to think well of her when she was gone.

'I guess I…I don't know how to explain it, really. It made me feel uncomfortable. All that history and opulence.'

Dominic frowned. 'Uncomfortable? Why? I mean,

I've had people be angry about the privilege, had people be jealous or bitter. But why uncomfortable?'

'Does it really matter?'

'It does to me.'

He was very close now, closer than even Jerry had been before she maimed him. When had she shifted so close? When had the hand on his arm become a gentle caress rather than a calming gesture? When had his thigh pressed so closely against her legs, his arm along the back of the sofa just behind her?

She didn't ask why it mattered to him; it was enough that it did. And she wanted him to know the truth, to have one moment of honesty from her before she left, taking all her lies and secrets with her.

'It made me feel trapped. Like all that history, tradition, expectation were weighing down on me, instead of you. Like there was no room for you to be yourself or explore what you wanted. Because the family name, upholding what that means, would always make you follow a certain course. That's why it made me uncomfortable.'

Dominic stared at her, realising too late that he was close enough now to see every fleck of green and brown in her hazel eyes. He could kiss her without moving more than a few centimetres.

But he wouldn't. Because of Jerry, because she was leaving, and because the very basis of his life made her 'uncomfortable'.

'That's not how it is.' Sitting back, he slid his arm back along the sofa, tucking his elbow in at his side, keeping his hands far away from her tempting skin. 'What I've done at Beresford Hall…that's all me. When my father died, he left things in a less than ideal condition.' Had she ever heard the story? he wondered. Everyone he met in society knew; he could see it in their eyes when he was introduced. After all, it was such a good story—the Lady of the Manor who went wild, running off to the Med with a billionaire tycoon, leaving behind two children and a distraught husband. A husband who barely got over the loss enough to look after the children, let alone the estate. Who could blame people for telling it over and over again?

Of course, they didn't see beyond the pictures in the society pages. His mother, living it up on some yacht, flaunting her adultery, her betrayal. And his mother never had to see what it did to the family she left behind. How Sylvia cried and screamed and then went silent for two long months. How the husband she left behind faded to a shadow of a man.

Or how Dominic dealt, every day, with the photographers and the journalists, at the door and on the phone. And with the constant humiliation of every single person in his life knowing how little he meant to his own mother.

It came up less in the business world, at least—one reason he preferred to keep his focus on building up the business and the brand, rather than attending the compulsory charity galas and events that he'd inherited with the title. But did ordinary people really care? Did Faith?

She raised her eyebrows at him. 'Less than ideal? What does that mean?'

Did it matter any more? The shame he burned with at the memories? Had he done enough, finally, to set it all behind him? Would he ever?

Faith was still waiting for an answer, though. He swallowed down the last gulp of his whisky, enjoying the slight burn in his throat. 'After my mother left…my father checked out of life,' he said bluntly. 'He didn't care about anything any more. Not even the scandal my mother left behind. The estate suffered.' He shrugged. 'When he died, he left us with nothing but our name.'

'And you fought back from that.' Faith's eyes were wide as she watched him. 'You built up the estate, the business…'

'I saved the family name,' he corrected her. 'The rest was incidental.'

'It meant that much to you. The name, I mean.'

'Yes.' He glanced away. 'It was all I had left, after all.'

She was silent for a long moment, but when he looked back her gaze was still fixed on him. Her teeth bit down on her lip, a flash of white in the dim lamplight of the darkening hotel room, and he wondered what it was she wanted to say. And whether she'd decide to say it.

'My father,' she said finally. 'He was—is—the world's most charming man. But…he gambled. Still does, I imagine. He…lost. A lot. Even if he'd never admit it. Life had to go on as if everything was normal, like we were as good as—better than—everyone else. Even if we couldn't afford to buy my school uniform. That's one of the reasons I moved away. I didn't want to watch him destroy himself, or our family.'

The words caught him in the chest, and it took him a moment to identify why. That was, he realised, the first real thing she'd ever told him about herself. He knew about the tours she'd led, the people she'd met. He knew her opinion on subjects as varied as clothes and theatre and London traffic.

And now he knew something of her. A small token, before she left him.

It wasn't enough.

'Didn't you ever want to just give up?' Faith asked. 'Just walk away from it all and start a new life?'

Had he? He couldn't remember. It had never seemed an option. From the moment he'd inherited the title, he knew exactly what he needed to do and he just got on with it. Besides... 'How could I? Sylvia was only ten, and we had nothing...I couldn't leave.'

Faith's smile was sad. 'No. No, of course you couldn't.'

Tipping the last drops of whisky down her throat, she placed her glass on the coffee table. Dominic stared at her lips and the way her tongue darted out to catch the last drop of liquid from them. He wanted to kiss her. And he knew, just knew, from the way she leant into him, close enough to touch, that she wouldn't pull away. She wouldn't say no, wouldn't pull any of her self-defence moves on him. She'd let him kiss her, and then what? He'd take her to bed, just to let her leave him in a few days' time? She wasn't going to stay. And he was already in too deep. He couldn't risk falling any further. Not after Kat.

'You never did tell me the real reason you left Italy,' he said. Maybe now she knew some of his secrets, his truths, she'd be willing to share some of her own. Let him in enough that he could stop worrying about her lies.

Faith pulled back, wrapping her arms around her knees. Suddenly, even though she still sat on the same sofa, she felt miles further away. How bad was her truth that she couldn't let it near him?

'That day we met, at the airport,' she said, her voice slow.

'I remember,' he said drily. As if he would ever forget.

'I'd just found out that the company I worked for had gone bankrupt. I got everyone in my tour group sorted out with flights and hotels but I…I was stranded. Until you offered me this job.'

'Until you demanded it, you mean.' She was telling the truth, he was sure. But he was equally certain that there was more, something she was still hiding.

'Hey, I'm doing a good job, aren't I?'

'You're doing an incredible job,' he said, and she looked up, wide eyes surprised. 'I just wish you'd stop lying to me and let me see the real you.' He got to his feet, ignoring her alarmed stare. 'You should get some sleep. Goodnight, Faith.'

CHAPTER NINE

'HOW ABOUT THIS one?' Sylvia asked, and Faith glanced up from the racks of overpriced, over-decorated dresses to shake her head at Dominic's sister for the tenth time that morning. And they were only on the second shop. Faith sighed. Dominic hadn't been kidding when he'd said this would be exhausting.

Sylvia hung the dress back on the rail with a clatter of metal on metal. 'You know, this would be a lot easier if you could tell me what you're looking for.'

Faith flicked past another few dresses. 'I told you, I'm not sure. I'll know it when I see it.'

'Utterly unhelpful.' Flinging herself into a cream leather armchair outside the fitting rooms, Sylvia pulled out a small pink suede notepad and a sparkly pen. 'Come on. Let's figure this out. First question: cocktail or ballgown?'

'Cocktail, definitely. No one wears floor-length to the theatre any more, do they?'

Sylvia shrugged her slim shoulders and made a note on the pad. 'Not anyone your age, anyway. Okay, black or colour?'

'Colour,' Faith replied. 'I'm sick to death of black after a week in that one dress.'

'Plain or decorated?'

'Plain. It'll go with more accessories that way.' If she was getting to buy a dress on Dominic's card, it might as well be something she could wear again and again.

She turned her attention back to the rack and was only half paying attention when Sylvia spoke again.

'Okay, most important question, then—how do you want my brother to look when he sees you in it?'

'Awed,' she said without thinking, then smacked a hand over her mouth. 'I didn't say that,' she muttered through her fingers.

Sylvia gave a gleeful grin. 'Oh, you did. You most certainly did.'

'Well, I shouldn't have.' Faith studied the dresses again with unwarranted attention, since they were all exactly what she didn't want, but did at least distract from the way her cheeks were burning. 'He's my boss.'

'Only for a few more days,' Sylvia pointed out.

'At which point I'll be leaving. Hardly a winning argument.'

'You could stay,' Sylvia suggested. 'Maybe Dominic could offer you a permanent job.'

'At which point he'd be my boss again.' Faith shook her head. 'Besides, he already did. I think he's much more interested in keeping me as an employee than anything else.'

'Given the way he was staring at you yesterday, I'd take that as a compliment,' Sylvia said, her tone dry. 'You must be incredibly good at your job.'

'I am.' Faith pushed the dresses back along the rail. 'Which is why we're going to try the next shop in the hope of finding a perfectly work appropriate dress for tonight, so I can go out and do what I'm being paid for. Nothing more, nothing less.'

'Are you sure?' Sylvia asked, holding the shop door

open for her. 'Because I have to tell you, Dominic never looked at Kat that way.'

Something froze inside her, and Faith was awfully afraid it might be her heart. Like it had been shocked into stillness by the idea that Dominic wanted her more than she'd ever dared to imagine.

He'd almost kissed her the night before; she'd seen it in his face. She still wasn't sure what had stopped him, although she could list a dozen perfectly reasonable options off the top of her head. Probably it was Jerry, she'd decided. Dominic would never try anything so soon after she'd had to fend off the attentions of another man. It wouldn't be Proper.

And Dominic was all about Proper.

Which was exactly why she couldn't let herself have him. She had given up any chance of a place in Dominic's world when she ran away, and that was a decision she had to stick by.

Besides, if they started something, anything real, the truth would come out. It always did. And she couldn't bear the thought of the disgust and disappointment on Dominic's face when he found out.

She ignored the small part of her brain that said she only had a few more days. Maybe she could have that, at least. Surely she could keep her secret that long...

It all came down to one simple fact. If Dominic knew who she really was, what she'd done, he wouldn't want her. And on the infinitesimally small off chance he did, if she wanted a real chance with Dominic, she'd never get to be Faith Fowler again.

Lose-lose.

Kind of like the shopping expedition so far.

She sighed as Sylvia dragged her into the next boutique, another tiny, expensive shop filled with incredible dresses Faith's mother would have loved.

'Do you really think we're going to find anything in here?' she asked.

'We won't know until we look,' Sylvia replied, already scouring through the individual dress hangers on the walls to find the perfect outfit.

Faith was pretty sure that not one of the dresses Sylvia was looking at would fit over her not exactly model-shaped frame. The women these dresses were intended for didn't have curves. She couldn't even swear they had hips, looking at the narrow cuts.

Still, Sylvia seemed happy browsing through the fabrics, so Faith let her attention wander, imagining what the evening ahead might be like if she did let herself be talked into some glamorous, fabulous dress that showcased all her best assets.

Would Dominic notice? Would he look her over in that way of his and take in her figure, rather than her inappropriate clothes? Would he sit beside her in the theatre, transfixed by the plunging neckline of her dress?

Probably not.

The bell over the shop door chimed and Faith looked up absently, then froze. Lady Ginny Gale. Her mother's best friend.

Her head felt fuzzy, as if every thought she'd ever had was buzzing in there, all at the same time. She couldn't let Ginny see her, recognise her. This was just what she'd been afraid would happen at the theatre that night.

Getting to her feet as casually as she could—jerky movements would only draw attention to her—Faith turned her body away from the door, where Ginny was talking to the assistant. Then, grabbing the first dress she came to, she murmured to Sylvia, 'I'm just going to try this on.'

Sylvia's eyebrows rose in surprise, probably because the dress was everything Faith had said she didn't want—full length, black and decorated with crystals in a fan pattern on the skirt—but Faith ignored her, moving serenely towards the safety of the fitting room.

Of course, once safely behind the heavy locked door, she collapsed onto the velvet padded seat and buried her head in her hands.

This was why she couldn't stay in London. This was why she couldn't consider trying to seduce Dominic that night. As if she needed the reminder. She wanted out of his world, not back in. She'd been crazy to even take the job, once she'd figured out who he was.

Still, she'd see it through now, of course. Which meant finding something utterly un-Faith-like to wear that night. She needed to be so unrecognisable even her own mother would walk past her in the lobby if she showed up. And she wasn't going to find that in any of the shops Sylvia was dragging her to.

'Faith? Are you okay?' Sylvia's voice rang through the fitting room, and Faith winced. Why hadn't she lied about her first name, too? Would have made things much easier. Except she'd always been Faith, and she hadn't wanted to lose that too, when she was letting go of everything else.

She'd probably forget to answer to another name, anyway.

'Fine,' she called back, her voice low. 'I don't think this is the one for me.'

'Well, I think we could have predicted that before you came in here,' Sylvia said drily. 'Lady Gale has left, by the way. She was just placing an order for a new jacket.'

Was she that obvious? 'Who?' Faith tried innocently but, as she unlocked the door to the changing room, Sylvia was standing on the other side, arms folded and eyebrows raised.

'Want to explain to me what just happened?' she asked.

Faith shook her head. 'Not really. It's old news now, anyway.' Which didn't mean anyone had forgotten about it. Certainly not the Internet.

'Former employer?' Sylvia guessed.

'Something like that.'

'I won't tell Dominic, you know. Not if you don't want me to.'

'There's nothing to tell,' Faith lied. Then, leaving the hideous black dress hanging on the rail, she headed back out into the shop and straight for the door. 'Come on; I think I've got a better idea of what I'm looking for now.'

Dominic was a busy man. He'd had important meetings all day, emails and calls to deal with, not to mention some valuable forward planning with Marie and Henry that afternoon. They'd made some real headway on the expansion plans, and Dominic could almost see his dreams coming to life.

Which was why it was particularly embarrassing to admit, even to himself, that he'd spent most of the day wondering what sort of a dress Sylvia would persuade Faith to buy for the theatre that evening.

He hadn't had a chance to see Faith all day, despite his attempt to catch her at breakfast. He had, however, seen Jerry, which had been entertaining enough in itself.

The man had turned white, then slightly green, then run in the opposite direction down the corridor away from him. Okay, maybe it was more of a power walk than a run, but when Dominic told the story to Faith he expected to make it more of a sprint.

When he finally saw Faith, of course.

Maybe he'd pushed her too far last night, letting on that he knew she was lying to him. Faith was like a small frightened animal at times, behind her confident exterior. Whatever she was hiding, it scared her, which in turn worried Dominic even more.

Two and a half days. That was all the time he had left to uncover Faith's secret. To find out if it was something he could live with. Something they could deal with together.

And if it wasn't...then he had two and a half days before he never saw Faith again.

The thought made him shudder.

By the time he made it back to the hotel that evening, he had a scant half hour to shower and change, but he still managed to make it to the lobby before anyone else, ready for their evening of theatre.

Faith was next down, as he'd expected. He'd come to value the brief, quiet ten minutes before they left for the evening's entertainment. Ten minutes when it was just them and they had a chance to catch up on the day, and the plans for the next one. It was work, of course, but somehow it felt more like play when Faith was there.

The lift pinged, and Dominic turned to see if Faith was on board, sucking in a breath as the doors opened. Would it be backless? he wondered. And surely not black. Whatever it was, she'd look fantastic. And he'd get to spend the whole evening looking at her. Almost as good as if it were really just them going out together for the evening.

But then Faith stepped out of the lift, into the lobby, and Dominic's breath slowly released in disappointment.

'Sylvia let you buy that?' he asked as she strode across the lobby in plain flat navy shoes. What happened to the glorious red heels of last night? Oh yeah. Broken, even before she stamped on Jerry.

'What's wrong with it?' Faith asked, looking down at herself.

Dominic searched for the right words. In lots of ways, it was perfect. Navy dress, cream cardigan and handbag. Nothing too revealing or showy, but smart enough for the occasion. Maybe Sylvia *had* chosen it. He had a hard time believing Faith would because, despite everything that was right with it…

'It's just…boring.'

Faith beamed. 'Thank you. That's just what I was going for.'

Dominic shook his head. He was beginning to believe that he didn't stand a chance of ever understanding what went on in Faith's brain. Especially if he only had two days left to learn.

The others arrived shortly after, and they piled into pre-ordered taxis to take them to the theatre. There'd be food at the after-show party later, so he'd told Faith not to bother with booking a dinner.

The press were out in force for the occasion, and he lost sight of Faith in the melee as they were shepherded through the crowds into the theatre. Inside, the place was crowded with half familiar faces, and Dominic quickly lost track of who he actually knew and who he just recognised from TV.

'I've arranged drinks with the barman over in the balcony bar,' Faith said, suddenly at his side. She was shorter without her heels, and had to stand on tiptoe and shout into his ear to be heard over the crowd. Someone brushed past her and knocked her balance and, without even thinking about it, Dominic wrapped an arm around her waist to keep her upright.

'Lord Beresford?' Dominic looked up to see the official photographer for the evening brandishing a camera at him. 'A photo, if you please?'

He hated this. Hated that his attending a play was the cause for photographs and reports. Hated that anyone cared.

Still, it was part of the deal. He knew this. And, even if he hadn't, his father had made it perfectly clear when he was growing up. Whatever else was going on, you played the part.

One of the many things his father forgot after his mother left. Including his children.

He gave the photographer a swift nod and let his arm fall from Faith's waist.

'With your friend?' the photographer asked hopefully.

Of course. 'Do you mind?' he asked, turning to where Faith had been standing, only to find that she'd gone. He caught a brief glimpse of navy disappearing into the sea of people, but didn't bother calling after her. 'Apparently not,' he told the photographer, who looked disappointed, but snapped away at a couple of shots anyway.

He eventually found Faith, along with Sylvia and his clients, in the upper balcony bar. 'What happened to you?' he asked, taking a glass of champagne from her hand.

'Just doing my job,' she said, smiling innocently. 'Your guests were thirsty.'

She was lying again. He almost wished he couldn't tell. The number of casual lies she told him in a day was honestly disturbing.

'So, what's this show about, anyway?' he asked, to distract himself from the fact that not only was the woman he'd fallen for leaving him in two days, but she'd been lying to him the whole time he'd known her and it was getting increasingly likely that he'd never get to know the truth.

'You don't know?' she asked. 'But you specifically asked me to arrange for us to see it.'

He covered a yawn with his hand. Apparently late nights and long days weren't compatible with theatre visits. 'Sylvia said it was the biggest show opening this week. Although I think she just told me that so I'd get her a ticket, too.'

She stared at him. 'You're going to sleep through the whole thing, aren't you? The lights will go down, the theatre will be warm, the seats will be cosy, and I'll spend the entire evening trying to pretend you're not snoring.'

Actually, that didn't sound all that bad. 'I'm sure I'll wake up for the interval drinks.'

Faith rolled her eyes, but then he felt her body tense beside his.

'Lord Beresford? Perhaps I could get that shot of you with your friend now?'

Photographers. Knowing his luck, they'd get one of him fast asleep halfway through the first act. And now worrying about that was going to keep him awake.

'Faith? Is that okay?' He turned to where she'd been standing just moments ago, but the space was empty.

Where the hell had she gone now? And why?

'Sorry,' he told the photographer unapologetically. 'She's camera shy.'

And then he set about finding Faith, and some answers.

CHAPTER TEN

FAITH HAD FIGURED that the tiny alcove on the back stairs leading up to the Upper Circle was a decent enough place to hide. Plenty of people passing by, none of them likely to recognise a used-to-be-notorious girl in a boring navy dress.

She hadn't counted on Lord Dominic Beresford's tenacity, though.

'What the hell are you hiding from?' He planted himself outside her hiding place, hands on his hips.

'I'm not hiding,' Faith lied. 'I just got a bit claustrophobic. You know, with all the crowds up there. Thought I'd get some air.'

A group of theatre-goers trying to reach their seats forced Dominic off the staircase and into her alcove, and suddenly Faith really couldn't breathe. He was too solid, too attractive—and too close! How was she supposed to keep her story straight when she was surrounded by the scent of his aftershave, when she could feel the heat of his skin through his shirt?

'Claustrophobic.' Disbelief coloured Dominic's words. 'So you hid here. In a ridiculously small alcove with hundreds of people walking past.'

'I was *trying* to get outside,' Faith said, knowing he didn't believe her. 'I just got a little turned around.'

'Then let's go.' Grabbing her hand, Dominic led her down the staircase and out through a side door. Faith sucked in the cool evening air, letting it fill her lungs and calm her.

That had been close. Too close. If that photographer had got her photo and run it with a caption about Lord Beresford…it wouldn't matter where she went next, Dominic would still have to deal with the fallout when someone realised who she was.

He'd still end up hating her.

'Feeling any better?' Dominic asked as the side door slammed shut behind them.

Faith nodded. 'But I don't think we're getting back in that way,' she said, motioning at the handleless door. 'And I left our tickets in my bag, upstairs in the bar.'

'I'm fairly sure they'll let us back in.' Dominic leant back against the brick wall of the theatre, arms folded over his chest. 'If I ask them to.'

He was watching her too carefully and his words from the night before flooded her brain.

I just wish you'd stop lying to me and let me see the real you.

How did he know? And how much did he suspect?

'Are you going to?' she asked.

'That depends,' Dominic said.

'On what?'

'On if you're going to tell me the truth.'

Fear crawled through her middle. 'I told you. I just needed some air—'

'Not about tonight. Well, not just about tonight,' he amended. 'You've been lying to me since the moment we met, and I want to know why.'

Faith stilled, and looked up into his dark eyes.

'No,' she said. 'You really don't.'

* * *

Her words hit him in the gut. That was it then. Whatever her secret was, it was too big for them to move past. Too huge for her to even trust him with.

It was over, before it ever really started.

He should walk away now. Head back into the theatre and his clients and his sister. Let Faith work out the rest of the trip, without letting her any closer to his heart. Then he should put her on a plane and resign himself to never seeing her again.

He knew exactly what he should do.

But instead he said, 'Then we're not going back inside.'

She looked desperate now, her eyes wide and pleading. 'Dominic, don't be ridiculous. We've got your clients to sort out; my handbag is in there...'

'I'll text Sylvia. She can deal with everything.' In fact, he rather thought his sister might cheer approvingly.

'So what are we going to do?' Faith asked.

It wasn't a plan, wasn't something he'd thought out or weighed up and decided on. And it might be the most un-Lord-Beresford-like thing he'd done in his entire life.

But somehow Dominic knew it was the only thing to do.

'We're going to take a night off.'

'A night off?' Faith's forehead crinkled up.

He nodded. 'One night. Just one night, where I'm not Lord Beresford and you're not my employee. One night to just be Dominic and Faith.'

She wanted it, he could tell. Her eyes were wider than ever, filled with amazement, and the slight flush on her cheeks told him she hadn't missed any of the possibilities of the suggestion.

'For just this one night,' he said, moving closer, 'it doesn't matter about the truth. Doesn't matter about our pasts, or our futures. For tonight, all that matters is us.'

He took her hand, rubbing circles on her palm with his thumb, and held his breath when she looked up at him, her lower lip caught between her teeth.

'Just one night?'

'Just one night,' he echoed.

'What will we do?' she asked, and Dominic's mind filled with possibilities, most including getting her out of that ugly dress as soon as possible.

No. Too quick. If he only had one night with her, he needed to do this properly.

'First, I'm going to take you out for dinner. Anywhere you choose.'

Some of the tension dropped from her stance at that, and she smiled. 'I know just the place.'

The crowds were still gathered out front, but by keeping close to the side of the building they managed to avoid them as they dashed across the street behind the theatre, the warm evening air smelling of freedom and possibility.

One night. Just one night. That was what he'd said. And even though Faith knew she shouldn't, knew that this could end in disaster, or at least a broken heart, she couldn't resist that kind of temptation. Surely she could keep her secret for just one night?

Covent Garden buzzed with life, filled to overflowing with tourists, buskers, after-work socialisers, people wanting to sell something and people looking to buy. Faith let the sights and sounds warm her, make her feel at home again. She hadn't realised she'd felt so out of place in her own London that week, until now.

'So, where do you want to go?' Dominic asked. 'Somewhere around here?' He cast an arm around him at the market piazza, almost hitting a tourist in shorts and a Bermuda shirt as he did so. 'Looks like there's plenty of places to choose from.' Seeing Faith's horrified look, he added, 'What? I know it's not exactly up there with the meals you've been organising this week—'

'That's not it,' Faith interrupted. 'Just...Covent Garden's for the tourists. It's the equivalent of eating pizza right next door to the Coliseum in Rome. You'll get perfectly ordinary pizza at three times the price.'

They'd stopped walking, Faith realised, and were standing still in a sea of people, swelling and ebbing around them. Dominic's hand came down to rest at her waist, pulling her in closer, anchoring her against the tide. Heat spread out through her body from the place where they touched, and she swallowed, hard.

'Follow me,' she said, and grabbed his hand with her own.

It was easy to get trapped in the slow-moving crowds if you didn't know what you were doing. Dominic would have been far too polite to do the essential barging through if she'd left him to his own devices. That was the only reason she held his hand, she reasoned.

Of course, once they'd escaped the market and were walking more casually away along Long Acre, she didn't let go. By that point, it felt far too natural.

'Where are we going?' Dominic asked, his thumb rubbing the back of her hand in a relaxing rhythm.

'A little Italian I know.' Marco had taken her there, back when he was trying to hire her for his fledgling tour company. He said it would give her a real taste of Rome.

Dominic's thumb stopped its comforting movements. 'Missing Italy already?'

'Not really,' Faith said, giving him a smile. 'Mostly just the pasta.'

He returned the smile and started stroking her hand again.

Faith suddenly found herself wishing that she'd bought the dress Sylvia wanted her to have, the backless, wine-red dress that cascaded down her legs and showed off every single curve, instead of the boring navy shift she'd chosen.

Tugging on his hand, she led him down a hidden backstreet into the cooler shadows where the sun never reached, even at noon on midsummer. Halfway down the alley, a tattered red sign hung above a dirty window, and read simply, 'Lola's'. No one would recognise them there.

'This is it?' Dominic asked, looking dubious.

'Trust me,' Faith said, and he sighed.

'Seems to me, trusting you could get me into a lot of trouble.'

Faith smiled brightly to try and pretend that didn't hurt, just a little. After all, he was right. 'Oh, I don't know. You're doing okay so far.'

'This is true.' He pushed against the door and a bell clattered tinnily. 'Come on, then.'

Inside, the restaurant was even darker than Faith remembered. But then, most of her memories were of the picture Marco had painted of Rome in the summer, and of the Italian lakes. Well, that and the fantastic walnut pasta and red wine that went down like water.

A waiter in jeans and a T-shirt led them to a table at the back, and Faith watched in amusement as Dominic realised nearly every other table in the place was already occupied.

'Am I the only person who doesn't know about this place?' he murmured as they took their seats.

Faith slipped her cardigan from her shoulders and placed it on the back of her chair. White cashmere didn't go well with red wine. 'There are a lot of people in London,' she pointed out. 'Not everyone can afford to eat at the finest restaurants every night. Besides, the food's better here.'

'Can we see a menu, please?' Dominic asked, as if looking for proof, but the waiter shook his head.

'No menus,' he said, his rich Italian accent adding extra amusement to his tone. 'We'll bring you the best we have.'

As he spoke, a younger girl appeared, also in jeans, and filled their glasses with red wine. Dominic raised his eyebrows, but lifted the glass to his lips anyway.

'Not bad,' he said as the servers disappeared.

Faith tried her own. 'Liar. It's gorgeous.'

The smile Dominic gave her was warm and intimate, and suddenly Faith knew it didn't matter if the food had gone drastically downhill since the last time she was there; this would still be a better evening than the one with Marco. Apparently all she needed for a fantastic evening was the presence of Lord Dominic Beresford.

She wondered if that worked for everyone. She could use him on all her tours...

'What are you thinking?' Dominic asked, and Faith shook herself back into the real world. He wasn't Lord Beresford right now, anyway. He was just Dominic. Maybe even *her* Dominic, just for the night.

'Absolute nonsense,' she admitted. 'And worrying a little about abandoning my post.' Getting out of the theatre had seemed like the best plan, given that dodging every single camera was probably impossible. But, on the other hand, she'd been hired to do a job and she wasn't currently fulfilling those obligations.

'I'm the boss,' Dominic pointed out. 'You can look on this as…a mid-project appraisal.'

'Is that so?' Faith leant back in her chair and watched as he nodded. 'In that case, how am I doing?'

'Fantastically.'

Faith hoped the candlelight was forgiving enough to hide her blush. 'Anyone would think you were biased.'

Dominic's eyes turned dark. 'Oh, but I am.' Reaching across the table, he took her hand again. 'Utterly, utterly biased. Because I want you to stay in London with me.'

Maybe it was the wine, but suddenly Faith felt reckless. They weren't at the hotel, or at an event. There were no clients around. There was no chance of bumping into anyone who might recognise Lady Faith Fowlmere at Lola's. This was their one night. There was nothing at all to stop her asking for the truth.

'Because you want me to work for you?'

His smile was slow. 'Faith. I promise you that, for once, work is the furthest thing from my mind tonight.'

It wasn't quite a lie, Dominic reasoned and, even if it was, she'd told enough of her own. He'd offered her a night off, a night away from who they really were, because he couldn't bear the idea of her leaving without doing *something* about whatever compulsion it was that burned between them.

It wasn't easy, though. Business, sure. He could forget about contracts and meetings in a heartbeat. But the title, the heritage, they were scored deep into him in a way she couldn't understand. You had to be born to that kind of obligation. Still, just being with Faith made it easier. It was impossible not to relax around her, harder still not to lean into her, touch her, flirt and caress, however much he'd planned to take things slow.

Around the third glass of wine, he stopped even trying.

The servers, for all they looked as if they'd been yanked in off the streets, knew what they were doing. Dominic barely noticed when they topped up his glass or cleared away their empty plates. The food—incredible-tasting food on plates for sample-sized portions—just kept on coming, course after course. Antipasti, pastas—three kinds—fish, meat, and then, when they were almost fit to busting, a sorbet so sharp it almost cut the mouth. The tiramisu to finish would have been beyond him, but Faith grabbed her own spoon and dug into the shared plate, and the expression on her face as she tried it made him want to know what made her look like that. If he could replicate the experience for her in other ways...

'Oh, that is good,' he admitted, taking his own bite.

Faith gave him a smug smile. 'I knew you'd enjoy letting go for once.'

Suddenly, his head was filled with all the ways he could make her let go. How she would look if he kissed her breathless. How he could touch her until she forgot who she was, never mind him.

He swallowed down the last of his wine. Too much, too soon. 'So, what do you want to do next?' he asked, as the waiter brought over two tiny glasses of Limoncello, along with the bill.

Faith picked up her glass, took a sip, then licked her sticky fingers. Dominic felt something tighten in his chest at the sight. 'Well, that depends on you,' she said.

'On me? How?'

'Do you think you've managed to suitably forget who you are for the night?'

Watching her across the table in the candlelight, Dominic thought he might actually be a whole new person, after all. 'I think I've managed it, yes.'

'In that case,' she said, pushing his liquor glass towards him with two fingers, 'drink up. Because I want to show you *my* London.'

CHAPTER ELEVEN

SHE STARTED ON the South Bank, because she loved the way it lit up and came to life at night. They crossed at Waterloo Bridge, with a crush of other people heading the same way, and walked west along the river, towards the London Eye.

'I've been on that, at least,' Dominic said, looping her hand through his arm. 'Does that earn me any points?'

Faith considered. 'Depends. Did you go on an ordinary day with ordinary people? Or were there champagne, strawberries and schmoozing involved?'

'The latter,' Dominic admitted. 'Does that mean I have to go on it again?'

'Probably. But not tonight.'

They walked further, staring back across the river at the lights of Westminster, watching Big Ben as it chimed the hour. It was already getting late, Faith realised. She wondered how Dominic would feel about getting the night bus back… She shook her head. A step too far for this trip, she decided. Besides, if the evening went the way she hoped, she didn't want to waste time on buses.

'You know, I don't think I've ever done this,' Dominic said as they paused at the railings, just taking in the skyline.

'Done what?'

'Just…wandered around the city with a beautiful girl on my arm.' He tugged her a little closer at his words, and Faith felt the warmth of him seeping through her dress. He thought she was beautiful. No one had ever called her that before. Sexy, yes. Gorgeous, yes. Beautiful? No.

'How long have you lived here?' she asked, hoping to distract from her blush. 'How is that even possible?'

Dominic shrugged, and shifted again, drawing her into the circle of his arms, making her feel warm and safe. 'I grew up on the country estate. Trips to London were always for a purpose. I went from car to hotel to venue or event, back to hotel then car and home again. I wasn't exactly encouraged to explore.'

Faith leant back against his chest, remembering how that felt, that being shuffled from one place to the next, more of an accessory than a person. Surely Dominic, of all people, could understand why she'd run?

'What about when you grew up?' she asked.

'It didn't occur to me,' Dominic said, amused honesty in his voice. 'I don't know why. No, I do. There was just so much else to do. I had an entire family name to save. Every single thing I did, for years, was about building up the estate, making new connections, finding new ways to use the land, the influence, the money that started coming in. I didn't have time for anything else.'

'Not even people?' He sounded so lonely. How could she leave him when he sounded so terribly alone?

'Just Sylvia, really. Until Kat came along.'

Ah, of course. Maybe he had a reason for wanting to be alone. 'I don't like to pry…'

'You love to pry. You're officially nosy.'

'Okay, yes, I am.' How had he got to know her so well, so fast? 'I saw the YouTube video.'

'You and every other person in the country with eyes.' There was a bitterness to his words Faith didn't like. Was he still in love with Kat?

She tilted her head round to see his face. 'Want to tell me what happened?'

'You want a blow-by-blow account?' he asked, eyebrows raised. 'I thought you saw the video.'

'Not that,' she said. 'Between the two of you. A woman doesn't just go off and betray her fiancé on the Internet for no reason.'

He sighed, and she could feel the air leaving his chest, leaving him smaller, sunken. 'She didn't know she was being filmed, apparently. Not that it's much of an excuse.'

'It really, really isn't.'

There was a pause, and for a moment she thought that was all he would say on the matter. Then he spoke again. 'She was unhappy. With me, mostly. She…she wanted me to let her in, she said. She never felt like she was a real part of my life.'

Faith winced. She could see that, could see Dominic defending everything he held dear, holding it so tight that there was no room for anything else. Until tonight.

'You loved her, though?'

Dominic shrugged. 'She seemed like a good fit. Similar background, similar ambitions. She'd have been a great lady of the manor.'

Faith frowned. 'You make it sound like you were marrying her to enhance your brand, not because you loved her.'

'Maybe I was,' Dominic admitted, and Faith's eyes widened. 'Not intentionally, of course. I thought it was the real thing. But now, I wonder… Maybe she's right. Maybe I never let her in.'

'Because then she couldn't really leave you.'

She'd turned almost completely round in his arms now, Faith realised too late. His grip had tightened too, and anyone seeing them would surely have no doubt that they were lovers, held close in a lovers' embrace. Her body pressed up against his chest, her hands at his back. Would he kiss her this time? Would she let him?

Somewhere, a car horn blared, a crowd of guys laughed out loud and music played. Dominic ignored all of it, staring straight into her eyes. Then, without giving any indication of what had changed between them, he said, 'So, what's next on this tour of yours?'

Faith blinked, trying to break out of the moment. And then she realised that there was still one very special place she wanted to show him. 'Let's go see the pelicans.'

'Are you going to make me break into a zoo?' Dominic asked as they crossed back over Westminster Bridge, the Thames gleaming with lights below them. 'Because I think not being Lord Beresford for the night stops at criminal behaviour.'

Faith rolled her eyes, then tugged on his hand to make him keep moving. 'Have you honestly never seen the pelicans in St James's Park before?'

'Didn't even know we had any.' How many times had he walked through that park, on the way to somewhere? A few, at least. Wouldn't he have noticed big white birds swooping overhead?

The gates to the park were still open, thankfully, which meant it couldn't be too late, even if it felt like some magical witching hour. That was probably just Faith's influence.

'What time does the park close?' he asked as they headed into trees and lush grasses, just moments from the busy city centre.

'Midnight,' Faith replied, her tour guide brain still working.

'Do you know everything about London?' He'd lived in the city most of his adult life, and apparently missed everything of any importance. He had to spend more time exploring. If he ever got the chance.

'I know that the park has been home to pelicans since 1664, when the Russian Ambassador gave the first ones as a gift. And I know that the city of Prague gave the park three new ones last year, and I haven't met them yet.'

She talked about them like friends or relatives, he realised. 'You like the pelicans?'

'They're my favourite part of the city,' she admitted, stumbling to a stop on the lakeside path. 'Look!'

Dominic's gaze followed where her finger was pointing, into a clump of reeds at the edge of the lake. It took him a moment to spot the white feathers in the moonlight. 'It's asleep.'

Faith gave him a scathing look. 'Of course he is. It's late.'

Glancing at his watch, Dominic realised she was right. 'Eleven-thirty. Cars should be picking up from the theatre around now. Heading to the after-show party.'

'Want to head back and catch up with them?' Faith asked.

Dominic didn't even need to think about his answer. 'No.'

'So what do you want to do?' She was close again,

too close. Closer even than she'd been as they'd looked out over the river, talking about Kat. Close enough to make him crazy. 'It's your turn to choose.'

'I want to spend tonight with you.'

So close he could see her eyes darkening, even in the faint moonlight under the trees. 'I thought that's what we've been doing.'

He shook his head. 'This was just the evening. I want the whole night.'

And he did. He wanted it so badly he ached. And he didn't care if she couldn't stay, didn't care if it could never go anywhere. Didn't care what the risk was. He just wanted her.

'Are you sure?' Faith asked, her lower lip caught between her teeth.

'Absolutely.'

'I'm leaving—'

'I know. We both know what this is, and what it isn't. What it can't be. I don't know what you're hiding from me, but I trust you it's better that way. And I can't let you leave without...' He stopped, trying to find the words. Wrapping his hands around her waist, he pulled her closer, close enough that she had to be able to feel every line of his body through that hideous dress. 'You've shown me your world tonight. All the things you love about a city I've lived in for years and never got to see.' No, that wasn't right. 'Or, worse, all the things I've seen every day and never felt the way you do. I want one night to see everything through your eyes. Just one night.'

Rising up on tiptoe, Faith pressed her lips against his and his whole body almost sagged with relief. Then his brain caught up and he hauled her closer again, practically lifting her off the floor as he kissed her properly, thoroughly. The way a woman like Faith deserved to be kissed.

'Back to the hotel?' Faith asked when he finally pulled away.

Dominic nodded. It was past time to take Faith home to bed.

They caught a cab back to the hotel, Dominic's hand at her waist the whole way, and Faith could feel the blood thrumming through her veins too fast, driving her on. He was Lord Beresford again now, she could tell, so there was no inappropriate behaviour in the taxi, much as she considered just climbing into his lap and kissing him speechless.

Or maybe she'd be the one without words. But the man could kiss! One touch of his lips and she'd forgotten anything she ever knew about any city in the world. If someone had asked her where she was right then, she'd have struggled to answer.

In a way, she was almost glad of the reprieve his propriety gave her. She needed a moment to gather her thoughts, to enjoy the anticipation of what was ahead. And besides, with only one night to enjoy with him, she wouldn't have wanted him to be pretending to be anyone else.

No, against the odds, and despite everything, it was Lord Dominic Beresford she'd fallen for, and Faith didn't want to even pretend otherwise.

The taxi pulled up outside the hotel, and Dominic handed over a couple of notes to the driver—too much, probably, not that Faith cared right then. She glanced around to check before getting out of the car, but there was no sign of the service she'd arranged to collect the clients from the theatre. She checked her phone quickly; no one had called, so hopefully that meant they were all still having fun at the after-show party, somewhere they wouldn't see her and Dominic heading up to his suite together.

Perfect.

Dominic took her arm as they headed into the hotel, and she felt a certain relief that he wasn't hiding this. Wasn't hiding her. She'd worried he might be…embarrassed, if not ashamed. After all, as far as he was concerned she wasn't in his social strata and besides, she was his employee. Dominic wasn't the sort to blur the lines of propriety that way, even without the secrets he knew she was keeping.

The doorman at the hotel foyer gave no sign of anything out of the ordinary when they walked in. The concierge nodded politely, but otherwise kept a blank face. The receptionist barely even looked up. Faith held her breath. This might really happen. One night: one perfect night. She'd earned this much over the last few years of voluntary exile, surely? He never had to know who she was. What she'd done.

They were silent in the lift, a respectable few inches between them. She wondered if Dominic really felt so keenly about keeping up appearances and respectability that he wouldn't even touch her in an empty lift. Or was he just afraid, as she was, that if they touched again they wouldn't be able to stop…?

She got her answer the moment the door to the hotel suite swung shut behind them.

'Faith…' His hands were on her waist in a moment, pulling her closer into him, his lips descending before she could even think, even comprehend what they were doing here.

He reached for the zip at the back of her dress, tugging it down with impatient fingers, and Faith breathed with relief to be out of the stupid thing. What had she been thinking, trying to be anyone but herself around this man? He might not know her true name or identity, but he saw exactly who she was. He'd found her, under the disguise, and wanted her anyway.

Kisses ran across her neck, her shoulders, and she realised Dominic was whispering between each one, murmuring words of affection and longing and desire. She bit her lip, tilting her head to give him better access, and wondered if she'd ever stop being surprised by this man. This man who had looked at her body with distaste when they met, but was now admitting exactly how much he wanted it. This man who appeared every inch the respectable aristocrat every moment of the day, but was currently whispering exactly what he wanted to do to her in enough detail to make her whole body pulse.

He was so much more than she'd ever imagined that night in Rome, and she wanted him more than she could have dreamt.

Reaching up, she trailed her own kisses across his jaw, to his ear, his hands gripping her tighter as she went. Then she whispered, 'Take me to bed,' and felt the floor disappear under her feet as he lifted her and turned them round, covering the space between them and the bed in a very few steps.

Faith's back hit the mattress and her greedy hands pulled him down on top of her, not wanting their bodies to be separated for a moment. This was it. Her one night with Dominic Beresford. One night to be entirely herself, whatever name she used. And she was definitely going to make the most of it.

Afterwards, in the dim light of the darkened room, Faith curled closer into Dominic's side and tried to control her

breathing. 'We definitely have to do that again,' she said
without thinking, then winced. 'Before I leave, I mean.'

'We really, really do,' Dominic said, and she relaxed.
But then he added, 'You have to leave?'

She nodded against his chest, pressing a kiss against
his breastbone as an apology. 'I do.'

'Why?'

It was easier, admitting things in the dark. 'I can't
be who I need to be, here.'

'With me?'

'In London,' she corrected him.

He sighed. 'And I can't leave. Not for ever, anyway.'

If he were anyone else, he could, Faith knew. Anyone but Lord Dominic Beresford, defender of reputation and honour across the British Isles.

'The estate.'

'My family.'

'Your name.' She hadn't meant it to sound bitter,
but it did.

Dominic shifted, turning onto his side and pulling
her closer against him. She could only just see his eyes
in the darkness, but she could feel his heartbeat against
hers. 'It's not just the name. It's who I am. Who I was
born to be.'

'You were someone else tonight,' she reminded him.

'Just for tonight. I wish…' He shook his head. 'I
know you don't get it, Faith. And maybe it is just the
way I was brought up, or my heritage. But…these things
matter to me. Responsibility. Trust. Duty. Reputation.
They do, and I can't change that. My mother…she didn't
take those things seriously. She put her own desires
ahead of her responsibilities and it almost destroyed us.
She betrayed all of us when she ran away, but the family
name most of all. I couldn't do that. And then Kat…'

Faith's heart grew heavy at the other woman's name. 'She betrayed your trust.'

'She did. But more than that… It wasn't just that she cheated on me. It was that she did it in a way calculated to cause the most damage to everything I hold dear. My family, my reputation. She hurt them. And she hurt me.'

He spoke simply, stating the facts, but the iron weight that had settled in Faith's chest in place of her heart pulled her down further at his words. Wasn't she doing the same? Whichever way things went. She was a runaway, a betrayer just like his mother. And she was making him take a risk of scandal and embarrassment, without even letting him know the danger was there, just like Kat. She should have told him, and now it was too late.

But if she'd told him…they'd never have had this night. And Faith couldn't give that up, even for honour's sake. Maybe that was the true difference between them.

A sharp ringing noise jerked her out of her thoughts, and Dominic reached across her body to grab the hotel room phone.

'Yes?' he said, then as he listened to the voice on the line his body stilled. 'We'll be right down.'

Hanging up, he pulled away from Faith, sitting with his back to her on the edge of the bed.

'What's happened?' she asked, her heavy heart beating too hard now.

Dominic's voice was calm and steady as he replied. Unfeeling. 'They need us in the lobby. There's someone down there asking for you. Apparently he's causing quite a scene.'

Oh no. Faith swallowed, reaching for her dress. 'Right, of course. I don't…I can't…' How could she explain that she didn't know who it was, because there were too many options to choose from? Her father. Antonio. Great-Uncle Nigel. Who'd found her? And who had such awfully bad timing as to ruin this night?

'I suppose we'll find out what this is about when we get downstairs,' Dominic said, and Faith nodded, a sick feeling rising up in her throat.

She didn't bother with her bra or tights, just pulled the dress over her head and shoved her feet into her shoes. She probably looked a state but, well, wasn't that just what people would expect anyway? Even Dominic, in trousers and an untucked shirt, looked less respectable than normal. Not as free and abandoned as he'd been half an hour before, but Faith knew, in her heart, that she'd never get to see that side of Dominic again. Whoever was waiting for her in the lobby had ruined that for her.

The lift ride down was silent again, but this time the tension between them was filled with questions rather than anticipation. Faith kept her eyes on the toes of her shoes and prayed that she'd be able to talk her way out of whatever this was.

But then the lift door opened and before they could even step out she heard her name being yelled across the lobby.

'Faith!'

She froze. The accent was wrong for Antonio, or her father, and Great-Uncle Nigel sounded like the fifty-a-day smoker he was, so...

'Lady Faith Fowlmere.'

Dominic froze beside her, and Faith made herself look across the lobby to see who it was that had unmasked her. Who had ruined her one night.

She closed her eyes against the horror as she recognised the photographer from the theatre striding across the lobby towards her. Then her brain processed what she was seeing and her eyelids flew open again. He had his camera. He had his camera out and pointed at them.

'We need to go,' Dominic said, grabbing her hand, but Faith knew it was already too late. The flash of the camera lit up the subdued lobby, light reflecting off the marble tiles and the mirrors on the stairs. There was no hiding this now.

'You need to come with me. Now!' Dominic's words fought their way out from between clenched teeth and Faith ducked her head, turning and following him towards the lift.

'Lady Faith! Would you like to make a comment on your whereabouts for the last couple of years?' the photographer called after them, still snapping away.

'Do not say a single word.' He sounded furious. She'd known he would be. She'd just hoped he'd never have to find out. Or at least that she'd be many, many miles away when he did.

'Or perhaps what made you want to come back?'

Faith couldn't resist a glance over her shoulder at that, even as Dominic stabbed the call lift button repeatedly. The reporter was smirking, obviously assuming he knew exactly why she was there: Dominic. Just as they'd been so, so sure they knew what she was doing in that hotel room with Jared three years ago.

They were wrong again.

She hadn't come back to London for Dominic, and there wasn't a chance in hell he'd let her stay now he knew the truth.

The lift pinged and the doors opened at last. Dominic hauled her inside, holding down the close doors button

before she was even through. All Faith could see was
the reporter's smile, even after the lift started to move.

And then she realised she was alone with Dominic. Again.

'My room,' he said, the words clipped. 'We don't
talk about this until we are safely behind a locked door.'

CHAPTER TWELVE

THIS WASN'T QUITE how he'd imagined having her in his room tonight.

Faith stood against the wall by the bathroom, arms folded over her chest, looking like a schoolgirl caught smoking. Like she was just anyone. Like she was still his Faith, only guiltier.

Lady Faith Fowlmere. How had he not known? Okay, so he didn't exactly study the social pages, but even he'd heard the story of the missing heiress, and the scandals she left behind. There must have been a clue, something that he'd missed. Probably because he was too busy being swayed by her curves and her enthusiasm for life.

A life away from the one he lived.

'Were you planning on telling me?' he asked, his eyes landing on her bra, still tossed across the arm of the chair. Just how had this gone so wrong so quickly?

Faith's head jerked up and she met his gaze head-on, her eyes wide but steady. 'No.'

Hope drained out of him. If she'd said anything else—that she was scared, that she hadn't known how, that she wanted to know how he felt first…anything else at all—maybe they could have worked it out. He could have understood, perhaps.

But she'd never wanted him to know who she was. Ever.

'Why?'

A half-shrug, one hunched shoulder raised. 'We agreed one night. Come on. You knew I wasn't going to stay, and you knew there was a reason. Look me up on the Internet and you'll see why. I'm a scandal; everyone knows it. And I know you. You'd have fired me if you found out. Too much of a risk. And, more than that, you'd have wanted me to talk to my parents, to reconcile, for the good of the family name. You know you would.'

She was right. She did know him. Better than he'd ever been allowed to know her. 'And you won't.' Not a question. He knew her that well, at least.

'I don't ever want to go back there.' The vehemence in her voice surprised him. He didn't know the Fowlmeres personally, but they were her family.

'You might have to. We need to put a respectable face on this, and "runaway heiress returns home" sounds a hell of a lot better than "runaway heiress found in high-priced love nest".' He reached for his phone, trying to keep his temper under control. He needed to think, not react. And he needed to ignore the part of his brain that was telling him that the secrets were out now. He knew the worst of it. Maybe he could salvage something from this.

But first he had to fix it.

'Here's what's going to happen now,' he said, scrolling through his contacts. 'I'm going to call my PR people, get them down here. I'll sit down with them, come up with a plan. Maybe we can talk to the reporter, or more likely the newspaper owner. Maybe we can get

an injunction. I don't know. But I am *not* going to let
your past ruin my future.'

Faith hadn't even moved from her position by the
door. 'And what am I going to be doing, while you set
about fixing my mistakes?' Her voice was cool, calm—
everything he didn't feel right then.

'You are going to be sitting in your hotel room, not
talking to anyone, not seeing anyone, not even *thinking*
about anyone. Do you understand me?'

Her eyes were sad as she spoke. 'Oh, I understand.
You're going to rewrite not just my history, but our entire past.'

'I've known you a week, Faith. I don't think what we
had qualifies as a past.'

'We had tonight.'

'And now we don't.'

Faith felt very cold, as if someone had left a window open
in winter and the icy wind was chilling her through,
layer by layer. Was this how it felt to freeze to death?
And, in the absence of both winter and wind, was Dominic's coldness enough to finish the job?

'You're treating me like a child,' she said, the words
hard lumps in her throat.

'I'm treating you like what you are,' he replied. 'A
scandal and a flight risk.'

Just like his mother, Faith realised. But knowing why
he was mad, expecting it even, didn't make it any easier.

And it didn't mean he got to take over her life.

'I understand,' she said again, wrapping her arms
tighter around her. 'You'd better make your phone call.'

Dominic gave a sharp nod. 'Go straight to your room.
I wouldn't put it past that photographer to have snuck
back in, assuming security kicked him out by now. He

could be anywhere. I'll call you in the morning,' he said, and she nodded as she collected her belongings and headed back towards the door, away from him, thinking hard.

He wanted her to stay hidden. Wanted her to let him fix her life for her. Wanted her to be a good, obedient Lady Faith.

It was as if he'd never known her at all.

This would be all over the Internet by the morning, however hot Dominic's PR team were supposed to be. And if she were going to be a story again, a scandal even, she was doing it on her own terms. She couldn't stay with someone who was embarrassed by her, ashamed of her.

Not even Dominic.

The story was out now, and that changed everything. What was the point of hiding when everyone knew where she was? This job had been her last chance. Without it—and without her salary for the week—she was out of options. She couldn't just hop on a flight to another country this time. Chances were, she'd be spotted at the airport, anyway.

No, Faith knew what she needed to do next. Even if it was the last thing she wanted.

Back in her hotel room, Faith packed quickly and economically. Three years as a tour guide had taught her the best way to roll clothes, as well as what was essential, and what wasn't.

She stripped off the hideous dress she'd bought for the theatre and left it folded on the chair. She wouldn't need it again. Instead, she pulled on an old pair of jeans, a T-shirt and a cardigan, loading her case with the rest of her clothes. She removed her make-up before packing her cosmetics bag, shoved her feet in her trainers and headed for the door.

As one final thought, she left Dominic's expenses credit card on top of the dress. He already thought badly enough of her. She didn't want him thinking she was a thief, too.

She kept the money in her purse though, the last remains of the petty cash he'd given her at the start of the week, to buy a train ticket back to the only place she had left.

Home.

Dominic was up early the next day, after a night spent liaising with his PR team and barely sleeping. He could still smell Faith on the bed sheets, and knowing she was only a few rooms away, awaiting his decision on her future, didn't help. He knew he couldn't really have handled it differently, under the circumstances. But knowing that didn't make him feel any better about it.

Now he just had to break the plan to Faith.

'We'll sell it as a rehabilitation,' Matthew the PR guy had said once they'd established there was no way to keep the news that the runaway heiress was back in town from breaking. 'You met in Rome and brought her back to try and reconcile her with her parents. There'll still be a lot of talk about her past, I'm sure, but as long as we present it right, get in early with the story, you should both come out okay.'

The first step, they'd agreed, was to get Faith to give an interview, with Dominic at her side as a sort of mentor. Then they'd stage the reunion with her parents, build it up carefully. After that, Matthew said, Dominic could wash his hands of her altogether, if he wanted.

It was a plan. It wasn't perfect, but it should at least

minimise the damage. Once he convinced Faith to play along.

Showered and dressed, he headed to her room, annoyed when she didn't answer his knock. He banged louder, and this time the door opened—only there was nobody on the other side. Anger and frustration started to build. The room was empty, with no sign that anyone had even slept in the bed last night.

Dominic swore. The runaway heiress had run again.

'I'm not staying,' Faith said, the moment her mother opened the door. Time was, there'd have been the butler to do that, but after Jenkins died when Faith was seven, there'd never been the money to hire another one.

Her mother raised her eyebrows at her, gestured inside with her glass and said, 'Then I assume you want money. There isn't any, you know.'

'Trust me,' Faith said, lugging her suitcase over the threshold, 'I know.'

Her father, at least, seemed pleased to see her.

'We missed you around here, you know,' he said, kissing her cheek and taking her arm as if she'd been away on holiday, not missing for three years. 'Nobody to laugh at my jokes!'

'I can't imagine that's true.' There had always been someone to laugh at the right time, to sparkle and smile when he wanted it. Lord Fowlmere had never needed his daughter—or even his wife—for that.

He laughed. 'Dahlia! Fix this girl a cocktail. She's probably been travelling for days to return to the bosom of her family.'

In fact, Faith had caught the first train north from King's Cross, studiously avoiding all the papers at the station and refusing to log into the train Wi-Fi. Instead, she'd slept all the way, then walked the three miles from the nearest station and arrived at Fowlmere late morning. Also known as cocktail hour to her mother and father.

While her mother fixed her drink, Faith took herself and her suitcase back up to her old room.

Now she was back, it almost felt as if she'd never left, except for the aching loss in her middle where thoughts of Dominic used to reside. If she thought about him, about the disappointment on his face or the feel of his body against hers, she'd cry. And if she started, she might not stop. So, no crying.

But, seriously, why was it she cared so much about his disappointment? She'd let down every single member of her family, scandalised the society in which they lived...why would she care about disappointing one man who she'd known for less than a week? Especially one who'd wanted her to stay put and stay quiet while he managed her life.

The answer whispered around her mind, but Faith refused to acknowledge it. That way lay madness, and probably a lot more cocktails than was advisable.

She managed to avoid most of her parents' questions by hiding in her room until dinner, ostensibly napping. Her father blamed jet lag and let her be, which was a blessing. But Faith knew she'd never sleep until she faced things head-on. So she pulled out her tablet, took a deep breath and checked out the damage.

The blogs and the websites had the news first, as always. The photo of her and Dominic in the lobby of the Greyfriars, looking as if they'd just rolled out of bed, was plastered everywhere. Faith scrolled past, wishing that every glimpse of the picture didn't make her remember exactly what they had been doing just before it was taken. How his body had felt pressed against hers. How perfect everything had been, for one fleeting moment.

The text below tended to be scant. Nobody knew anything except that she had been seen in London with Lord Dominic Beresford. Which was, she supposed, all there really was to know—especially if Dominic's PR team had got to work. There was speculation about where she'd been, and whether she was still holed up at the Greyfriars, but that was it for new news.

So, of course, they rehashed the old news instead. Faith buried the tablet under a pile of blankets on the trunk at the end of the bed when she reached that part.

Dinner with her parents was a stilted affair. Dad would try to make jokes, telling anecdotes that grew more obscure and confused with every glass of wine, but neither her mum nor Faith laughed. When he pulled out the whisky after dinner, Faith thought of Dominic and declined.

'I need an early night,' she said.

Her mother frowned. 'You slept all afternoon.'

'Jet lag, Dahlia,' Dad said, and Faith didn't disagree.

She wandered through the halls of the manor towards the main staircase, her gaze alighting on the holes in the carpet, the empty spaces on the shelves where expensive trinkets once sat. In some ways, it was hard not to compare Fowlmere with Beresford Hall. In others… there just was no comparison.

Fowlmere was decaying, ruined. Over. Just like her relationship with Dominic.

Tucked up in her childhood bed, the old feelings of isolation and hopelessness pressed in on her, but she willed them away. She'd escaped from this place once. She'd do it again. This was merely a temporary stop, until everything blew over and she was employable again. That was all.

She would never have to be that Lady Faith again. The girl with no place in the world, whose very home was falling apart around her, whose parents couldn't see past their own problems to see her misery. She was an adult now, and she got to choose her own life.

And nobody in their right mind would choose this.

The next morning, Faith pulled her tablet out from its cocoon and braved the news sites again. Nothing much new, except a note that Dominic had checked out of the Greyfriars, but with no sign of her. There was a new photo, showing Dominic stalking out of the hotel, dark eyes hard, ignoring every single reporter and photographer waiting for him. Something pulled at Faith's insides at the sight of him.

How he must hate her right now.

She shook her head. She had more practical matters to worry about. The news would have made it from the Internet to the papers this morning, which meant that her father would read it. And if the world knew she was no longer at the Greyfriars, the paparazzi would be coming here next. She needed to warn her parents, see if they were willing to stick with a 'no comment' rule until the reporters got bored. After all, none of them were very likely to want to sit in a field outside a crumbling mansion for more than a day or two, even if it meant getting a photo of the Runaway Heiress.

But before she got further than pulling on her dressing gown against the pervasive chill of Fowlmere Manor there was a sharp rap on the door and a mug of tea poked into the room, followed by her father.

'Am I allowed in?'

'Of course.' Faith took the drink and sipped. Milk and two sugars. She hadn't taken sugar for years.

Entering, he moved to the bed and sat, bouncing a little on the mattress. 'I haven't been in here for a while,' he admitted. 'Your mother, she'd come and sit in here whenever she missed you, but I found it easier just to stay away. Much like yourself.'

Faith blinked. 'She missed me?'

'Oh, very much. We both did. Not just for the laughing at jokes thing.' He gave her his trademark lopsided smile. 'And then when I saw that business in the papers this morning...I understood. No jet lag then, I suppose?' A blush heated Faith's cheeks. 'Shame you couldn't bring Lord Beresford with you, really. I wouldn't mind picking his brain on a few subjects.'

'It's not...we're not...' Faith swallowed. 'It wasn't how I imagine they made it look. Not really. And anyway, it didn't end well.'

'But it is ended?' her father asked. 'That's a pity. He's done incredibly well, really, given what he started with.'

Faith rather thought that Dominic had done incredibly well for anyone, but that wasn't her main concern. She could see her father calculating what he could do with access to a fortune like the Beresfords'. How there might be the chance of a little loan, something between friends. She'd seen it before. But not again.

'No. It's definitely over,' she said.

'Ah, well.' He shifted on the bed, kicking up his feet. 'Your mother tells me you're not planning on staying.'

'That's right.' Faith sat down on the dressing table stool and took a sip of her too sweet tea. 'I've just finished a job down in London. I should be able to pick up another one fairly quickly.' As long as they didn't want references from Dominic. Or Marco... 'Once I'm sorted, I'll move out again. But I might be able to send some money home, to help out.' It would just go onto the gin budget, she knew, but at least she might feel a little less guilty.

'What sort of a job?' her father asked, curiosity in his gaze. When she gave him a look, he threw up his hands to protest his innocence. 'It's not like we have any idea what you've been doing for the last few years. Or even where you've been, except for the news that you apparently somehow fell in with Beresford.'

Guilt pinged at her middle again. Okay, so they'd been lousy parents for the most part, and it hadn't really occurred to her that they might be worried about her whereabouts, but she could have at least dropped them a postcard, or something.

Except they'd have dragged her back. Although, right now, she wasn't sure if that might not have been a good thing. She'd never have met Dominic. Never ended up in this hideous mess.

But she could never really wish not to have met Dominic.

'I've been working as a tour guide,' she said, reaching for her mug again. 'In London, and in Italy.'

'A tour guide?' Her father looked fascinated. The idea of work had always been interesting to him. Just a shame he'd never had the desire to actually do any himself. 'Showing people around things?'

'And organising their hotels, their travel, looking after their needs, their trips and so forth. Yes.'

'Sounds like being a servant,' her father said, and laughed. 'Did you have to wear a uniform?'

Faith nodded. Who was he to suggest that her job was below her station? At least she was doing more than sitting around drinking in a decaying relic of an earlier era. 'I did. And actually it was fun. I liked it, and I'm good at it. So I'll find another job doing the same sort of thing, uniform and all if required, and send some money home for the drinks cabinet. Okay?'

'Whatever makes you happy, buttercup,' he said, instantly making her feel bad for acting so defensive. It really was just like old times. 'Only I was just thinking that it might be you don't have to go all that far to find that new job of yours.'

Faith felt her parental sixth sense tingle. This wasn't going to be good. 'I was thinking London...close enough to visit, right?' Not that she intended to. But if she could borrow the car to get to the station, she could commute from Fowlmere until she had enough cash to find a place of her own.

Her father shook his head. 'I've got a better idea. You want to be a tour guide? You can do that right here. At Fowlmere!'

Faith thought of the entrance hall, with its dingy lighting and faded and fraying curtains in the windows. So different to the bright open halls and lovingly restored features at Beresford Hall. 'Dad, I really don't think anyone is going to want to tour Fowlmere at the moment.' The whole house was in the same state. Who paid money to see mould and decay?

'Not yet, maybe, but I've got a plan.' He tapped the side of his nose.

Faith bit her lip to hold in a sigh. Just what she needed. Another one of Dad's plans.

'Perhaps, in the meantime, it might be better if I—'

'You want to go to London; I understand that.' Dad waved a hand around. 'That's fine. I need you in London. You can come to my meetings with me.'

'Meetings?' Dad's meetings only usually took place

in the pub, with men who knew exactly which horse was going to come in, really this time, honest.

He nodded. 'I've met with a young guy who is helping me save this place—for a cut, of course. Still, it might fill the old coffers again.'

Because that was what it was all about for her dad, wasn't it? Living the life he truly believed he was entitled to, even if they couldn't afford it. 'What does he intend to do?' she asked, as neutrally as she could manage.

'Do this place up. Use the land for corporate activities, events, the whole deal. Like Beresford did down at his place. I'll introduce you tomorrow; he can tell you all about it.'

The image of Beresford Hall, all clean and crisp facilities, clashed horribly with Fowlmere in Faith's memory. 'I think it might take a bit more work than you're anticipating, Dad. I've been to Beresford Hall. It's pretty spectacular.'

Her father smiled a beatific smile. 'That's why it's so wonderful that you're home to help me. Serendipity, don't you think?'

Fate was playing with her, just like it had at that airport bar in Rome. Her father looked so excited, so full of self-belief. But all Faith could feel was her escape routes closing in on her with every word.

CHAPTER THIRTEEN

THREE WEEKS LATER and still the world didn't seem ready to let him forget about Faith and move on.

The first week had been the worst. Once the picture of Dominic and Faith looking dishevelled together at the Greyfriars hit the Internet it was in every single paper by the evening editions. And then came worse—the photographer who'd caught them leaving the theatre hand in hand. Footage of Westminster Bridge that evening where someone's camera phone just happened to catch them embracing in the back of a photo. An anonymous source—Dominic suspected Jerry—who detailed how long Faith had worked for him and claimed 'they always seemed like they had some big secret. Like they were laughing at us behind our backs.'

There were more stories after that. Someone—presumably a friend Faith had spoken to when setting up the events that week—told the story of Faith talking her way into the job over drinks at the airport. It read as far more sordid than Dominic remembered the reality being, and even Sylvia had called him up and squealed at him, demanding to know if that was really what had happened.

And then Faith's apparently numerous ex-boyfriends

had started getting in on the act, and Dominic had stopped reading the stories.

But he couldn't avoid the headlines. Ridiculous puns and alliterations that no one showed any sign of getting bored with. 'Runaway Heiress, Runaway Bride?' was the latest one. Dominic hadn't quite managed to restrain himself from reading the entire speculative article that followed that one, suggesting that Faith had left him just after he'd proposed marriage.

The worst of it was, with every article he learned something new about Faith—although he'd probably never know for sure what was truth and what was pure fabrication.

He'd learned about her family, finally making sense of the bits and pieces she'd told him. No wonder she'd hated being at Beresford Hall. By all accounts, her father had spent his way through the Fowlmere fortune in record time. He must have been a constant reminder of what she'd lost.

He'd followed the story of her misspent youth, too. The media had happily mined the photo archive with every article, although Dominic had barely recognised his Faith in the scantily clad, drunken society girl falling out of nightclubs and being caught on camera with the hot young celebs of the day.

His Faith. That was one thing she'd never been, not really.

In fact, if the papers had it right, if she was anyone's Faith it was Jared Hawkes's, the married rock star with a notorious drug problem who had, apparently, left his wife and kids for Faith, before she skipped the country.

She looked more like he remembered her in the photos of her leaving the hotel with Hawkes, which somehow made things worse.

He'd tried to keep his head down and focus on work, wait for it all to blow over like Matthew the PR guy advised. But even if Sylvia was reporting record numbers of visitors to Beresford Hall, the Americans had returned home leaving the contracts unsigned, after many awkward conversations and superior looks from Jerry. So now he was waiting. Waiting to see if his professional life could move past this scandal. Waiting to see when the next comparison piece between his mother and Faith would appear in the papers. Waiting, against reason, for Faith to suddenly appear in his life again, the way she had the first time.

Because, the truth was, London wasn't the same without Faith. She'd already been gone longer than she'd been with him, but in three weeks that feeling of something being missing hadn't faded. In the office, he missed her snarky emails pinging through every so often. In his apartment, he missed the idea of her sprawled across his sofa, tablet on her lap, sipping whisky. And in the city…well, that was the worst.

It seemed that everywhere he went there were reminders of her. A poster for a show she'd wanted to see. A view of Tower Bridge and the memory of the dress she'd worn to dinner that night. A tiny backstreet Italian restaurant that was never Lola's, but often looked close. A pelican staring balefully at him in St James's Park.

He seemed to be, inexplicably, spending a lot of time walking through St James's Park these days. He couldn't even remember how he used to get from one place to another, before Faith introduced him to the pelicans.

The most embarrassing part was that he kept thinking he saw her. All across London, any time he spotted a woman in a red cardigan, or wild dark hair, his brain screamed 'Faith!' Several times, he'd found him-

self halfway to accosting a curvy stranger before he realised that, even if it was her, she'd betrayed him, she'd
run away from him, and they were done.

He had a list of things he wanted to say to her,
though. A mental list he added to each night when he
couldn't sleep, remembering the feel of her body against
his, under his.

It started with the obvious. *Why couldn't you just do
as I asked you for once?* If she'd just stayed, he could
have fixed things. She knew that, surely? How desperate must she have been to get away from him that she
ran anyway?

Just one night. That had been the agreement. Which
led to the second item on his list. *Why didn't you want
to stay?*

Except that sounded too desperate, as if there were
a hole in his life waiting for her to fill it, even after all
that she'd done, so he always mentally scratched that
one off again.

The list went on and on, through anger, pain, loss
and outright fury. But the last question was always the
same. *Why couldn't you have just left me alone in that
airport bar?*

Because if he'd never met Faith, his life wouldn't be
so disordered, so confused. And people wouldn't be
discussing his private life again, the way they had after
the revelations about his mother's affair.

And that, he had to admit, was the part that made
him angriest of all.

But the dark-haired woman across the street, or the
park, or the shop was never Faith, so he never got to
ask her any of the things on his list.

No one seemed to know where she was, but Dominic
assumed she'd skipped abroad again. The reporters had

staked out Fowlmere for a few days after he checked out of the Greyfriars and it became clear she was no longer there with him. He'd read a brief statement from Lord Fowlmere saying that his daughter was just fine, thank you, but taking a little time off. No hint on where she might be doing that. Dominic couldn't even be sure that the man really did know where Faith was.

The search for the runaway heiress had reached a dead end.

Until, unexpectedly, one evening, at a charity ball Sylvia had insisted he attend, the woman across the room really was Faith, and he didn't even recognise her.

'Look!' Sylvia nudged him in the ribs, hard, just in case he'd missed her not-at-all-discreet attempt at a stage whisper.

Dominic straightened his dinner jacket. 'Where, exactly, am I looking?'

'Over there! Cream dress. Gorgeous skin. Hair pinned back.'

He followed her also-not-discreet pointing finger with his gaze. 'Still not getting it,' he said. Except he was. There was something. Not in the polite expression of interest on the woman's face as she listened to some bore drone on. And not in the high-cut evening dress, complete with pearls. But underneath all that…

'It's Faith, you idiot!' Sylvia prodded him in the ribs again. 'You need to go and talk to her.'

Around him, the room was already starting to buzz. Whispers of his name and hers. Those looks he thought he'd left behind years ago, the ones that said: *We know your secrets.*

What was she doing here? Shouldn't she be in Italy or Australia or anywhere by now? Not standing next to her father at the most glamorous, most publicised and photographed charity ball of the year.

Had she really gone home? The journalists must have grown bored of staking out a crumbling estate in the middle of nowhere pretty quickly not to have noticed. But if her big plan was to go home anyway, why couldn't she have just stayed long enough for him to fix things?

He had to leave. He'd drop a large enough donation to the charity to excuse his absence at the ball, and he'd be gone. No way he was providing entertainment to a room full of gossip hounds by actually talking to Faith.

'People are starting to stare,' Sylvia pointed out, as if he hadn't noticed.

'Let them.' Dominic slammed his champagne flute onto a passing waiter's tray. 'I'm leaving.'

'Dominic, no.' Sylvia grabbed the sleeve of his jacket and held on, her brightly polished nails digging into his arm through the fabric. 'Look, the only way this blows over is if you and Faith act like it doesn't matter. You can't be all affronted and embarrassed. You have to bore them out of it.'

'I'm not talking to her.' Just looking at her, acting the perfect heiress she'd never been before, had made it perfectly clear she couldn't be for him… It made his teeth ache his jaw was clenched so hard.

'Well, if you won't, I will,' Sylvia said, marching off across the room before Dominic could react.

Any eyes that weren't on him before swivelled round to catch the scene.

Bore them, she'd said. Somehow, Dominic suspected that wasn't the most likely outcome of this situation.

'Of course, I've always found…' Lord Hassleton said, and Faith tuned out again, secure in the knowledge that the peer liked the sound of his own voice far too much to ever expect her to comment on what he was actually saying. As long as she nodded occasionally and kept a polite smile on her lips, she'd be fine. And maybe one day, if she was really lucky, one of those waiters with the trays of champagne would come her way and give her another glass. Or brain Lord Hassleton with the silver tray. She wasn't fussy.

This was her role, for now. She'd got her parents to keep quiet about her return, hiding out in her room until the photographers outside Fowlmere Manor grew bored. But it seemed her father was deadly serious about them working together on the regeneration. She couldn't hide for ever, not if they were going to save the Manor, he said. They needed to get out there, meet people, start making new connections, new networks. And no one pulled a guilt trip quite like her father, so here she was, shaking hands, smiling politely and wishing she was anywhere else in the world.

It was only until her father got everything up and running, she told herself. After the intense interest about her return in the media, she needed this new boring Faith to make people forget her past. Then she could get on with fixing her future.

'Faith!' The bright voice to her left made Faith freeze. She didn't relax one iota when she realised who it was.

'Oh, Lord Hassleton,' Sylvia said, her tone light and happy and lots of other things Faith wouldn't really expect from Dominic's sister. 'I'm *so* sorry to interrupt. But you don't mind if I steal Lady Faith away from you for just a moment or two, do you? It's been an *age* since I saw her, and I'm *dying* to catch up.'

Lord Hassleton looked down at Sylvia's petite hand on his chubby arm and said, 'No, no, of course not. You gels go and…talk, or whatever.' He turned to Faith, and she quickly twisted her lips back into the fake smile she'd perfected in the mirror. 'We'll continue this another time, Lady Faith.'

'I look forward to it,' Faith lied.

But as she turned away from Lord Hassleton and let Sylvia lead her across the room, she started to think she might have had a better time listening to another hour's rambling on sewage works near his estate, or whatever it was the man had been going on about.

Just steps away stood Dominic, watching her with wary eyes. How had she not noticed him come in? Too busy trying to stay awake while listening to Lord Hassleton drone on, she supposed. But now… Now she could feel the stares on her back, the anticipation in the room. Everyone knew they'd been together. Everyone knew she hadn't been seen again since, until tonight. And everyone was waiting to see what would happen next.

'I don't think this is a good idea, Sylvia,' she said, slowing to a halt.

'Trust me, it is.' Sylvia tucked a hand through Faith's arm and dragged her forward, smiling like a politician. 'Like I told him, the only way this ends is if you two act like it doesn't matter.'

But it does matter, Faith didn't say.

'Faith,' Dominic said as they reached him, his voice cold and clipped. 'I wouldn't have expected to see you here.'

'I lost a bet,' Faith joked, and watched as Dominic's eyebrows sank into a frown.

Sylvia glanced between them, eyes wide. 'You know what? I think maybe I'd better leave you two to this.'

'Probably safest,' Faith agreed with a nod. Then,

glancing around the room, she watched as every person there suddenly pretended not to be staring at them.

'Actually,' Faith said, turning away so most people couldn't see her face, 'why don't we take this conversation out onto the balcony, Lord Beresford? Fewer witnesses that way.'

Sylvia's eyes grew wider still, but Dominic just gave a sharp nod and took her arm. 'Let's go.'

CHAPTER FOURTEEN

WITNESSES. SHE WAS worried about witnesses. Dominic supposed that he should be grateful she wanted to take the conversation out of the public domain, but instead all he could think about was what on earth she had planned she didn't want witnesses for.

Or perhaps she was more afraid of what he might do. His list of questions rose up in the back of his mind but, in the end, the moment the balcony door swung shut, the first thing he said was simply, 'Why?'

Leaning back against the balcony rails, too high up above ground for Dominic to really feel comfortable with her lounging over them, Faith raised an eyebrow. 'Why what? Why did I leave? Why did I lie? Why am I here?'

'Yes,' he said. He wanted answers to all of them. He also wanted to know how he could be so furious with her and yet so desperate to kiss her at the same time, but he suspected she wouldn't have the answer for that one.

Besides, fury was winning by a comfortable margin.

'You ran away,' he said, the words hard in his mouth. 'I was going to fix this. I could have stopped all of... this.' He waved an arm at the expanse of windows between them and the ballroom, where a host of well-connected people in evening dress were barely even pretending not to be watching them any more. 'All you had to do was stay put and—'

'And let you fix my life?' Faith's voice was cool, colder than he thought he'd heard it before. As if she thought she had some right to be angry with him, after everything that had happened. 'No thank you. My life, my problems, my solutions.'

'Solutions? Since when did running away solve anything?'

Faith tilted her head as she looked at him, and Dominic couldn't tear his eyes away from the lovely line of her neck above her dress. 'That's what this is really about, isn't it? You're mad at me for leaving you.'

His gaze jerked back to her face. 'No! I'm furious because you lied to me. You risked my reputation and you ruined a deal I've been working on for years.'

She stilled, and for a brief moment he thought he saw something like guilt in her face. 'The Americans didn't sign?'

'Not yet. They want to see where we are when things have "settled down".'

Faith winced. 'I'm sorry.'

'*That's* the thing you're sorry for?' He laughed, even though it wasn't funny. 'Of course. The job always meant more to you than I did.'

'No.' Her eyes jumped up to meet his and for a second he almost believed her. 'I'm sorry I couldn't tell you the truth. But I knew how you'd react, what would happen if it got out. I couldn't risk it.'

'Because you needed me. You needed the job.'

'Yes.' Her gaze dropped to her shoes. 'I didn't know who you were either, when I met you. Not when I first asked for the job. And even then...it wasn't until later that I realised what me being, well, me, could do to you. And by then, things between us had become…more.'

Dominic pushed away from the wall and paced across to the edge of the balcony. From there, he could see all over London, all the places he'd never again be able to look at without thinking of her. But it was still better than looking at her face. 'It was never more. The first sign of trouble you ran away, like you always do.'

'I went home.'

'I know.' He shook his head, leaning against the rails as he stared down at the street below. 'Letting me help you was such a terrible prospect that you ran straight to the place you'd been trying to get away from all along.'

'I didn't have a lot of options.' There was an edge in her voice now. Good. She should be angry too. Between them, they'd messed this up good and proper. And even if it was all her fault, he wanted her angry. Wanted her to hate the way their one night had ended.

He shouldn't be the only one being eaten up by the fury.

He couldn't show it anywhere else. To the rest of the world, he needed to be the same in control Lord Beresford he'd always been. This couldn't be seen as more than a tiny blip on his life radar.

But to her…she knew. And so she was the only person he could tear apart.

'You had my credit card,' he pointed out. 'You could have gone anywhere in the world if you'd really wanted.'

Faith gave him a scornful glare. 'You think I'm a common thief, now? Gosh, you really don't have any respect for people outside your social sphere, do you?'

'But you're not outside it. You're Lady Faith.' He spat out the last two words. 'And I've learned a lot about what that means in the last three weeks.'

'Don't believe everything you read in the papers,' she said, as if it were a joke. As if it were even the slightest bit funny.

He turned to face her. He needed to see her reacting to this one. 'Maybe not. But a picture is worth a thousand words, don't they say?'

There. A tremor of something, under the bravado. But still, she tried to excuse herself. 'Like the picture of us?'

'We can't deny what happened just before it, however much we might want to,' he said. 'And it seems like it wasn't your first time in that particular situation.'

That was it. That was the line that got to her. Her whole body, usually so kinetic and full of energy, stopped cold. The only time he'd ever seen her so still was in his hotel room, just before she ran.

Dominic half hoped she might just run again. But she didn't.

'You mean Jared,' Faith said, proud that she could even find her voice. Did he truly think this was the same? That she had some habit of causing scandals for guys and then skipping town?

She'd hoped he knew her better than that. Apparently her real name wasn't the only thing he hadn't realised.

'I heard the poor guy left his wife and kids for you, before you ran. Guess I should be grateful that all I had to lose was my reputation.'

'Funny. I always thought that was all you cared about anyway. If it wasn't, maybe you'd have the wife and kids already and would never have to have worried about me at all.' Ouch, that hurt. It hurt her, and she was the one saying it. But if he honestly believed everything they printed about her…well, a little insult was nothing, surely.

And Dominic wouldn't let her see, even if it did sting. His expression was back to that robot look of the early days, the one that didn't let anything show. The one that had almost convinced her that he wasn't interested in her, didn't want her the way she wanted him.

But she knew better now. She knew him, even if he'd never really known her.

He drew back, leaning away from her against the railings. He wasn't going to rise to the bait. Of course not. As much as she'd love a knock-down drag-out fight with the guy, just to get it all out, to clear the air, maybe even let them start afresh…Dominic would never let go like that. And he'd certainly never do it where they had an audience. Through it all, he'd kept his voice low, his hands clenched at his sides or holding the railings. No outward sign of the fury burning in him.

Well, the crowd behind the glass might not be able to tell, but Faith knew. She knew he was every bit as angry as she was. And she knew he'd never let himself show it.

'So. What are your plans now? Will you stay at Fowlmere as the happy heiress?'

'You mean, will we be required to make polite conversation at every social function until the end of time?' Faith shook her head. 'Thankfully for both of us, no. Dad needs a little help setting up a new project, something to get the estate running properly again, and then I'll be on my way. Fowlmere is only ever a temporary stop for me.'

'You'll be running away again, then. Of course.'

Faith bristled at that. 'I'm not running *from* anything. I'm running *to* something new. My new life. A life where I don't have to answer to people like you.'

He raised an eyebrow. 'People like me?'

'Yes, people like you. And them!' Faith swept an arm out to encompass their audience, just a window pane away. He was the only one on that balcony who cared if they knew they were talking about them. 'All you care about is what other people think about you, what they say. Your precious reputation.'

'What's left of it now you're done with it,' Dominic muttered and grabbed her arm, trying to keep her calm, undemonstrative. Docile.

Ha!

Faith wrenched her arm away. 'Why does it matter to you so much what people think? So your mother left. That's her story, not yours! So you slept with a scandalous runaway heiress. Who cares? And what makes it any of their business anyway?'

'You cared,' he pointed out. 'Or are you trying to tell me that when you ran away the first time it wasn't because of what people were saying about you and Hawkes?' He shook his head. 'All that time I wasted trying to figure out what dreadful secret had made you leave Italy, when all the time I should have been trying to find out why you left Britain in the first place.'

'It wasn't because of Jared,' Faith said, remembering how it had felt, then, to be on the receiving end of that media fever. At least this time she'd actually slept with the guy. 'Not entirely, anyway. I just wanted to be somewhere—someone—else. I wanted people to not care what I did, to be able to live my own life.'

'Without caring what you left behind.'

'That's not true,' she said, but she knew he was never going to understand. 'And you never answered my question. Why does your reputation matter so much to you?'

His lips curved into a cruel smile. 'Didn't you say it yourself? It's all I have.'

'No, it's not.' She looked up at him, willing him to understand this one thing, even if everything else between them would forever be a battleground. 'You have so much more. I saw it, that night in London. The real you. You're more than just Lord Beresford. You're Dominic, too. And you're denying the real you just to keep up a façade in front of people who don't even matter!'

'Whereas you don't even bother with the façade,' he snapped back. 'You just run away when things get hard. You pretend to be anyone except the person you really are. Don't talk to me about denying my true self, *Lady Faith*. I doubt even you know who you really are any more. But it sure as hell isn't this woman in pearls and evening dress.'

Faith's skin burned pink above the fabric of her gown, and Dominic took a perverse pleasure in knowing he could still affect her that way. 'Maybe not. But I know something else I'm not. I'm not going to be your scapegoat any longer. I'm not taking the blame for this. Life is risk. You fail. People leave. And until you take that chance, you'll never be happy. You wanted one night with me, and you got it.'

'And you always told me you were going to leave,' Dominic said. 'At least that was one thing you didn't lie to me about.'

'What, you expected me to stay? As your events co-ordinator, right? No thanks.'

'I might have wanted more if—'

'If I weren't such a scandal? An embarrassment?'

'That's not it,' he said, but even he knew he was lying.

'Yes. Yes it is.' Faith shook her head and reached for

the balcony door. The buzz and noise of the ballroom filled his ears again as she stepped through. They were talking about them again. It seemed to Dominic they might never stop.

'Goodbye, Dominic,' Faith said, and he had to grip onto the railings to stop himself hauling her back, from making her finish this. He needed her to understand what she'd done to him, what it meant...

He watched as she made her way back into the crowd. Saw her put on her smile, the one that looked completely different to the quick, bright grins he'd seen when she was just Faith Fowler. And nothing at all like the slow, secret smiles she'd given him between kisses, on that last night.

He studied her a little closer. The tension in her shoulders, the slant of her head. The desperation in her eyes. All things he'd never seen before she became Lady Faith again.

She looked as if the walls were closing in on her, bricking her up alive. How hadn't he seen that before? This life, here, was killing her. And he didn't know how to live anything different.

No wonder she'd only ever wanted one night.

'You know,' Sylvia said, sidling up to him, 'that wasn't entirely what I meant when I said "be boring".'

'Faith doesn't know how to be boring,' Dominic said.

'No,' Sylvia agreed, staring out across the ballroom at Lady Faith Fowlmere, too. 'I always liked that about her.'

'Me too,' Dominic admitted.

CHAPTER FIFTEEN

'So. That was an interesting little show you and Lord Beresford put on for us all.' Faith scowled out of the taxi window at her father's words. Bad enough that the whole of London society had been watching through the glass. She didn't need to deconstruct the misery with her father, too.

'It wasn't meant to be for public consumption.' It should have just been her and Dominic, working things out. Making sense of everything that had happened between them. Not just trying to hurt each other without anyone else noticing.

'Wrong venue then, buttercup.' He patted her knee. 'Come on. You know people are fascinated by you. By all of us, really. But especially by you.'

'Maybe that's why I left.'

'And here I thought you didn't care what people thought about you. Wasn't that always what you used to say, when your mother would complain about another photo of you showing your knickers outside a nightclub?' He spoke the words lightly, as always, but Faith thought perhaps there was something harder underneath this time.

'I'm not that girl any more.'

'No, you're not.' Her father smiled at her. 'After all,

you came home this time.' He stretched out his legs as far as the taxi seats would allow and folded his hands behind his head. 'So, are you ready to tell me why you did leave? Really, this time?'

Faith shrugged. 'Nothing complicated. I wanted to be myself, and I felt I couldn't be that with the title round my neck and everyone watching my every screw-up.'

Except Dominic had been right about one thing. She would always be Lady Faith, however much she pretended otherwise. Maybe she really was no better than him. Hiding from her true name wasn't very different from hiding behind a reputation.

'And now?' her dad asked. 'Now you're back. What do you want to be now?'

'Still myself,' Faith replied, because that was always, always going to be true. But... 'Lady Faith, I guess. Whoever she turns out to be.'

'Well, if you really want to find out, seems to me the best place to learn is Fowlmere Manor.'

'I suppose it is.' Could she stay? Should she? Not just for a quick pit stop, but long enough to figure out what it really meant to be Lady Faith Fowlmere, here and now.

'I've got a meeting with Jack tomorrow. We're going to be talking about some of the plans for the estate. You should come with me.'

Was she ready? Getting involved with Dad's scheme...that wasn't something she could just run away from. If she committed to it, she'd have to see it through. Not doing so would mean leaving her parents in the lurch, more than ever before.

Was she ready to take on the responsibility she'd always avoided? Yes, maybe her parents had been responsible for running down the estate. But did that mean she shouldn't help build it back up?

'There'll need to be some changes…' she said.

'I know, I know.' He gave her a self-deprecating smile. 'I know I haven't always done right by you. Or your mother. But we've been trying, you know. When you left…things were bad for a while. But we've turned a corner, I think. And having you home…maybe we can all make it work. Together.'

She'd heard it before, plenty of times. But something in her wanted to believe it was true this time. 'How do I know you won't gamble it away, or get bored and find something better to do?'

'You don't.' He took her hand and squeezed it lightly. 'But, buttercup, what you do know is that it's a lot more likely I'll make a mess of it without you.'

That was true.

Maybe this was something she could do. Something she could be good at.

Maybe, against the odds, the place in the world she'd been searching for, the space she needed to feel at home was, actually, home.

Faith bit her lip. Then she said, 'Give me the guy's number. I'll call and tell him I'm running the project with you now.'

Her father beamed, and Faith hoped she wasn't making a colossal mistake.

'You really should talk to her,' Sylvia said, and Dominic sighed into his paperwork. Was even the office not safe now?

'I can't help but feel we've had this conversation before,' he said, shifting a pile of folders to the middle of his desk, making a wall of filing. 'Don't you have a tea room to run, or something?'

'Russell is taking care of it for the day.' Sylvia

dropped into his client chair and kicked her feet up on his filing wall. 'Which leaves me free to bother you.'

'How wonderful and special.' Dominic reached for the next folder in the stack. He had no idea what it contained, or what he might need it for, but if it meant not talking to Sylvia, he was all for it.

Except she was still sitting there. Watching him. Waiting for him to crack.

'What do I have to do to get rid of you?' he asked.

'Talk to Faith,' she replied promptly.

He sighed and put down the file. 'What on earth could I possibly have to say to her that wasn't already covered, in excruciating public detail, at the event last month?' And in the gossip rags the next day. Everyone was speculating about their mythical on-again, off-again romance. Some even dared to speculate that Faith had spent the last three years in their private love nest on the Continent.

If only they knew the truth, he thought. They'd be so disappointed. Not unlike him.

'That doesn't count,' Sylvia said, which made no sense at all.

'Trust me. It was the most honest conversation we've ever had. Possibly the only honest one.' He shook his head. 'I don't think there's anything left for Faith and I to say to each other.'

'Except that you're in love with her.'

For a moment it seemed so obvious, so profound a truth, that Dominic couldn't speak. Then reality reasserted itself.

'Of course I'm not,' he said, grabbing another handful of files. Where did all these bits of paper even come from? And what happened to them normally, when he wasn't using them to help him ignore his sister?

'Oh, Dominic.' When he looked up, Sylvia was shaking her head sadly. 'Are you really *that* stupid? I mean, I always knew I got the brains in the family. But really?'

'Hey,' he said, a little sharper than he intended.

'Well, right now you are being officially stupid!' Leaning forward to rest her wrists on her knees, Sylvia stared at him so intently he felt obliged to put down the files. 'Listen. She's great. She's honest—fake identity notwithstanding—bright, efficient, gorgeous. She's everything you've ever wanted in a woman.'

'She's a liability,' he countered because he couldn't exactly claim that any of the above weren't true. 'She'd ruin us.' Just like their mother almost had.

'How? By speaking her mind?' Sylvia shook her head. 'You wouldn't want a docile miss who never said what she was really thinking. It would drive you crazy, trying to figure out what she wanted.'

'She's a scandal,' he offered. 'She was caught having an affair with a married man. A drug addict. No one knows where she was for three years. There are all sorts of stories…'

'You know where she was,' Sylvia pointed out. 'Does any of it bother you?'

Yes, Dominic wanted to say. The idea of Faith being with another man, living with him. Loving someone who wasn't him. But he couldn't help but think that might bolster Sylvia's argument more than his own.

Which only left him with the truth.

'She'd leave, Syl. It's what she does.'

Sylvia's face fell, her eyes suddenly very wide. 'Oh, Dominic. You can't possibly think that's true.'

'I don't need to think,' he said, shuffling his files again. 'I know. And she's already done it once! You saw her at the gala last month. She hates that sort of thing.

She hates our whole world. Why else do you think she ran away?'

'But she came back,' Sylvia pointed out. 'She's at Fowlmere right now. It's been weeks and she hasn't left. So maybe she changed her mind?'

He shook his head. If only it were that easy. 'She told me herself, Syl. As soon as she sorts out the mess her father's made of the estate, she's out of there. She'll be back in Florence, or India, or Australia before you can speak. She's not the staying kind.'

'Maybe she just hasn't found something worth staying for yet,' Sylvia suggested in a small, quiet voice.

He gave her a lopsided smile. 'Yeah, well. I think she's made it pretty clear that's not me. Don't you?'

'Faith? It's Sylvia.'

Faith didn't bother asking how Sylvia had got her number—she just assumed she'd stolen it from Dominic's phone. It seemed like a Sylvia thing to do. So, instead, she motioned to Jack to keep walking the hedgerow between the lower and upper fields without her. He knew what they were looking at, and looking for, far better than she did anyway.

'Sylvia. What can I do for you?'

'Oh, I was checking in, see how you're getting on. You're still at the old homestead, I understand?' Sylvia spoke airily, as if it was a matter of no consequence, but Faith knew that if she'd spoken to her brother at all, she had to know that it was.

And yes, she was still at Fowlmere. And, against the odds, actually enjoying being there for the first time she could remember. Which wasn't to say that her parents weren't still capable of driving her crazy at times, but working towards something, as a family, seemed to be making a difference. Even her mother was hard at work pulling out long lost heirlooms and trying to restore them to their possible former glory. Maybe all they'd needed all along was a shared goal.

Maybe that was all she had needed, too.

'I'm still here,' she told Sylvia. 'Actually, it looks like I'll be staying for a while.'

'Helping your father with the estate, I understand?' Faith wondered where she'd heard that. Well, news got around, she supposed. Even when it was a lot more boring than scandalous nights in hotels and missing heiresses.

'Trust me, he needs the help,' she joked.

It was never going to be Beresford, but Faith was discovering that Fowlmere had its own charms, and its own opportunities to shine. To her surprise, she was even excited about them, far more so than planning a tour of some foreign land. This was her home, her heritage, at last. And, for the first time, she wanted to share that with other people.

'So…you think you'll be staying, then?' Sylvia asked.

Suspicion started to prickle at the back of Faith's neck. 'Yeah, it seems like it. Look, Sylvia, not that it's not lovely to hear from you, but was there something that you actually wanted?'

Sylvia sighed down the phone line. 'He's miserable without you.'

'No. He's safe without me. Respectable. Just like he wanted.'

'He was wrong.' Hope tugged at her heart at Sylvia's words, but Faith stamped it back down.

'I can't imagine him saying that.' Or even admitting it to himself.

'Maybe not. But I'm his sister. I know these things. So, you know, bear it in mind.'

Bear it in mind? What did that even mean?

But then a car pulled up on the driveway, just across from the field where she stood, and Faith knew, even before he got out of the car, exactly who the driver was.

CHAPTER SIXTEEN

'BETWEEN YOU AND your sister, this is all starting to feel a little stalkery,' Faith said, folding her arms over her chest as she reached the car.

'My sister?' Dominic asked, cursing Sylvia mentally in his head. This was all her fault, somehow. If it hadn't been for her with her insinuations and questions the day before, he'd never have felt the strange compulsion that led him to check up on Faith. Just to make sure she was okay. And maybe, a little bit, to find out what was making her stay at Fowlmere. 'What did she do?'

'She called. Apparently to check I was still here.'

'And you thought I'd asked her to do that?' Dominic asked.

Faith raised her eyebrows and indicated his presence. 'Not looking entirely far-fetched. Except that I'd have expected it to take you longer to get here.'

'I didn't ask her to call. I imagine she was just concerned for your wellbeing and wanted to see how you are. She's nice like that.' Which sounded much better than, *She's overly invested in our non-existent relationship.*

'Which still doesn't explain what you're doing here.'

'You wouldn't believe the same?' She raised her eyebrows at him. He got the message. 'Fine. I heard you were still here at Fowlmere. And I didn't want to leave things between us as they were. The papers seem to have lost interest, so—'

'So it was safe to come see me. I get it.' There didn't seem much point denying that one.

'I thought maybe you might need some help.' He hadn't been able to get the image of her, confined by evening wear, desperation in her eyes, out of his head. He needed to know she was still here because she wanted to be. Not because she didn't have any other options. 'Word is that you're trying to renovate the Fowlmere estate. Open it for business, like Beresford.'

'I'm not *trying* to do anything. I *am* doing.'

'Right. I just…I didn't expect you to stay this long.' Not voluntarily, anyway.

'You mean you didn't expect me to stay at all.' She looked away, staring out across the fields at some guy with a tape measure. 'Maybe something of what you said stuck. Maybe I'm done with running away.'

'Really.' Stood to reason she wouldn't decide to stay somewhere until *after* she'd run away from him.

'You don't believe me.' She didn't give him time to answer. 'Well, it doesn't matter what you believe. You, or your sister, or the papers, or my parents' friends. I'm back and I'm staying.'

'Why?' Dominic asked, just like he had on the balcony. Would this woman ever stop making him question things?

'Because I found something to stay for,' she said simply, and Dominic stared at the open truth in her face.

She'd found a reason to stay. But it wasn't him. It was never him.

'You were right about one thing,' Faith said. 'Pretending to be someone else, living in hiding, that wasn't being me. I'm Lady Faith Fowlmere, and nothing I do or say will change that. And nobody can take it away from me, either. So I'm here, where I belong. I'm making my own place in the world, not looking for it everywhere else.'

His heart weighed heavy in his chest. He wanted to be happy to see her so free, so alive again. But he couldn't help wish she could have found that happiness with him.

'That's great,' he said. 'And really, I can…I can help. If you want. I've got contacts, been through a lot of the stuff you're going to come up against…'

'Thank you, but no.' She smiled as she spoke, but the words still stung.

'Why not? Because you're too stubborn?'

She shook her head. 'Because I can't have someone in my life who is ashamed of me. I'm done being ashamed of myself. I've made mistakes, sure, but…' She took a breath. 'That's not who I am any more. And I can't have you reminding me at every turn what an embarrassment I am.'

He winced at the reminder. 'When I said…I didn't mean to…'

'Yes. You did.'

'You weren't exactly complimentary to me, either,' he pointed out, and she sighed.

'Look, Dominic, it's okay. Really. We knew each other for, what, a week? It's crazy to think it was anything more than a flirtation. We barely even made it to fling status. It was a one-night stand. Yes, things ended badly, but it's over. You don't have to check up on me, try to help me. You don't even have to feel guilty about the things you said. It's over. We just…move on.'

It was all perfectly reasonable. Almost as if she did

this sort of thing all the time. Rational, even. The sort of sensible argument he'd normally be the one putting forward, not her.

The only problem was, it was a lie.

Whatever had been between them in that week, it was more than a flirtation. More than a fling, even if they never made it past one night together before everything fell apart. And it meant more to him than she could possibly know.

But the most untrue part of all was something he'd been lying to himself about, right up until the moment he saw that tilted chin, the pride in her warm hazel eyes.

He couldn't move on. He needed her in his life. No matter what her past, or who she was. No matter what the papers would say, or his mother's friends, or anyone else.

He needed her. Even more than he wanted her.

Now he just had to convince her of that.

'Dominic?' she asked, and he realised he was staring at her.

'Sorry. Just…thinking.'

She shook her head. 'You think too much. Look, I mean it. You can go.'

He didn't want to. But he needed time. He needed a plan.

Across the field, the burly guy with the tape measure beckoned to her.

'That's Jack,' she said. 'He's helping me with the estate. I've got to go. Thanks, though. For coming and talking to me. It's good to…' she let out a breath '…I don't know. Have closure, maybe.'

'Closure is good,' Dominic agreed. If she wanted to think that this was it, that this was the end for them, fine. It would make it all the more fun to prove her wrong.

Faith bit her lip, then jerked forward suddenly, wrapping her arms around him for a very brief moment. Her body felt stiff, unsure—so unlike the way she'd melted against him in the park at almost midnight, or the way she'd come apart in his arms in bed that night.

A clear sign that this was just not the way it was meant to be.

'Take care of yourself,' she said, stepping back. 'And…I don't know. Try not to overthink things. And loosen up, sometimes, yeah?' She sounded as if she thought she'd never see him again.

'I will,' he promised, watching her walk backwards away from him. His heart hurt just to watch her go, but he held firm. He had to do this properly. He had to find a way to convince her that it didn't matter who she was, where she'd been, what she'd done, or how she might ever embarrass or humiliate him in the future. He loved her. And none of the rest was worth anything, without her.

'Faith?'

She paused. 'Yeah?'

'One more thing. What really happened? With you and that rock star?'

'Jared?' Her eyebrows shot up. 'Didn't you learn everything you needed to about that from the papers?'

He shook his head. 'I don't believe them. You wouldn't do that.'

She bit her lip and he wanted to kiss her, so very badly. 'You're right,' she said. 'It wasn't what it looked like. His wife had just walked out on him, taken the kids, and he'd got himself into a hell of a state at some club. He called me—we were friends, before everything that happened. I picked him up, got him back to his hotel and spent the night sobering him up and listening to him wail about his life. I was taking him home to call his wife and beg her for another chance when they took the photos.' She looked up at him. 'Satisfied?'

'Yes,' he said. He should have known. Should have trusted her. She thought she was a scandal, but really... she was just his Faith. And, for the first time, it didn't matter what anyone else believed about her. 'And thank you. For telling me the truth.'

She shrugged. 'It's a new thing I'm trying. And tell your sister to stop checking up on me, yeah?' Faith added with a grin as she walked away. 'I'm fine.'

Sylvia. She'd help him fix this. Of course she'd also tease and probably hit him, but he could take it.

'Trust me,' he said, smiling at Faith as he climbed back into his car. 'I'm going to go have a long talk with my sister. Right now.'

Faith turned, halfway across the field, and watched his car as it pulled away, trying to ignore the emptiness that threatened to fill her. She'd see him again, she knew. If she was staying at Fowlmere, in society, it was inevitable. But they'd never be just Dominic and Faith again. She'd never get to take him to see the pelicans or eat at Lola's. She'd never feel his lips against hers, or his body over her.

She'd never get to tell him that she loved him. And she'd given up any chance of ever hearing him say it back.

Loss coursed over her in waves, as if she'd lost her whole life, her whole future, instead of just one man.

It was for the best, she reminded herself, wiping away the tears that dampened her cheeks. She didn't even know if he wanted more—certainly not after everything that had happened. How could she possibly work alongside him, day after day, without giving into the desperate desire for him? And how could she let him help her when she knew he'd be putting his professional and personal reputation on the line to do so?

There was a chance that her plan to save Fowlmere would fail. She wasn't stupid; she knew that. And she couldn't let everything that Dominic had worked for at Beresford be dragged down with it.

Besides, like she'd told him, she was done being ashamed. Done with seeking a place in a world that didn't fit her. She was making her own place, and Dominic Beresford could never understand something like that.

No, this was the perfect ending. A little bittersweet, sure. But they both knew it was the right thing, they had closure, they'd said goodbye.

Now she could move on with her life.

Without the man she loved.

With a shuddering breath, Faith called out to Jack. 'Okay. What's next?'

'You want to do what?' Sylvia screeched to a halt in the middle of the pavement when Dominic announced his intention. He smiled apologetically at the irritated pedestrians who crashed into them.

'Marry Faith,' he said again, his voice calm. It was strange how, once you figured out what needed to be done, the doubt and the worry faded away. All that mattered now was the plan. The right steps he needed to take to make her say yes. 'I'm pretty sure it was your suggestion, actually.'

'I said you were in love with her! I figured you'd date her first. Like a sane person.'

Dominic shook his head. 'It has to be all or nothing.'

'Why?'

'Because she won't say yes to anything else. Actually, she probably won't say yes to this. Which is why I have to get it exactly right.'

Sylvia stared at him, sighed, then started walking again. 'You know, when you said we should go shopping, I was hoping for something more in a shoe line.'

'You don't want to help me choose a ring?'

That changed her mood. 'Yes. Absolutely I do. You're bound to get it wrong without me.'

'So you are in favour of my plan.'

Sylvia lifted a hand and wobbled it from side to side. 'Maybe.'

'How can I convince you?'

Halting in front of the first jewellers shop on the row, Sylvia paused with her finger on the doorbell. 'Tell me why you're doing this.'

Dominic considered. It was one thing to know it was the right move in his head, another to articulate exactly why. Finally, when it became clear they weren't going anywhere until he answered, he said, 'I love her. I'm pretty sure she loves me. I know, in my heart, we belong together.'

'So ask her out. Go for dinner. Take it slow.'

Dominic shook his head. 'Won't cut it. Slow means… it means her worrying I'm going to end things if she does something I find embarrassing. It means leaving an escape route, a way out if she leaves me. A way to pretend it didn't matter. And it means leaving open the chance that we can walk away if things get hard. It means stories and rumours and whispers designed to try and split us up. And it doesn't show her how I feel. That it doesn't matter who she is, what she does, any of it. As long as she's with me. I'll take any risk—even the risk of her leaving—if she'll give me a chance.'

'A lot of those things can still happen, even if you're married,' Sylvia pointed out. 'In fact, there'll probably be more talk if you just rush in like this.'

'I don't care,' Dominic said. 'It won't matter.'

'Because you'll have your ring on her finger.'

'Because she'll be my wife,' Dominic amended. 'Exactly.'

Sylvia rang the bell. 'Then we'd better go choose you one.'

'Thank you,' Dominic said, grinning. 'For helping.'

'Oh, you're going to need my help with a lot more than this,' Sylvia said as the jeweller came and opened the door. 'Have you even thought about how you're going to propose?'

Dominic smiled. 'Trust me. That part I've got covered.'

CHAPTER SEVENTEEN

IT HAD BEEN a week. One whole long, boring week since they said goodbye. Faith had tried to keep busy, knowing that the only way she was going to get over Dominic was by stopping thinking about him. When she was knee-deep in dusters, polish and tarnished brass, it was harder to remember nights in luxury hotel suites, working together, both watching for a sign of something more…

No. Work was the thing. She couldn't daydream when she was discussing the estate plans with Jack, or working with her parents to clear decades' worth of junk from the attics. Jack had the first round of potential investors visiting at the end of the month—and she had tons of work to do before then.

Work was the way forward. Not worrying about her parents, who seemed a little saner every day. Not thinking about Dominic, who was gone. Not even wondering why Sylvia kept ringing. Faith ignored the calls. She'd moved on. She had closure. No point ruining all that now.

Except it seemed Sylvia wasn't very good at taking a hint.

'Sylvia!' Faith said, hopping down the steps of Fowlmere Manor to meet the car. 'I wasn't expecting you.'

'That's because you don't answer your phone any more. I've come to take you down to town for the day.'

Faith groaned inside. 'That's very kind of you, but I've got a lot on here at the moment...'

'Exactly why you need a day off! Come on, we can go shopping again.'

Faith didn't have especially fond memories of their last shopping trip, but she did like Sylvia and she really didn't want to hurt her feelings. Besides, she did need a new suit for the investors meeting...

'I've got Dominic's credit card,' Sylvia said, waving the card temptingly.

'I don't need that.' Faith was pretty sure there was a little bit of room left on her own.

'Just jump in,' Sylvia urged, and Faith gave up the fight.

'Okay. Let me just settle up a few things here...'

With hindsight, she should have been more suspicious from the start. If not then, certainly when Sylvia drove them straight to the Greyfriars Hotel for their lunch. But Sylvia kept chatting about nothing and keeping everything light and unimportant, so Faith's suspicions only really started to grow when they stepped outside at the exact same moment a red double-decker tour bus pulled up.

'What fun! A tour!' Even Sylvia didn't manage to not sound fake at that one.

'What's going on?' Faith said, rounding on Dominic's sister.

'I've always wanted to take a London bus tour,' Sylvia said, obviously lying. 'Come on, you can be my tour guide! You can stand up front with the microphone and everything.'

'They normally hire someone in to do that,' Faith

said as Sylvia dragged her up the bus steps and grabbed the microphone from its stand, handing it to her. 'Besides, it's been years since I did a bus tour. I've probably forgotten everything...'

She trailed off. She wasn't suspicious any more. Because she knew beyond a shadow of a doubt that she'd been set up.

Lord Dominic Beresford sat in the bus driver's seat.

'What are you—' The words echoed around the bus and she fumbled for the off switch on the microphone. 'What are you doing here?' she whispered.

Dominic grinned at her. 'Sylvia's always wanted to take one of these tours. So I commandeered a tour bus. We figured you could do the guide bit for old times' sake.' As if that were the most normal thing in the world.

Faith glanced back. A bus full of tourists stared at her, cameras and guidebooks at the ready. 'For the love of... You stole a tour bus? You? Lord Beresford?'

'Borrowed,' Dominic corrected. Starting the engine, he checked his mirrors and put the bus in gear. 'You remember that night you showed me your London?'

As if she could ever forget. 'Yes.'

'Well, today I'm going to show you mine.' The bus pulled away from the kerb. 'Come on, tour guide, aren't you supposed to be talking into that thing?'

Faith stared at the microphone in her hand. 'I don't know where we're going.'

'Yes you do,' Dominic said, and started to drive.

Dominic wiped the palm of his hand against his trousers before grabbing the steering wheel again. In his pocket, the hard lump of the ring box dug into him, a sharp-edged reminder of exactly what craziness he was pursuing. Oh, not the proposal, exactly. That, he was certain about. But the method… How had he thought this was a good idea?

Maybe it wasn't. But it was the only chance he had of convincing Faith he was serious. If nothing else, she couldn't worry about his fear of embarrassment any longer. Nothing she could ever do could humiliate him more than what he was about to do. Especially since he suspected his sister would be secretly filming the whole thing to share with the Internet.

Beside him, Faith had begun her tour, talking in only a slightly wobbly voice about the landmarks they passed. He'd decided to start off with the usual tour route, down past St Paul's and Fleet Street before he detoured over the river after the Tower of London. Faith still knew this route backwards, she'd told him on their tour of her London, and, for now, he was happy to let her talk, feel comfortable. As if this really was an official tour with an unusual driver.

'The Tower of London has a long and varied history,' Faith said, and Dominic risked a glance out of his window at the landmark. Maybe he'd take her there one day, just to listen to her get excited about the stories the building could tell. 'Most notably, of course, it's known as the site of the murder of the princes in the tower…'

Not romantic enough, Dominic decided. Time to start the plan properly.

Swinging the bus over to the other lane, he headed for the bridge over the Thames, ignoring Faith's murmured protest. Then, as they crossed over the water, she put her hand over the microphone. 'You're going the wrong way.'

'I'm really not.'

'They usually go along to Big Ben and the Houses of Parliament next,' she argued.

Dominic flashed her a smile. 'Trust me. I know exactly where we're going. Now, give me the microphone.'

'What?' She grabbed it closer to her chest at his request.

'Put it on the stand there so I can talk into it,' he said, nodding towards the steering wheel.

'What are you going to say?' she asked, but she did install the microphone as he'd asked.

'I'm not a hundred per cent sure yet,' Dominic admitted. 'But I'm sure I'll figure it out as I go along.'

Figure it out as he went along. Faith was pretty sure Dominic had never figured out anything as he went along. The man liked to have a plan. A fixed, unchanging, reputation-saving plan. So what on earth was he doing?

Sinking down into the guide's chair at the front of the bus, hands gripping the arm rests too tightly, she waited to find out.

'Hello, everyone. I'm your driver, Dominic. I'm afraid that today's tour is going to be taking a little bit of a detour. You see, not very long ago, your tour guide, Faith, introduced me to a side of London—and a side of myself—I'd never seen before. Then, for reasons we really don't need to get into, but suffice to say it was mostly my fault, she left me here alone in this big city. And now I want to show her my London, and how it looks without her.'

Faith's cheeks burned at his words. She couldn't look at him, couldn't even acknowledge what he was saying. Was he trying to humiliate her? Was this some sort of ridiculous revenge? No. This was Dominic. Whatever might have happened between them, he wouldn't do that to her.

'And, Faith?' he said. 'Trust me, this is going to be far more embarrassing for me than it is for you.'

Somehow, she wasn't entirely convinced.

'On your right, you can just about still see the River Thames.' Dominic's voice automatically took on the cadence she'd heard when he was presenting at meetings, or holding court over debate at the dinner table. 'We're now officially on the South Bank. Coming up, you'll see the back of Shakespeare's Globe Theatre, amongst other things. We can't really get close enough to the river in this big old thing, but that's okay. All you really need to know is that every single time I walk along this river, I think about Faith. I remember walking along the South Bank with her, practically in the middle of the night, looking out over the London skyline.'

Faith was pretty sure that wasn't all he remembered. Whenever she thought of it, her body remembered his arms around her, his chest under her cheek, the way he'd kissed her as if she were the air he needed to breathe...

'As we swing around here,' Dominic said as the bus lurched around the corner, 'we can head back over the river. From here you can see the London Eye, and across the way the Houses of Parliament. But what really matters is, if you look back along the river the way we came, you can see Tower Bridge in the sunshine.'

Tower Bridge. The place they'd first had dinner with all his clients. What on earth did he remember about that night? Behind her, the tour group were all whispering, chatting and giggling. About her, Faith assumed. Well, at least they were having fun. And it wasn't as if she hadn't had more embarrassing moments in her life. Even if she wasn't exactly sure what this one was leading up to. Another way to convince her to let him help with Fowlmere? A really weird first date?

'Tower Bridge was where I first realised how incredibly smart, intelligent, organised and good at her job Faith is. How she could take on my job in a second if she wanted. Anything she sets her mind to, this woman can do.'

Faith tilted her head to stare at the ceiling, trying to ignore the blush burning her cheeks.

'Is it working, love?' the old woman sitting behind her asked. 'Have you forgiven him?'

'It's not about forgiveness,' Faith muttered, sitting up straight again. 'We agreed this was a bad idea, is all. I'm not going to work with him.'

'I don't think that's what he's asking, dear,' the woman said. 'Besides, I don't think he's finished yet.'

As Dominic steered the bus back across the river, he pointed out the spot where they first kissed, giving her a lingering look as he spoke that nearly resulted in them crashing into a bollard.

'Eyes on the road,' Faith screeched.

Dominic laughed and, before they'd gone very much further, pulled into a bus stop and pulled on the brake. 'Okay, ladies and gentlemen. This is where we need to continue our tour on foot, I'm afraid.'

'Dominic!' Faith said, even as the tourists started gathering their bags and cameras. 'These people have paid for a bus tour, not a walking tour. That's what they expect.'

'They'll like this more,' Dominic promised her, planting a swift kiss on her lips. 'And I hope you will too. Come on!'

She couldn't help but jump down off the bus after

him, her lips still tingling from his kiss. But then she stopped on the pavement.

'Wait. Just… Dominic. Wait.'

Twenty paces up ahead, at the front of the gaggle of tourists in their cagoules, cameras at the ready, Dominic stopped, turned and looked at her.

'I just…I don't understand what's going on. I don't know what you want.' Tears burned at the back of her eyes, and Faith blinked them away. 'Why are you doing this? We agreed…'

'We were wrong.' Dominic walked back towards her, and held out his hand. 'We were stupid to think we could just put this away in a box and ignore it. I'm never going to be able to walk through St James's Park without thinking of you. Without wanting you in my life. It's not possible.'

A small, sharp flare of hope burst into life in her chest. 'So, you want…'

'I want you to come with me to see the pelicans,' Dominic said.

'Okay.' Faith nodded. She could do that.

CHAPTER EIGHTEEN

GETTING THE WHOLE group of them across the road and into the park was quite an operation. Dominic would happily have left them to find their own way there—they all knew their jobs, after all—but Faith was in full tour guide mode again, shepherding them all across and stopping traffic just by standing in the middle of the road. It made Dominic's heart clench just to watch.

But finally they were all through the gates of St James's Park and the last, most important part of the plan was in motion. Maybe the first part hadn't gone quite as well as he'd intended when he'd described his plans to Sylvia; her storyboard for the afternoon—which Dominic fully intended to frame and give to Faith on their first anniversary—had included Faith swooning into his lap with delight before he'd even started driving.

This part, though, he had faith in. How could she resist pelicans, the perfect ring, and the most romantic, embarrassing proposal of all time?

This was weird. This was officially the weirdest thing any man had ever done for her. And she still wasn't entirely sure what exactly was going on. All she knew was that she was walking around St James's Park with the man she loved, and fifty total strangers, looking for pelicans.

Totally normal.

'There's one!' one of the tourists yelled out, and suddenly everyone was crowded around the edge of the lake, staring at it. Faith hung back, Dominic beside her, and watched. Then, without warning or any obvious sign, the whole group turned back to face them, grinning manically.

'What's going—' Faith started, then stopped as she heard music. Impossible, lilting music coming from some sort of sound system somewhere. She looked around, trying to spot where it was coming from, to figure out what everyone was looking at—

'It had to be you,' Dominic sang, his voice strong and sure and only slightly off-key.

Faith froze, even as he smiled at her. And then he started to dance. Faith clapped a hand to her mouth as Dominic foxtrotted around her with an imaginary partner as he sang. It was, by far, the most surreal moment of her life.

Around her, the tour group picked up the tune to the classic song and supported Dominic as he dropped to one knee. And then, like some sort of crazy dream, they started to move, stepping in perfect unison to the side, then into pairs, clearly rehearsed and planned and anticipated by everyone who wasn't her.

Their dance, choreographed to the last step, swirled around them, the words coming clean and strong in sopranos, altos, tenors and basses. Faith blinked with disbelief, even as she watched. Crowds were forming on the paths beyond, staring as the bus of people she'd tried to tell about the Tower of London foxtrotted in perfect time through the park, singing as they went.

Bystanders were joining in now, and right by the lake Faith spotted Sylvia, hand to her mouth with excitement. Even the pelicans seemed to be enjoying themselves.

And there, at her feet, was Dominic, holding out a ring box.

'Too much?' he asked.

'Um...'

'Only I wanted you to know. You're worth any embarrassment. Any story in any paper. I can ignore any of it if I have you with me.' He sounded so earnest, so open. Faith couldn't remember ever seeing him like that, except in this place. And one precious night when he'd let himself go, only to have everything ruined.

'Even if I'm a scandal?' Because she was. And probably always would be. If he wanted her, he had to want all of her, even the parts that were too brash, or showed off too much cleavage, or walked up to strangers in airport bars and demanded a job.

'I don't care,' he said, so swiftly she couldn't help but believe him.

'I suppose no one is going to ever find anything to laugh at you for more than this,' Faith mused as the performers reached the climax of the song.

'Unless you say no,' Dominic pointed out.

'I should, you know,' Faith said. 'Just to be sure you can really take the humiliation.'

Dominic flipped open the ring box, letting the sunshine sparkle off a diamond that could probably fix the roof of the west wing at Fowlmere. 'Are you going to?'

Faith looked down at him, into his warm eyes, his raised eyebrow, and thought, *How I love this man.* He was, by turn, ridiculously stiff and unyielding, then hilariously open and embarrassing. She might never get a handle on him completely. On how to make him open up when he needed to, and how to know when something was too much.

She'd probably embarrass him a thousand times over, and he'd probably drive her crazy at least once a day. The society pages would talk of nothing else for weeks. He'd want to interfere in everything she did at Fowlmere, then forget to ask her advice at Beresford.

But they'd sneak off to Lola's once a month, and book a suite at the Greyfriars when they needed to get away from it all. She'd get to be herself, not Lady Faith, not Faith Fowler, just her. Because she knew, beyond anything else, that was who he loved most.

There was a lot they'd need to figure out. But they'd get there. She had faith.

'You're not afraid I'll run away?'

He shook his head. 'I'll take the chance. Besides, I don't care where you go, as long as you always come back to me.'

The song finished and the dancers crowded round them, panting slightly, not adding anything at all to the romance.

'So. What's your answer? Are you going to say no to test my humiliation level?'

'Yes,' Faith said.

Dominic's brow crumpled. 'Yes, you're going to say no? Or yes, you'll marry me?'

Faith laughed, her hair blowing in the breeze, and reached down a hand to pull him to his feet. 'Yes, I'll marry you. Even though you hijacked a bus and proposed to me by flash mob.'

His arms were around her waist in less than a second, before the crowd even started cheering.

'It was the only way I could think of to convince you,' he murmured as he leant in to kiss her.

'Well, it worked,' Faith said, stretching up on tiptoe. 'Remind me not to let you search for wedding speeches on the Internet?'

'Will do.' And then he kissed her and she forgot her sister-in-law-to-be, filming everything from the side, forgot the flash mob, forgot the crowds; she even forgot the pelicans.

She only knew she'd never need to run away again.

* * * * *

THE RANGER'S SECRET

BY REBECCA WINTERS

Rebecca Winters, whose family of four children has now swelled to include five beautiful grandchildren, lives in Salt Lake City, Utah, in the land of the Rocky Mountains. With canyons and high alpine meadows full of wildflowers, she never runs out of places to explore. They, plus her favorite vacation spots in Europe, often end up as backgrounds for her romance novels, because writing is her passion, along with her family and church. Rebecca loves to hear from readers. If you wish to email her, please visit her website, www.cleanromances.com.

Chapter One

The bride had just fed wedding cake to the groom. Now the photographer grouped the wedding party for one more set of pictures. "You're in this last one, Nicky. Come and join your parents. Everyone smile and keep smiling. I'm going to take several shots in succession. Say cheese."

Nicholas Darrow, the precocious six-year-old wearing a tux, didn't need any urging. Happiness radiated from his cute face and eyes. Nicky was now the adoptive son of his aunt Rachel Darrow Rossiter and his new adoptive father, Vance Rossiter, the chief ranger at Yosemite National Park in California.

A half-dozen rangers from Yosemite had gathered for the late September wedding and reception at Rachel's father's home in Miami, Florida. Chase Jarvis chuckled over Nicky. The boy was so crazy about his new daddy, all evening he'd been skipping around the flower-filled house and could hardly stop long enough to pause for a picture. Yet no one could be happier for the three of them than Chase, Vance's best friend and his best man for the church ceremony.

By this time, most of the guests had gone and the festivities were fast coming to an end. Chase, Vance's second in command, had been named acting head ranger while Vance was on his honeymoon for the next three weeks. As such, Chase and the others needed to head for the airport and fly home. First, however, he had to change out of his tux in the guest bedroom.

"Uncle Chase?" The boy came running after him.

"Hey, Nicky—" They high-fived each other. Vance had taught his new son to call him Uncle Chase. Amazing what power the words *I do* could wield. In spite of no blood ties, Chase had become a part of the Rossiter family and loved it.

"Are you leaving now?"

"Afraid so."

"I wish you didn't have to go yet."

This was progress. From the time Nicky and his aunt had first come to Yosemite, the boy hadn't wanted anyone around Rachel except Vance. Chase had been a pariah— but no longer. Now that everything was legally signed and sealed and Vance and Nicky were now truly father and son in every sense of the word, the boy had finally accepted Chase. It was a great relief in more ways than one.

"Believe me, I'd like to stay longer. But somebody's got to run the Park until your daddy gets back."

"Mommy and I will be coming with him."

Chase laughed. "Don't I know it! We're all going to live right by each other. I can't wait!"

Nicky beamed. "Me neither." For the first time since Chase had met Rachel and her nephew in early June, Nicky threw his arms around Chase's legs. It brought a lump to his throat. He picked him up and gave him a long, hard hug. They'd all been through many painful moments together to get to this joyful place in time.

"Maybe you'll see the Queen while you're in London," Chase said. Nicky loved the Harry Potter story and wanted to see the train station where the children took off for Hogwarts wizard school.

"Yup. And castles and tall red buses and white owls."

"If you see a white owl, you have to be sure and tell me about it in a postcard."

"I will! Daddy says they're not as big as our great horned owls in the park. When we get back I want to watch the bears go to sleep."

More laughter rumbled out of Chase as he changed into trousers and a sport shirt. "It's pretty hard to catch them going to bed," he teased.

"Daddy can do it! We'll use our binoculars and sneak up on them!"

Yes, Vance could do anything in Nicky's eyes. In Rachel's, too. Vance was a lucky man to have that kind of love. For a moment, waves of longing for the happiness he'd once known with Annie Bower swept over him, catching him off guard.

Even after ten years, thoughts of her and the life they'd once planned together assailed him, but evil forces had had a way of destroying that dream, snatching away his heart's desire. By now his beautiful Annie was probably married with several children.

"Nicky?" a familiar voice called out. They both turned to see Vance in the doorway.

"Uncle Chase has to go back and run the park now," Nicky announced.

A broad smile broke out on Vance's face. "Yup. It's all on your more than capable shoulders. I leave its headaches to you with my blessing."

Nicky frowned "Headaches?"

Chase rubbed a hand over Nicky's latest marine haircut. "He means the problems that come up."

"You mean like the bear that climbed in that lady's car and wouldn't come out?"

"Yes, and a six-year-old boy named Nicky who hid from everyone because he didn't want to go back to Florida."

A giggle escaped. "Daddy found me!"

Vance laughed before looking to Chase. "Good luck on your first meeting with the new superintendent. Bill Telford's a recent widower with a son and daughter away at college. I understand he's a real go-getter, full of new ideas. Rumor has it he wants to turn the park on its ear. I'm glad you'll be breaking him in instead of me."

"Let's hope he's not as grumpy as the last one."

"Amen to that."

"So *this* is where everyone is!" Rachel swept into the room in her white wedding dress. She was a vision with her gold hair and lace veil. Rachel's charm and personality reminded Chase of Annie. With hindsight he realized those similarities had caused him to be drawn to Rachel when she'd first arrived at the park with Nicky. But she'd only had eyes for Vance. When she looked at her new husband like she was doing now, the love light in her jewel-green eyes was blinding.

Pain twisted his gut. Annie's smoky-blue eyes used to look at Chase like that… He had no doubt that somewhere in the world she was getting ready to go to bed with her husband and love him the way she'd once loved Chase.

Did she ever think about him?

He wondered how long it was going to take him to get over her and fall in love with someone else. Heaven knows he'd tried. The thought that it would never happen frightened him.

On his flight back to California with the other rangers, he'd tell Ranger Baird to go ahead and set him up with his wife's cousin. For over a year the couple had been pushing to get Chase and her together. Why not relent this once? Seeing Vance and Rachel so happy brought on a terrible hunger for that same kind of fulfillment. He needed to try…

Rachel rushed over to hug him. "Thank you for everything. We'll be back at the park before you know it. Take care, dear Chase."

He grasped her hands. "When is your father's operation?"

"The day after we get back from London. We're leaving tomorrow, but we'll only be in London a week. Then we'll spend the next two weeks in Miami to be with my parents. If all goes well with Dad's heart, we'll bring them to California with us."

"Everyone's pulling for him."

"I know. I can't thank you enough." She hugged him one more time.

Vance signaled to him. "Your taxi's here, Chase. I'll walk you out."

He grabbed his suitcase and followed Vance through the house to the driveway where a couple of cabs waited. One of the drivers put his suitcase in the trunk of the first car. Chase turned to Vance. "Enjoy your honeymoon. If you need a couple more weeks than you planned, you've got them."

"Thanks. We'll see how things go, but I appreciate it. Good luck. I'm going to miss you."

Chase grinned. "Sure you are." He climbed in the back with one of the other rangers and told the driver to head for the airport.

THOUGH IT WAS THE SECOND WEEK of October, the days were still hot in Santa Rosa, California. Annie Bower turned on the air-conditioning and waited in her compact car outside Hillcrest elementary school. It was three-thirty. Any second now class would be over for the day. She had mixed emotions about the news she had to tell her ten-year-old daughter, Roberta.

While she pondered the unexpected job offer that had come in the mail, students poured out the doors of the school. Five minutes later she saw her slender daughter walking toward the car with her dark ponytail swinging. Debbie, her outgoing best friend ran to catch up with her.

Debbie's mother, Julie, a single mom like Annie, drove the girls to school in the mornings. Annie picked them up afterward and kept Debbie at their condo until Julie came for her daughter. The system had been working well for the past two years.

To imagine Roberta having to make new friends in a new environment was troubling to say the least, especially since she was a quiet child who didn't have a large group of friends. However, this new job was something Annie had been hoping to get for a long time. In fact while she'd worked for the California Department of Forestry as an archaeologist for the last five years, there'd never been this kind of opening until now.

The pay wasn't that great, but if she didn't grab it, she could lose out on an unprecedented opportunity to do fieldwork on the Sierra Indians, her particular expertise.

Ten years ago Annie's parents, who lived a hectic social life in San Francisco, had welcomed her back from the Middle East with open arms. They'd tried to comfort her over the loss of Robert and his family. No two people could have been more kind and understanding when they'd learned she was pregnant with his child, but they'd expected her to live with them and couldn't countenance the kind of work she wanted to do, certainly not with a baby on the way.

Her goals were so different from those of her parents'. She'd rented a small apartment, taken out a loan to finish her education and had put her daughter in day care after she was born. When Annie received her anthropology degree, she moved to a condo in Santa Rosa where she'd gone to work for the CDF. Slowly she worked her way up the scale while being the best mother she could be to her daughter.

Every month she spent a weekend in San Francisco so Roberta could visit her grandparents, but they continued to complain about Annie's choices and this created more tension, something she knew Roberta could feel.

If Annie took this new position, her parents would throw up their hands in dismay, indicating their disappointment over her doing something so unorthodox while she had a child to take care of. It was either their way, or no way. Since there was no use discussing it with them, she and Roberta were on their own.

So far they'd been doing fine. Other people had to move where their jobs took them if it meant doing the work they wanted to do. Her father's pharmaceutical corporation meant many thousands of people had to relocate to work for him, but that argument didn't fly when discussing his only daughter and granddaughter's future.

What the decision really came down to for Annie had everything to do with Roberta and how she took the news.

"Hi, girls."

"Hi!" Debbie answered, and got in the car first.

Roberta climbed in the back seat with her, both of them lugging their backpacks.

Annie waited until the school crossing guard allowed her to pull out of the drive and onto the street before asking, "How was school today?"

"Good."

"We had a substitute," Debbie offered.

"Did you like her?"

"She was okay, but she made two of the boys stay in for recess."

"What did they do?"

"They laughed at her because she limps."

"Jason and Carlos are mean," Roberta explained.

Annie stared at her daughter through the rearview mirror. "That was mean."

"I'm going to tell Mrs. Darger when she gets back."

"Good for you." The school had a no-bully policy. That went for teachers who were targets, too. Everyone needed to be on the watch for it.

"You might get in trouble if they find out."

"I don't care," Roberta told Debbie.

And her daughter *didn't*. Roberta stood up for injustice no matter the situation. How Annie loved her!

A few minutes later she pulled into the carport of their unit in the eightplex. "I'll make dinner while you two get started on your homework." They always ate an early meal because that was when Roberta was the hungriest.

Annie's daughter was a funny little thing. So far this year the lunches she'd made for her remained in her backpack virtually untouched. Roberta's only explanation was that bullying extended to the lunchroom. If you didn't bring a juice box and packaged snacks of a certain brand, some of the popular kids made fun of you. When she finally admitted what was wrong, Annie was disgusted, but she took her to the store and let her pick out some items that would keep the negative comments down.

If Annie sent a check with her for school lunch, she later found it in Robert's her pack, uncashed. Apparently Roberta was too embarrassed to go through the cashier line. Her shyness might have come from not having grown up with a father. Deprived of a father, as Annie was of a husband. The thought of him came into Annie's mind, and she put it away again because of the pain of that ghastly day in Kabul.

Annie had been walking to the dig site from the hotel when an explosion rocked the whole area. In the aftermath there was chaos. She soon learned that Robert and all those with him, including his parents, had been killed. Even the thought of it was still too excruciating to contemplate.

"The substitute didn't give us any work, Mom. Mrs. Darger will be back tomorrow."

Since Roberta didn't lie, Annie had no reason to disbelieve her. "Then you two can help me make tacos."

"Can I grate the cheese?"

Debbie asked the question first, but Roberta loved to do it and her friend knew it.

"Of course." Again Annie looked through the mirror to see her daughter having a private talk with herself. Her rigid idea of fairness won out and she didn't say anything. A trait that had probably come from Roberta's father. An admirable one.

If Roberta were a boy, she would look exactly like a young Robert. She had his straight nose. It gave both of them character. She also had his wide mouth and dark brown hair. The parts of her features belonging to Annie were a softly rounded chin and blue eyes.

Robert's had been gray with flecks of silver that lit up when he looked at her. During their passionate interludes they turned iridescent, letting her know she brought him as much pleasure as he brought her.

"Be sure you guys wash your hands first," she admonished before opening the front door of the condo.

"Why do you always say that, Mom? We're not babies."

Uh-oh. "You're right. I'm afraid I'm still in the habit of treating you like one." In ways her daughter was growing up too fast, but maybe it was a good thing considering the conversation they would have later when they were alone. A certain amount of maturity was needed for Roberta to consider moving to a unique location.

"My mom says the same thing. Be sure and brush your teeth and say your prayers."

While they ran off to Roberta's room, Annie freshened up before putting some frozen ground beef in the microwave to thaw. Yesterday she'd shopped for groceries and pulled all the necessary ingredients from the fridge.

The girls joined her. While they chopped and grated, she fried the tortillas and browned the meat. Before long she'd whipped up a fruit salad.

No sooner did they sit around the table to eat than Julie arrived. She'd forgotten Debbie had a violin lesson and they needed to leave immediately. Annie jumped up and packed a couple of tacos in foil for her to take with her.

"Thanks, Annie. See ya tomorrow, Roberta."

"Okay. Bye."

Once they'd gone, Roberta came running back to the table to eat. "I'm glad you didn't make me take violin."

"Everyone should learn some kind of instrument. Since I used to play the piano, I thought of renting one so you could start taking lessons this year, but before we talk about it, there's something else we need to discuss first."

Roberta finished fixing herself another taco. "What is it?" she asked before biting into it with enthusiasm. "Did you and Grandma have another argument?"

Annie stopped munching. "Is that how it sounds to you?"

"Sometimes," came her quiet answer.

"I'm sorry. When we talk it may sound as if we're arguing, but sometimes that's just how we communicate. They love you and wish we lived in San Francisco." She studied her daughter. "Do you ever wish we lived there?"

"Maybe. Sometimes." After another swallow she said, "Do you?"

"Sometimes, but I can't do my work there."

"I know. If Daddy hadn't died, we'd live with him and you could do it." Her logic couldn't be disputed.

"That's right, honey." Annie had told Roberta the truth. She and Robert hadn't had a chance to get married before he was killed, but they'd planned to because they'd been painfully in love. He was every bit her father, even if there hadn't been an official engagement or wedding ceremony. "We would have always been together."

Now was the time to broach the subject of her new job offer, but the turn in the conversation had made her reticent. Was she hurting Roberta by living away from her parents? Would her daughter be better off being close to the grandparents who adored her?

"If I were willing to do another kind of work entirely, we could live in San Francisco."

"Like what?"

"I—I don't know yet," she stammered. Roberta sounded interested in the possibility.

"Grandpa said he'd take care of us and you wouldn't have to work."

She let out a heavy sigh. "When I was a girl he took care of me, but now that I'm all grown-up with a daughter of my own, do you think he should still have to take care of me?"

After a period of silence, "If Daddy hadn't died, he would have taken care of us."

"But he did die, and that was a long time ago."

From the beginning Annie had done everything possible to help her daughter know and understand the wonderful, adventurous man who'd fathered her. It had been easy to do because Robert had been a breed apart from other men, academically brilliant yet fun loving and kind. Annie had made certain Roberta understood he was courageous to work in a relatively hostile environment and had made her feel perfectly safe.

She'd assured Annie that he'd looked forward to getting married and having children. The two of them had had dreams of the family they planned to raise. Her photographs revealed a strong, handsome, vital male any girl would love to claim for her father.

As a result, Roberta never forgot for a second that he would have loved her and would have been the most terrific dad in the world to her if he hadn't been killed.

After such praise, to remind Roberta that Annie had been taking care of her since she was born didn't mean the same thing in her daughter's mind.

She straightened in her chair. "How come Julie and Debbie don't live with Julie's parents?"

Roberta shrugged. "I don't know."

"It's probably because Julie likes to take care of her daughter just like I like to take care of mine." Now, no matter the consequences, it was time to ask the definitive question. "Would you feel better if Grandpa took care of us?"

Those clear blue eyes stared at her. "Not if *you* wouldn't."

"Oh honey—" She reached out to grasp Roberta's hand. "Please be honest with me. Do you want to move to San Francisco? We can, you know. I'll find a job there."

"You mean and live with Grandma and Grandpa?"

She bit her lip. "Not exactly. We could find our own place, but that way you could visit them a lot. Maybe ride your bike to their house after school and on weekends."

"Don't you like it here?"

"Yes. What about you?"

"I just want to be with you."

Humbled by the answer, Annie had to believe that sentiment came from her daughter's heart. "Then let me ask you another question. How would you like to live someplace else, just for a year? We'd be together a lot more because I'd do most of my work at home throughout the winter."

"Would it be a long way away from Debbie?"

"No," she said without hesitation. "She could come

and visit you on weekends. So could Grandma and Grandpa. Sometimes we could visit them."

"Where is it?"

"Yosemite National Park."

"That's where they have those big sequoia trees. I think they look like giants."

"Yes. How did you know that?"

"I'm in fourth grade, Mom. We're studying California history. Mrs. Darger showed us a video the other day. We're going to go on a field trip to Yosemite next year near the end of school."

Of course. On back-to-school night the teacher had passed out copies of the fourth-grade curriculum. Annie had only given it a cursory glance. "The park is very famous."

"She said part of our water comes from a dam built in the park. It's in a funny-sounding place. People are fighting about taking it down."

"I know. You're talking about the Hetch Hetchy Valley."

Roberta nodded. "How did you know that?"

"Your grandparents took me to the park a lot when I was young. It's an amazing, beautiful place."

Annie's parents had bought an original black-and-white photograph of Yosemite's Half Dome taken by Ansel Adams from a collector back in the early forties. It was worth a fortune now and hung in her father's den.

"What kind of work would you do?"

"What I always do. Archaeology."

She cocked her head. "In the park?"

"Yes. The Yosemite Valley is designated as an archeological district. It's listed on the National Register of Historic Places in the United States. That's where I developed an interest in archaeology. Do you know it has more than one hundred known Indian sites that give information about prehistoric lifeways?"

"Do Indians live there now?"

"Some. Because of timber falling and rockfalls or slides, the park has archaeological treasures hidden in the ground. My job would be to catalogue data and, when possible, try to unearth some of them."

Annie could hear Roberta's mind ticking. She had her interest now. "Where would we live?"

"Somewhere in the park. I've been waiting years for the opportunity. Finally a letter has come in the mail telling me I could have the job. If I'm interested, the Forestry Department will fly me there for a one-day orientation to see if I want to take it. While I'm there, the director of archaeology will give me all the information we need to know."

Her daughter slid off her chair. "Can I go with you?"

"Not for the fly over. I'd leave early Monday morning and be back that night. If you want, you can go to Grandma and Grandpa's, or we'll make arrangements for you to stay with Debbie or Penny. But I won't do any of it if you don't want me to."

Roberta suddenly darted out of the kitchen, causing Annie's spirits to plummet. "Where are you going?"

"To look up the park on the Internet!"

Her little bookworm was very savvy when it came to grazing Web sites. Annie followed her into the dining room where they'd set up the computer for Roberta's homework and her own work at the CDF in Santa Rosa.

She stood in the doorway, waiting until her daughter figured out the right spelling of Yosemite and pulled up the site on the park. It seemed an eternity before she exclaimed, "You can ride horses there!"

Annie wasn't surprised to hear excitement in her voice. Before the Harry Potter books had arrived to absorb her daughter, Roberta had gone through a reading phase on animals—everything from cats and dogs to wolves and polar bears. However, her favorite animal was a horse.

In another life she would have wanted to be born on a horse farm in Kentucky. Robert had loved horses and would have been thrilled to know their daughter had an affinity for them. Annie had taken them riding at a local stable a couple of times and both of them had loved it.

"That sounds fun."

"This says there are miles and miles of horse trails." After a few minutes she lifted her head again. "I don't see any schools."

"Well, since school is for the children whose parents work there, they wouldn't advertise it on the Internet."

"I forgot about that. They don't want predators finding kids." Her daughter sounded a hundred years old just then.

A shiver ran down Annie's spine. If nothing else, she could be thankful her daughter's school was teaching them awareness of the ugly side of society. To do her part at home, Annie had put a filter on their Internet server to help keep them both safe.

"What do you think?" She held her breath. "Should I go and find out about it or not?"

Roberta was glued to the screen. "Yes. After Debbie's violin lesson, I'm going to call her and tell her to look up Yosemite Park. This says some of the rangers ride horses. Debbie could go horseback riding with me. I'll ask her if I can stay at their house until you get back."

Annie couldn't believe it. Her daughter hadn't said no. Of all Yosemite's wonders, who knew it would be horses that spoke to Roberta. Maybe it was in the genes.

"While you do that, I'll send an e-mail to the director and tell him I'll be ready to go on Monday." That was five days away. Enough time to read up on the latest information he'd sent about a project she would be working on along the Tuolumne River. The Awahnichi had lived there in 500 A.D.

Now that she had a chance to do some fieldwork, she was starting to get excited. Except for Roberta, who was the greatest joy of her life, she hadn't known true excitement since before losing Robert.

AFTER LUNCH, Beth poked her head in the door of Vance's office. "Chase? Ranger Baird is on line two. He says he'll hold until you're off the phone."

Chase nodded to Vance's personal assistant before finishing up his call with Ranger Thompson about the fall cleanup and repair of several of the camping areas. This was Chase's least favorite time at the park. The waterfalls were a mere trickle of their former selves and the trails were well worn from the locustlike traffic of summer crowds. Without rain this season, the controlled forest fires left a smoky smog over everything, especially while the weather was still warm.

Nicky wanted to watch the black bears go into hibernation, but that wouldn't be for a while. Right now they were so active, they broke into cars and camps where they could smell food and stuffed themselves.

His thoughts went to Vance, who would be back at

the park with his family tomorrow afternoon. Chase planned to pick them up at the Merced airport. Where had the three weeks gone? He'd been so busy doing the work of a dozen men, he hadn't noticed the time passing. His respect for Vance just kept growing.

The one dinner he'd had at the Bairds' house last night to meet his wife's single cousin had gone well enough. Susan was a dentist in Bishop, California, and a very attractive woman. Though she'd dropped hints she'd like to see Chase again, he had no desire to encourage her and couldn't pretend otherwise. Frank Baird was a straight talker and so was Chase. He'd understand. Still, Chase didn't like hurting anyone.

Once he'd hung up with Ranger Thompson, he clicked on to the other ranger. "Frank? Sorry to keep you waiting."

"No problem. I figured if there'd been a spark last night, I would've heard from you early this morning. You know—in case you didn't want Susan to leave for another day."

Chase heaved a sigh of relief. "I'm sorry to say you figured right. She's a talented, beautiful woman, but—"

"Don't bother to explain. I've been there and know what it's like. Before I met Kim, I went through women like water. Your problem is, you were married once." *Not quite.* "I think it's harder to go through all that rigmarole again."

A sardonic laugh escaped Chase's lips. "I planned to call you tonight and thank you and Kim for going to all that trouble for me. The Sunday dinner was delicious by the way."

"Kim appreciated the bottle of wine you brought, so we're even. Better luck next time."

"You know what, Frank? No more going into things blind. After Vance gets back from Miami, I'm leaving on a long vacation. Who knows? I might actually meet someone." Yet deep in his gut he didn't quite believe it.

The old blackness was starting to seep in, robbing him of even small pleasures. As Vance had expressed after his grandmother, the last member of the Rossiter family, had been buried at the beginning of the summer, he felt empty. Chase could relate. Something had to change.

"I hear you."

"Talk to you later." He rang off and buzzed Beth. "What time is my meeting with Superintendent Telford tomorrow?" The man's ideas for advertising the park's attractions could take them into a lengthy discussion.

"Ten-thirty in the morning."

"Would you call him and ask if we can start at nine-thirty?" Vance's flight was due in at 4:10 p.m. Chase didn't want to be late.

"I'll take care of it. Will you want goodies?"

He chuckled. "Do you have to ask? Bring on the works and plenty of coffee!"

"You're as bad as Vance. I'm going to miss you when you're not sitting in his chair."

"You're full of it, Beth. In case you didn't know, the sacred chair is his with my blessing."

"You mean you don't want to be Chief?"

Chase grunted. "If anyone needs me, I'm leaving for the Lower Pines Campground to inspect the latest damage."

"Good luck."

Laughing because they both knew it was in the worst

shape of all, he hung up and headed out the back door of the visitors' center for his truck. No sooner had he climbed inside the cab than another call came in. It was a typical Monday. The phone had rung off the hook since early morning. He clicked on. "Ranger Jarvis here."

"Chase? It's Mark. Five minutes ago Tom Fuller was at the controls of a forestry helicopter when it went off radar somewhere over Mount Paiute. There's been no contact since. We know that means it's down." Chase groaned. "I've called out air and land rescue units, but it will take a while to get to the crash site. I left word for Tom's wife to phone me immediately."

His hand tightened on the receiver. It was the flight that Superintendent Telford had asked Chase to authorize. He wanted more archaeologists working with the park director of archaeology and had come up with the funding.

"Let's pray they're found soon." Dead or alive, Chase didn't want to think what could happen to them while the bears were actively foraging. "Give me the name of the passenger."

"Margaret Anne Bower from Santa Rosa, California." *Bower?*

Just hearing that name after all these years squeezed the air out of Chase's lungs. His mind reeled in shock. It couldn't be Annie. It wasn't possible. Still…

He raked a shaky hand through his hair. His thoughts went back ten years. She would have told him if she'd been named Margaret. He would have remembered. They'd shared everything. And surely by now she would be married with a different name.

"If you've got a phone number on her, better call her family." Chase didn't dare do it or his caller ID would show up and that would involve him personally.

"I already did. An answering machine came on and a man's voice said no one was home. I left a message for her husband to call me."

She *was* married then.

Maybe she went by her maiden name. "That's all you can do for now, Mark. Keep me posted."

"Will do."

After Chase hung up, he started the truck with the intention of talking to the rescue units before they took off, but the hairs stood on the back of his neck when he realized his assumption about Annie being married might be wrong.

Just because a man's voice came on the line, it didn't necessarily mean it belonged to her husband. In order to prove a man lived in the house, she could have asked a male neighbor or friend—or a lover—to program her phone. Even her father. San Francisco wasn't that far away from Santa Rosa.

This woman was an archaeologist. She'd probably been to the park many times. If she were Annie, then he *knew* she had.

Was it possible she'd spotted Chase on one of her recent visits and realized he was alive? Could it be the reason she'd applied for the position Superintendent Telford had opened up, so she could find out the truth without letting anyone else know?

But that didn't make sense. If she'd seen him, she wouldn't have been able to hold back from responding. They'd been too deeply in love. He ruled out that theory.

He shook his head in despair. There were too many questions with no answers. He thought of the downed helicopter. Visions of Annie's lovely body mangled and burned or worse bombarded him until he broke out in a cold sweat and found himself screeching toward the helipad.

Before jumping out of the truck to join the others, he made a call back to Mark. "I'm flying up to the crash site. Tell Beth you're in charge until further notice!"

Chapter Two

Every so often Annie heard a moaning sound. She wished she could see who was making it, but there was something covering her eyes. When she tried to remove it with her hand, red-hot pain shot through her upper arm, causing her to gasp. Her other arm lay trapped beneath her body.

The moaning sounds continued. She could smell smoke. It was as foul as the taste of blood in her mouth. A terrible thirst had come over her. If she could just have a drink of water.

She heard vibrating sounds, which she thought must be coming from inside her head. They'd been growing in intensity and wouldn't stop. Maybe a woodpecker was trying to crack her skull open. It pecked faster and faster, tap, tap, tap, tap, driving her mad.

"There she is." A male voice reached her ears. She heard footsteps coming closer.

"Easy," another voice spoke to her.

"I've got a pulse. She's alive."

"Thank God." Yet another male voice that had a gut-wrenchingly familiar timbre, rousing her more fully.

"She has a possible broken arm. I see a scalp

wound. Could be internal injuries. Let's get her to the hospital pronto."

Whatever had blinded her was taken away. Through veiled eyes she found herself surrounded by men in uniform. Above her a helicopter hovered. There'd been an explosion. It was the rotors she'd heard inside her head. Her adrenaline surged. She had to find Robert. He hadn't died after all. He was here. In the confusion she'd heard his voice.

"I've got her neck and back braced. Ready to lift her into the basket?"

"Take care with that arm," Robert said.

She felt herself being moved, causing her to groan from the pain. Her heavy eyelids fluttered. For an instant she looked into a pair of silvery gray eyes trained on her. They were *his* eyes.

"Robert?"

Suddenly she was hoisted out of sight. They were taking her away from him again. She couldn't bear it.

"Robert!" she screamed, trying to look back, but she couldn't move her head. Searing pain engulfed her. "Don't let me go! Don't let them take me away—" She screamed wildly until she knew nothing more.

CHASE COULDN'T BREATHE.

He heard his name being screamed over and over until it grew faint above him. Each cry staggered him a little more. From the ground he watched the guys ease the basket into the chopper. The other crew was bracing Tom in another basket farther up the slope for the lift into the second helicopter. By some miracle neither person had died in the crash.

Annie was alive. She'd come to the park to work.

Their chances of being together here at this moment in time were astronomical.

He buried his face in his hands. Before long a third helicopter carrying an inspection team would descend to rummage through the smoldering wreck. Chase stayed behind, ostensibly to wait for them and make out the preliminary report.

In truth he was so shaken to discover it had been Annie lying there like a beautiful broken doll tossed out a window, he needed this time alone to recover. The rescue team were professionals trained to hide emotion, yet they too had been noticeably disturbed to see an attractive woman passed out hurt and bleeding in this unforgiving wilderness.

When she'd recognized Chase and cried his name with all the emotion of her soul, he'd come close to losing any composure he had left. More than anything in the world he wanted to go in that helicopter with her and never let her out of his sight again, but he couldn't do that. No one had any idea he was a wanted man. It needed to stay that way. Let her believe she'd been hallucinating. Let the others think the same thing.

There'd been no wedding ring or band on her finger to indicate she had a husband, no suntan mark to prove she'd worn one recently. Did it mean what he thought it meant? That she, too, had never been able to fall in love with anyone else?

Annie, Annie... Those blue eyes with their tinge of wood smoke had deepened in hue the second she'd recognized him. The contrast of shoulder-length hair glistening like dark ranch mink against the pallor of a flawless complexion assailed him with exquisite memories. Though blood had run down the side of her face onto her lips, its stain couldn't disguise the voluptuous curve of the mouth he could never get enough of.

Ten years had added more womanly curves to her body encased in a knit top and jeans that outlined her long, shapely legs. He'd been aware of everything while he and Ranger King had worked to stabilize her.

Forcing himself to do his duty, he walked around the crash site making notes to turn over to the federal authorities, yet all the while he was dying inside because once again—when he least expected it—his heart had been ripped out of his body.

Still drained by shock, he finally drew his cell phone from his pocket and called Mark. "Good news here, under the circumstances," he said. "Both victims are alive and in flight to San Gabriel hospital in Stockton. Until you hear otherwise, they're in critical condition."

A shudder racked his body. If Mark could see the mess the helicopter was in, he wouldn't believe anyone could have survived. Chase tried in vain to quell the tremor in his voice. "God was good to us today."

"Amen," Mark whispered. "With the chief coming back tomorrow, this wouldn't have been the best homecoming, if you know what I mean."

"I know exactly," Chase muttered with his eyes closed. The deaths of Nicky's parents eighteen months earlier on top of El Capitan would always live in the memories of those who worked in the park.

"Thanks for the update. Tom's wife will be overjoyed to know he's alive at least."

Chase cleared his throat. "Any word back from the Bower household?"

"Nothing yet. I checked with the CDF in Santa Rosa.

They have an emergency number for her parents in San Francisco and have already put in a call to them. I expect to hear from them at some point."

Annie's parents were in for a terrible shock. So was the man who was in love with her, whoever he was. Whether married or not, there had to be a man in her life. After seeing her again, the thought of her giving herself to anyone else tore up his insides.

In the distance he could hear the sound of rotors whipping the air. "Mark? I'm going to be here at the crash site for a while. When the inspectors have finished, I'll fly back to headquarters with them. Keep me posted with updates on the patients' conditions." *Annie had to be all right.*

"Will do."

SOMEONE CAME IN THE ROOM. Annie opened her eyes. "Hello."

"Hi. Are you Ms. or Mrs. Bower?"

"I'm not married. Just call me Annie."

"My name's Heidi. I'm your night nurse. How's the pain? On a level of one to ten, ten being the worst, can you give me a number?"

"A two maybe."

"Good. Glad to hear that arm fracture isn't giving you too much grief."

"Not as much as the gash on the side of my head."

"Those stitches always sting for the first little while. Do you want more painkiller? The doctor says you can have what you need."

"I'm all right for now, thank you."

"Are you sure? Your blood pressure's up a little. What are you anxious about? Everything else is fine and you'll be out of here in no time." She proceeded to take the rest of her vital signs.

Annie squeezed her eyelids together. No, everything else was *not* fine.

Unless Robert had an identical twin, and she knew he didn't, Robert was *alive!*

She'd heard and seen him after the helicopter crashed. It wasn't a dream. It was Robert's voice she'd picked out first. She couldn't be mistaken about that. A voice was like a fingerprint, only one individual set of tones per human being.

It was Robert who'd helped place her body in the basket with infinite care, a Robert who'd matured into a gorgeous, bronzed male. If anything he was more attractive now with those lines of experience bracketing his hard mouth. In the past it could soften with such tenderness it made her cry.

Once he'd worn his dark brown hair overly long, but today it had been short cropped. There'd been a lean, hungry look about him. Those characteristics had been absent ten years ago. In one illuminating moment this afternoon she had the strongest impression he rarely smiled anymore. He looked tough. Forbidding. A man who walked alone. With robotlike perfection he'd cold-bloodedly rescued her, never showing the tiniest sign of human emotion.

But all this she kept to herself as she told the nurse, "I'm waiting for my daughter, Roberta."

"How old is she?"

"Ten."

"Ah. Now I understand your agitation."

"My parents are bringing her. I thought they'd be here by now."

"I'll ask the desk if they know anything." She raised the head of the bed a bit for her. "Do you feel up to talking to an official from the CDF? He's right outside and only needs a minute of your time to finish up his report."

"Send him in." Annie had some questions herself.

"Shall I bring you back more apple juice?"

"Could I have a cola instead?"

"Of course. I'll get it right now."

She heard voices in the doorway before the man approached her bed. "Please forgive me for disturbing you. This won't take long."

"It's all right."

"Can you tell me what happened when you knew you were in trouble?"

"Yes. Tom had flown us as low as we could go to give me a look at one of the Indian sites. All of a sudden the helicopter spun around, but it wasn't because we'd hit anything.

"I've been going over it in my mind. It reminded me of the way it is when you're flying a kite and it's riding a current and everything's perfect, and the next second it suddenly does all these crazy spirals for no reason. Tom was amazingly calm. He said we were going to crash and told me to get into fetal position. The next thing I knew I was lying in the brush and smelled smoke."

"You and Tom had a miraculous escape."

"How is he?"

"Other than a broken leg, he's fine."

"Thank heaven!"

"He said the same thing when he heard you were all right."

"What did he say happened to the helicopter?"

"Without a thorough inspection, no one knows

anything official yet, but he's been in other crashes like it in the navy and felt it was an interior malfunction."

"I'm sure he's right. I can tell you right now it had nothing to do with his flying expertise. He kept me from panicking and showed remarkable courage."

"Thanks for your cooperation. As a final note, the CDF will be paying all your medical expenses."

That was a relief. "Thank you for coming."

Alone again, Annie lay there in a frozen state beyond anguish. If Robert had wanted to end their relationship, he could have gone about it like most people and simply told her it was over. Yet for some reason she couldn't comprehend, he'd used the tragic event of his parents' deaths to make the grand exit from her life ten years ago.

It was the perfect plan to bring her permanent closure. No messy explanations had been sought or required. Of course that was when she'd thought he was dead.

If she had the opportunity to confront him right now, would she find herself talking to a true amnesiac? He'd behaved like one during the rescue, but she didn't believe it. In the moment when she'd had a glimpse of him, his eyes had looked fierce, not vacant.

Ruling out that particular mental disorder as the reason for his lack of reaction, she had no explanation for his disappearance from her life. But it was clear he'd wanted no part of her. What a shock to have been found out at the crash site of all places!

She had no doubt he'd already disappeared from the park, but he needn't have bothered. If he thought she would make frantic inquiries and try to track him down after the lie he'd perpetrated, then he'd never known the real Annie.

In the most graphic of ways, the terrifying crash had reminded her of her mortality. One's life could be snuffed out in an instant. By some miracle she and the pilot had survived. She'd learned nothing was more important to her than staying alive to raise her darling daughter. Since Robert had chosen to be dead to Annie for the past ten years, he could continue to remain dead for the rest of her life.

If Roberta were to learn the truth, it would extinguish the flame of love in her heart for the dad she'd never known. Her world would be blighted forever. Annie determined never to tell her or anyone what had transpired on the mountain. That secret would go to the grave with her.

"Mom?"

Her splotchy-faced, tear-ravaged daughter came into the hospital room ahead of Annie's parents and rushed over to the bed. Between the cast on her left arm and the drip on the top of her right hand, there wasn't a lot of space to work with, but Roberta found a way. While she buried her head against Annie's chest and quietly sobbed, Annie's parents looked on through their own tears.

"I'm all right," she assured them before anyone else spoke. "Thanks to the pilot who had the presence of mind to tell me how to protect myself, I only have a fracture in my arm."

"Did he die?" Her father asked the solemn question.

"No. I just found out he has a broken leg. We were both so lucky. It's probably because we were so close to the ground looking at an Indian site when the helicopter malfunctioned and we more or less rolled out before it crashed. The doctor says I'll be able to go home day after tomorrow."

Her parents kissed her cheeks. "You're coming home with us to recuperate. Thank heaven you're alive!" her mother cried. "We couldn't believe it when we got the news from the police."

"I've never known that kind of terror before," her father confided in a low voice.

Moisture bathed Annie's cheeks. "Neither have I." She patted Roberta's head. "I know you were frightened."

"I wish you hadn't gone to Yosemite. Please don't go back." Another burst of tears resounded in the room. Roberta's slender body shook.

Her daughter's heartfelt plea, plus the pain in her parent's eyes, made up her mind for her. "Guess what?"

Roberta lifted her head. "What?"

"I've decided I'm not taking the job. We're going to move to San Francisco."

"Annie—" her mother cried out in a mixture of joy and disbelief.

Roberta's grave eyes studied her. "You mean to live?"

"Yes."

Her dad stared at her as if he'd never seen her before. He knew something earthshaking would have to happen for her to make an announcement like that. Naturally he would attribute her near fatal accident to the reason for this about face.

"If you'd said anything else…" He stood there and wept. So much happiness for the family rode on her decision. No more looking back.

For ten years Robert had been alive! In all these years he hadn't *once* tried to contact her.

It reminded her of a story on the news about a man who'd faked his own death to get away from his wife and family. Twenty years later his wife saw him. He was married to someone else and had another family.

Annie couldn't comprehend anyone doing that, but *Robert had done it*. Her summer in Afghanistan ten years ago had been nothing more than an intermezzo in her life. He'd proposed and she'd accepted. Still, they'd never made it to the altar.

But it had produced her beautiful baby. From here on out she would devote her life to Roberta's happiness and make her parents happy in the process.

"What job are you going to do?"

"I don't know yet. Maybe I'll go back to university and become a schoolteacher." Something unrelated to archaeology and memories. She'd spent too many years honoring a man who'd turned out to be unremarkable after all.

Her dad put his arm around his granddaughter. "The important thing is that we're all going to be together, sweetie."

She looked up at him. "Can I sleep by Mom, tonight?"

"We'll ask the nurse as soon as she comes back in."

"I'm sure it will be okay." Annie's gaze flicked to her mother. "Where are you staying tonight?"

"At a hotel just around the corner from the hospital."

The door opened and the nurse came in with Annie's soft drink. "Looks like everyone got here," she said with a smile.

Annie nodded. "Could a cot be set up so my daughter can stay with me tonight?"

"Of course. I'll see to it right away."

"Thank you. You've been wonderful to me."

"We aim to please. I bet the rest of you could use a soda. How about you?" she asked Roberta, who nodded, causing her ponytail to wiggle. "What's your favorite? Sprite? Cola? Orange soda? Root beer?"

"Root beer."

"Cola for us," Annie's mom spoke up.

"Got it," she said and was gone once again.

Annie's eyes filled with tears. Everyone she loved was assembled around her bed. This morning she'd set out on a new adventure, unaware that before the day was over, her entire life would undergo a dramatic change.

The crash had given her clarity about her priorities. Robert's return had rewritten history, closing the door on the past. From now on she would live for these three precious people and ask for nothing more.

"There's Uncle Chase!"

Nicky broke away from his parents and came running toward the car, his cute features alive with excitement. A tortured Chase had been resting against the passenger door waiting for them. He scooped the boy from the ground and hugged him close, so full of conflicted emotions he was dying inside.

"Did you get my postcard? It was the Tower of London!"

"I did and I loved it."

"They used to torture people in it."

"That's what you told me."

Nicky gave him a peck on the cheek. "I brought you a present, but it's in my suitcase."

"I can't wait to see it."

His hazel eyes twinkled. "You'll *love* it."

"You *will*," Vance assured him.

Chase turned to his best friend, who'd never looked better. Happiness radiated from his eyes. In fact, Chase would say marriage had taken five years off him. As for Rachel, she exuded that aura of true fulfillment you felt when you knew you were loved beyond all else.

When Chase left the park tomorrow, this picture of them would be indelibly impressed in his mind and heart. He hugged Rachel extra hard. He was going to miss his friends like crazy. "How's your father?"

"He's fantastic!" she cried. "The surgery was a complete success. They'll be moving out here before we know it."

"That's wonderful," he whispered, but he was functioning on automatic pilot. Since yesterday when Mark had told him the passenger in the helicopter was named Margaret Anne Bower, Chase's life had been turned inside out.

He could feel Vance's eagle eye on him. Already the Chief could sense Chase wasn't being himself. The two men had never been able to hide anything from each other, but this was one time when he'd have to bluff his way through.

"You guys get in and I'll stow your bags." He moved to the rear of the car and opened the trunk. Vance followed him. For the moment they were alone.

"Pardon my English, but you look like hell."

Yup. Chase had been one of hell's occupants since yesterday. It was Mark Sims who'd provided him his only lifeline to the world of the living. Through their communication he'd learned that Annie had come out of the crash with nothing more than a fractured arm and a few stitches in her head. Thank God for that.

"Being chief ranger of Yosemite Park was a lot harder than I thought it would be. Your shoes are too big to fill."

Avoiding eye contact, he shut the trunk lid and got

in the driver's seat. Nicky and Rachel had installed themselves in the back where Chase had put Nicky's car seat. Vance climbed in front. Again Chase felt his friend's laser-blue glance doing a full probe while they fastened their seat belts.

Once they left the airport Chase purposely engaged Nicky in conversation. "Did you see any white owls?"

"I got to see Hedwig!"

"The real Hedwig?"

"Yup."

"The one in the movie?"

"Yup. Except they used seven different owls. The one I saw was really called Oak."

"How did you manage that?"

"Mommy and Daddy drove us to this town. I don't remember what it was called."

"Walsall," Rachel interjected.

"Yeah, and this lady came to the library with some animals. She brought Oak, who was really snowy."

"Well, lucky you."

"Yup. We got pictures of me standing next to her and I also got to touch a pygmy hedgehog."

Chase chuckled in spite of his pain. He'd learned to love Nicky and couldn't imagine not being around him anymore. "I can't wait to look at your pictures."

"Have you ever seen a pygmy hedgehog?"

"I don't think so."

"They're really little."

"I bet. You didn't happen to see the Queen too, did you?"

"Nope, but we saw the guards guarding her with these huge hats. What were they called again, Mommy?"

"Beefeaters."

"Oh yeah, and we rode the red double-decker buses all over London. You can see the river and everything upstairs. Oh, and guess what else?"

"What?" Keep it up, Nicky.

"We rode on a train."

"Did it take you to Hogwarts?"

Nicky giggled. "Hogwarts isn't real. You're funny, Uncle Chase."

Their little blond chatterbox entertained them until they reached the entrance to the park. Chase wouldn't have stopped, but Jeff Thompson, the ranger manning the guard station, had seen them coming. When he spotted Vance, he stepped out to say hello. Chase had no option but to apply the brakes.

"Glad to see you back, Chief."

"It's good to be home."

Jeff tipped his hat to Nicky and Rachel seated in the rear. "Just so you know, Ranger Jarvis did such a great job, no one would know you'd left," he added.

"That's laying it on a little thick don't you think?" Chase scoffed.

"It's the reason I left him in charge," Vance followed up. "What's new with you?"

"Not a thing, but I guess you know all about the forestry helicopter crash over Mount Paiute," he said in a quieter voice.

Vance's head swung toward Chase in consternation.

Chase almost bit his own tongue off. *Thanks a lot, Jeff.* "Let's talk outside," he muttered to Vance, who nodded. They both got out of the car, not wanting Nicky to hear anything.

"When was this?" Vance asked. A grimace had broken out on his face.

"Yesterday."

"Why didn't you tell me?"

"If there'd been fatalities, I would have. Fortunately, the pilot and passenger on board came out of it with only a broken leg and a fractured arm."

"It was miraculous they survived in such great shape, all things considered," Jeff said.

Vance was waiting for a more detailed explanation from Chase. "So far the inspectors think it was a tail rotor malfunction or an in-flight mechanical malfunction. There's no other logical explanation for what happened."

"Who was at the controls?"

"Tom Fuller," Jeff supplied.

Chase elaborated. "The good news is that pilot error has been ruled out. It happened around noon in perfect weather, providing optimum conditions for a happy outcome."

"Who was the passenger?"

The blood pounded at his temples. "A new archaeologist from the CDF on an orientation flight."

"A *new* one—"

"It was Superintendent Telford's idea to hire an additional archaeologist. He found the funding for it."

"The rescue guys said she's a real looker," Jeff said.

"What's her name?"

"Margaret Bower. The guys are lining up to meet her, but I plan to be first to nail a date."

Chase could feel his blood pressure rise.

"She's single then?" Vance muttered.

Jeff nodded. "She has a daughter who'll be living in the park with her."

A daughter? For the first time in Chase's life he nearly passed out from shock.

"How old is she?"

Jeff shrugged. "I don't know. You'll have to ask Mark for those details."

Chase eyed his friend. "I'd hoped to spare you that information until tomorrow, Vance. Welcome home."

"I'm glad I found out tonight. Forewarned is forearmed. I presume it's been plastered all over the news here."

"Of course, but the positive outcome has caused the clamor to die down."

"The new superintendent must have come close to having a coronary."

Jeff nodded. "It's safe to say we all did until they were taken off the critical list. Superintendent Telford felt so responsible, he wrote out a statement for the park publicist to give to the press so we're covered."

"That's a relief."

Chase couldn't take any more. "It's great talking to you, Jeff, but they've had a transatlantic flight and need to get home." *I have to talk to Mark.*

They both got back in the car. Jeff waved to the two in the back seat. "See you around, Nicky!"

"See ya!"

He backed away so Chase could drive the car on through.

For the rest of the drive to Yosemite Valley they talked shop while Chase brought Vance up to speed. Rachel and Nicky held their own conversation in the back seat. Before long Chase turned into Vance's driveway and shut off the motor.

"I'll help you with the luggage." Chase couldn't talk to Mark fast enough, but that wouldn't happen until he was alone.

Vance helped his family into the house then came back to the car. Together they carried the bags inside the door. As Chase turned to leave, Vance caught his arm. "Hey? Where's the fire? We want you to stay. Rachel's going to fix us a snack. Come on in."

Chase flashed him a wry smile. "This is your first night home with your bride. Four's a crowd, if you know what I mean. Don't forget I'm still in charge until you show up for work tomorrow, so enjoy yourselves."

After clapping a hand on Vance's shoulder, he walked back to the car. Though he felt like running, he controlled the impulse. When he looked through the side-view mirror he noticed Vance still standing in the doorway with a deep frown marring his rugged features.

After rounding the corner, Chase turned into his own driveway and pressed the remote to enter his garage. He hurried inside the house and pulled out his cell phone to call Mark from the kitchen.

"Mission accomplished. Vance and family are back home and safe. All is well."

"Terrific. How does he look?"

"Better than a man who just won the ten-billion-dollar lottery."

"That's very good," was Mark's emotional response. Like all the rangers, the head security officer for the park thought the world of Vance.

"Did Nicky enjoy himself?"

"He's been chattering nonstop. You're going to be hearing all about his trip."

Mark laughed. "I'm crazy about that little guy."

"Everyone is." Until he had the answer to one specific question, Chase's anxiety was so severe he could hardly breathe. "Speaking of children, Jeff told Vance that Ms. Bower has a daughter."

"That's right."

"I didn't realize. By any chance is she Nicky's age? If so, that would be nice for him to have a friend. We'll be in short supply around here this winter."

"According to the information sheet provided by the CDF, she's ten years old, my Carly's age. It says she's in the fourth grade and her name is Roberta."

The phone slipped from Chase's fingers and fell to the floor.

He'd made Annie pregnant. They had a child together—

"Chase? Are you still there?"

A girl—he had a daughter!

"Hello? Chase?"

He had to reach down for the phone, but his hand trembled like a man with palsy, making it difficult. "Yes," he murmured in a daze. "Sorry about that. The phone dropped. Thanks for the info, Mark. Feed all emergencies to me. Vance won't be back on duty until tomorrow. Stay in touch."

"Will do."

The second they hung up, Chase braced himself at the sink. While he stared blindly out the window trying to come to grips with the fact that he was a father, someone knocked on the front door. It was the kind of summons you couldn't ignore. One of the rangers, no doubt, but this was one time when the intrusion seemed more than he could handle.

Still, he strode through the house and flung the door

open wide. Vance took one look at him and said, "I thought so." Sidestepping him, he moved inside.

Chase shut the door. They faced each other like adversaries.

"I'm not leaving until you tell me what's going on."

Chapter Three

A full minute passed while Chase stared at him. It was truth time. "You're not going to like what you hear. When I've told you everything, you're not only going to hate my guts for lying to you, you'll be enraged that my being here has put the park in danger."

All animation left Vance's face. "Why not let me be the judge of that. Let's hear it."

Taking a fortifying breath, he began. "For starters my name is Robert Myers. I was born in New York City, not San Diego. There's no Barbara in my life. I was never married or divorced. Never a navy man.

"Like my parents I too received my Ph.D. from Duke University in archaeology, but I need to backtrack. I didn't grow up in the States. Before I was a year old, my parents left for China. We virtually lived our lives following the Eastern to Western outposts of the Silk Route from the Orient to Afghanistan where we ended up in Kabul to do an excavation.

"As you know from being a marine in Iraq, archaeologists often have entrée into countries where few others can get in. I was a young boy when the CIA approached my parents to do intelligence gathering for them. At the time I didn't understand the significance. All I knew was that I was warned never to talk to anyone about our activities."

Vance shook his head in amazement.

"When Afghanistan was under Russian occupation and subsequent Taliban rule, their national museum in Kabul was looted of its treasure, but it never showed up in the Western auction houses or in Russia. The world was stumped.

"To make a long story short, it was learned that the Afghan government had hidden it in an impenetrable vault beneath the presidential palace complex in Kabul. After the Taliban were expelled, a team of locksmiths were called in to open the seven locks.

"Save for a few pieces, the fabulous Bactrian Gold treasure was all there along with the priceless two thousand coins dating from the fifth century B.C. showing the profiles of successive kings. Other teams of archaeologists including ours were sent in to verify the authenticity of the contents, proving a central Asian identity midway on the Silk Route."

"*You* got to examine it?"

Chase nodded. "A part of it, but victory came at a price. An Al-Qaeda cell still working with the Taliban got their revenge against anyone connected to the find. They set off an explosion at our excavation site, killing my parents and thirteen others. I was given up for dead too, but I survived and was flown to Switzerland by the CIA for rehabilitation.

"I was in the hospital a year to recover. Besides the massive scarring and skin grafts from successive operations, I was told I wouldn't be able to have children. And one more thing…"

Chase could tell Vance was holding his breath.

"There was an inoperable piece of shrapnel lodged in my heart. If it moved, I was a dead man. Knowing it could happen at any time, my life wasn't worth two cents so I agreed to go back to work for the CIA. It was better than waiting around for the end to come. Because of my knowledge of Arabic, Punjabi and Persian Dari, my job was to infiltrate and gather intelligence for them.

"The taste for revenge was strong. To my shock, my heart survived the training. The doctor just scratched his head. I ended up giving them six years of my life. On my last mission where I was embedded with a group of special forces, my cover was blown by a double agent who recognized me from the Kabul disaster. They immediately put me in the witness protection program here at Yosemite where I could fade into the woodwork.

"In case you're wondering how I made it through my physical, the powers that be planted someone else's chest X-ray during my park service physical. For three years nothing has disturbed the tenor of my existence...until yesterday."

Vance folded his arms. "I knew there had to be a reason I felt an affinity to you from day one." He gazed at Chase with a mixture of fascination and admiration. "Go on."

Chase swallowed hard. "I'm in trouble, Vance."

"You mean your identity here has been compromised?"

"Not yet." He rubbed the side of his jaw. "But this is something related and deeply personal. A little while ago I found out I'm a father."

Those blue eyes squinted. "Say that again?"

"I can't believe it either. Apparently I have a daughter. Her mother happens to be the woman who was in the helicopter yesterday, Annie Bower. She's the woman I fell in love with in Afghanistan. She was there as an undergraduate archaeology student from UCLA volunteering for credit."

The news brought Vance to his feet.

"When Annie first appeared at the dig site, no male working there could keep his eyes off her. I took one look and felt an immediate attraction that only grew stronger the instant she smiled."

Her intelligence had fascinated him, drawing him to her. The warmth of her personality captivated him. "We became inseparable…until the day disaster struck and separated us permanently. Thank God she'd stayed at the apartment that morning." His voice trembled.

"Thank God," Vance echoed.

"We'd planned to be married at the end of the summer, but now you know what happened. She went back to California believing I was dead. I'd taken precautions, so I had no idea she was pregnant when she left.

"With Al-Qaeda cells active everywhere in the U.S., I was terrified they'd track her down because she'd been part of the excavation team. I had no choice but to remain dead to her. And let's face it. Who would want a scarred shell of a man who could drop dead at any moment?"

Vance grimaced. "I hear you," he whispered.

"The CIA has kept her under surveillance all these years, but they've never given me any knowledge of her. I guess they knew that if I found out we had a daughter, I wouldn't be able to stay away from her." He sucked in his breath. "Can you imagine how I felt yesterday when I flew to the crash site and there was Annie lying crumpled in the brush?"

"Chase—"

"It's one of those coincidences that has defied all logic. As we lifted her into the basket, she looked at me and cried my name. The guys figured Robert must be her husband's name and didn't find it unusual she'd called out to him."

Vance was quick to put two and two together. "So it was Ranger Thompson who unwittingly broke the news to you tonight that she had a daughter. I swear you turned into a different man just then."

Chase nodded. "I phoned Mark a few minutes ago and found out my little girl is ten years old."

"Did he tell you her name?"

"It's Roberta."

A low whistle escaped Vance's lips. "That's better proof than DNA," he teased. "If Nicky were here he'd say *whoa!*"

His head reared. "What am I going to do?"

"What do you want to do?"

"That's a hell of a question—"

"I was going to tell you the same thing," Vance retorted.

"You don't understand. Even though my heart's still pumping, that piece of shrapnel could suddenly move and that would be it."

"True, but it hasn't happened in ten years. I'd say you've beaten the odds."

"Maybe, but my CIA contact keeps me updated and the fact remains that Al-Qaeda operatives are still searching for me. We know their patience is legendary. Though being in the witness protection program has kept us all safe so far, I'll always be a fugitive looking over my shoulder. Better for Annie and Roberta if I disappear into another world before she leaves the hospital."

Vance shook his head. "Your particular war has been over for a long time. The chances of either of you being traced here is a million times less likely than her being involved in a helicopter crash over the park. What better place for you to protect her where she and Roberta can live in relative seclusion? No way are you leaving here! I won't let you," he vowed with satisfying ferocity.

Chase's eyes smarted. "You have every right to despise me for pretending to be someone else all this time."

"Don't be an idiot. Would you despise *me* if the shoe were on the other foot?'

"You already know the answer to that."

"Then we understand each other. Now that I'm back to being the Chief again, I'm giving you as much time off as you need to take care of unfinished business. I'd say ten years' worth." He headed for the door. "To think Rachel and I were talking the whole trip about how to find you the right woman…"

"Surely not the *whole* trip."

He grinned. "No. I have to be honest about that. Good night, Robert, or should I say Dr. Myers."

"Do you know how weird that sounds to me now?"

"Probably not as weird as the name 'Chase' will sound to Annie. She's going to have to learn to call you that. Of course Roberta won't have any problem. She'll just call you Dad."

"Let's not get ahead of ourselves. Annie knows I'm alive." He sucked in his breath. "I have a gut feeling she'll never forgive my long silence no matter the reason."

"Then make her fall in love with you all over again. Rachel says you're a real heartthrob. By the way, I don't think I had a chance to tell you about my conversation with Chief Sam before I left on my honeymoon."

The old Paiute chief was a visionary man. Whenever he spoke, he gave Chase gooseflesh.

"After he thanked me for fixing the photo of the Paiute lodge in the library, he said he saw a peregrine falcon flying faster than an arrow to her mate nesting in the cliffs overlooking the valley. You realize we haven't seen any falcons nesting there in a decade or more. Kind of gives you chills, doesn't it?"

Before he closed the door behind him he added, "Remind me to give the Superintendent a bear hug for opening up a slot for a new resident archaeologist to the park."

After Vance left, there was no sleep for Chase. For the rest of the night he downed coffee and wrestled with a dozen ideas on how to approach Annie. By morning he'd come to the conclusion that the only thing to do was phone her before she was released from the hospital. It was a place to start. If she refused to take the call or shut him down flat, then he'd find another way to reach her.

At eight in the morning he couldn't wait any longer and rang information for San Gabriel hospital in Stockton. Eventually he reached the hospital operator who told him she was in W423 and rang her room. Between caffeine and adrenaline, he was so jumpy he paced the living room floor while he waited for someone to pick up.

"Hello?" said a young female voice.

If he didn't miss his guess, it was his daughter who'd answered. Unbelievable. "Hello," he said back, breaking out in another cold sweat. "Is this Ms. Bower's room?"

"Yes?"

"May I speak to her please?"

"She can't come to the phone right now. Who's calling?"

"Ranger Jarvis."

After a brief silence she said, "Are you one of the men who rescued my mother?" Her sweet demeanor melted his heart.

"I am." He cleared his throat. "How is she doing?"

"The doctor says she can go home this afternoon."

He swallowed with difficulty. "That's wonderful news. Who are you?"

"Her daughter, Roberta."

His eyes closed tightly. *Roberta...* "That's a beautiful name."

"Thank you. I was named for my father whose name was Robert. He died before I was born."

Chase covered his face with his hand. "I'm glad your mother is all right. Have you been staying with her the whole time?"

"Yes. My grandparents wanted me to stay at the hotel with them, but Mom needs me to do things for her."

"She's very lucky to have a daughter who loves her so much. Do you think she'll be able to talk to me later?"

"If you'll hold on, I'll find out."

"Okay. Thank you."

"You're welcome."

What an amazingly polite, charming girl! He could tell she'd had the right training from her mother. To think she was blood of his blood, flesh of his flesh. Already, he was bursting with pride.

"Ranger Jarvis?" She'd come back to the phone.

"I'm still here."

"Mom's busy with the nurse. She says that if you'll leave your number, she'll call you back in ten minutes."

Annie had guessed who it was.

It appeared she'd decided to face Chase head-on. That put the fear in him. She wasn't twenty years old anymore. She was a thirty-one year old woman who'd been the head of her home for ten years and had carved out an enviable career for herself and Roberta.

"Do you have a pen to write it down?"

"Yes. Go ahead please."

He smiled through the tears and gave it to her. She made the perfect secretary. Such a serious head on those young shoulders. Who could blame her after almost losing her mother? Chase shuddered because Annie had come so close to death. Visions of the twisted wreckage refused to leave his mind.

"I'll read it back." She'd gotten it right. "Don't worry. She won't forget to call you. She said her rescuers were angels."

Except for one… "Thank you, Roberta. I'll be waiting."

"Okay. Goodbye. Thank you for helping my mom." She hung up before he could say anything else.

Chase sank down in the nearest chair, shaken and humbled by the first conversation with his only offspring.

A RANGER JARVIS WANTED Annie to call him back?

Along with flowers sent from friends and staff at the CDF, she'd already received two gorgeous flower arrangements from the park superintendent and the chief ranger wishing her a full and speedy recovery.

So why this phone call from a ranger? Unless it was an official follow-up courtesy call on the part of the park service to anyone who'd been injured within its borders. She had no idea of park protocol and couldn't say with any authority what they did one way or the other.

It led her to the conclusion that if it wasn't their policy to call in these situations, then Robert had initiated it because he knew *she* knew he hadn't died. Out of desperation he'd called on a fishing expedition to find out what she was going to do about it.

How she would have loved to be a fly on the wall when he discovered he was talking to his own daughter! A normal man might have come close to cardiac arrest. But considering Robert was capable of the worst cruelty, nothing short of liquid nitrogen could run through his veins.

Now that the anesthetic had left her body, rage began to take its place, along with aches and pains starting to come out in every part of her. She was infuriated to think it might have been Robert talking to her sweet, innocent girl just now. He didn't deserve to have a conversation with her, let alone be anywhere near her!

Once out of the shower, the nurse had helped Annie dress in a loose-fitting top and skirt, then Roberta took over. She put toothpaste on Annie's brush, then dried her wet hair with a towel.

"Thank you, honey. I don't know what I'd do without you." Annie hugged her with her free arm before more or less shuffling into the other room. She sat down in a chair so her daughter could put her hair in a ponytail. It felt good for someone else to brush it. "Ah, this is sheer luxury."

Roberta laughed gently while she did an expert job on her mom, taking care not to touch the area with the stitches. The two of them had always been close, but this experience had bonded them in a more profound way. Roberta fastened the elastic in place. "I'm all finished."

"You did a perfect job. I love you."

"I love you, too." She walked over to the table by the bed and brought her the cell phone and notepad. "Now you can call that ranger back."

Annie would do it right in front of Roberta. Regardless of whoever answered on the other end, her daughter would never know anything was out of the ordinary. In light of the fact that her parents would be here soon to take her home, she hoped it was Robert so she could get this out of the way once and for all.

She pushed the digits and waited three rings before he picked up.

"This is Chase Jarvis."

No matter how ready she thought she was to handle the call, she hadn't counted on the way Robert's deep voice resonated with her insides, calling up memories she was fighting with all her might to repress.

Her body went rigid. How did he have the gall to do this to her, to them! "I understand you asked me to return your call."

"Annie?" He sounded haunted. No doubt he was. It had taken ten years, but he'd finally been snared in a trap of his own making. "Don't hang up," he begged. "We have to talk."

"I agree," she said. Roberta might be watching TV, but her tender ears picked up on everything. "It would be remiss of me not to express my gratitude to all of you brave men for rescuing me and the pilot. I'll never be able to thank you enough.

"When I'm a little better I'll send an official thank-you to each of you for your extraordinary courage. It took courage to fly up there and perform those rescues knowing what had just happened to the helicopter we were in."

"Annie—" He said her name again, this time in a voice an octave lower and saturated in some indefinable emotion. She hardened herself against its insidious power to break through her defenses.

"If you'd be kind enough to tell the chief ranger I've decided not to take the job after all, I'd appreciate it. He sent a note with his flowers welcoming me to the park. Yesterday I spoke with my boss at the CDF and let him know I've changed my mind. I'm sure the word will be passed along, but since you work under Chief Rossiter he'll probably hear it sooner if you tell him.

"Goodbye, Ranger Jarvis, and thanks again for your uncommon act of valor. It will never be forgotten by me or the pilot." She clicked off, breathing in huge drafts of air to gain some semblance of control.

The moment Roberta could see that she'd hung up, she turned off the TV. "That ranger was nice."

Oh Roberta…

"Yes he was."

"Can we sleep at our house tonight? I want Debbie to come over."

The girls had a lot to discuss. "We'll probably stay there through the rest of the week and leave for San Francisco on Sunday."

"Are Grandma and Grandpa going to stay with us till then?"

"Tonight certainly. Then they'll probably drive back and forth. You know Grandpa. He has a hard time staying put for long."

"Yeah. He always walks around and it drives Grandma crazy."

Annie smiled at her observant daughter. "Now he'll have you to take with him. What you and I should do is get organized and make sure we've packed what we need to stay at Grandma's until our big move."

"When will we do that?"

"We can't move everything out until this cast comes off in six weeks. I don't even want to try. What we'll do when we get to Grandma's is enroll you in school near their house and start looking for a place to live that's close to them. Once that's accomplished we'll go from there. I don't expect we'll leave Santa Rosa for good for at least two months."

The lease on their condo wouldn't be up until the end of December. That gave her enough time to set up a new household in San Francisco without feeling rushed. Right now Annie was jobless, but she'd worry about that later. She had enough savings to take them into the first few months of next year.

"Can I invite Debbie to stay at Grandma's on the weekends?"

"Debbie and maybe Penny."

Penny was a girl who lived in the eightplex, but went to a private school. Annie and Roberta liked her a lot. "We'll ask Julie to come too and sometimes you can stay with them." Julie rented a house only a block away from the condo. In time Roberta would make new friends in San Francisco, but for now this would work.

She heard footsteps and saw her parents come in the room. Roberta ran to hug her grandma. Annie's dad beamed when he saw her. "Looking at you, you'd never know you've been through such a horrendous ordeal. Do you feel as good as you look?"

"Better," Annie lied, giving him a kiss on the cheek.

Every bone in her body ached and the one-sided conversation with Robert had shaken her to the core. Though he'd only said a few words, they'd been enough to disturb her at her deepest level. "The doctor has discharged me. I'm ready to leave."

Roberta gave him a hug. "I've got our suitcases ready."

"Then let's go."

"What are we going to do with the flowers?"

Annie studied her daughter. "We can't take them with us. Shall we ask the hospital to give them to some patients who could use cheering up?"

She nodded. "Here's your purse."

"Thank you."

Her mother peeked out the door. "The nurse is coming with your wheelchair."

"Can I push you, Mom?"

"We'll ask the nurse, but I don't see why not."

FRIDAY MORNING Chase sat in his car in one of the guest parking stalls at Annie's condo. Agent Sid Manning, his contact in the CIA, was parked around the corner waiting for Chase's signal to join him.

The phone conversation with Annie on Wednesday had been a lesson in futility. He'd known it in his bones before he'd picked up the phone. In truth he didn't have much faith in what he was about to do now, but it was necessary if he expected her to listen long enough to hear him out.

Since yesterday he'd been watching the activity at her condo. Last night he saw a man and woman leave her place in their luxury car. They had to be Annie's parents. Both had attractive physical traits she'd inherited.

A few minutes ago he'd had his first glimpse of his daughter. At eight-thirty a woman driving a Toyota pulled into the parking area with a blond girl in the back seat. In another minute a brunette of medium height flew out the front door in a blue and green top and jeans, carrying a backpack. While her ponytail swished back and forth, she waved to her friend waiting in the car.

Chase's hungry gaze took in her slender frame. She moved with nimble grace, like Annie. As she drew closer, he could see her facial features. His heart jolted to realize she bore an almost uncanny resemblance to his family, to him. Tears welled in his eyes. Roberta—his little girl. She was *adorable*.

The moment the Toyota disappeared down the street, Chase phoned Sid. "I'm going to approach her now."

"I'll be right there."

He'd decided to show up without warning. He realized it would be another strike against him. For all he knew Annie was still in bed, recuperating. But this was a life-and-death situation.

His life.

Knowing what he knew now, existence would have no meaning if he couldn't take care of them and love them for as long as he was granted life.

After drawing in a deep breath, he levered himself from the car and walked toward her condo. Sid pulled his car around and met him at the front door. He rang the bell. To his surprise she answered it faster than he would have expected.

"Honey?" she cried. "Did you forget something?"

But the minute she saw Chase, a gasp escaped her throat. She backed away from him. Beneath her mane of dark, glistening hair still in slight disarray from sleep, her features took on a chiseled cast.

"How dare you come here."

She wore a simple pink sundress, no doubt easy to put on over her cast. At second glance he noticed she was barefoot and beautiful. More beautiful than she'd been ten years ago if that were possible.

"Ms. Bower?" Sid spoke up. He took out his ID and held it in front of her. "I'm Agent Manning from the CIA. I need to have a word with you. It's for the safety of you and your daughter as well as Dr. Myers, who worked for us for a time."

"Of course he did," she mocked with a cruel laugh.

"May we step inside please?"

"No," she responded without hesitation or hysteria. "You can say what you have to say right here." She stared directly at them without the flicker of an eyelash to reveal any angst she might be hiding.

Chase wasn't surprised. There were degrees of betrayal. His qualified at the bedrock level. You couldn't go any lower.

Sid remained calm. "This will take some time."

The curve of her normally provocative mouth thinned to an angry white line. "You said you had something to say, so say it, otherwise I'm shutting the door."

"I was only thinking of your physical comfort."

"You people don't give a damn about anyone's comfort."

Sid flashed Chase a covert glance of surprise.

"Agent Manning is my contact here in the States," Chase explained. "I realize I'm dead to you, but as he explained, an Al-Qaeda cell is still hunting for me. For a long time we've feared you and Roberta might be a target. Now that you've learned I'm alive, it's important you know exactly what happened before Roberta was born. The explosion that killed everyone at the site wasn't an accident."

Her eyes darkened to an inky-blue. Finally a connection.

"He's right, Ms. Bower. Both he and his parents were operatives for the CIA helping gather intelligence while they worked undercover as archaeologists. They served faithfully many years until their true agenda was discovered and they were wiped out along with a dozen others.

"Only two bodies in the rubble were found still alive. Both had been given up for dead, but one of the doctors literally brought Dr. Myers back to life. Our people got him out of the country to a hospital in Switzerland where he spent over a year learning to walk again, not to mention undergoing several operations in order to recuperate from serious chest and stomach wounds."

Her face paled. Chase saw her sway and was ready to steady her, but she leaned against the doorjamb. "I don't believe any of it."

Sid reached inside his suit jacket and pulled out an eight-by-ten envelope. "These photos will convince you otherwise. They were taken after the explosion and at the hospital after Dr. Myers was flown there for surgery." When she wouldn't make a move to touch it, Sid tossed it onto the hall floor behind her. It slid across the tile.

"Knowing your relationship with him," Sid continued, "you were flown home immediately and put under protective surveillance in case Al-Qaeda operatives traced you here for retaliation. Because your life was in danger, Dr. Myers had no choice but to stay away from you. He gave up his work as an archaeologist to go to work for us full time."

Chase saw the muscles working in her throat. "I've given you more time than you deserve. You've had your say, now get out!"

His hands formed fists. "I need to talk to you, Annie."

Her face closed up. "I've needed to talk to you for ten years. Now it's too late." She shut the door in his face.

Sid turned his head toward Chase. "I've been in this business a lot of years, but I never met anyone as hard to crack. I'm not sure it's possible."

"It isn't," Chase whispered in shock. When he'd told Vance he feared she wouldn't be able to forgive him after she'd learned the truth, even he hadn't counted on the depth of her trauma. Pain consumed him.

He *was* dead to her.

Chapter Four

Annie stared at the brown envelope lying at the edge of the tile. Wherever she moved, it followed her like a living thing. Her survival instincts told her to burn it without viewing the contents.

If by any chance Agent Manning had told her the truth, more than ever she had no desire to see pictures of the man who'd never once tried to contact her since he'd been released from the hospital, not even through a third party.

Danger be damned! He'd seen a way out of their relationship and he'd taken it. There was only one reason he was making contact with her now. He'd found out he had a daughter. On Wednesday he'd spoken to Roberta on the phone. This morning he'd been stalking them out in front and had seen her leave the condo and get in Julie's car.

Who did he think he was to be absent for over a decade, and then swoop in to demand he and Annie talk?

There was no way she'd let him have access to Roberta. Annie needed to talk to her father's good friend, Clive Radinger. She'd met him several times at her parents' home when they'd entertained. He was supposed to be the best attorney in Northern California.

She would hire him to put a restraining order on Robert, but she'd keep it a secret from her family.

If Robert was so paranoid he'd actually chosen to remain dead to her until now, she reasoned he would shy away from undue publicity that could attract public attention to him or Roberta. Not wanting to waste a second, she snatched the envelope from the floor and went into the bedroom to make that phone call.

In a few minutes a receptionist answered. "Radinger and Byland."

"Hello? This is Annie Bower, Joseph Bower's daughter." She couldn't remember the last time she'd used her father's name for an entrée, but this constituted an emergency. "Is Mr. Radinger in?"

"He is, but he's with a client."

"If you'll put me on hold, I'll wait for him. This is extremely urgent."

"It could be a while."

"I don't care."

"Very well."

While Annie waited, she put her phone on speaker and sank down on the side of the bed. In case he wanted to know what was in the envelope, she thought she'd better open it. With only one arm free, it took some ingenuity to undo the seal. Out fell six glossy black-and-white photographs.

Her gaze fell on them. All she could see was a blood-spattered male body lying on his back with his arms and legs flung wide. The huge, gaping wound in his chest looked like a heap of spaghetti. It brought bile to her throat. There was so much blood on his face, she wouldn't have known who it was if she hadn't recognized the shape of Robert's head.

Her eyes traveled to another photo showing him lying on a stretcher facedown. The base of his spine looked like someone had taken a hacksaw to it. His trousers were totally drenched in blood.

Her cry resounded in the bedroom before she rushed to the bathroom and lost her breakfast. Five minutes later Annie returned to the bedroom, shaking like a leaf. For a moment she didn't realize the sound she could hear was a dial tone. She put a hand to her mouth, having forgotten all about the call to the attorney.

On rubbery legs she moved to the bed to hang up, then redialed the number.

"Radinger and Byland."

"H-hello. It's Annie Bower calling back."

"I'm glad you phoned. He's still on that other call. Do you really want to wait?"

She swayed in place. "N-no. I've changed my mind about talking to him. Please don't say anything. If I need him, I'll call and make an appointment."

"You're sure?"

"Yes. Thank you."

Annie clicked off. She was in shock over the pictures spread out on the bed. One photo showed a close-up of his bloodied face covered in cuts. This picture was exceptionally gory because he was such a striking man. The sight of him riddled with bits of the bomb brought home as nothing else could the evil of those who'd caused the mutilation done to him.

By rights he should have died with the others, yet it was no dead man who'd appeared at her door a little while ago.

She shoved the pictures under her pillow out of sight, not knowing what to do or where to turn. In agony she collapsed on her back and sobbed. This was a new horror on top of the old.

When her cell phone began ringing she was in no shape to answer it, but the person on the other end wouldn't give up. Using her free arm for leverage, she sat up and checked the caller ID in case it was her parents or the school phoning, but she knew full well who it was. Naturally the ID was blank.

Annie feared he was still outside the condo. What if he waited until Roberta got home from school and then approached her, forcing a confrontation of the three of them.

Today Annie's mother planned to pick up the girls and bring dinner home with them. She started to panic because, if either of them saw Robert, they'd recognize him at once.

She'd brought back photographs from Afghanistan. Most of them had been framed and were placed around Roberta's bedroom. Annie kept several framed pictures on her own dresser and by the bed. The rest had been put in an album Roberta went through all the time and showed her friends.

Robert had put her in an untenable position. She was damned no matter what she did, but if she refused to talk to him, he was capable of anything and it could affect Roberta. She would do whatever it took to protect her daughter.

Her hand reached for the phone and she clicked on. After a brief hesitation she said, "What is it you want?"

"To talk."

"There's nothing to discuss. I could have done without the photographs and am deeply sorry for the horror you went through, but have no fear. You're still dead to me and Roberta. That's the way I want it to stay."

"At any moment you might get your wish."

His comment brought her up short. "You mean you're going to be disappearing again? If that's the case, why bother telling me?"

"I'm not going anywhere, but there's something else you need to know about me. Unfortunately when we came to the door earlier you were so upset, I held back."

"Held back what?"

"Let me backtrack for a minute. When I heard you had a daughter and learned that her name was Roberta, I realized she was my daughter, too. Knowing I'd made you pregnant, I wanted to be a part of her life and help care for her. But you need to know about my medical condition. It might influence you not to tell Roberta about me. I would understand that and leave you alone."

His words rocked her. "That sounds very noble. What medical condition?"

"There's a piece of shrapnel lodged in my heart." When the words sank in, Annie felt a tight band constrict her lungs. "It's in an inoperable position. As long as it doesn't move, I'm all right. After ten years I'm still here, but there are no guarantees. Roberta would have to know that."

Annie could hardly swallow, let alone respond.

"Every two months I have it checked at a private clinic. No one knows about my condition except Agent Manning and Chief Rossiter. Because ten years have gone by without incident, it gives me hope for a few more. How many, only God knows. At this point you deserve—no, you have the right to know everything about me before you decide to let Roberta know I'm alive. I'm aware it could influence your decision."

A cry escaped her throat. "Are you telling me you

were afraid you might die of your injury and that's the reason you never tried to contact me?"

"No. I've already given you my reasons for remaining dead to you, but now that I know I have a daughter…everything's changed," he said emotionally. "I know you're going to say that it hardly makes sense for me to show up now and endanger both your lives, but I've talked with my superiors.

"We've come to a consensus that ten years has minimized the threat of danger as long as I remain at the park. The uncanny coincidence that you applied for the archaeology position will make it possible for me to see our daughter on a daily basis."

"That's out of the question. I've already withdrawn my application."

"If you take the job," he said, ignoring her, "there'll be no safer place in the world for all of us where I can protect you. Homeland security is especially tight there. I want to get to know my daughter, Annie. As long as she's told the whole truth about me and you think she can live with it, then this is the one way we can be together."

By now she was shaking. How could she tell Roberta her father was alive in one breath, and then in the next, tell her he could die any time from an injury to his heart? This was insanity! "I've told you I don't want anything to do with you."

"I'm well aware of that fact, but would you punish Roberta who has her own father ready and willing to love her? How do you think she'll feel if later on she finds out you made the decision to keep her away from me after you found out I'm alive?"

Her breath caught. "The only way she'd find out would be if *you* told her!"

"I've already told you I wouldn't do that, but can you be positive there won't be another coincidence down the line that brings an accidental meeting of the two of us?"

Her thoughts flicked back to a recent conversation she'd had with Roberta. *We're studying California history. Mrs. Darger showed us a video the other day. We're going to go on a field trip to Yosemite next year near the end of school.*

Annie shook her head. "This is a nightmare."

"Why? What did you tell her about her father? Does she even know the truth?"

"Yes—" she almost shouted in defense. "Yes," she mumbled, trying to calm down.

"Then why is this a nightmare? Unless you're on the verge of marrying someone else and she already thinks of him as daddy."

Her hand tightened on the phone. "There isn't anyone else," she admitted in a weak moment. She'd dated other men, but she'd only allowed those relationships to go so far before she backed off because she couldn't commit.

Only now did it occur to her Robert was probably involved with some fascinating female. The women she knew in Kabul, foreign or American, had coveted her relationship with him. Since she'd been younger than any of them, she couldn't believe it when he'd singled her out. He was one man who could have had any woman he wanted and was an even more arresting male now. How many had there been since he'd left the hospital in Switzerland?

"When will Roberta be home from school?"

The unexpected question set off alarm bells. "Why?"

"Because I'm walking up to your door as we speak.

In case you feel she can handle all the truth, we need to work out a plan face-to-face before I meet her for the first time. In the event you don't end up taking the job in the park, we have to talk about visitation rights."

"No—"

"Don't you think her input will be crucial when she learns she can visit me at the park any time she wants to? It's your choice how we handle it."

"Robert? Please don't do this—" she begged frantically.

"My name is Chase Jarvis. It's just one of the many things about my fictional background Roberta and her grandparents will have to have explained to them. I saw them leaving the condo last night, by the way. Ages ago I told you I was looking forward to meeting them, but I didn't realize it would take ten years before I had the opportunity. There's no time like right now to talk this through."

He'd run her to ground. "Y-you'll have to give me five minutes."

"No problem. I'm not going anywhere."

Annie knew that. The ramifications terrified her.

WHEN THE DOOR OPENED and a pale Annie with her arm in a sling stood back so Chase could enter, he could breathe again. He saw no change in her except she'd put on sandals and had run a brush through her glossy hair.

Once inside the condo he noted the yellow-and-white color scheme in the front room with its splashes of blue. She'd placed potted plants around with an artistic eye. A basket of fresh violets sat perched on the coffee table in front of the yellow-and-white-striped couch. Two French provincial chairs in a taffeta plaid of blue, yellow and white completed the living room arrangement.

Everything reflected the warm personality of the woman he'd fallen in love with. She'd decorated her condo along traditional lines, creating a cozy, comfortable atmosphere for herself and their daughter. Give her free rein with his house in the park and they'd have a showplace.

It had been needing a woman's touch. Her touch. He'd needed, craved her touch for too long. Being with her like this again made him want to catch up on ten years all at once. He wanted an on-the-spot fix that would obliterate the pain of the past so they could take up where'd they'd left off before the explosion, but he knew it wasn't possible. He had to slow down and let her set the pace.

She shut the door behind him. "Come in the living room."

As he moved out of the foyer, he felt inquisitive eyes wander over him, undoubtedly trying to see through his sport shirt and trousers to the massive scars on his torso and lower back. The shrapnel in his heart wouldn't be visible without an X-ray, of course.

Several plastic surgeries had helped make the damage somewhat more presentable to human eyes, but even the doctors who'd attended him had to admit those photographs weren't a pretty sight. However, their shock value had at least made a fissure in that wall of ice encasing Annie, otherwise he wouldn't have made it inside her home.

Standing in the middle of the room, he said, "I fell in love with our daughter over the phone. When I saw her leave the condo earlier, my entrancement was complete. She has a faint look of me, but all the important parts are you. To say that you've done a superb job raising our child would be a colossal understatement."

She stood opposite him. He noticed her breathing had grown shallow. "The last thing I want is for her to be hurt!" she cried. "You suddenly show up back from the dead with your pretty speech, not having a clue what this could do to her."

"I know what it has done to me," he said calmly, "so I think I have some idea of the impact it will have on her. But if we do this right, then she'll have the benefit of being loved by the two people who love her more than anyone on earth. I'll love her and protect for as long as I'm granted breath."

He could see she was trembling. "How do you do something like this *right*?" She was fighting for Roberta's life. The anguish in her tone cut him to the quick.

"You're still recovering from the crash and look pale. Before we talk about it, I'm going to get you a glass of water."

Despite her protests, he walked through the dining room to the sunny kitchen. He checked a couple of cupboards until he found a glass. As he turned on the cold water tap she joined him. One glimpse of her drawn features and he forced her to sit on one of the white wood-and-wicker chairs placed around the breakfast table.

"Drink this, Annie. You look ready to pass out."

Incredibly, she did as he asked.

"Do you need more painkiller for your arm?" When she didn't immediately answer, he told her he'd get it and headed down the hall to her bedroom. Going on instinct he found the medicine on an end table next to her bed.

Beneath the lamp he saw a framed picture of the two

of them with their arms wrapped around each other. He remembered when and where it had been taken as if it were yesterday. His heart gave him a karate-sized kick, sending him back to the kitchen.

He opened the bottle and shook out the prescribed two pills for her. She swallowed them with the last of her water.

"More?"

She shook her head.

"You need to be in bed. I'll help you."

"No—you've done enough. The weakness has passed."

Her color had improved. It was the only reason he didn't pick her up and carry her to the bedroom.

Chase stood next to her chair. She refused to look at him. "I realize the shock has been too much for you so I'm going back to my motel. It's only a mile from here. Just understand that I want to have a full relationship with our daughter, but I'll honor your wishes if you decide she can't handle learning about my heart condition.

"Please let me know one way or the other. Depending on your decision, we'll come up with a plan to be introduced. I'm on vacation and will wait as long as it takes for your phone call."

"I can't give you a timetable for anything."

"You need to keep in mind there's an endless line of archaeologists waiting for the opportunity you've been offered to work in the park. Roberta's too young to know you were singled out from all the others because of your outstanding credentials and experience in Afghanistan. Superintendent Telford is counting on you to vindicate him in adding an archaeologist with your particular expertise."

She made no response, indicating she was barely

tolerating his presence. He doubted she'd been listening.

He ground his teeth in frustration. "Before I leave, is there anything else I can do for you?"

"Nothing." It was clear Annie wanted him gone.

"Don't forget I'm only five minutes away if you need anything." With those parting words he strode from the kitchen to the front door and let himself out. From now on it was a waiting game.

LATE SATURDAY AFTERNOON, Annie poked her head inside the door of Roberta's bedroom. The girls had been playing with their Polly Pocket figures. "Debbie? Your mom's here."

Roberta looked up from the bed. "Does she have to go?"

"I'm afraid so."

"Mom's boyfriend is taking us for pizza and a movie." She put the figures she brought in a little case and jumped off the bed.

"Do you like him?" Roberta asked as they walked through the house. Annie followed them.

"Not very much. When he comes over he always turns off my show so he can watch sports."

"That's not fair."

Annie could have predicted her daughter would say that. They waved Debbie off and shut the door. "How soon are Grandma and Grandpa coming?"

"They're bringing Chinese for us and should be here by seven." It was four-thirty now, giving Annie a two-and-a-half-hour window to talk about the elephant in the room, the one Roberta didn't know had been living with them since Monday.

She made a detour to the laundry room to pull the clean clothes out of the dryer. "Would you mind carrying the basket to my bedroom so I can fold them?"

Roberta did as she was asked and trudged behind Annie with it. "I'm glad you don't have a mean boyfriend." Roberta set it on the bed. Her daughter had just given Annie the opening she'd been searching for since Robert had made his demand before leaving the condo yesterday. No matter how he'd couched it, he'd let her know he was going to have his way and there was no escape.

"Would you like me to have a nice one?" she teased.

"Would *you*?"

Either Roberta was a crafty soul or unsure of herself. Maybe she was a little of both, because she often answered Annie's questions with another question, thereby excusing herself from incrimination.

"I haven't given it a great deal of thought. We've been happy together, haven't we?"

Roberta nodded. "Nobody would be like Daddy."

Annie struggled to breathe normally. "How do you know that?"

Roberta gave her one of those innocent stares that seemed to go clear through to Annie's soul. "Because you *loved* him."

In an abrupt move, Annie turned the basket upside down on the bed and started separating their clothes. Halfway through the process she sank down on the edge, praying for inspiration.

"Honey? Let's play a game."

"Which one?" She was carefully folding her tops and stacking them. Roberta was a much neater person than Annie.

"It's one we've never tried before."

"Okay. What's it called?"

"What if?"

"We used to play that in kindergarten."

"Can we do it anyway?"

"Okay."

"I'll start." Annie's heart hammered so hard, she wondered if it would pound her right into the floor. "What if you found out a miracle happened and your daddy didn't die in that explosion?"

She'd begun folding her school pants in another pile. "I'd be the happiest girl in the world."

"I know that. What if you learned he had a piece of metal in his heart from the explosion that the doctors couldn't get out?"

Her hands stilled on the clothes. "You mean he could die."

"It's possible."

"But he hasn't died yet so maybe he won't."

Oh, Roberta... "What if it took him ten years before he could let me know he was alive?"

She lifted her head. "Why would he take so long?"

"Because he was in a war and bad people were looking for him. He didn't want to put you and me in danger." For the time being she had to accept Agent Manning's explanation.

Roberta went perfectly quiet. "Are we still playing what if?" Her daughter knew the answer to that question before she'd asked it.

Annie shook her head. "No."

Solemn eyes mixed with fear clung to Annie's. "Is he still in danger?"

"Not in the same way he once was. That was a long

time ago, but he's been using a different name for years just to stay safe."

She twisted her hands together like she often did when she was her most insecure. "Does he know I was born?"

"He does now."

Roberta bit her lip. "Does he want to see me?" she asked in a quiet voice.

"Oh yes, darling. The second he found out he had a daughter, he phoned me in the hospital." She tried to swallow but couldn't. "Do you remember Ranger Jarvis? The one you said was so nice?"

She nodded.

This was it. "He's your father."

Annie could hear her mind trying to take it all in. "The ranger who rescued you?"

"Yes. He's been a park ranger for three years, but I didn't know it. I only saw him for a moment when they were lifting me into the helicopter. H-he wants to meet you as soon as possible." Her voice faltered. "How do you feel about that?"

Her daughter blinked. She was in a daze. "Is he at the park now?"

An adrenaline rush made Annie so jumpy she stood up. "No. He's staying at a motel here in Santa Rosa waiting to meet you."

"Do you think he would come over?" Her daughter was holding in all her feelings of excitement. Annie could tell she didn't quite believe this was happening. Who would? The whole situation was too surreal to comprehend.

"Why don't you call him? I have his phone number, the one you wrote down. It's in my purse." Before she could ask Roberta to hand it to her, her daughter rushed to the dresser to get it. Annie handed her the cell phone lying on the bedside table. "If he doesn't answer, leave him a message. I know he'll return it."

Roberta punched in the number and put the phone to her ear. Annie held her breath.

CHASE HAD JUST PULLED AWAY from a drive-through when his cell phone rang. One glance at the caller ID showed it to be Annie's number. His heart thudded against his ribs. This call had come sooner than he'd anticipated. How would he handle it if she shut him out for good?

He rested the sack of food on the seat and answered. "Annie?"

After a silence, "It's Roberta."

Warmth flooded his system. This could only mean one thing. Annie had told their daughter about him. That meant she'd told her about his heart condition. He didn't know how much other information she'd given her, but under the circumstances it was a miracle she'd unbent enough to let them get acquainted.

"Hi, sweetheart."

"Hi," came the timid greeting.

"I can't wait to meet you."

"Me, too," she admitted quietly.

"Are you afraid?"

"Kind of."

"So am I. What if you don't like me?"

A nervous little laugh escaped. "I have pictures of you."

"I wish I'd had one of you all these years. I'm afraid I look a lot older now."

"Like my grandpa?"

He chuckled. "Maybe not quite that old."

"Mom told me about your heart. Does it hurt?"

Chase had to clear his throat. "No, sweetheart. I feel perfectly normal."

"That's good. Can you come over to our house?"

There was no other place he wanted to be. "I was hoping you'd ask. If you want, I'll drive there right now. What do you think?"

"Mom says you can come for a little while."

Chase took that to mean they were expecting company later, probably the Bowers. "I'm on my way. See you in a minute."

"Okay."

He didn't remember the short drive to the eightplex or the walk from the guest parking stall to the condo. Before he reached it, he saw her standing in the open doorway wearing a pair of jeans and a bright red cotton top.

As he approached, they studied each other for a long time. Now that he had a frontal view of her, he detected a lot more of Annie in the oval shape of her face and the feminine way she stood and moved.

"Do I look like a grandpa to you?"

"No."

That was something anyway. He smiled. "With those sky-blue eyes, you're even more beautiful than I had imagined. Am I the luckiest father in the world or what?"

Her Myers mouth curved into the sweetest smile he'd ever seen.

"I never got to change you or feed you when you were a baby. Would you mind very much if I gave you a hug?"

She shook her head, causing her dark brown ponytail to swish.

He made the first move, but when he swept her into

his arms and lifted her off the ground, she lost her reserve. Her arms crept around his neck and clasped him tightly. The slight weight of her body satisfied a deep ache that had been gnawing at him since he'd been torn from Annie.

"Roberta," he murmured against her temple, giving her kisses. "I love you." He could hardly bear it that he'd missed her first ten years.

"I love you, too."

She broke his heart with her unqualified acceptance. "Will you be my big girl from now on?" He felt her nod. "Some of my ranger friends have children. They won't believe it when they find out I have a daughter. I guess you realize we look alike."

"That's what mom says."

He lowered her to the ground. "Where is she?"

"Inside." She stared up at him. "Do you want to come in?"

"If it's all right with her."

"She said you could."

"Then I'd like to." Before he walked inside with her, a girl Roberta's age came skipping down the sidewalk from another condo and asked if she wanted to play.

"I can't. My dad's here."

The auburn-haired girl gazed at him in shock. "I've seen your pictures. I thought you...died."

He laughed inwardly. She'd said it the way it was. "I was in an accident and Roberta's mother thought I was dead. When I woke up in the hospital I had amnesia and didn't know who I was. Over the years I eventually regained my memory." That was the story he and Sid had come up with to tell everyone. "Roberta, sweetheart? Who's your friend?"

"This is Penny."

He smiled. "How do you do, Penny."

"Hi." She kept looking at him. This was what it felt like to be an alien.

"Have you two been friends a long time?"

Penny nodded.

"Penny's dad is the football coach at St. Xavier high school."

"That's exciting," Chase replied. "Do you attend all his games?"

She nodded. "Sometimes Roberta goes with our family and Dad takes us for hot dogs after."

He glanced at his daughter. "Lucky you."

Roberta nodded. "My dad's a ranger at Yosemite Park," she announced unexpectedly.

To hear her say "my dad" filled him with joy.

"You are?"

Chase chuckled at the expression of amazement on Penny's face. Kids often responded that way. Soon after he'd started working at the park he discovered there was something of a mystique about the rangers in tourists' eyes.

"That's right. You'll have to come horseback riding at the park with me and Roberta sometime. We'll take a picnic with us and I'll show you a fabulous beaver pond. There's an old granddaddy beaver we've named Methuselah because he's been around so many years. When he slaps his big tail, it's so loud it scares all the animals away."

Suddenly it was his daughter who looked awestruck. "How soon can we go?"

"Whenever you want."

Out of the corner of his eye he saw Annie appear in

the entry. He'd been waiting. Every time he saw her, those old feelings of desire took over.

"Hi, Penny. How are you?"

"Good. Does your arm still hurt?"

"Not when I wear the sling."

"Mom!" Roberta cried. "Dad's going to take us horseback riding!"

"So I heard."

Chase had a feeling she'd been listening and had decided to break things up when the conversation started to get out of her control.

Roberta must have heard Annie's guarded answer. On cue she said, "I have to go in now, Penny, but I'll call you later."

"Okay. See ya. Don't forget."

"We won't," Chase assured her. "It was nice to meet you, Penny."

"You, too." She hurried down the sidewalk.

Annie flicked him a glance out of shadowed blue eyes. "Come in. We need to talk."

His words exactly.

He ushered Roberta inside and shut the door. It was déjà vu except that they congregated in the living room. Roberta sat next to him on the couch. Annie stood behind one of the chairs. Negative tension radiated from her.

"Honey?" she began. "Before you start making any plans with friends, we have to be very careful about what we say. Not even your grandparents know your father is alive yet. Whatever we tell people has to be the same story. No one can know he was once Robert Myers."

"Your mother's right," Chase corroborated. "We'll tell everyone I lost my memory and barely got it back. That's all people ever have to know. As for you,

Roberta, you have to be told the truth. You know there's a war in the Middle East, right?"

She nodded.

"After the explosion, I was in a hospital in Switzerland for a long time. After that I fought in the war for our country."

"You did?"

"Yes. But one of the terrorists who'd planned the attack on my parents recognized me and word went out that I was still alive. That's when the CIA flew me to the States and turned me into a park ranger to keep *me* safe. For three years everything has been fine, so I don't want you to worry about being in danger.

"When you visit me, it will be in the park where my colleagues are on the alert for all bad people and terrorists living in our country. In fact you'll probably be safer at my house than here in Santa Rosa because of the tight security. Chief Rossiter was a marine in Iraq. He knows the danger to me and has heightened security to keep us all safe."

Annie finally sat down in the chair. "After we move to San Francisco, we'll work out a schedule so you can go see your father when it's convenient for us and for him."

"But now that Daddy's here, I don't want to move to San Francisco."

Chase kept his head bowed. *Did you hear that, Annie?*

"It's all decided," she declared in a no-nonsense tone. "Grandma and Grandpa have been making plans for us."

Roberta slid off the couch and stood up. "I know I told you I didn't want you to work in the park, but I've changed my mind."

"You can't just change your mind. I've already turned down the job offer."

Her daughter's eyes filled with tears. "Can't you get it back? All you have to do is call them up and tell them you're feeling better now."

Nothing pleased Chase more than to watch Annie squirm over this.

He raised his head, focusing on her. "It's not too late. For the last three weeks I was acting head ranger for the park while the Chief was on his honeymoon. I'm the one the new superintendent asked to arrange for your flight over the park. All I have to do is say the word and the position is still yours."

"You were the head of all the rangers?" Roberta questioned while her mother looked poleaxed.

"I'm the assistant head ranger. When the Chief has to leave the park or go off duty, I'm in charge."

Her face beamed. "I can't wait to tell Debbie."

"Who's Debbie?"

"My best friend."

"I'd like to meet her. In fact I'm anxious to get acquainted with all your friends. They can come to my house anytime and sleep over with you. Of course if you lived in the park too, your house would be right around the corner from mine and you could run back and forth between us."

She gave a little jump of happiness.

As long as he'd gone this far to undermine Annie's plans to stay away from him, he might as well go all out. "You'll be a welcome addition to the school. The kids in the Yosemite Valley are homeschooled."

"You mean they get to study in their own house?"

"Not exactly. Ranger Farrell's wife, Kristy, is a professional teacher from the Mariposa County school district. You attend school at her house just like you go to school here. It's about two blocks away from mine. If you end up living in the park, that will make ten students for this school year."

"Are there kids my age?"

"Yes. Ranger Sims has a daughter named Carly who's your age and Ranger King has an eleven year-old boy named Brody. You'd like both of them."

At this point Annie had vacated her chair. "I'm afraid we're getting way ahead of ourselves."

Roberta ran over to her. "Mom—please say yes! Please! Grandma and Grandpa can come and stay with us all the time. I want to live by Daddy."

Satisfied to have created this much chaos, Chase rose to his feet. "Roberta? Your mother was kind enough to let me come and meet you, but I'm going to leave now. This is a situation you two need to discuss in private. You can call me anytime."

She looked alarmed. "Are you going back to the park?"

"Yes, but I'm only as far away as a phone call." He turned to Annie, who couldn't sustain his glance and had averted her eyes. "Annie? You'll never know what this day has meant to me," he whispered. "I'll let myself out."

He walked to the front hall. Roberta darted after him. "You promise you won't go away from the park?"

"I promise, sweetheart. It's my home." As if he'd been doing it all his life, he hugged her hard and was rewarded with a surprisingly strong squeeze. It came so naturally to him, he marveled. When he raised up he caught a glimpse of Annie, whose tortured expression he carried with him as he strode swiftly to his car.

Chapter Five

After Annie heard the front door close, she hurried into the kitchen to get herself a drink of water. It was an excuse to gather her wits, but Roberta stuck to her like glue.

"Daddy said you could work in the park if you want to. Don't you want to?"

She drained the glass she'd poured before turning to her daughter. "Actually I don't."

"Because of the accident?"

"No."

"Then why?" she persisted.

"Roberta, I realize this is hard for you to understand, but your father and I have led separate lives since before you were born. The park is his home now. I have to respect his privacy."

"Why? He wants us to come."

"No, he doesn't." The bewilderment on Roberta's face prompted her to sit down and draw her daughter to her. She brushed the tears off her cheeks with her free hand. "There's something you need to know. After you left for school this morning, he came to see me."

"You didn't tell me that. Neither did he."

"I know. He was trying to respect my feelings. We

talked for quite a while. A lot has happened in ten years. We're different people now. Everything has changed except for one thing. He loves you more than anything in the world and wants you in his life."

Roberta looked heartbroken. "Don't you love each other anymore?"

Annie had to be honest with her. "We have our memories, of course. No one can take those away from us, but we've both moved on. He said he never contacted me in all that time in order to keep me safe. I think that's a wonderful, noble excuse, the best excuse there could be, but I don't think it's the real reason he let me believe he had died."

Her daughter's blue eyes implored Annie. "What's the real reason?"

"If he'd truly been in love with me, I don't think he would have been able to stay away from me. When two people love each other more than anything in the world, nothing can separate them."

"Oh." Roberta's lips trembled.

It killed Annie to have to be this brutally honest with her, but it was the only way. "While he was rescuing me, he pretended he didn't know me. Honey, he was ready to leave the park and go someplace else without ever talking to me again, but by then one of the rangers told him I had a daughter. That changed everything for him. You see, I didn't know I was pregnant with you when I left Afghanistan, so of course he didn't either."

"I know. You told me that before."

This was developing into a new nightmare. "It's his love for *you*, not me, that brought him to the condo this morning, otherwise he'd be somewhere else far away from here by now. No one but his own little girl could have made him decide to call me at the hospital. That's because he wants you in his life and the only way he can make that happen is to talk to me and work things out."

Tears poured down Roberta's cheeks. "But he wanted to marry you."

"We said a lot of things to each other once. That was a long time ago. The fact that he hasn't ever married proves to me he's happy with his life the way it is and doesn't want a wife.

"You have to understand that before he fought in the war, he was an archaeologist who traveled from China to Afghanistan. In many ways, it's a lonely occupation. He lived in far-off places where the dig sites were hard to get to and he kept strange hours. Robert isn't a man like Penny's father, who has a normal kind of job with normal hours and time for his family."

"He's not an archaeologist anymore," Roberta said. She wasn't willing to let this go.

"That's true, but as you can see, he still lives alone because it's difficult to change old habits. In ways a ranger's life isn't that conducive to having a family either." She needed to squelch Roberta's hope that the two of them would get together.

"He said some of the rangers are married."

Annie sucked in her breath. "I know, but the last thing he wants is to see me working in the park, wishing I weren't around. He used the explosion that ended our relationship to make certain the situation remained permanent, but that was before he was told he had a daughter. We'll work out visitation for you to see him."

"Don't you even like him anymore?"

"Roberta, this doesn't have anything to do with liking him. He was a part of my life. Of course I like him, but to find out he's alive has been a great shock to me. I know you've always wanted your Daddy and by some miracle he's here for you, but our lives are more complicated than that."

"Daddy said he would protect us. Are you scared those terrorists are going to hurt you now?"

"Oh no, honey—"

She frowned. "Then I think you're being mean."

In Roberta's vocabulary the word *mean* had many definitions depending on the situation, but she'd never used it against Annie before. It was like a dagger plunged in her heart. "In what way?"

"If we lived in the park, I could see him every day. I don't want to live in San Francisco and have to wait all the time to be with him. He said he loves me more than anything." Her body shook with emotion. "When I talk to him again, I'm going to ask if I can live with him." On that note she ran out of the kitchen, leaving Annie absolutely devastated.

To her dismay the doorbell rang. Her parents' timing couldn't be worse. Thank goodness, Robert had already left. Attempting to pull herself together, she walked through the house to the entry, but a tear-ravaged Roberta had beaten her to it.

"Daddy?" she cried as she flung the door open. Obviously she thought he'd come back for some reason.

Caught off guard, Annie's parents' shocked gazes traveled from their granddaughter to Annie, who groaned in reaction. With that one telling word, the water had spilled over the dam, never to be recovered.

While her father stood there holding a sack of

Chinese takeout food, her mother bent over Roberta. "What's going on, dear?"

"Daddy didn't die in that explosion!"

She cupped Roberta's face in her hands. "I don't understand."

"Grandma—Daddy's alive! He's the assistant head ranger at Yosemite who helped rescue mom. He wants us to live in the park!"

Her father shut the door. He shot Annie an inquisitive glance mixed with hurt surprise that she hadn't confided any of this to them earlier. "Is this true?"

More groans.

"Yes. I—it's a long story," she stammered.

AFTER THE DRIVE from Santa Rosa, Chase let himself in the rear door at headquarters and entered Mark's office. Since he knew he wouldn't be able to sleep, he'd phoned Mark to tell him he would cover the Saturday night shift so the chief security ranger could have some much needed time off.

Vance had told Chase to go on vacation, but being alone in a motel waiting for the phone to ring was the kind of torture he couldn't tolerate.

The other man tried in vain to hide his excitement. "You're sure you want to do this?"

"Get out of here, Mark."

He grinned. "I'm going. I'll be back on duty at noon."

"Show up at two instead." While Chase waited for Annie to make the next move, the only panacea was to stay too busy to do a lot of thinking.

"You're on!"

Ten minutes after he left, the rangers stationed

around the park phoned in their status reports. The last one to come in was Ranger Farrell on duty at the base camp of the Tuolumne Meadows.

"We've got a situation, but I don't know how serious yet. There's been an outbreak of gastrointestinal illness."

"Who's been affected?"

"Some of the lodge employees and hikers."

"How many?"

"At least thirty so far. Three people were sick enough to be taken to the hospital in Bishop."

"I'll get right on it. Give me an hour-by-hour report."

"Will do."

After hanging up, Chase phoned the hospital to talk with the lab. In a few minutes he learned they suspected it was a norovirus infection illness. So far no fatalities. They didn't expect any.

Chase asked them to phone him when they had more information, then he left word for the county health inspector to get busy on it. He made a third call to the lodge to offer any assistance they needed, then he phoned Vance.

"At last! I've been waiting to hear from you. Have you met your daughter yet?"

"I'll tell you everything in a minute. Business first."

"What are you talking about?"

"I gave Mark the night off."

"You're here?"

"Drove in about a half hour ago."

"I'll be right there."

Within five minutes Vance walked into Mark's office. Chase was on the phone with one of the rangers reporting on a deserted car found on the road near Wawona.

While he told the ranger to impound the vehicle and send out a search crew for the missing driver, he handed Vance the faxed report from the lodge about the outbreak. Once he hung up, Chase brought him up to speed.

"Okay—" Vance sat back in the chair facing him. "Now that we've got business out of the way, I want to hear it all."

It was a relief for Chase to unload. "My Roberta is adorable. Perfect."

"Yeah?" Vance was grinning. "Has she called you Daddy yet?"

Chase nodded, still incredulous he was a father.

"So how soon can we expect her and her mother? Rachel and I are dying to meet them."

His smile morphed into a grimace. "That part isn't resolved. Annie's fighting it all the way."

"Is there another man?"

"No. I'm dealing with something much more formidable. She won't consider taking the job. We're down to visitation rights."

Vance sat forward. "Your daughter holds all the power right now. Do I have to remind you that Nicky was the one who brought Rachel back to the park a second time when she had no intention? Give it time."

Chase needed to hear that about now.

"You'll hate me for saying this, Chase, but patience is the key. I know because I've been there."

Chase shook his head. "After ten years, I don't have any." Just then the phone rang. "Let me get this."

"I'll go find us a couple of sodas."

Chase nodded and picked up. "Ranger Jarvis here."

"This is the hospital lab in Bishop calling." Chase

was crushed it wasn't Annie or Roberta on the other end. "What's the verdict?"

"Our assumption about the virus was correct. It comes on fast but everyone should recover without problem."

"I'll get the word out."

Good news for the park, but he needed even a modicum of good news from another quarter or he wasn't going to make it. He hoped to heaven Vance was right about Roberta working on her mother. Like Nicky, who'd been Vance's cheering section and had brought Rachel around, Chase's daughter was the key to his happiness.

ROBERTA ALWAYS GOT in bed with Annie in the mornings, but not this Sunday morning. All the way around, last night had been a total disaster. After she'd sat down with her parents to explain the incredible news that Robert was alive, Roberta had been so upset with Annie for insisting they were moving to San Francisco anyway, she'd gone to bed utterly inconsolable. Not even her grandparents could get her to come out.

Every time Annie peeked in the bedroom, she heard Roberta crying into her pillow. With each quiet sob it tore her apart a little more and she tiptoed back to the living room to talk to her parents. Mostly they listened while she unburdened herself.

"Do you have any idea how hard it would be for me to live at the park in such close proximity to him after what's happened?" Her voice throbbed in pain. "All these years I've kept a myth alive for Roberta. I've been such a fool."

"No, Annie," her father said. "He intended to marry you before terrorists destroyed his world. They could have destroyed you too if he hadn't protected you the way he did. The way he still has to!"

Annie hid her face in her hands. Somewhere deep down her father was making sense, but the shock of seeing Robert alive had prevented her from taking it all in.

"Don't blame him for deciding not to recognize you in front of the other rangers at the accident scene," her dad continued. "He was trying to protect you until he got you to the hospital, but the moment he felt it was safe, he phoned you. I'd say he's been perfectly clear about his intentions. He wants to be a father to Roberta now that he knows of her existence."

"Your father's right," her mom agreed. "When he first saw you, he could have asked the witness protection program to hide him away at another undisclosed location. Instead he called his superiors and now he has told you he wants you and Roberta near him, but he can't leave the park. My advice is to take the job. You have to admit it would make the problem of visitation a lot easier."

She stared at her mother. "I thought you were on my side. Don't you want us to live by you?"

"Margaret Anne Bower, that question doesn't deserve an answer." Her mother hadn't called her that since she was Roberta's age. "Do you honestly believe you'd be happy in San Francisco when you know how unhappy it would make your daughter? From day one you put her father on a pedestal and now he's here to claim her. You're changing the rules and she doesn't understand."

Annie didn't want to think about her parents' logic. She was in a kind of hell where there was no way out.

"All we're suggesting is that you don't let your pride get in the way of making such a vital decision where Roberta is considered," her father reasoned.

"Pride?" Annie questioned in surprise.

"Isn't that what this is all about?" He studied her for a moment. "If he'd come right out on the phone and declared that he was still in love with you, would you have given him the time of day…considering your frame of mind?"

The question went to the heart of the matter.

Her mother's eyebrows arched. "Where you're concerned, no one can presume to know what's in his mind and heart right now, but if I were you I'd show Robert you've matured into a woman who moved on a long time ago. He can see you've been leading a fulfilled life without him. Prove to him you'll continue to do what's right for your daughter. The future will take care of itself."

"Let him spend time with Roberta," her father said. "That will relieve you to enjoy yourself in the process. Have fun for the first time since you came home from Afghanistan. He'll soon realize you haven't lost that sense of adventure he was drawn to in the beginning. If you and Robert aren't meant to be, don't shut yourself off to other possibilities. You might meet someone exceptional while you're working in the park."

Annie wasn't a complete fool. She knew that deep down they worried she would never get married. Thirty-one wasn't an old age, but if she didn't put herself in a position to meet men, opportunities would be missed.

Her dad got up from the couch and came around to kiss her cheek. "We're going to the hotel, but we'll be back in the morning. The offer still holds to drive you to the park tomorrow. Roberta's never been there. It wouldn't hurt for her to see if she even likes it."

"Oh, Dad—with Robert there you *know* Roberta will love it."

That salient fact had kept Annie tossing and turning all night. Needing to talk to her daughter before any more time went by, she moved carefully off the bed and headed straight for Roberta's room.

She was still burrowed under her covers, but Annie knew she was awake. Her daughter was an early riser, always had been. When she was a baby, Annie would discover her in her crib in the wee small hours wide awake and playing with her toes. When she moved into the toddler years, she would be standing at the bars talking unintelligibly to herself before the sun was up.

Finally came the morning when Annie heard a loud thump and went running to Roberta's room. Her little girl had climbed over the railing and landed on the floor. Instead of a cry, Annie had been met with a smile and it was only six o'clock. It wasn't much past that time now.

"Roberta? Time to get up."

"I don't want to," came the smothered response.

Annie moved over to her and sank down on the bed. With her free hand she pulled the covers back so she could see her. "Do you know last night was the first time we ever went to bed without kissing each other good night?"

When she encountered only silence, Annie leaned over and kissed her brow. "In a little while your grandparents will be coming to take us to Yosemite for the day. We both need to get up and eat breakfast so we'll be ready."

Movement at last. Roberta shot up in the bed, her eyes shining from a puffy face. "Does Daddy know?"

"Not yet. I have no idea if he's on duty or not. We'll call him after we get there. If I'm going to take the job, I thought we'd better look at the house we'd be living in."

Roberta threw herself into Annie's arms. Tears of joy spilled everywhere, wetting them both.

Courage, Annie. You're about to go onstage in a new role. It will have to be so convincing, even you will be blessed in time with the gift of forgetfulness.

BETH SLIPPED inside Mark's office. She put coffee and a paper plate filled with breakfast fare on the desk for Chase. He'd just answered the phone and mouthed her a thank-you before she left.

"What were you saying about the abandoned car?"

"A tourist ran out of gas and hitched a ride back to Wawona. Problem solved."

"Good. How's the smog from the burn in that section?"

"Average."

"We can be thankful for light wind today. Keep in touch."

Chase clicked off and reached for a slice of toast. His gaze flicked to the clock. Ten to ten. Four more hours before he went off duty. After working all night he ought to be exhausted, but his inner turmoil over Annie had sent out hot, wirelike tentacles to every atom of his body, preventing him from relaxing.

A call from the hospital indicated no more new patients had been admitted because of the virus outbreak in the park. Chase sent a fax to the superintendent with the latest update, then settled down to eat his breakfast.

While he was swallowing the last of it, Jeff Thompson phoned in. Curious to know what was up when he'd just talked to him a half hour ago, he clicked on.

"Ranger Jarvis here."

"I thought you should know the park's most famous female just passed through the entrance."

He frowned. "Whom are you talking about?"

"Margaret Bower."

The disposable cup slipped from Chase's fingers. Fortunately he'd drunk the contents.

"Her daughter and parents were with her. Because of her cast, her father's driving. She said they were visiting for the day. For somebody who was in a crash just a week ago she looks fantastic, you know what I mean?"

Chase shot the cup in the direction of the waste-basket and missed. He couldn't answer. Too many emotions had seized him at once.

"Thought you should be informed in case they show up at the Visitor's Center. The Chief will want to meet her."

"He's off today. Got another call coming in," he lied, and ended the conversation before he had to listen to anything more that idiot had to say about Annie.

Last night Chase had been so negatively charged, he'd told Mark not to report for duty until two today. He groaned to realize Annie and Roberta would in all probability be arriving shortly and he couldn't leave his post.

He didn't know what was behind Annie's agenda. Chase would be a fool to assume she'd done a 360-degree turnaround. In all likelihood she wanted Roberta to get a feel for the park before she allowed visitation. To ask for more than that would only result in dashing his dreams. For the moment he had to squelch the desire to phone her. Until she made contact with him, he had no choice but to wait.

Everything seemed to be working against him. For once things were slow around the office despite the fact that this was one of the biggest traffic weekends for the park would have until spring.

At eleven-thirty he sent out the latest weather report to each ranger station. In the process, Cindy rang him from the information desk in the visitor's center.

"What's happening, Cindy?"

"There's a cute young lady out here named Roberta Bower who's asking for Ranger Jarvis." Elation brought him to his feet. "She says you're one of the rangers who helped rescue her mom from the helicopter crash and she wants to thank you." Clever girl. "What should I tell her?"

"Bring her back to Mark's office."

"Will do."

He walked around the counter to the door and opened it. A few seconds later he saw them coming down the hall. His first reaction was to run out and sweep her into his arms, but he restrained himself.

Cindy smiled at Chase. "Ranger Jarvis? Meet Roberta Bower."

He tried to dislodge the lump in his throat, but it was no use. "We met once before didn't we, Roberta."

"Yes."

They were both playing a game in front of Cindy. Behind Roberta's reserve, her blue eyes glowed like hot stars. As she surveyed him in his ranger outfit, he saw her heels go up and down, as if she were barely holding on to her excitement. Join the club.

"Where's your mother?"

"Outside in the car with my grandparents. She said I could visit you for a minute if you were free."

"You picked the perfect time. Come in." He flicked his gaze to Cindy. "Thanks for bringing her back."

"You bet. See you later, Roberta."

"Thank you for helping me."

His daughter's excellent manners delighted him all over again. He shut the door so they could be alone. Smiling down at her, he said, "Aren't *you* a sight for sore eyes!"

She looked so cute in her long-sleeved pullover and jeans, he couldn't resist picking her up to hug her. Roberta was right there hugging him back with all her might. She smelled fragrant, just the way her mother always did.

Naturally the phone rang while they clung to each other. "I've got to answer it." He carried her around the counter with him and set her on one of the stools before he picked up. "Ranger Jarvis here."

"It's Ranger Hawkins reporting from Tamarack Flat. I found five dead skunks in the latrines. This is a new one on me."

It surprised Chase, too. The park's chief biologist would need to investigate. "I'll get right on it. In the meantime, seal them off to the public."

He hung up, then called Paul Thomas's office and explained the situation. "Give me your best theory after you've investigated. Mark will need to know if they wound up in there because of a malicious prank."

"That was my first thought. I'm leaving now."

"Thanks, Paul."

Finally he could give Roberta his attention. "Is your mom still out in front?" She nodded. "Maybe I'd better talk to her."

"She wants to know if you have to work all day."

"I'll be off at two, then I'll show you where I live."

Roberta slid off the stool. "I'll run out and tell her, then I'll come right back.'

"Okay."

She darted around the counter and out the door. A couple of staff came and went from the room. He answered another call. The next time the door opened he thought it would be Roberta. Instead, Nicky popped in carrying a long, thin, gift-wrapped package.

"Hi, Uncle Chase!"

"Hi, yourself! Did you come over with your dad?"

"Nope. He's home with Mom. We wanted you to come for dinner so I could give you my present, but Daddy found out you had to work. He said I could come over and give it to you, but first I have to call him and tell him I'm here."

Chase handed him his cell phone. "Press two."

While Nicky was making the call, Roberta came running inside. She swept right past their visitor and hurried around the counter. "Grandma and Grandpa have to get back to San Francisco so Mom says we have to leave the park by three."

Stifling his disappointment, he said, "Then we'll have an hour to talk. What does she plan to do in the meantime?"

"We're going to look at the falls and walk around, but I'd rather stay here with you."

"Then run back out and tell her I'll keep you with me."

"Can I?" she cried with excitement.

"I want you to. At three we'll meet in my office with your mom and talk."

By now Nicky was off the phone. He stared from her to Chase. "Who's that?"

This was going to be fun. "Nicky Rossiter? I want you to meet my daughter, Roberta Bower. Roberta? Nicky's father is Vance Rossiter, the chief ranger and my best friend."

Nicky giggled. "You don't have a daughter, Uncle Chase."

Chase put an arm around her shoulders. "Are you sure? Take a close look." He lowered his face next to hers. "What do you think?"

At least a half minute passed while Nicky scrutinized them. "You kind of look like each other. Is he really your daddy?"

Roberta nodded. "He had amnesia for ten years and didn't know I was born until a few days ago."

"What's amnesia?"

Chase straightened. "Tell you what, Nicky—I'll explain all about it in a minute. First though, why don't you go with Roberta while she runs outside to talk to her mother. On your way back, show her where my office is and then stop in at your dad's office and get both of you a soda from his mini fridge."

"Okay." Nicky put the unopened present on the counter. "What kind of soda do you like?" he asked as they started to leave the office together.

"Root beer."

"So do I! It's my favorite! Have you ever been to the park?"

"No."

"What grade are you in?"

"Fourth."

"You're old. I'm only in first. Are you scared of bears?"

"I'm scared of grizzlies."

"Don't worry. We only have black bears. Yosemite doesn't have any wolves."

As their voices faded, Chase broke into a broad grin because Nicky would be pure entertainment for his daughter from now on. That is, if Annie allowed him liberal visitation rights.

His hands tightened into fists. To think she was right outside the building behaving as if they'd never known each other. How ironic when in reality their precious go-between was no one less than the child they'd created together.

Annie couldn't have forgotten those early mornings of passion years ago before they left for work. They took turns fixing each other breakfast, then went back to bed, unable to leave each other's arms. Once at the site they had to be careful not to give in to their desires around the others. Knowing this, they made the most of every moment alone.

Annie's open, loving nature had been a revelation to him on a spiritual as well as a physical level. No woman since had the depth of character to tug so powerfully at his emotions. Having seen her again, her magic was stronger than ever. She'd given birth to their beautiful daughter. This new dimension of motherhood left him in awe that she'd had sole responsibility of their daughter from the moment she'd conceived.

Chase knew it was late in the day, but everything in him yearned to be a part of their lives. He ached for what he'd been missing. No matter how hard Annie fought him, he intended to live the life with them that had been denied him.

As he was making that vow to himself, the young lady who was going to help him achieve that joy came into the office with Nicky, both of them drinking root beer. From the way he was still chattering, it sounded like he'd been giving Roberta the guided tour.

"Hi, sweetheart. Did your mom say it was all right to stay with me?"

Roberta darted him a glance. "Yes. She says she'll be in your office at two."

Good. He wondered if her parents would come in with her. It was long past time they all met.

"Here." Nicky picked up the present. "This is for you. I hope you like it."

"I'm sure I will." Chase removed the wrapping paper and opened the long box. Inside the lining lay a silver, batonlike object, smooth and slim. "What is it?"

"It's your wizard wand. The man put your name on the handle. See?"

Chase lifted it from the box and examined it. Sure enough the words *Uncle Chase* had been engraved. "I love it! How did you know this is exactly what I wanted?"

Roberta looked fascinated. "Where did you get it?"

"In London at the Harry Potter shop. We all bought one."

"You went to England?"

Nicky nodded.

Pretending he was a wizard, Chase wove it around in the air. Making his voice scary he said, "Double, double toil and trouble, fire burn and caldron bubble— cool it with a baboon's blood, then the charm is firm and good."

While the children laughed, someone started clapping. Chase looked up to see Vance in the doorway. "Well, well, well. Shakespeare at Hogwarts. I believe you've missed your calling."

Chase chuckled. "Something my English tutor in Pakistan had me memorize, but I only remember the last four lines." He rubbed the top of Nicky's head. "Thank you for the terrific gift. I'm going to keep it on the desk in my office. When the rangers get out of line, I'll put a spell on them."

"You can't really do that." But he looked at Vance before he said, "Can he, Daddy?"

"I guess we'll have to wait and see," he teased. His gaze fell on Roberta. He studied her before sending Chase his nod of approval. "I'm already crazy about your little acorn," he murmured quietly. Then he turned to Nicky. "Aren't you going to introduce me to your new friend?"

He took another sip of his soda. "This is Roberta. Uncle Chase is her daddy."

Vance hunkered down in front of her. "I can see the resemblance, but you're the pretty one." Roberta blushed. "It's a pleasure to meet you."

"Thanks. It's nice to meet you, too."

"You've made your dad very happy by coming to visit him."

Nicky put his arm across Vance's shoulder. "Daddy? What does amnesia mean?"

The two men exchanged meaningful glances. "In Uncle Chase's case it means he had an accident ten years ago and it took away his memory. When he woke up in a hospital, he didn't know where he was or who he was."

By now Nicky was mesmerized. He eyed Chase with a worried glance. "Were you scared?"

"Very." *In fact you'll never know, Nicky. For years I had petrifying dreams that Annie had been found and tortured.* "Roberta's mother thought he died and she moved back to California," Vance continued. "Then just the other day she was in that helicopter crash and Uncle

Chase found her. Suddenly he remembered who he was, and to his joy he found out Roberta was his daughter."

After the explanation sank in, Nicky stared at Roberta. "Are you glad your daddy found you?"

She nodded.

"Next to Daddy and my grandparents, I love Uncle Chase best."

Chase's eyes smarted. "Ditto, sport." Just then Roberta slid her hand into Chase's.

She looked up at him. "I love you, too."

He squeezed her fingers. Those words had just melted his heart.

"Are you going to live with him?" Nicky asked.

Vance got to his feet. "Nobody knows what's going to happen yet. That's why Roberta's mother has come to the park today." He picked him up. "Now that you've delivered your present, we're going back to your mom and let Roberta and her father spend some time together alone."

"Okay. See ya, Roberta."

"See ya."

When the door closed Chase looked down at his daughter, who was drinking the rest of her root beer. "Now where were we?"

Chapter Six

"Hi. My name's Cindy. What can I do for you?" The cute, blond female ranger taking in the sling holding Annie's broken arm, had a charming Southern accent.

"I have an appointment with Ranger Jarvis at two."

"You have to be Roberta's mother. She's a darling girl."

Annie warmed to her. Anyone who liked Roberta was an automatic friend. "Thank you. I think she is, too."

"We're all so sorry you had to be in that crash. I'm sure it was horrible for you, but everyone's thankful you survived. I must say you look wonderful."

"Thank you, but the credit goes to the pilot. He told me what to do and it saved both of us."

"Tom was a crack naval pilot."

"So I've heard. I'm just glad he was at the controls."

"You were doubly lucky that day. Ranger Jarvis is a natural-born hunter. He's the one everyone wants on a rescue like yours. Chief Rossiter says he has superhuman instincts. Coming from the Chief, that's real praise."

A shiver ran down Annie's spine. Now that she knew Robert had trained with the Special Forces in Afghanistan, nothing surprised her. The look in the female

ranger's eyes as she spoke about Robert told Annie a lot.
So did the fact that there was no engagement ring or
wedding band on her finger.

Annie probably had that same look in her eyes when
she'd first met him. It seemed a century ago. "I realize
I was very lucky. Do you think he's free now?"

The other woman checked her watch. "He's just
going off duty. Why don't you walk back to his office?
Go down that hall on your left and you'll come to
another hall. His is two doors down on your right."

"Thank you. I'll find it."

She looked around the visitor's center filled with
tourists checking out the exhibits and getting information. Slowly she threaded her way through the crowd to
the hallway in question. It was almost impossible to
believe this had been Robert's world for the past three
years. His life here was far removed from the work he'd
done as the brilliant archaeologist with whom she'd
fallen in love.

Only now was she starting to recognize the sacrifices
he'd made to prevent disaster from striking again. For
him to live and work in this environment when it was
so foreign to him helped her to see what she couldn't
see or accept before now.

*He'd wanted to get in touch with her and would
have.* She was beginning to understand. Deep in
thought, she almost ran into him in the hall outside his
office.

With or without his ranger outfit, his striking
physique and features caused her to stare at him the way
she'd once done. He was such an attractive male, she'd
been caught off guard and didn't realize Roberta was
already waiting inside.

"Hi," he said in his deep, husky voice. His questing gaze wandered over her figure clothed in pleated tan pants and cotton sweater in a tan-and-white print. Roberta had been the one to tie her hair at the nape with a white scarf.

She took a steadying breath. "I'm sorry if we disturbed you while you were on duty."

He put his hands on his hips in a purely male stance. "Let's get something straight. Roberta's our daughter and is a permanent part of my life any time of the day or night."

Averting her eyes, she walked into his office ahead of him and found her daughter sitting on a chair playing with a silver baton. Annie sat down on another chair next to her. "What's that, darling?"

"It's a wizard's wand Daddy's friends brought him from England."

Annie examined it and saw the engraving *Uncle Chase*. "This is beautiful."

"I wish we could go to the Harry Potter shop, too. Nicky was so lucky."

Robert closed the door and sat on the corner of his desk, bringing him much too close to Annie. "Do you love those books?"

Roberta nodded. "I've read all of them."

"Nicky loves them as well. I think his mother has read every one of them to him. Did you know he met the real Hedwig while they were on their trip?"

Her eyes rounded. "How did he do that?"

"The next time you see him, you'll have to ask him about it."

"Speaking of next time," Annie broke in. Her heart was racing. "I phoned my boss at the CDF and told him that after consideration I've decided to take the park job after all."

There was a palpable silence before he said, "That's great news for the park. I'll inform Superintendent Telford." His silvery eyes swerved to Roberta. Their luminescent color revealed his satisfaction. "For me personally, I'm thrilled to know you'll be living so close."

"Me too, Daddy. Now we can be together all the time."

Annie cleared her throat. "Would it be possible to see the house Roberta and I will be living in before we drive back to Santa Rosa?"

"We'll do it in a minute, but first we have to decide how to proceed. From here on out my name is Chase Jarvis. For reasons of safety, the name Robert Myers no longer exists."

"We know, don't we, honey?"

Roberta nodded.

"Good. When we walk out of this room," he continued, "I'll be introducing Roberta as my daughter and you, her mother. Among the park personnel Vance will spread the news that following an accident, I had amnesia and was confused about my past until the helicopter crash."

Annie had so much energy to expend she recrossed her legs. "In case someone asks, we need to agree on where your accident took place."

"At Newport Beach in Southern California," he said without missing a heartbeat. "We met there on vacation from college. When I got run over by a speedboat way offshore, my body was never found and authorities theorized sharks might have been responsible."

"Dad!" Roberta cried in reaction.

Annie shuddered. The scenario he'd just painted was ghastly, but nothing could compare to the unspeakable horror of what had literally happened that day in Kabul.

"Any other questions?"

When Annie realized he'd been staring at her and had seen more in her eyes than she wanted him, she said no and looked at Roberta. "What about you? Is there anything else you want to ask your father?"

"No. I just want to go see our house."

"We'll do it right now." He stood up. "Come down the hall with me while I get the key, then we'll leave through the rear door and walk over there."

"I didn't know the houses were so close to your work."

"Years ago the planners built everything that way on purpose. The rangers have to be ready at a moment's notice."

Roberta followed him out the door. "You're like a fireman."

"That's right."

Their conversation floated back as Annie put the wand in the box and hurried after them. Robert appeared to be in high spirits. So far everything was going according to his wishes. Annie had to pretend she didn't mind the way things were turning out because she had her own life to lead. However, that was easier said and done in theory.

She had to admit it hurt to see how quickly Roberta had bonded with him. He held her hand as they stepped outside, as if they'd been doing it for years. Of course Annie wanted them to bond, but that insidious emotion called jealousy had squeezed in there to add to her turmoil.

Someone else in her daughter's world now had a claim on her heart. A legitimate claim. Annie had to learn to share her daughter. Correction. *Their* daughter. Somehow she hadn't expected to be pierced by this new form of pain.

It took only a few minutes walking through the pines to reach the cluster of houses used by the rangers. The forties ranch style was typical of the many tracts of housing built throughout California seventy years earlier.

Robert—Chase, she corrected herself mentally—led them to the end of a street where three houses stood. He walked up the steps of the middle one-story house and unlocked the front door.

Once inside, Roberta darted through the rooms making excited noises while Annie surveyed the living and dining room. She wandered through the rest of the house. Most of the rooms were carpeted. The maple furnishings were fine…homey, but the orange and brown decor was something she would change in a hurry.

Chase followed her around. They ended up in the postage-stamp-size kitchen. It meant their meals would have to be eaten in the dining room, but she couldn't concentrate on much of anything because of his close proximity.

"What do you think?"

She pinned on a smile and turned to him. "I think Jack Frost lives here."

His dark brown head reared back and he laughed that deep laugh she hadn't heard in years. Just then he sounded younger. It brought back too many memories, wounding her all over again.

Roberta came running to find them. "What's so funny?"

He threw an arm around her shoulder. "Have you ever heard of Jack Frost?"

She shook her head.

"Jack's a little elf who paints all the leaves in fall colors. Your mom thinks this is his house."

Annie could hear her mind digesting everything. "When we bring our things, it won't look so bad, Mom."

Chase burst into more laughter. Annie had to fight not to break down, too.

"Can I have the room next to the bathroom? There's a cute little squirrel running up and down the tree outside the window. Come and look!"

Relieved to put distance between herself and Chase, Annie followed Roberta down the hall past the bathroom to the bedroom she'd chosen. They moved beyond the queen-size bed to the screened window. Roberta's pink and white quilt would do wonders for the room.

"See!"

"There's a family living up there," Chase informed her. "You'll have to invite Nicky over. He has a pair of powerful binoculars. The two of you can watch them for hours."

"He's funny. How come he doesn't look like his daddy?" Annie had wondered the same thing.

A shadow darkened Chase's eyes, drawing her attention. "His real parents flew out here from Florida a year ago last spring. I was on duty when a freak winter-type storm was forecast. We warned everyone off the mountains and formations, but the Darrows didn't obey it. They were caught in a blizzard on top of El Capitan and died of hypothermia."

"That's awful," Roberta whispered, echoing Annie's thoughts.

"It was terrible for a lot of reasons. Vance went up in a helicopter to rescue them, but it was too late. We all knew they had a five year-old boy at home. Last June Nicky's aunt Rachel brought him to the park so he could see where the tragedy had happened. It was hard for him to understand that his parents had died. He'd been having nightmares and never wanted to go to school or play."

Roberta's lower lip trembled. "I don't blame him."

"But then a miracle happened. Vance became Nicky's hero and the three of them fell in love with each other. In time they decided to become a family and get married. Now they've adopted Nicky as their son. To make it fun for him, they took him to England on their honeymoon and just barely got back."

Annie lost the battle of tears. "What a touching story," she whispered, wiping her eyes with the back of her free hand.

Chase's solemn gaze switched from her to Roberta. "Nicky needs good friends. I know you're older, but you were very accepting of him today. I can tell he likes you already. Thank you for being my wonderful girl."

She hugged him before looking at Annie. "How soon are we going to move in?"

"Sometime next week. Your grandfather is arranging for a moving truck to bring the things we want here. The rest we'll put in storage."

"I wish it were tomorrow."

"Do you know what?" Chase intervened. "You'll probably need a few days to decide what you want to keep with you. If there are some things you want moved out of here to make room for your furnishings, I'll take

care of it. This is going to be your new home. You need
to feel comfortable."

Chase was behaving exactly like the accommodat-
ing, sensible man she'd once loved. In fact he was being
so reasonable and understanding without trying to take
over, Annie wanted to scream.

She checked her watch. To her shock, the time had
flown. "You know what? It's ten after three right now.
Your grandparents will be waiting for us."

"But I want to see Daddy's house first."

"We don't have time today."

"Your mother's right, sweetheart. After you move in,
we'll have the rest of our lives to do everything."

Roberta wiped her eyes with the end of her sleeve.
"Okay. I'll call you when we're coming. I've memor-
ized your number."

"I was hoping you would. I'll be waiting to hear
from you."

Annie started for the front door ahead of them. When
he'd locked it behind them and they'd walked down the
front porch steps, he turned to her and handed her the
key. "The place is yours."

As their hands brushed, she felt the contact like a hot
current of electricity. The same thing had happened
when she'd first met him. "Thank you for making this
so easy for us. I appreciate it."

His eyes gleamed silver. "You're welcome."

Roberta hung on to his arm. "What are you going
to do now?"

"Run home, have a shower and go to bed. I've been
up close to twenty-four hours and need sleep."

"Where's your house?"

He pointed to his left. "Right around the corner."

That brought a smile to her face.

"Come on," Annie urged.

"Okay. See ya, Dad."

While they hugged, Annie began walking in the direction of the visitor's center. His charm was lethal. In that regard nothing had changed in ten years.

ON THURSDAY MORNING Chase was in his office dealing with the latest faxed reports when Vance came through the door. They eyed each other for a brief moment. "Isn't this the big day or did I get it wrong?"

"You know it is."

"It's after ten now. What are you still doing here?"

"I've got to be careful, Vance. Roberta phoned to let me know the day and time, but Annie was coaching her because there was no invitation for me to be a part of things. Let's face it. I had nightmares at the thought of working out visitation, never dreaming Annie would take the job.

"We might be living around the corner from each other now, but if she thinks I'm trying to manage her in any way she'll shut me out so completely I'll never get to first base."

Vance smiled out of one corner of his mouth. "I'd say you've already done that."

"Not because of me," Chase muttered in a morose tone. "She wants this job no matter what. To be frank, I'm terrified of doing something wrong."

"I hear you, so this is what we're going to do. My wife's making food for them."

He sat back in the chair. "She's incredible."

"I agree. Rachel can't wait to meet her. We've arranged for Nicky to come home from school at noon.

He wants to help. We thought we'd go over there around twelve-thirty. I'll give her an official greeting. If you're with us, Annie can't object."

"You mean even if she wants to." Chase let out a sigh of relief. "You've just solved my immediate dilemma. While we're there, I'll take care of anything that needs doing."

"Good. See you later. For the moment I've got a camper accident to investigate.

He got up from the desk. "I'm headed into a meeting in the conference room."

"The new housing project controversy?"

"I'm afraid so. As you know, the arguments never end. I'll put the report in your basket." Chase followed him out of the office, grateful to Vance for helping him make it through the last few endless days of waiting. It was a miracle he and Rachel put up with him.

Chase still had a hard time believing this day had come. Once the news got out that his daughter and ex-lover were living in the park, the three of them would be an item of speculation and gossip.

He'd give anything to spare them, but nothing short of marriage could stem the tide of curiosity. That was the bad side of living in a closed community. But there was an upside. One way or another he'd be seeing both of them on a daily basis. For now he'd take whatever he could get.

Two hours later he left headquarters and sprinted through the trees to the housing complex. When he rounded the corner, he saw a small moving truck in her driveway. The front door of the house was open. He noticed her blue Nissan parked in front. He'd seen it in her parking stall at the condo. There was no sign of Vance yet.

As Chase approached the entry he slowed his pace, unwilling for Annie to detect the degree of his need for her. Nothing would turn her off faster.

A couple of men came out the door with a dolly. They nodded when they saw him.

"How's it going?"

"We just finished." They slid the plank into the truck and shut the back. As Annie came down the steps wearing a pair of jeans and a yellow top, one of them reached inside the cab and pulled out a clipboard. "Someone needs to sign. Are you Mr. Bower?"

"No, I'm not. You need to get Ms. Bower's signature." Chase remained in place while she walked toward the man and signed the release form with her free hand. "Thank you." Her crisp remark of irritation was wasted on them.

To his chagrin Chase was afraid he'd be silently blamed for showing up at the wrong moment. He was damned either way.

"Daddy!" Roberta came flying out of the house into his arms. She saved the day.

"How are you, sweetheart?" He swung her around and kissed her. In the excitement, Vance showed up. He waited for the truck to back out and drive away before he pulled into the driveway. After shutting off the engine, everyone got out of the car carrying sacks.

Nicky made a beeline for Roberta. "Hi! We brought your lunch. Where do you want me to put the bread sticks?"

Rachel must have just taken them out of the oven. Chase could smell the aroma and started salivating.

"Mom? Where should they put the food?"

It was clear the arrival of company had caught Annie

off guard. "Well, how about the dining room? There's no room in the kitchen until we get things put away."

"I'll show you," Roberta told Nicky. The two of them walked up the porch steps into the house.

Chase stepped forward. "Annie Bower, I'd like you to meet my closest friends, Rachel and Vance Rossiter."

"Hello," she said, shaking both their hands. Her hair swished like a glossy dark pelt against her cheek. "You've already done enough with the gorgeous flowers you sent. I can't believe you've come over with food, too."

"It's our pleasure," Rachel assured her. "Another neighbor is really welcome around here."

"Thank you. I feel the same way. Roberta's already charmed by Nicky. For one thing, they have Harry Potter in common."

"Don't forget root beer," Vance interjected with a warm smile. "I wanted to see our newest resident archaeologist in person. Let's hope that fractured arm and the attendant memories will be the only unpleasant moment you experience here."

"I'm hoping for that as well."

"Vance and I knew you'd get hungry at some point. If you don't feel like eating right now, that's fine. I'm aware how busy you are today and thought you'd like something to munch on."

"To be honest, I'm starving. We had breakfast with my parents before leaving Santa Rosa at six. They're taking charge of putting the rest of my things in storage and won't be visiting until tomorrow. Please, come in and eat with us."

Even with the invitation extended, Annie hadn't looked at Chase yet. He needed to get used to being invisible if he was going to survive.

Vance turned toward the car. "I'll get the casserole out of the back."

"Let me do it," Chase insisted.

Their eyes met in quiet understanding. In the next instant Vance escorted the women into the house while Chase walked across the street and opened the rear door of the car. The large covered casserole had handles, making it easy for him to carry the delicious smelling lasagna. Rachel had gone all out.

No sooner had he entered the house than Nicky came darting toward the front door with Roberta behind him. "Where are you two going? We'll be eating in a minute," Chase said.

"Roberta's running home with me so I can get my binoculars! We'll be right back!"

Watching them together, Chase's thoughts flew to a week ago last Monday when he'd been in such a severe depression he didn't know how he was going to make it through the rest of his life. Then came the phone call about Annie, followed by the news that they had a daughter.

Instant fatherhood. As if by magic a whole family came into being, illuminating his world. The only thing missing was his wedding ring on Annie's finger and all that went with it.

"Put the casserole here," Rachel called to him. She'd placed a hot pad down on the round maple table. While he did her bidding, he noticed there were only four matching chairs. He'd seen two of Annie's white chairs in the living room and brought them into the dining room.

As he fit them around the table, his arm brushed against Annie's, sending a rush of fresh longing through his body. She jerked away from him. Whether anyone else noticed her reaction or not, it left him pondering two possibilities. Either she didn't welcome his touch, or it had electrified her because she still felt an attraction.

It was a subject he intended to explore at a later date. Again he had to remind himself this was only her first day here. She might tolerate one accident, but he didn't dare start to experiment with another one yet.

When the kids came back to the house, he arranged for Nicky and Roberta to sit on either side of him. That way Annie couldn't accuse him of purposely manipulating the situation to his advantage.

Once the salad was passed around and everyone was served, Nicky lifted the binoculars to his eyes and surveyed each person.

"That's not polite. Put the binoculars in the living room for now," Rachel admonished. Darting Annie a covert glance, Chase saw a smile break out on her flushed face. She found Nicky as funny and irresistible as the rest of them did.

"Okay," he said in a pretend grumpy voice and got out of the chair. In a second he was back to make inroads on his breadstick. "This is fun." He munched a little more. "I wish we could eat together all the time, don't you, Roberta?"

While the others chuckled, Chase exchanged a private smile with his daughter. For the next half hour Nicky kept them laughing in his inimitable way. As Chase was thinking that he hadn't known this kind of happiness since sharing all his meals and the aftermath with Annie, there was a knock on the front door.

His first instinct was to answer it, but this wasn't his

home. He watched Annie get up from the table. Maybe her parents had decided to come after all.

It had been so different back in Kabul. Though they'd had their own accommodations, they'd been like a married couple. To go from that kind of intimacy to this situation was killing him.

Bill Telford's voice preceded his eventual entry into the dining room. The mid-forties superintendent had a golfer's build and most of his blond hair. He couldn't seem to take his eyes off Annie. "I only came to welcome our new resident archaeologist to the park. I don't want to intrude," he insisted.

The hell he didn't. The man hadn't wasted any time. The widow and the widower.

"You know everyone here except my daughter. Roberta? This is Bill Telford, the superintendent of the park. He made it possible for your mother to have this job."

"Hi! It's nice to meet you."

"It's a pleasure to meet you too, Roberta." He moved around the table to shake her hand. He hid his surprise well as his gaze traveled over Vance and Chase who got to their feet. "You're in celebrated company."

"What's celebrated?" Nicky piped up.

"Very famous," Bill explained.

"Oh." He wiped the milk off his mouth with a napkin. "Did you know Uncle Chase is Roberta's daddy?"

Nicky had just given Chase another reason to love him so much.

Bill's head jerked toward her. "Were we misinformed? I didn't realize you were married." The man looked as if he'd just been hit in the jaw by Tiger Woods's line drive.

Chase shot Vance a glance. This was a job he

intended to leave for the Chief. Annie would appreciate Chase's absence.

"Bill? Why don't you take my place and enjoy some of Rachel's fabulous lasagna. I'm going to help the kids sneak around the tree outside and look for squirrels."

Nicky clapped his hands. "Hooray! Come on, Roberta. I'll get my binoculars."

Chapter Seven

"Rachel, after bringing over the delicious meal, I won't have you helping me with the dishes, too," Annie declared.

"I want to. The guys are busy putting all your electronic equipment together in the spare bedroom and loving it. I'm afraid Nicky is driving Roberta crazy while she's arranging her room. That leaves *moi* with nothing to do. If you'll give me directions, I'll empty a few boxes and start putting dishes and pans in the kitchen cupboards."

"If you're sure."

"Of course. That cast on your arm is there for a reason. If you'll let us help, we'll have you settled in no time. It isn't as if you've just moved into the Palais Royal with a hundred rooms to fill."

Annie laughed. "No, but it's cozy and it's our new home for now."

"You don't plan to stay here for long?"

"I've signed a year's contract. At the end of that time the superintendent will decide if the progress made warrants more funding."

Rachel eyed her speculatively. "I'm pretty sure that won't be a problem. I've only met Bill Telford one other time, but if I don't miss my guess, he showed an inordinate interest in you today. I heard him ask you to go to dinner with him next week. It might have been a purely professional invitation, but in case you didn't know, his wife died of cancer last year."

"Thanks for telling me." That missing piece of information hadn't passed Chase's lips, but in all fairness she hadn't encouraged conversation with him. Her boss at CDF hadn't mentioned it either.

"Earlier today Vance came home from headquarters and let me know you were gorgeous." Annie shook her head. "I've discovered he was right, so I'm pretty sure you'll be seeing a lot more of Bill. That is, if you want to. His house is only three blocks away."

"My boss at the CDF says he has impressive credentials."

"He's attractive, too, if you're partial to blond men."

Annie took a steadying breath. "If I could speak frankly with you for a minute, I'm sure you're wondering about Chase and me."

"Listen," she said in a quiet voice, "you don't owe anyone an explanation, least of all me. Vance told me the whole story. To be honest, I would feel so betrayed if Vance had been alive ten years without telling me, especially if we had a child between us, I'm not sure what I would do."

Annie's eyes smarted. "At first I was in shock and so hurt, I was convinced Chase couldn't have been that in love with me."

"And now?"

She lifted her chin. "Now I understand why he didn't ever get in touch with me, but the fact still remains that after ten years we're strangers to each other."

"Of course you would be," Rachel agreed.

This woman understood and could be a real friend to Annie. "Thank you, Rachel," she whispered.

"Just know I'm around if you ever need a shoulder to cry on."

"Careful." Annie sniffed. "You may live to regret that offer. You don't know how grateful I am over your being so candid. I'm aware you've been through a horribly painful experience yourself. Chase told me about your brother and his wife. Poor little Nicky. I understand he went through a terrible struggle."

"He did. My parents and I almost lost our minds wondering how to help him. Then I flew him out here and he met Vance."

Annie smiled. "I can tell they're joined at the hip."

"One day I'll fill you in on the details."

"I think I can guess. Your husband has the most beautiful blue eyes I've ever seen. When he looks at you, they glow."

"I love him so much, it hurts."

Annie bowed her head. She and Chase had once felt that way about each other. Now that he was back in her life she hurt all the time, but that was because… because she wanted him to love her that way again, but she didn't dare think it might happen. The difference in Annie's and Rachel's personal lives was off the charts.

"Annie?" At the sound of Chase's low voice, her pulse raced. It seemed her body recognized it whether she tried to shut him out or not. She turned around to meet a pair of shadowed gray eyes. No silver in them right now. "We've finished setting up your computer. Where do you want the television?"

"I think against the wall opposite the couch. Thank you."

He glanced around. "It looks like all the boxes have been emptied. I'll get my truck and we'll cart them away. The kids want to go with us. Is that all right with you two?"

They nodded.

He made quick work of removing the cartons. After he left, she could breathe more easily. A few minutes later the kitchen had been put in order and the dishes were done.

Annie turned to Rachel. "I can't believe how fast everything's been set in place. Without your help, Roberta and I would have been putting things away for days. Thank you for all you've done, including that delicious meal."

"You're welcome."

"I owe you. If you're free on Sunday afternoon and your husband isn't on duty, I'd like you to come over for dinner."

"That sounds wonderful. When I know his schedule, I'll call you. It changes all the time depending on emergencies."

"So I understand. Let's go to the other room and take a break. You've worked long and hard enough for one day."

They moved through the dining room to the living room. Already it looked better, with her occasional pieces of furniture placed around and her framed prints hanging on the walls.

Rachel went over to the Renoir. "I love this one of the mother and daughter."

So did Annie. "My mother gave it to me after Roberta was born."

"Roberta is so sweet to Nicky. I'm really glad you've

moved here. He needs friends. I'm hoping to provide him with a brother or sister."

"Maybe that will happen one day."

"We're trying," Rachel confessed. "Vance's first wife served in the military when he did, but she was killed during the war in the Middle East. They'd wanted children, but there wasn't enough time."

A hand went to Annie's throat. "I didn't know he'd been married before." Vance had lost his wife the same way Annie had thought she'd lost Chase.

"That was a little over five years ago. He loves Nicky like his own, but he's such a wonderful father I want him to experience the whole business of childbirth. Needless to say, I can't wait to have a baby."

Annie took a deep breath. "There's nothing like it." Chase had missed out on it. He'd missed Roberta's first ten years. It was time to change the subject before she broke down. "I understand you're barely back from your honeymoon. Are you still moving in?"

"Not in the way you mean. My father just had a heart operation which was successful. They're moving out here from Florida right before Halloween and will be bringing my things in the van with them. Then Vance's house is going to undergo a big renovation. It needs it."

They both laughed as they looked around Annie's living room, observing its lack of a uniform theme or decor.

"Will your parents live here in the park, too?"

"No. Vance owns a house right outside the park entrance in Oakhurst. It was his grandparents'. They raised him. In June his grandmother passed away and willed it to him."

"That's wonderful you'll be so close to them," Annie

cried softly. "My parents live in San Francisco so it'll be a bit more of a drive for all of us, but not impossible."

"Family's everything. That's why Chase—" She suddenly stopped talking. "I'm sorry. I didn't mean to bring him up."

"Please, Rachel, it's all right to talk about Chase. He and Vance are best friends so it's inevitable."

"I was only going to say that for him to discover *you* again has caused as dramatic a change in him as turning on a blowtorch in a pitch-dark room. He's overjoyed to realize he has a daughter."

"It's been a shock for all of us." Annie's voice trembled.

"My husband told me Chase was in a depression when he came to work at the park three years ago. Over time it had gotten worse. When I met him in June, I liked him very much, but I sensed a deep sadness in him and thought it was due to his divorce."

Annie blinked. "What divorce?"

"The one he manufactured as part of his fake persona once he was put in the witness protection program."

"I had no idea. Naturally he would have to create a background for himself."

Rachel nodded. "You know what's odd? Even though it was fiction, I bought the emptiness I heard in his voice. Something was definitely missing. Now that I know the whole truth, I understand it. In order to keep everyone safe, he's been forced to deny his whole former existence for years. I can't imagine anything worse."

Their conversation was throwing Annie into more turmoil. It had only started to dawn on her he'd put his life in jeopardy every day while he'd worked undercover. He'd seen so much of war. It had to have changed him in so many ways and she hadn't been able to share any of it with him.

"What does Vance think now that he knows everything?"

"The only argument Vance and I have come close to having is the one over whether it was wrong of Chase not to contact you from the hospital in Switzerland. If you're asking me if Vance would have chosen to remain dead to his wife, Katy, under Chase's circumstances, the answer is yes. He's seen the evil of the enemy in the Middle East firsthand. It's the warrior in them that vows to protect their women at all costs, I guess."

"Women can be warriors, too."

"You and I know that, but Chase and Vance are honorable to a fault. It puts them in a class by themselves. You should have seen how angry I was when I first met Vance. I blamed him for my brother and sister-in-law's deaths. He was the chief ranger and they died on his watch. I was ready to prosecute him for criminal negligence."

"You're kidding!"

"Afraid not. We got off to the worst start imaginable. I stormed out of his office in a fury."

"I can't imagine it."

"You don't know the half of it. Later that night he found me and Nicky eating dinner at the Yosemite Lodge with Chase."

Annie fought to hide her dismay. "You mean you and Chase went out together?"

"Yes. It was all very innocent. He offered to watch Nicky while I was in with Vance. When I left, I was in turmoil and Chase knew it. He asked me if he could meet us for dinner at the lodge. I said yes, but Nicky didn't like it at all.

"Then Vance came walking into the dining room. Ignoring me, he got down in front of Nicky's chair and started talking to him about what happened. I learned it was my brother who decided not to heed the blizzard advisory.

"While I sat there feeling like the world's greatest fool, Vance was able to explain things in such a way that Nicky broke down and they ended up hugging each other. From that moment on, my nephew started to heal and they bonded.

"After Vance left, Chase asked if we'd like to go horseback riding the next morning. Nicky didn't want to, but I accepted. A huge mistake. Nicky was positively atrocious to Chase. The reason I wanted to go was because he was easy to talk to. You see, I'd broken my engagement to my fiancé and he was begging me to get back with him.

"Chase said he had the same problem with his ex-wife. We talked about our emotional problems. At the time I didn't know he'd fabricated the story about his divorce. We commiserated. I told him I was going back to Miami and, on the advice of my psychiatrist, I was going to make an effort to talk to my ex-fiancé and see if anything could be salvaged.

"I knew in my heart it wouldn't work because I was already attracted to Vance. What an irony when you consider we started off striking sparks against each other. He didn't show me anything but professional courtesy, but the way he treated Nicky was another story.

"The reason I'm going into all this detail is because

I want you to know the truth of everything. I liked Chase a lot because I could tell he's an exceptional man, but when I came back to the park a second time, it wasn't just for Nicky's sake. I couldn't wait to see Vance again. I knew when he picked us up at the airport in Merced, that I'd fallen hard for him.

"It took forever for him to reciprocate because he thought I hadn't let go of my ex-fiancé. I, in turn, was afraid he would never get over Katy. Of course we were both wrong. During a hike in the mountains, Vance kissed me for the first time and suddenly we were pouring out all our feelings. That was a glorious day."

"I can imagine," Annie murmured, but she was strangely conflicted. She already liked Rachel so much, but apparently Chase had been drawn to her, too. Even if it was one-sided, was it possible he still had feelings for Rachel? They were all exceptionally close.

Swallowing hard, she said, "I'm so glad everything turned out for the three of you, Rachel. I—" She stopped talking. "Uh-oh, I can hear them in the driveway." They both got up from the couch and walked out onto the front porch.

With the boxes disposed of, the men helped the children down from the empty truck bed. Chase gave Roberta a long hug before lowering her to the ground. The part that had been missing in her daughter's life was now complete. She had her very own father and a built-in set of new friends.

Vance hoisted Nicky onto his shoulders. "Rachel? I have to get back to headquarters. What would you like to do?"

"I'm coming."

Nicky frowned. "Do we have to go?"

"Afraid so," Rachel answered. "You still have a little homework to do for school in the morning."

"Is Roberta coming to school?"

Annie nodded. "She'll be there."

Rachel turned to her. "If you want, Nicky and I will come by for you at eight-thirty and we'll all walk over."

"Terrific. We'll be ready. Thanks again for all the help and the fabulous lunch."

"It was really good," Roberta called to her. "See ya tomorrow, Nicky."

"Okay. Bye."

After they drove away in their car, Chase turned to Annie. "Roberta wants to come to my house. Why don't you come in the truck with us so you can see where she'll be spending some of her time."

Annie wanted to see where he lived, *how* he lived. "I'll be right with you. Let me get my purse and lock the door."

A minute later she joined them. Always the gentleman, he helped her into the cab. When his arm accidentally brushed against her thigh before shutting the door, she hoped he hadn't felt her quiver in response. Roberta sat between them with a smile of contentment on her face.

Chase backed the truck out of the driveway and they headed for his house around the corner. On the way they passed a ranger who stared at them and waved. He waved back.

"Who's that, Daddy?"

"Mark Sims, the head of security. He's Carly's father. You'll be meeting her at school tomorrow. She only lives a half a block from you. Kind of like you and your friend Penny."

They headed for the house on the next corner. He pulled into the driveway and pressed the remote above the visor to open the garage door. From the outside at least, all of the houses looked pretty much the same.

Annie jumped down before Chase could come around. She didn't want any more contact with him. Twice today was enough. She could still feel his touch. It would stay with her and conjured up intimate memories. Within five minutes she'd walk back to the house and Roberta could come home later.

She waited till he'd opened the door to the kitchen, then followed Roberta inside. Right away she noticed differences. His kitchen could accommodate a break-fast table and the attractive sage and wood décor throughout the main rooms came as a surprise. She assumed the contemporary dark brown leather furniture facing the fireplace was his own.

"Look at all the books!" Roberta cried. Annie *was* looking. Walls of them from floor to ceiling in the living room. It took her back to his apartment in Kabul, which had been more library than living quarters. They spent most of their alone time in hers. "Have you read every one?"

Chase laughed. "That's the idea, sweetheart. Most of them are historical journals of the explorers and early frontiersmen who came to Yosemite. The rest are reference materials for a series of books I'm writing on the park for people who enjoy hiking in the wilderness."

"Mom said you're the smartest man she ever knew."

Yes. Annie had told her daughter that and couldn't take it back. He scoffed. In that regard he hadn't changed. Chase had always been a modest man.

"It's true, Chase. To be honest, I'm not surprised you've immersed yourself in another field besides archaeology. Are you published yet?"

He stood in the middle of the room with his hard-muscled legs slightly apart. "I haven't even picked an agent yet."

"With your credentials you don't nee—" She suddenly broke off talking. Heat crept into her face. "I forgot you've had to give up that whole life."

A grimace marred his rugged features. "I wish I could."

In that moment Annie heard a bleakness in his tone that haunted her. Once again it hit her that the explosion had not only robbed him of his parents, he could no longer continue to pursue archaeology, his life's work and passion.

A lesser man might have given up, but not Chase. The dining room was the proof. He'd turned it into an office with file cabinets and state-of-the-art electronic equipment. On two walls hung several giant U.S. geological survey maps of Yosemite with all kinds of colored pins he'd placed to set off various coordinates. Fascinated, Annie walked over to study one of them.

"I love your house, Daddy!"

"That's good, because it's your house too when you want to come over. Would you like to see your bedroom?"

"You made a bedroom for me?" She squealed for joy. That didn't sound like the more sober minded daughter Annie had raised. Chase's advent in her life was transforming her.

"Who else? I used it for a storeroom, but as soon as I found out you'd be coming for visits, I cleaned it out and got it ready for you. Come on and take a look."

Roberta walked off with him, leaving Annie drowning in a flood of new feelings and sensations. Since Rachel had confided in her, jealousy had reared its ugly head again. She needed to get out of there before her natural curiosity took over and she gave herself away.

"Hey, you two—" she called after them. "I've got a lot to do back at the house so I'll see you later. Okay?"

"Okay!" Roberta shouted back.

She heard nothing from Chase, but then why would she? Upset with herself for even questioning it, Annie left his house via the front door and hurried home. Except that once she was safe inside, her house didn't feel like home. Though she'd brought their most important possessions from Santa Rosa, she realized inanimate objects didn't mean anything without her daughter here.

From now on Roberta would want to spend equal time with Chase. Annie couldn't blame her. He'd embraced her so completely, you would never have known they'd been apart since her birth. Moreover, he was a striking man any child would be thrilled to claim as her father.

Realizing she was spending too much time focusing on Chase rather than her new job, she got busy arranging her bedroom the way she wanted. By the time she was ready for bed, darkness had fallen over the park. She was about to phone Chase when she heard the front door open and close.

"Mom?"

"In the bedroom!"

She ran down the hall to Annie's room. "Daddy's outside. He wants me to call him and tell him you're here before he leaves."

Annie handed her the phone. She appreciated Chase being so careful, but again it didn't surprise her. He'd always been protective of Annie. Naturally he'd be even more so with their daughter

"I will," she heard Roberta say. "I love you, too. Good night, Daddy. See you tomorrow." After she hung up, she grabbed Annie. Her eyes were dancing.

"Daddy's going to take me and Nicky horseback riding on Saturday! Is that okay?"

If it weren't, Annie wouldn't have the heart to tell her. "Of course!"

"He loves horses just like me! I can't wait!"

While Annie locked up and turned out lights, her daughter bubbled over with excitement. "I wish I could call Debbie tonight."

"It's too late. You can phone her after school tomorrow."

"Okay."

Later, after they'd both gone to bed, Annie turned on her good side, wishing she weren't tormented by memories of one glorious horseback ride with Chase in the Khyber Pass. They'd camped out several nights in a row, eating food they'd packed and making love while their handpicked guides kept guard over them. She'd never known rapture like that. On one of those two nights she'd gotten pregnant.

Had his horseback ride with Rachel this past summer become a standout memory for him? In the dark hours of the night did he envy Vance?

Salty tears trickled from the corners of her eyes. "Chase—" she half sobbed, "Is it too late for us?" She could hardly stand it. After everything they'd shared, how was she going to live this close to him? Every time he hugged or kissed Roberta, she remembered how his arms had felt around her, how his mouth had devoured her, sending them both into euphoric oblivion.

To think he now lived around the corner from her and

Roberta! For the past three years he'd been hibernating here in relative contentment, obviously dating other women. He'd wanted a relationship with Rachel. She could hardly bear it, but she had to.

What was it Sid Manning had said? *Because your life was in danger, Dr. Myers had no choice but to stay away from you.*

Since that was true, it meant Chase had loved her more than his own life. Did it mean now that they were together again and his secret had come out, he would end up fighting for her in this presumably safe haven? Or was it too late. Love had to be fed and he'd gone hungry too many years. So had she…

Pain ripped through her body. Annie flung around in bed, forgetting the cast on her arm. It cost her as she cried out in discomfort. Another night like this and she'd have to have it reset.

Tomorrow couldn't come soon enough. Her parents were going to stay with them through the weekend. However, before she'd left Santa Rosa this morning her dad had said, "Don't you think it's time we met Roberta's father?" She'd put it off as long as possible while she'd sorted out her feelings, but there was an inevitability about anything having to do with Chase.

THE CHILDREN RODE on either side of Chase as they left the beaver pond and headed back to the stable. They'd been discussing their Halloween costumes. Halloween was only three days away. Nicky had decided to be Harry Potter and Annie was going as Hermione. Chase couldn't wait to take them trick-or-treating with Vance and Rachel. This was the kind of fatherhood experience that had passed him by, but no longer.

Today he was especially proud of how well Roberta handled her horse. She was a little camera buff, too. She'd taken pictures of everything.

"Can we come again next Saturday, Uncle Chase? That Methuselah's funny. He got me wet when he slapped his tail."

Chase smiled. The beaver wasn't half as funny as Nicky. "I'll check my schedule."

"Maybe my friend Debbie could come with us?"

"Since that's the only day your friend's mom can bring her, I'll trade with one of the guys for some time off." He glanced at his daughter, who'd started school yesterday. "What did you think of Carly?"

"She's okay."

That didn't sound very enthusiastic. When they were alone Chase would find out what was wrong.

"Do you guys like Mrs. Farrell?" They both nodded. That was a plus. "Is it strange only having a few kids at school?"

"Kind of."

"I like it," Nicky exclaimed.

"What did you think of Brody?"

"He's *mean*." Again this from Nicky.

"What does he do?"

"He's eleven. And when we have recess out in back he always gets to choose what we're going to do, huh Roberta."

"He tells everybody what to do, Dad."

"Yup. He said his dad was more important than *my* dad. I said he wasn't and he almost hit me."

That didn't sound good. "Brody has two older brothers, sport. They probably boss him around. Did you tell Mrs. Farrell?"

"If he's mean again, I'll tell her," Roberta said.

Good for her. "Looks like you two will have to stick up for each other."

"Yeah. Can I play at your house when we get back, Roberta?"

"I'm staying at my dad's today." She looked over at Chase. "Do you think Nicky could come over for a while?" She obviously liked him a lot. Nicky won everyone over.

"Sure."

"Hooray! Where's your mom?"

"In Wawona." Chase didn't know that. "What's she doing there?" Nicky asked.

"To have lunch with the other archaeologist. He just got back from a trip to Mexico."

Nicky sidled closer to Chase. "In class I heard Brody tell Carly he got a divorce. What does that mean?"

Gossip always abounded among the park employees, but that was news to Chase. He'd assumed Ron Saddler and his wife had a solid marriage. Annie would be working with him all the time. He took a shuddering breath. "It means his wife and children aren't going to live with him anymore."

"Oh."

On the trip back Roberta remained unusually quiet, causing him concern. When they reached the stable, he helped Nicky down. Roberta got off the horse on her own. She was already independent, just like her mother. Chase needed to find a way to get to Annie.

They piled into the truck and headed back to the house. When they walked in the kitchen, Chase told Nicky to go in the bedroom and call his parents to let them know where he was.

While Roberta washed her hands in the kitchen sink, Chase took advantage of being alone with his daughter for a moment. "I know something's wrong," he murmured. "Did Carly ignore you yesterday?"

She shook her head.

"Well, she did something."

Without looking at him, Roberta said, "She asked how come my parents didn't live together."

His heart thudded. "What did you tell her?"

"That they didn't want to." She finally lifted her head. Those pure blue eyes were swimming in tears. "She asked me if you two got a divorce."

"How did you answer her?"

"I told her no."

Chase had known there'd be talk, but he hadn't counted on it reaching Roberta's ears through Carly. He'd hoped the two girls would become friends. In time they probably would, but it didn't make Roberta's first days happy ones.

He hugged her before letting her go. "I'm sorry she made you uncomfortable."

She wiped her eyes. "Dad? Do you like Mom?"

Roberta, Roberta. "I never stopped, but I hurt her without intending to. I don't think she'll ever be able to forgive me." He waited for the protest from her telling him he was wrong in his assessment, but one never came, because Roberta knew exactly how her mother felt.

"I wish we all lived together."

"So do I," he whispered.

She looked stunned. "You do?"

"What do you think?" He tugged on her ponytail. "You're my daughter. All these years I'd given up hope of ever having a child. There's nothing I'd love more, than to be surrounded by my family in my house."

"Mom, too?"

"I loved her before I loved you, sweetheart. To have my own beautiful women living with me would be my heart's desire."

They heard feet running through the house. "Mommy said I can stay until she picks me up in an hour. We're going shopping."

"Terrific. What do you guys want for lunch?"

"Can I have a peanut butter and jelly sandwich?"

"Sure." He got busy fixing it. "What about you, sweetheart?"

"I just want a glass of milk. I'll get it."

Chase didn't press Roberta to eat. After telling her how he felt, he'd lost his appetite, too. Once the news reached Annie's ears—and it would—he feared she'd keep putting emotional distance between them because she couldn't love him the same way anymore.

His admission might spell the coup de grâce for Chase, because he knew he shouldn't have revealed his deepest feelings this soon. He'd promised himself to go slowly and give it time, but he hadn't been able to hold back any longer, not in front of Roberta.

While Nicky finished off half a sandwich, Roberta poured them each a glass of milk. Chase eyed the two of them. "When you're finished, do you guys want to go out in back and play a game of horseshoes with me?"

His daughter nodded. "I've never done that before."

"It's fun!" Nicky cried, "but it's kind of hard."

"There's a knack to it, but anyone can learn. I'll teach you." Chase needed to keep busy so he wouldn't think about Annie spending time with every damn man in the park except him.

Chapter Eight

After the drive from Wawona, Annie drove straight to Chase's and honked the horn for Roberta. It was after five o'clock. There'd been so much to talk about with Ron, time had gotten away from her.

What a difference it made to live here. If she happened to be late for Roberta, which she didn't intend to happen again unless it was unavoidable, she knew Chase would always be available to their daughter.

A few minutes later Roberta came running out to the car. "Honey," she called to her from the open window. "Your grandparents are waiting for us at the Yosemite Lodge for dinner. Do you want to ask your father if he'd like to join us? I don't know if he's free or not."

"He doesn't go on duty until tomorrow."

"In that case, your grandparents would like to meet him."

"Okay. I'll be right back."

Annie only had to wait a minute before her daughter got into the front seat. "Dad said he'll shower and be right over."

"Good." She backed out of the driveway. "Did you have fun horseback riding?"

"I loved it!" In the next breath she gave Annie a rundown of everything she'd done all day. She was still talking when they reached the village and parked near the lodge. Chase was responsible for the light in her eyes. Only the father who loved her could have put it there.

No matter what, Annie had to concede that the move to the park was already good for her daughter in the most fundamental of ways. There was no substitute for one's own daddy, especially not Chase, who was an exceptional man. Nicky adored him, too. You couldn't fool a child. As for Annie's parents, they'd see through to Chase's core right away and be impressed.

Roberta got out of the car ahead of her. Together they entered the hotel and made their way to the dining court. Through the crowd Annie saw her parents waving them over to their table. After hugs, they sat down and a waiter brought menus.

"I thought your father would be with you."

"He'll be here in a minute, Nana."

Annie's father studied her. "How's everything going?"

"Good. Ron Saddler and I outlined a work schedule. Until my cast comes off in another month, I'll be recording data while he's out in the field. Most of the time I'll be home for—"

"There's Dad!" Roberta slid from her chair, all conversation forgotten. She hurried toward the tall, fit man who'd drawn every eye in the room. He walked toward them wearing a stunning pearl-gray suit paired with a white shirt and striped gray-and-silver tie. Annie's breath caught because it had been so many years since she'd seen him formally dressed.

His dark hair and tanned complexion provided the perfect foil for his pewter eyes. Ten years ago she'd thought him incredibly handsome in the guise of archaeologist and, how, more recently as a park ranger. But tonight he gave off an air of urbane sophistication that did away with labels and distinguished him from the other men in the room.

Though her parents had seen pictures, she could see in their eyes that they hadn't been prepared for the attractive, compelling reality of him. Roberta gazed up at her daddy in hero worship. To Annie's dismay she was caught staring, too.

"Annie," he said in a deep, husky voice before walking around the table to shake her parents' hands.

"Mom and dad? This is Chase Jarvis."

"Mr. and Mrs. Bower? Meeting the two of you is a great honor and pleasure. Once upon a time I'd hoped to marry your daughter and become your son-in-law."

The use of the words *I'd hoped* put in the past tense caused Annie's heart to fall into the pit of her stomach.

"After the explosion, I never could have anticipated this moment. Though I'd go undercover again to protect her, my sorrow for all the pain I've caused will never leave me."

Despite her renewed pain, his soul-felt delivery shook her to her foundation. Judging by her parents' silence, the words had made an indelible impression on them as well.

Her father recovered first. "I'd say the smile you've put on our granddaughter's face has gone a long way to dry up the tears. Tonight should be a celebration of life."

Annie's misty-eyed mother nodded. "My husband

just took the words out of my mouth. Please sit down. Roberta has been living for tonight."

"She's not the only one." The smile he flashed their daughter lightened Annie's mood.

"I can't get over how much you two look alike," her mother commented.

Chase winked at Roberta. "I don't know about you, but I'll never complain."

Roberta's gentle laugh coincided with the waiter's arrival to take orders. From that point the dinner conversation centered on Roberta's new world with her daddy. Aching with the pain of Chase's first remarks to her parents, Annie mostly listened, only here and there offering a comment as they ate.

While she battled with her emotions, she heard Chase's cell phone go off. After he answered, lines darkened his face. Before he'd hung up, he'd already gotten to his feet.

"What's wrong, Daddy?"

"I have to go, but I'll tell you about it later, sweetheart. Sorry everyone. I hope to see all of you again soon." His sober gaze met Annie's for a brief moment before he strode swiftly from the room.

"I wish he didn't have to go."

Contrary to her daughter's desire, Annie was relieved he'd been called away. To be all together at last like they were a real family hurt too much.

Her mother patted Roberta's hand. "It's nice that you live here now and can see him whenever you want."

"No I can't," she corrected her grandmother.

"What do you mean?"

A tear trickled down her cheek. "We don't live with Daddy. Can we go home now?"

Annie's parents didn't try to respond to Roberta or ask her if she wanted dessert. "I'll take care of the check," her father murmured.

"We'll see you back at the house. Come on, Roberta." Annie reached for her daughter's hand and they hurried out of the lodge to the car. The old adage that hope sprang eternal was still alive in her broken heart.

"Do you think Daddy's going to be okay?"

"Of course. He's just doing the job he's been doing for the last three years."

"I wish I knew where he went."

Roberta wasn't the only one. Chase's reaction revealed more concern than usual. It would take time for her and their daughter to acclimatize to his world of emergencies. A ranger never knew what situation he was going to face.

Annie pulled into the garage and shut off the engine. "Have you forgotten your daddy was in the military?" She asked the question to reassure both of them. "He can take care of himself better than anyone."

"Except he couldn't save my other grandma and grandpa."

"Honey—" Devastated by Roberta's fears, she reached across the seat and pulled her against her chest. "I thought you weren't worried about that anymore." She pressed kisses on her head. "The rangers protect each other and everyone in the park, remember?"

Roberta's slight body trembled as she sobbed. Annie had no idea all this had been going on inside of her daughter. It was too late to wish they hadn't moved here. Whatever they did now, they were caught in an emotional trap.

Roberta eventually eased away from her. "Why can't we live together? Daddy wants to."

"No he doesn't."

"Yes he does!" she argued in a louder voice than Annie had ever heard before. "He told me today!"

Her daughter was overwrought. *How to get through to her?* "Okay." Annie wiped the moisture off Roberta's cheeks. She didn't want to get into a battle with her. "Tell me what he said. Take your time."

"After we came back from riding, Daddy and I were in the kitchen and I told him I wished we all lived together and he said 'I do too.'"

A frustrated cry escaped Annie's throat. "Don't you think he was just saying that because he loves you?"

"He loves you too, Mom!"

How many more nightmares were in store before any normalcy dominated their lives? "Why do you think that?"

"Because he called us his two beautiful women. He said he loved you before he loved me and he wants us to be a family."

Annie started to tremble. Did he really mean it? It was evident that Roberta believed he did. Before any more time passed Annie needed to have a private talk with him. Tonight, if it was possible.

"Your grandparents have driven up. Will you let them in the house? We'll talk about this later, all right?"

Roberta's glum expression was her only answer before she got out and hurried into the kitchen. Annie remained in the car and phoned Rachel. *Please be home.*

After four rings the other woman picked up. "Hello, Annie?"

"Hi. I'm so glad you're there," she said in a shaky voice.

"You sound upset. What's wrong?"

"I — it's a long story," she stammered. "First I need to ask you if Vance is there."

"No. He's on duty tonight."

"Could you do me a favor and find out what emergency caused Chase to leave dinner tonight? Roberta has some deep-seated fears and it upset her terribly. If he isn't gone too long, I need to talk to him when she's not around. Since my parents are staying overnight, this would be a good time to have a much needed conversation with him."

"I'll call Vance right now and phone you back."

"Thank you so much."

She clicked off and waited, not wanting to go inside the house until she was armed with some information that would reassure Roberta. One minute passed, then two. She was about to get out of the car when Rachel rang her back.

"Hi! Did you find out anything?"

"Yes. Vance said there was a very small rockslide at Curry Village a little while ago. Nothing serious. No one hurt, but he wanted Chase with him while they took a look around and made recommendations. He said it wouldn't take more than an hour or two at the most."

Annie let out a sigh. Under the circumstances she'd probably be able to talk to him before he went to bed. "I'm relieved everything's all right."

"So am I. Vance said you should explain to Roberta that slides happen quite often because the granite walls are so sheer. In fact it's amazing there aren't a lot more of them."

"Thanks, Rachel. I'll tell her. I'm indebted to both of you."

"Nonsense. Call me anytime."

"You know I will. The same goes for you. Good night."

She rang off and hurried in the house. Though her parents liked to stay at a hotel, Roberta had talked them into sleeping at their house tonight. Annie had given up her bed for them and would sleep with Roberta.

When she walked in the dining room, they were already seated around the table. Roberta had the Monopoly game set up ready to play. Annie took an empty chair next to her.

"I just talked to Rachel. Everything's fine with your dad. There was a small rock slide they needed to investigate." After she told her what she knew, Roberta seemed to relax, but she still wouldn't look at her. Annie exchanged silent glances with her parents, who were aware Roberta wasn't acting like herself.

The game took a long time. Annie's mother turned out to be the winner. When her father declared he was ready for bed, Annie suggested Roberta get into her pajamas. "You've had a big day considering you started out with a long horseback ride."

That brought her head up. She stared at Annie. "Daddy says I'm a natural rider."

"I'm not surprised. He did a great deal of riding years ago and is an expert horseman himself. You're a lot like him."

Her eyes filled. "I'm glad he didn't die." She put the top on the Monopoly box and hugged it to her chest. "Good night."

"Don't I get a kiss?"

She gave her a peck.

"Good night, honey. Sweet dreams."

Annie's father followed Roberta out of the room. That left her mother who gazed at her with troubled eyes. "What can I do to help?"

"Keep being there for me."

"Always that."

"I know. I don't deserve you."

"What in heaven's name are you talking about?"

A noise sounded in her throat. "I adore my daughter, but I made a serious mistake when I slept with Chase. You raised me differently than that. I was so in love that in my weakness, I let my emotions rule my good sense. Who would have thought that ten years later there'd be a price to pay…"

"Because?" her mother prodded.

"You already know the answer to that question."

"You mean that you're still in love with him?"

She smarted. "Is it that obvious?"

"Yes, but that's because I'm your mother. If it makes you feel any better, I almost had a heart attack myself when he walked into the dining room tonight. You wouldn't have been human if you hadn't been attracted to him. He's everything you claimed him to be, and maybe more."

Annie sat up straighter. "More?"

"He's been through hell, darling. You can see it in his eyes. There's a desperation in the way he clings to Roberta. When he looked at you before he left the table tonight, I saw a flash of fear."

She lowered her head because she'd seen it too, but she didn't know what it meant. Was he afraid she would change her mind and leave the park, taking Roberta with her? She sensed he walked on eggshells around her. In that regard he was so unlike the decisive, take-charge male she'd once known and loved. That man laughed in the face of danger. His highly adventurous nature had drawn her to him.

Maybe he was afraid that he really wouldn't be able to protect Roberta if his cover at the park were ever compromised. What if he was living with a new nightmare that the unspeakable would happen and she'd disappear?

Annie needed answers to so many questions she didn't know where to start.

"Mom? Roberta confided some things to me earlier. For her sake I've got to talk to him tonight if I can. Do you mind if I slip over to his house? It's just around the corner. He may not be there, but if he is you'll understand why I might not be back for a while."

"Go ahead. If Roberta asks where you are, I'll tell her the truth. That will comfort her more than anything." Annie's mother understood a lot.

After getting up to hug her, she went to the hall closet for her parka. The temperature outside had to be in the upper thirties and was still falling. She put one arm in the sleeve and pulled the other over her shoulder. Once she left the house, she jogged around the corner to Chase's.

When she reached it, there was no light on. Maybe he'd already come home and was in bed. After a slight hesitation she knocked on the door several times. No answer. She tried the bell. Nothing. Disappointment washed over her.

She could wait on the porch, but the cold would get to her before long. On a whim she tried opening the front door. It was locked. Annie would give it ten minutes before she went back to her house.

THE CLEANUP PHASE HAD STARTED. Vance walked over to Chase. "All things considered, what do you think?"

"As long as even one tent cabin was damaged, I think

we were wise to evacuate everyone in the perimeter. I say we keep these dozen or so cabins in the vicinity closed until next summer."

"Agreed." Vance looked at the sky. "Our first snowfall in the valley is forecast for tomorrow night. From then on, the cliffs will be at their most vulnerable."

"Yup. If there's going to be another slide, it'll happen now that the weather's starting to turn cold. It's good the people in that cabin were out to dinner when it occurred."

"You can say that again. As it is, it'll be all over the news. I'll phone Bill Telford when I get home."

Chase nodded. Right now he wasn't in the mood to talk to the superintendent. He didn't want Bill anywhere near Annie and Vance knew it. "Are we all set for Halloween?"

"I've arranged the watch in two shifts so the rangers with children can do the trick-or-treating with the kids. That means you and me." Vance flashed him a grin. "Last year you and I volunteered to cover for everybody because we didn't have any little Rossiter or Jarvis goblins of our own. Remember? My how things have changed."

"It's so incredible I still don't believe it," Chase whispered.

His friend studied his taut features. "How did it go with Annie's parents?"

"Now I know why she's so remarkable. Unfortunately, the slide happened before I had much of a chance for an in-depth conversation."

"Sorry about that. Can't run this place without you."

"That's good to hear. I like my job."

"But—"

He sucked in his breath. "But my life's not going to turn out like yours. I feel it in my bones. Don't get me wrong. Roberta's the blessing I never expected. Annie…is a different matter. She'd just as soon I faded from existence."

Vance cocked his head. "If that's true, then how come Rachel got a frantic call from her a few hours ago wanting to know where you went in such an all-fired hurry?"

Chase blinked. "Say that again?"

"You heard me."

He shook his head. "If she did that, it was because she was calling for Roberta's sake."

"I don't think so, otherwise Roberta would have called Nicky herself. As you well know, my wife's pretty intuitive. She asked me not to tell you this, but I'm going to anyway. The other day she had a talk with Annie and got the impression you're the one keeping a distance."

"That's because I am! Hell, Vance. One misstep with her could spell disaster."

Those brilliant blue eyes stared him down. "Maybe in the beginning you had to be careful, but the shock has worn off. Rachel could be wrong of course, but I say it wouldn't hurt to turn the tables on Annie and see what happens. It couldn't be any worse than the way things are going now. In any case she'll never take Roberta away from you. She needs to be reminded that once upon a time you two were lovers."

"That's right, until I stayed away from her for ten years!"

"And she knows why. Maybe you should show her some pictures of families of other CIA operatives who were butchered because they *didn't* enter the witness protection program."

"I've thought about it," Chase said.

"Good. Now go on home and think about it some more."

"I'm going."

Vance eyed him narrowly. "You're brooding again. What else is bothering you? If you think Annie will be turned off by your scars, then she's not the woman you thought she was."

Chase couldn't hide much from his friend. "As the doctors told me, I'm not a pretty sight."

"Let her be the judge."

Terror filled him whenever he thought what her reaction would be.

"See you tomorrow, Vance." He wheeled around and headed for his truck. If there was any truth to what Rachel had told Vance—if Annie did worry about him a little—he needed to explore it. Having his darling daughter restored to him wasn't enough. Not nearly. He wanted the woman who bore his child.

Chase rounded the corner of the housing complex in time to see a feminine figure leaving his property. As he drew closer and noticed the cast, he slowed down and lowered the window.

"Annie?" She looked up. "Turn around. I'll meet you at the house."

"It's late and you're probably tired."

"I've never been more wide awake." He drove past her and pulled in his driveway. Shutting off the motor, he jumped out of the cab. "Come on. I'll let us in the front door."

She followed him inside. He turned on the light and

shut the door. "Excuse me for a minute while I shower. If you're hungry or thirsty, help yourself to anything in the fridge."

"Thank you."

"I'll hurry."

AFTER HE DISAPPEARED, Annie eased off her parka and put it over one of the leather chairs. She'd been wearing the same tan pleated pants and white cotton sweater since morning and could use a shower herself.

Another time and she'd pore over the titles on his bookshelves, but tonight she was too restless to concentrate. Maybe she'd take him up on his offer and get herself a soda if he had one. Anything to keep busy while she waited.

One lone can of cola among several root beers beckoned to her. She didn't recall that he drank root beer. They had to be for Roberta. He wasn't a big soda drinker. The only kind she liked was cola.

Her thoughts drifted back to Kabul. When they'd come home to either of their apartments at the end of the day, he'd crush her in his arms and say, "My kingdom for a drop of cold water, but first I have to have this." They'd kiss until there was no beginning or end. Inevitably they gravitated to the bedroom. The water and room-temperature cola came much later.

So deep was her reverie, she didn't realize Chase had come into the kitchen until he turned on the cold water tap and drank for a good half minute. When he lifted his head, his glance fell on the can in her hand. "Some habits never change."

Annie realized he remembered too. "No," she whispered.

"Thank you for that much honesty."

Her pulse picked up speed. He smelled and looked wonderful. The black T-shirt and well-worn jeans molding his powerful thighs took her back in time. He needed a shave. He always did at the end of the day. It added to his sensuality, making her ache to the palms of her hands. She had to take an extra breath to regain her equilibrium.

He lounged against the edge of the counter. "What brought you over here tonight?"

"I need to talk to you about Roberta."

"Go ahead."

He stayed where he was, which was too close to her. Right now he reminded her of the old Robert. The only way to describe him was that he seemed more aggressive, yet he'd done nothing overt. She drank nervously from the can.

"She has this fantasy about you and me."

"So do I," came the quiet assertion. He put his hands on either side of her neck, rubbing his thumbs in circles over her tender skin. His touch hypnotized her. "You and I haven't had a chance until this minute to give each other a proper hello," he whispered against her lips. The warmth of his breath seemed to ignite her whole body.

"Robert—" she gasped softly.

"The name's Chase. An hour before the explosion that changed our world, we had just made passionate love. It was the morning we set the date to leave for the States and get married."

"I remember."

"So do I. Every detail," he insisted. "Afterward I very reluctantly left your arms for work and let you sleep in.

My mind was so full of the future and how gorgeous you were, I didn't notice until the second before oblivion hit that a couple of unfamiliar trucks had pulled up to the site."

The moan she heard was her own, resonating in the kitchen.

"It's taken longer than I expected to get back to you, Annie, so don't refuse me now. I couldn't take it."

There was no escape route as his lips closed over hers and she was pulled into his embrace. Ten years might have gone by, but her mouth and body recognized him and responded as if it had only been an hour since he'd left their bed. The frustration of not being able to use both her hands and arms was driving her insane. She realized the only difference between then and now was that her cast prevented their bodies from achieving a total melding.

He kissed her with a hunger that kept growing more voracious even while it was being appeased. How she'd lived this long without knowing his possession again was anathema to her. She could no more stop what was happening than she could stop breathing. There was a reason she shouldn't be doing this, but so help her, coherent thought had fled and she couldn't remember why.

Somehow her back ended up against the counter until there was no air between them. Without conscious thought her free hand slid up his chest and started to wind around his neck, but the pads of her fingers had run over ridges and bumps beneath his T-shirt that hadn't been a part of his torso before.

Visions of the photos Sid Manning had tossed on the floor illuminated her mind. Horrified once more, she gave an involuntary gasp and slid away from him, forcing him to relinquish his hold. She started to lift his shirt so she could see, but he took her wrist in a firm grip, preventing movement.

"No, Annie. Not yet."

She stared into his eyes and saw the same fear she'd seen in them earlier. "What do you mean not yet?"

"You don't want to look. Trust me." He averted his eyes.

"But I've seen the pictures."

"Those are nothing compared to what's left."

"That's ridiculous. The blood-spattered man I saw riddled in bomb fragments had been given up for dead. You're alive!"

He rubbed the back of his neck in a gesture she interpreted as a sign of insecurity. She couldn't comprehend him falling victim to that weakness. Not Chase.

"You mean what's left of me."

Her hand knotted into a fist. "I didn't think you had a vain bone in your body."

"I don't remember thinking much about it either until I looked into a full-length mirror and found myself staring at one of Dr. Frankenstein's experiments."

"Don't say that, Chase! Don't ever speak like that again." Her body shook so hard she had to hold on to the sink for support. "No one would ever guess in a million years."

He smirked. "With clothes on, you mean?"

She had trouble swallowing. "What do you do when you swim?"

"I don't."

Annie bit her lip. "Are you telling me you've never been with a woman since?"

"No, I'm not telling you that," he came back with brutal honesty.

"Does that include Rachel?" she asked before she could stop herself.

Chase had enviable control. "Rachel was never interested in me. It was Vance from the moment tempers flared in his office. If she told you anything different, she was lying."

"No," Annie answered honestly. "She said as much to me, but evidently you were interested in her."

His eyes narrowed. "You want your pound of flesh, don't you. Well here it is. Rachel had a sweetness about her including an inner strength that made her attractive to me. The truth is, she reminded me of *you*, but Vance had already gotten under her skin. There was no contest. Does that answer your question?"

She looked away, ashamed she'd brought Rachel up to him.

"Why don't we talk about the number of men who found you attractive over the intervening years. Roberta has told me about one of them. Greg somebody? The whiz kid from Pennington Mutual your parents introduced to you? She said he flew the two of you to his yacht moored in the San Francisco Bay area several times.

"I also remember her talking about a professional golfer named Lucky Sorenson who invited you to see the PGA Open at Pebble Beach. I understand you stayed overnight at his home in Carmel."

She should never have opened this up. "You've made your point, Chase."

"Did you sleep with *them*?"

Annie would love to lie to him, but she couldn't. "No," she answered in a quiet voice, "but you've been with other women who've seen your scars."

"They could handle it," he fired back.

"But not me."

"Especially not you."

Flame stained her cheeks. "Why?"

"I'd rather you remembered me the way I was."

"If you mean dead, it's too late for that now!"

His eyes grew bleak. "I know."

Full of pain she cried, "Evidently you always thought of me as a high-maintenance princess who needed to be pampered all the time and couldn't take anything the real world handed out."

She watched his features harden. "I asked you to marry me a long time ago and you said yes. Shall we see if your answer is the still the same now?"

In front of her eyes he pulled his T-shirt over his head. Next came his jeans, leaving him stripped down to his boxers. "Behold the man you once said was the embodiment of your every fantasy."

Looking at Chase was like looking at a picture taken at a carnival. The kind where you stood behind a cardboard stand-up that distorted a portion of your body. She'd always considered him the personification of male beauty. In her eyes he always would be.

"This is only the frontal view."

He turned around so she could see his back all the way to where the scarring was covered up by the waistband. "More plastic surgery might make me a little prettier, but with all my dreams obliterated, I never had the incentive to do anything about it."

When he faced her again, his hands were on his hips in that warriorlike stance she and Rachel had talked about. One brow dipped. "What do you think? Shall I have it done for your wedding present, or don't I stand a chance in hell?"

Annie couldn't talk. It wasn't the scarring that stopped her, although it was massive and no doubt represented years of pain and anguish while he healed. What wounded her was the darkness that had crept into his psyche over the intervening years. A menacing grimace distorted his smile.

"I'm waiting for an answer, my love. Even if our dreams were shattered, do you have the guts to make our daughter's come true?"

Suddenly she was reminded of Roberta the first year she took swimming lessons. All the other kids in her class had finally learned to dive off the side. When it came to her turn, she backed away from the edge. The teacher urged her to try it.

Roberta had denied that she was scared and insisted she didn't feel like diving right then. That look in her eyes was identical to the one in Chase's. Pure, unadulterated, defiant fear.

Chase had said he still wanted her, that he wanted to marry her. He'd kissed her tonight as if he'd never stopped wanting her. If marriage could take away his inner demons, maybe it could heal her demons, too. Nothing mattered except that he was back in her life, a man who'd faced terror and was still standing.

Her chin went up. "I do if you do. Your scars change nothing. I love you, Chase. How soon do you want to plan the ceremony?"

"Annie—" he cried, but as he reached for her, his cell phone rang.

She felt as well as heard his frustration at being interrupted. It frustrated her too because she knew he had to answer it. With one arm still around her, he reached for the phone lying on the counter, and clicked on, but whatever he heard on the other end changed his entire countenance. His arm slowly fell away

Even in the light she could see he'd paled. All the joy in his expression of moments ago was gone. Extinguished. Annie felt sick to the pit of her stomach.

He covered the phone. "I'm afraid this is going to take some time," he said in a gravelly voice she didn't recognize.

"You want me to leave?"

She'd never seen Chase look more tormented. "It's the last thing I want and you know it. But under the circumstances it would be better. I'll come to your house later."

He gave her a swift, hard kiss on the lips before she grabbed her parka from the chair and left the kitchen. All the way to her house she hugged her cast against her chest to subdue the fierce pounding of her heart. She had the awful premonition something was about to threaten her happiness all over again.

Chapter Nine

Annie slipped in the house, relieved to discover everyone had gone to bed. She wasn't in any condition to face her parents or Roberta. Tonight she'd known such intense joy in Chase's arms, and the shock of having to leave him the second she'd told him she'd marry him had filled her with paralyzing fear.

Once before he'd left her to go to work, and he'd never come back. It couldn't have been normal ranger business making demands on his time tonight; for that, he wouldn't have lost color or sent her away.

He'd said he would come to the house later.

She glanced at her watch. Now it *was* later. What was going on?

If he didn't knock on her door in five minutes, she would run back to his house to find out why. While she was pacing the living room floor, her cell rang. Annie lunged for her purse lying on a chair. She pulled out the phone and clicked on.

"Chase?" She hadn't even looked at the caller ID.

"It's Vance."

"Oh, Vance. Forgive me. I—I've been waiting for Chase."

"That's why I'm calling. He's dealing with an emergency in another part of the park and doesn't know how long he'll be. Since he knew you'd be worried, I told him I'd call you."

She gripped the phone tighter. It was much more serious than Vance was making it out to be or Chase would have called her. Maybe there'd been a bear attack on a camper, or a shooting he had to investigate. As much as she wanted to ask Vance for details, she held back. He'd been kind enough to phone and assure her everything was all right.

What kind of a ranger's wife would she make if she fell apart every time Chase had to respond to a crisis? "You don't know how much I appreciate your call. Thank you for being so thoughtful, Vance."

"You're welcome. We'll be seeing each other soon. Nicky's living for Halloween."

"So is Roberta."

"Tonight he reminded us it's only three days away."

She laughed in spite of her anxiety. "We've been going through a similar countdown here."

"It'll be a fun night for everyone. Don't tell Nicky, but I'm just as excited as he is." Vance was a wonderful man. "Good night, Annie."

"Good night."

Once she'd hung up, she got ready for bed and slid in next to Roberta. But after an hour of tossing and turning she grabbed a blanket from the hall closet and spent what remained of the restless night on the couch instead.

When morning came, Roberta was up and ready for school, none the wiser that Annie had gone over to Chase's last night. By the time Annie had prepared breakfast, her parents had joined them.

Her mother gave her a searching glance. Naturally she wanted to know the outcome of last night's visit, but she didn't say anything in front of their sober granddaughter.

"Aren't you going to finish your toast?"

"I'm not that hungry, Mom." She looked at her grandparents. "I wish you didn't have to go back to San Francisco today."

"Don't you worry. We'll drive up here next week," Annie's father assured her.

"Okay." She slid out of the chair and kissed them, then grabbed her backpack from the chair in the front room.

Annie followed and gave her a hug. "See you after school."

"Daddy said Nicky and I could drop by headquarters for a root beer on our way home."

"That sounds fun." What else could she say? Hopefully Chase was back at his house in bed by now.

"Bye!"

All three of them watched her from the porch until she disappeared around the corner, then they went inside. "I guess we'd better get going too," her dad muttered without his usual enthusiasm.

"Before you do, I have something important to tell you." That got her parents' attention in a hurry. "Last night Chase asked me to marry him and I said yes."

Their eyes lit up. "That's the best news we've ever heard." The next thing she knew they were hugging her, cast and all. While she wiped her eyes, her mother said, "Why didn't you tell Roberta this morning?"

"Chase and I want to do it together." Their conversation hadn't gotten that far last night, but she knew *him*. He'd missed out on everything else to do with their daughter. Annie wasn't about to take that moment away from him.

Her father kissed her cheek. "How soon do you plan to be married?"

"Soon—" she blurted, feeling her face go hot. They hadn't talked about that either, but their hunger for each other demanded nothing less. She couldn't wait to go over to his house later.

"Well, don't keep us in suspense long."

"I promise to phone you the moment we've set a date. Last night he had to go out on an emergency before we could make plans."

"Oh, Annie!" Her mother embraced her again. They'd all been through so much since her return from Afghanistan. She knew what her mom was saying without any more words having to be said.

A few minutes later she walked them out to their car. "Drive safely."

"I will." Her dad gave her another long hug. "Tell Chase we said welcome to the family."

Annie nodded. She couldn't wait!

Once they'd gone, she rushed inside to do the dishes and take a shower. Though she couldn't do anything about being ten years older than she'd been when they'd met, she intended to make herself look as beautiful as possible for him.

By the time she was ready, she phoned headquarters first, just to make sure he wasn't in his office. The dispatcher, Ranger Davis, said he hadn't been in and she didn't know when to expect him. Annie had thought as much.

Five minutes later she discovered his truck wasn't in the driveway, nor did he answer the door. If he was in a deep sleep, she didn't want to rouse him from it. It looked like she had no choice but to go back home and start doing the job she was getting paid for.

The minutes crept into hours while she waited for him to phone at least. When the call never came, she phoned headquarters again. Still no sign of Chase being in his office. By quarter to four she was ready to call Vance when Roberta ran into the house. "Mom?"

Annie hurried down the hall from the room she'd turned into an office. "Hi, honey! How was school today?"

"It was okay, but Dad wasn't at headquarters. Can I go over to his house?"

"Of course," she said, not having to think about it, "but he might not be there."

"I know. If he's not, I'll come right back." She dropped her pack on a chair and took off out the front door.

Please be home, Chase.

Fifteen minutes passed, long enough for Annie to assume all was well. Giddy with relief, she had decided to walk over there and join them when Roberta came through the front door with a long face. "You were right. He wasn't home. Has he called?"

"Not yet, but I know he will the minute he can. Vance said he was called out on an emergency last night, so we don't know how long he'll be gone. Do you want some fruit or a sandwich?"

"Maybe some string cheese."

Good, Roberta wasn't too upset to eat. Annie was determined to keep things normal no matter what. "Why don't you ask Carly to come over. I'd like to meet her."

"I don't know her phone number."

"I'll get it from Ranger Sims. He's probably on duty."

She walked back to her office for pen and paper. While she was at it, she'd find out if he knew Chase's whereabouts.

Carly's father was clearly pleased that Roberta wanted to play with his daughter. He gave her their home phone number but, to her disappointment, his explanation didn't help her.

"He's been working on a big case with the feds to arrest the men responsible for growing marijuana in the wilderness areas. I happen to know they have a manhunt on to ferret them out and need Chase's help. That's probably what's keeping him."

"I'm sure you're right. Thanks, Mark. Talk to you soon."

Annie clicked off, but she wasn't reassured. Mark had been too ready with an easy answer. She knew what she'd seen last night. Chase's sudden pallor had given him away.

"Here's the number." She'd crossed over to Roberta's room to hand her the paper and phone. "I'm still working if you need me."

"Okay. If she can come, can we make popcorn?"

"Sure," she said, convinced his emergency didn't have to do with park business. The pit in her stomach had enlarged to a cavern.

"AREN'T YOU READY YET, honey?"

"I don't want to go trick-or-treating without Daddy," Roberta called out from her bedroom. "Do you think something bad has happened to him?"

"No, I don't."

"But he's been gone three days," she said in a mournful tone.

"He's a federal park ranger with important responsibilities. Sometimes he has to be gone on business he can't discuss with us. I'm afraid it's something we're going to have to get used to." This speech was for Annie's benefit, too. "If you stay in your room all night, you're going to disappoint Nicky, not to mention that you'll be miserable. Do you think that would make your father happy?"

After a silence, she finally said, "No."

"So what do you say?"

"Okay. I'll come."

"Have you taken out your curlers?"

"Yes. I used your hair spray to fluff it."

"I bet it looks perfect. I can't wait to see you and Nicky in your wizard robes. Luckily you can wear your coats under them."

"Rachel bought him a wig and glasses. He looks just like Harry and practices walking around like in the movie."

Annie chuckled. "You two will be the hit of the night."

"Daddy was going to bring my wand from his office."

Don't think about Chase right now. "Maybe it's better you don't have it. All the children will want to hold it."

"I know. Nicky's bringing his." Roberta opened the door, but it was Hermione who marched toward Annie with her Myers nose slightly in the air. The white blouse with the pointed collar was perfect beneath her black robe.

"Oh honey, you look just like her!"

Still staying in Hermione's character, her daughter eyed Annie up and down. "You must be some kind of Indian princess. Who are you precisely?"

"It was supposed to be a secret. I wanted to see if your father could figure it out."

"My father is brilliant," she stated in a superior tone. "Of course he would figure it out, *if* he were here."

They both broke into laughter. Bless her daughter for deciding to be a good soldier. It helped release some of the tension they were both feeling with Chase gone. This was the most animated her daughter had been in several days. Annie hoped this new mood would last, at least for tonight. They hugged, but not too hard. She didn't want her makeup to get on Roberta.

Heavy eyeliner and darker pancake makeup helped create the rest of the illusion that she was Princess Tee-Hee-Neh. Ron Saddler had managed to borrow the dress for her from a friend. Much as she would have loved to wear the moccasins she'd bought in the gift shop, she would have to save those for the party at Mark Sims's house after trick-or-treating because it had started snowing.

The only authentic part of her costume was a woven headband worn by the Ahwahnee women once living in Yosemite. After a couple of tries with her free hand she lowered it around her head so it gripped her forehead without dipping in the wrong place. As the legend went, Tee-Hee-Neh had long, dark hair. Annie wore hers the same way. She hadn't had this much fun in years, hoping to impress Chase, even if she was in a cast.

As if her thoughts had conjured him up, the doorbell rang. "I'll get it!"

Roberta zipped out of the room. With her heart in her throat Annie hurried after her. When she opened the front door, a freezing blast of air blew in. There stood Harry Potter carrying a plastic pumpkin to hold his candy. He was accompanied by a witch and a grim reaper in black, at least seven feet tall.

"Oh my gosh!" Roberta took the words right out of Annie's mouth. Vance was frightening!

"Come in, everyone, and shut the door," Annie urged. They all had a slight dusting of snow. "Well, Mr. Potter, I can't believe I'm not at Hogwarts."

Nicky giggled. "Thanks. You look pretty."

"Thank *you*. Roberta? Give Nicky some candy, then I think we should start our trick-or-treating."

"Goody!" Nicky took two Tootsie Pops before darting out the door first.

"Let's leave the rest of them on the porch for the other children when they come."

"Okay."

Soon everyone had gone outside. Annie followed with her parka around her shoulders and locked the door. They stepped into a winter fairyland. Magic filled the air. With everyone in costume, the scene could have been taken right out of a fantasy where anything was possible and wonders were expected to happen.

Where was Chase? How would she stand another night without him?

After stops at the various houses, they ended up at the Sims's house with plastic pumpkins full of goodies. There had to be a good thirty people assembled. Between all the food and the prizes to be given out, everyone would be on a sugar high for days.

Among the many awards, the most hideous costume went to Vance, of course. Rachel was dubbed the best "bewitched" witch. Nicky and Roberta garnered the "most lifelike impersonations of the cinema" award. Carly won the prettiest award for her Tinkerbell outfit. Three of the kids came as vampires. Brody won the bloodiest award, the other two walked away with the creepiest and the scariest. Everyone won something. Annie was given the best award for an historical figure.

After she'd been given a prize of a free coupon to rent a movie, she wandered over to the punch bowl. While she was helping herself, the grim reaper appeared at her side.

"You're terrifying me again, Vance."

"I was just going to say that if Princess Tee-Hee-Neh looked as beautiful as you, then I can understand how the legend got started."

"Chase!" she cried, so overjoyed he was here she almost spilled her punch on the floor.

He put it back on the table. "Come with me," was all he said. To her shock he led her to the laundry room between the kitchen and the garage. Once he locked the door, they were alone.

"Before we do anything else, I have to have *this*." Off came the fake head of his costume. She caught the gleam of his silvery eyes, then he was kissing her the way he used to do after they got home from the dig site. Their hunger for each other had been insatiable then and was worse now.

For a few minutes they fed from each other's mouths, needing this rapture after three days' deprivation. Transported by desire, neither of them was aware of the passage of time.

Finally he allowed her to come up for air. "I've been worried sick, darling."

"I know," he whispered against her lips. "Forgive me again."

"There's nothing to forgive—" she cried. "I'm just happy to be holding you again."

"I never wanted to let you go. That phone call the

other night came from Sid Manning. Since Vance knows about my being in the witness protection program, Sid worked out an emergency code among the three of us. It was a necessary precaution in case of other people present or electronic surveillance on our phone lines. I'd hoped none of us would ever have to use it, but it happened."

Annie hugged him tighter.

"Right after you left, Vance came for me and drove me to the pad. He said Sid would meet my helicopter in Bishop. The pilot was told it was emergency ranger business."

"Did Vance say anything else?"

Chase grimaced. "I'm afraid so." She shuddered. "Sid told him to be prepared in case Vance had to make someone else his assistant head ranger."

She drew in a sharp breath.

"At that point I told him to turn around because I was taking you and Roberta with me. I'd already been to hell and back. No way would I ever leave you again, but Vance was way ahead of me. He said it was *me* Sid wanted to see, that every safeguard had been put in place to keep you safe while I was gone. Not to worry."

His hands gripped her shoulders tighter. "Can you imagine Sid saying that when you'd just told me you'd marry me?"

"You went so pale," she whispered. "It was an awful moment."

Their eyes met in pained understanding. "For the last few days I've been sequestered with men from counterintelligence reviewing tapes that picked up chatter relevant to the planting of the bomb in Kabul ten years ago."

"Why now, when we've just been reunited? Is that the reason?"

"No, darling." He hushed her with his lips. "This had to do with Lon Wiseman."

"I remember him. The Israeli from Jerusalem University working at the site."

He nodded. "Lon's the other man who escaped death like me. Lately his name has come up in the chatter. It seems they finally have proof he's hiding back in Israel. Clearly the terrorists have never given up hunting for him or me, but the arguments have been loud and long as to where I'm hiding."

"So they're still actively looking for you."

He drew her head against his chest. "They never stop. One of the most outspoken operatives insisted that the double agent who recognized me before I left the military believes I'm being protected by friends in China. Another one is convinced Pakistan. Still another is clinging to the theory that I'm back in the States, yet none of them can be sure I'm not still embedded with American troops."

"Thank heaven they don't know anything yet."

"It's clear they don't, but those killers are some of the best trackers in the world. Though I've been at the park three years without incident, the day could come when a lead might bring them to Yosemite. Knowing Al-Qaeda hasn't relented in their pursuit makes it imperative we be proactive."

Annie looked into his eyes. "What are you saying exactly?"

"That this menace isn't going to go away. When we tell Roberta we're getting married, we have to let her know that the situation we're in means we might have to relocate at a moment's notice. In the meantime you and I have to decide if we're going to continue to stay here at Yosemite or not."

"Because of the danger to everyone else."

"Yes. Our friends, your parents."

"Oh Chase!" She wept quietly against him.

He rocked her in place. "How to protect all of us...that's my torment."

She sniffed and finally lifted her head. "We're together again, aren't we?"

"Yes."

"That's the most important thing, isn't it? We have time to decide what we're going to do?"

"Yes, yes, yes!" His eyes burned with love for her. "You're so strong, Annie. With you I know we're going to make it."

As his mouth descended once more, they became aware someone was trying to open the door. With reluctance Chase eased her out of his arms. "When we're back at your house, we'll pick up where we left off. Right now, let's enjoy the party."

He put the top of his costume back on before unlocking the door. Mark's wife stood at the kitchen sink. Annie flashed her a guilty look. "Sorry about that."

The other woman in the vampire outfit grinned. "No problem. Here—" She handed Annie a napkin. "Your makeup's all smeared."

By now Chase was chuckling. He took the napkin and fixed her face before declaring she was presentable. When they joined the others he whispered, "Do you know every man in the room is envious of me?"

It appeared Chase and Vance had planned ahead of time to wear the same costume. Now there were twin terrifying figures in the house.

"Thank you for the compliment. I wish I could return it, but I have to agree with the MC. Vance won the award for the most hideous costume. You two should be banned to extinction."

His husky laugh played havoc with her insides, turning her legs to mush. While she was trying to recover, Roberta ran up to them. Nicky was right behind her, casting spells on everyone. He was hilarious as usual. Evidently they didn't know what to think with two grim reapers in the room.

"Hi, sweetheart." He picked her up and hugged her.

"Dad!" she squealed in delight and hugged him back. "When did you get here?"

"A little while ago. I came in through Mark's garage."

So that was where he'd come from. Nicky looked shocked. "I've got to tell Daddy you're here!" Everyone was relieved Chase was back, but no one more than Annie.

While he ran off to find his parents, Roberta showed him the coupons for ice cream she and Nicky had won for their costumes. Chase was like a magnet. The rangers congregated around the witch's brew punch bowl to talk to him. Annie didn't mind.

Nothing mattered now that he was back. Before long they'd be alone.... Her body filled with heat. What if she'd stayed home wallowing in pain like she'd wanted to, like Roberta had wanted to do? His arrival had turned the place into a real party that went on for another half hour before some of the rangers had to leave to go back on duty.

Vance gathered up their party of six. After saying goodbye to their hosts, they started walking home. En route their group agreed it had been a perfect Halloween. The kids groaned when Annie and Rachel reminded them they had school in the morning and needed to get to bed. The two families parted at the corner.

"See ya tomorrow, Roberta. Be sure and bring your candy. I'll bring mine."

"I don't think so," Vance interjected.

"How come?"

"Because Chase and I plan to eat all of it at work."

Chase burst into laughter. It sounded so funny, especially while he was still in costume, but Nicky didn't find it at all amusing.

"Mom? Can he do that?"

"I'm afraid so. He's the chief ranger."

"But that doesn't give him the right to eat our candy," Roberta whispered to Annie. It was always the fairness issue with her.

"He's only teasing."

"Oh." Roberta was still a little in awe of Vance. "See ya, Nicky," she called over her shoulder.

As they went their separate ways they heard Nicky giggling again. "You see? Vance adores Nicky."

Roberta nodded.

"What are you two whispering about?" Chase wanted to know.

Annie winked at him. "We were hoping you'd come home with us. We're going to make a fire and watch *The Great Pumpkin.*"

At the unexpected invitation, Roberta looked like she was going to explode with joy. This was only the beginning. Annie couldn't see Chase's face to register his expression, but she knew how he felt.

"I haven't seen a Charlie Brown cartoon in years. Let's

do it." He reached the front porch first and scooped up the bowl she'd left out for the kids. It had one Tootsie Pop left.

Once inside the house she said, "I'll change my clothes and be right out."

He took off his costume, revealing the man she loved beyond comprehension. His eyes swept over her in intimate appraisal. "I like you the way you are," he murmured.

Roberta smiled up at him. "Have you guessed who she is?"

"Could she be the Princess Tee-Hee-Neh?"

"How did you know that?"

"I know many things," he teased. Yes he did, Annie mused excitedly to herself. "She was a beautiful princess, the fairest of the daughters of the great chief Ahwahnee. She captured the heart of every young chief in the Yosemite Valley. Legend has it she was erect as the silver fir and supple as the tamarack. Her raven hair was silky as milkweed's floss, her movements graceful as a fawn's."

Annie trembled. When had he taken the time to learn that particular legend by heart?

"Each morning she stepped from her wigwam and would go to her secret place to meet her beloved. But one morning she found him dead from a fallen piece of granite where he'd been shooting arrows. She knelt down beside him. When he wouldn't wake up, she died, too. From then on the place with the giant slab above them was known as Lost Arrow."

While Annie realized it could almost be their story, Roberta looked mesmerized. "Nicky told me Lost Arrow is up by the falls. Are we going to climb up there someday?"

"We'll do it all, sweetheart."

"Roberta? Why don't you change into your pajamas before we start the movie."

"Okay. We'll be right back, Daddy. Don't leave."

"I'm not going anywhere."

Chapter Ten

A few minutes later the sight of Annie in the blue velour robe he'd once given her took him back ten years, causing his pulse to race. The dim light from one of the lamps threw her features into exquisite relief. She'd removed the pancake makeup that had turned her into an Indian princess. He desired her either way. It hurt to breathe.

"Annie?" His voice sounded hoarse even to him. Out of need he grasped her free hand, drawing her over to the couch where he sat down and pulled her onto his lap. Unable to resist, he brushed his lips against the soft warmth of her throat and mouth.

"There's something else I have to tell you before Roberta comes in."

Annie's body quivered. Her solemn eyes, almost a lavender-blue in the semidark, stared into his. "How could there be any more?" A haunted look had entered her eyes.

"This has to do with my physical condition."

Her eyes glistened with unshed tears. "Do you have a disease or some such thing you picked up in the Middle East?"

Close. "I still have the ability to make love to you but, according to the doctor, I'll never be able to give you more children. In case you were hoping for more, I need to know how you feel about that before we talk to our daughter."

She stunned him by wrapping her arms around his neck. After pressing her mouth to his, she said, "You already gave me the most wonderful child in the world. If we decide we want more, we can always adopt. How do you feel about that?"

He buried his face in her neck. "I think I can't believe this is happening at last."

Unable to hold back any longer, he kissed her with a hunger that was growing out of control. "You're beautiful beyond words, Annie. I need to love you so badly."

"I need you so much I'm in pain," she whispered and proceeded to show him. With his passion ignited he forgot where he was. In the next breath she was covering his face with feverish kisses the way she'd done years ago.

"Don't you want to watch the movie?"

Exulting in her love, he didn't realize Roberta had returned to the living room. Chase lifted his head in time to see his daughter standing by the TV in pink pajamas. Her Hermione hairdo still bounced.

"Put the DVD in, sweetheart, then come and sit down by me."

A slow smile broke the corners of Annie's mouth, captivating him. Easing out of his arms, she got to her feet. "I'll microwave the popcorn."

"Sounds like a plan."

He had a surprise plan of his own and would implement it during intermission. Annie knew it was coming, but she was letting him pick the moment. Chase checked his watch. It was ten-fifteen. He would announce the break in ten minutes. That was all the time he could stand to wait. Just thinking about it changed the rhythm of his heart, that violated, vulnerable organ he'd thought would have let him down by now.

Roberta took over. All he had to do was sit back on the couch and get comfortable. He played with her ponytail while they began chuckling over the charming characters. Chase saw a little of Nicky's and Roberta's most endearing qualities in them.

Annie came into the room with the popcorn and sat on the other side of their daughter. It was a good thing their offspring was around, considering his desire for her.

This was heaven, the kind of scenario he'd dreamed of so many times in the past ten years.

"I wish Snoopy were my dog, Mom."

"Every child who sees this film wishes the same thing."

Chase pressed the pause button. "Why don't we get one?"

Roberta leaped to her feet. "You mean and keep it here?"

"If this is where we decide to live."

"But you live around the corner."

"True." He could see he was confusing her. "I've decided I don't like going from your house to mine. What if we decide which house we like the best and all live in the same one together? Would you like that?"

Shock rendered her speechless for a moment. He saw fear creep into her eyes as her focus settled on Annie. "Would *you*, Mom?"

The blood pounded in his ears while he waited for Annie's answer.

"It's what I want more than anything in the world."

"You mean it?" she cried in joyous disbelief, throwing herself at Annie.

"Your mom and I are going to get married as soon as possible." He reached in his trouser pocket and pulled out a ring. "I've been wanting to give this to her since I first came to your condo in Santa Rosa."

He looked straight at Annie. "Before the explosion I asked the question and you said yes. Now I'm making it official in front of our daughter. Be very sure what you answer because this is forever."

"Say *yes*, Mom!"

"Yes," Annie answered in a tremulous voice.

"I'm planning to get two weeks cleared from the duty roster for our wedding and a honeymoon. It'll start Thanksgiving weekend."

"That's in about three weeks!" Roberta squealed. Now he was the one being hugged to death.

"By then your mother's cast will come off."

"Where will you get married?"

"Here in the park in a very small, quiet ceremony with only a few rangers to witness it. I wish it could be in a church and we could all go to some exotic place for our honeymoon, but that wouldn't be wise."

"So what will you do?"

He kissed her forehead. "We'll get married here at the house and honeymoon here. I'm thinking your grandparents could come and stay in your house while your mom and I get to know each other again in mine. After I'm back on duty we'll decide where we're going to live permanently."

Annie caught his hidden message before she put her arms around Roberta. "I think we're going to have to take a little shopping trip to San Francisco to find us something beautiful to wear for the wedding. Your grandmother will know the exact place."

Roberta cried with happiness against her. Annie's eyes, almost a violet-blue in the light from the television, stared into his without fear or striving.

This was the supreme moment of his life. He moved to Annie's other side and slid the solitaire diamond home on her ring finger. Once Roberta went to bed, he would show this amazing woman what she meant to him. The sooner the movie was over, the sooner he could get her in his arms.

"Darling," she said, pressing an avid kiss to his mouth.

"We'll celebrate after she's asleep," he whispered.

They all settled back on the couch. He had reached for the remote to release the pause button when a sound like the crack of thunder overhead went out like shock wave. It shook the ground. Roberta jumped and cried out at the same time.

Annie stared at him. "Was that an earthquake?"

Chase was already on his feet, putting on his parka. "No. A rockslide. It has a distinct sound. That one came from Curry Village."

"Wasn't that where the other one happened?"

He nodded. "I had a gut feeling it might happen again, but this was a much bigger one." Hopefully the tent cabins still available to the tourists had escaped catastrophic damage. He knew Vance was praying for the same thing.

"Don't either of you go out. When moisture gets in the cracks and a slab falls and breaks up, it sends pulverized debris called granite flour into the air for several hours. I don't want you breathing it."

"What about you?" Annie cried.

"I keep a mask in the truck. We'll do the rest of the movie tomorrow evening and invite the Rossiters. Be my good girls and mind me."

"Be careful, Daddy."

"That's my middle name." He gave her a hug, then caught Annie's face between his hands and kissed her thoroughly before taking off out the door.

The drive to Curry Village didn't take long. Already some of the guys were on the scene. It looked like a war zone. As he drew closer he saw Vance helping a dazed tourist out of her damaged tent. He reached for the mask in his toolbox and raced toward the others, grateful Annie and Roberta weren't anywhere near.

By morning he and the others had helped evacuate the 400-plus tourists to other lodgings. Only two had needed medical assistance, and they weren't seriously injured. As he was climbing back into the truck, Vance approached. "I guess you saw the damage to the tent cabins we closed off the other day."

He nodded. "If that first slide hadn't happened, we would have been digging for bodies. We dodged another bullet tonight."

"Yup." The chief wiped some of the powdery substance off his lips. "It's time to go home, but I'm afraid Nicky will think I'm the abominable snowman."

Chase let out a low laugh.

His friend's eyes flashed an electric blue. "I had the time of my life earlier tonight. How about you?"

"You don't know the half of it. Bring your family over to Annie's tomorrow night. I guess that means tonight. I've lost track. We'll watch *The Great Pumpkin*."

"That'll be a hit with Nicky. I'll tell Rachel."

Drained physically yet emotionally hyper where Annie was concerned, Chase drove home at a fast clip. She would be getting their daughter ready for school before she put in a day's work. He couldn't wait to be with her, but first he needed food followed by a shower and sleep. Their honeymoon couldn't come fast enough.

"MOM?" ROBERTA CALLED from the living room. "Nana wants to talk to you."

That was the second call today from her. Though her parents remained calm, she knew they were concerned about the rock slide. Annie on the other hand was coming to learn that something was always going on in the park, but she was so in love with Chase, nothing seemed to faze her.

"Bring the phone to the kitchen, will you?" She had decided to make a big dinner for them. The potatoes and carrots had been cooking around the lamb roast. After school Roberta had peeled the vegetables while Annie had made rolls. They'd be able to eat soon.

"Here."

"Thanks." She grabbed hold with her free hand. "Hi, Mom."

"The news on TV is full of the story about the rock slide."

"I know. I drove over to see the damage on my way to the store. It's pretty terrifying to think huge parts of boulders just fall away."

"What does Chase say about it?"

The mention of his name set her pulse off and running.

She stared at her diamond. "I don't know. I haven't seen or talked to him since last night, but the rangers worked till this morning so I'm sure he's still asleep."

Bill Telford had called her earlier in the day, reminding her they were having dinner tomorrow night. If he tried to turn it into something more than business, she would tell him she was getting married, but it was still a secret. For Roberta's sake she asked him if they could eat earlier than later. He was agreeable and they settled on six o'clock.

She had no way of knowing if Chase would be available for Roberta tomorrow evening. In case he had to be on duty, Rachel said Roberta could go over to their house and play with Nicky.

"You sound happy, darling."

"I am, Mom. He and Roberta are my life."

"That's the way it should be. Well, keep us posted."

"I promise to call you after I've heard from Chase."

"Good."

"Mom?" Roberta said after she'd hung up. "Can I call Daddy and see how soon he's coming over?"

"Go ahead. Dinner's ready." After pulling out the roast, she put the raised rolls in the oven to bake.

"I don't think he's there. It just keeps ringing."

"Then phone headquarters. They'll know where to find him."

"Okay." A minute later she said, "Daddy's off duty until tomorrow."

"I'm sure he's sleeping, so I have an idea. Let's pack up the food and take it over to his house. We'll drive over as soon as the rolls are done."

Roberta didn't need any urging. "I'll bring the key he gave me to get in."

"While we're loading the car, bring *The Great Pumpkin* movie with you."

"Okay."

In a few minutes they backed out of the garage and drove over to his house. If both his vehicles were in the garage she couldn't tell because the snow had melted on his driveway.

They phoned again and rang the doorbell, but there was no answer. Roberta looked up at her. "I'll let us in."

"Go ahead. If we have dinner waiting for him, he'll be thrilled." Together they carried the food to the kitchen. "Why don't you set the table? I'm going to tiptoe down the hall and see if he's asleep."

"Do you think he still is?"

"Or maybe he's in the shower. I'll be right back." The last thing she wanted was for Roberta to find him. If he were uncovered, the shock of his scars would be too much. When he decided to let her see them, he would have to talk to her about them first and prepare her.

With her heart in her throat, she peeked inside his room. To her relief she found him sprawled on top of the bed on his stomach, the sheet twisted around his long, hard-muscled legs. Realizing his back was exposed to his hips, she closed the door and collapsed against it.

"Chase?" she called out softly. At the sound of her voice, he flung out an arm of whipcord strength. "Darling?" she said a little louder.

He stirred before sitting up in the bed, taking the sheet with him. "Annie?"

"I'm sorry, but it's six o'clock. We brought you dinner. If you're not ready to eat, we'll leave you alone so you can go on sleeping."

He raked two bronzed hands through his hair. It was dark and rich, like the color of coffee beans. "I actually slept eleven hours?" he muttered. "I don't believe it." That aura of vulnerability he rarely showed to anyone tugged hard on her emotions.

"You needed it."

"Roberta's here?"

"Yes. She's going to hold you to that movie. Right now she's busy setting the table. I made sure she didn't find you first."

Their eyes met in silent understanding. His gave off a clear silver-gray. It appeared his sleep had done him a world of good. He rubbed his jaw. "I'll shave and join you in a few minutes."

Annie would have preferred to stay and feast her eyes on him. That summer in Kabul they'd gone without a lot of sleep in their desire to bring each other pleasure. Too many times she'd seen him in bed just like this, waiting for her to come back so they could love each other all over again. Stifling a moan, she slipped out the door to find Roberta.

"Your dad *was* asleep."

The tension lines in her face relaxed. "He must have been really tired."

"He was up all night. Do you think you can find some butter for our rolls?"

"I already have. Some jam too."

"Perfect."

A FEAST FIT FOR A KING.

That was Chase's first thought when he entered the kitchen wearing khakis and a sport shirt. His long sleep had made him feel like a new man.

The aroma of lamb roast flavored with fresh mint filled the room. Annie remembered. How many times had they camped out and eaten lamb kabobs roasted over the fire? It was his favorite meat, though he'd rarely eaten it since he'd come to the park. That was because he liked sweet onions and carrots with it and those items took additional preparation.

A few minutes later he caught hold of Roberta's hand and squeezed it. "This is the best meal I've ever eaten."

Her guileless smile got to him every time. "I peeled the vegetables."

"Well, they're perfect. So's everything." His gaze swerved to Annie. *"So are you."*

Their eyes held. "The feeling's mutual."

"I brought the movie over, Dad."

"Perfect," he said, still looking at Annie. "Roberta?"

"Yes?"

"Will you do me a favor and call Nicky? My phone's in the bedroom. Press two. I invited them to come over to your house tonight to watch Snoopy. Tell them to come here instead."

She let out another sound of happiness and ran to the other room to find the phone.

"Annie, come here to me. We never have a second alone."

They reached for each other at the same time. Chase didn't try to talk. All he could do was tell her with his lips and his body as he drew her into him, forgetting there was a cast between them.

Eventually they ended up in his living room on the leather couch. She looked beautiful and sophisticated in a navy blouse and tailored gray wool pants. He couldn't get enough of her.

Too soon for Chase his euphoria was broken by the sound of voices at the front door. He fought against relinquishing her mouth for any reason.

"Hey—" Nicky's bright voice filled the room. "How come they're kissing?"

Chase's body started to shake with laughter. So did Annie's. Slowly he raised his head. In that moment before he looked at the others, he saw the love light in her gorgeous eyes. If he could always have this effect on her, he wouldn't ask for anything else.

He turned to their friends, smiling at Nicky. "How come your dad kisses your mom?"

"'Cause he loves her!"

"And how come she kisses him back?"

"'Cause she loves him."

Annie decided to help him out. "I love your uncle Chase very, very much, so we're going to get married. He just gave me this diamond. Do you want to see it?"

He ran over to look at it.

"Would you like to be in our wedding?" Annie asked him.

Nicky gave a little shriek of excitement and turned to his parents. "Can I?"

Pandemonium broke out as Vance grabbed Chase and they gave each other a bear hug. She couldn't hear all they were saying, but she'd never seen two men so happy.

Annie shared a private glance with Rachel. In a short time they'd become good friends. Nicky's mother moved closer. Her eyes glistened with unshed tears as she inspected the one-carat solitaire.

"Thank heaven you've found each other again. Tonight Chase is such a different person from the man

I met last June, I hardly recognize him. I can see that you're changed, too."

She nodded. "We've had a lot to work out." They still did. Annie wasn't unaware Chase would always have certain demons to deal with from his past. But there was great satisfaction in knowing she would be there to love him through all of it.

"I want to help with your wedding any way I can."

"We both do," Vance declared, giving Annie a big hug. "Congratulations," he whispered. "You're about to be married to the greatest man I know." She nodded. Coming from the chief, there was no greater praise.

After putting his arm around his wife, Vance said, "Since your wedding has to be low-key, why don't you get married at our house? The minister in Oakhurst would be happy to officiate."

Annie checked with Chase. His wide smile said it all. "That sounds wonderful to us, Vance. Thank you so much."

"It'll be our pleasure, believe me. We'll keep everything quiet until the big day. Did you hear that, sport?"

When Annie looked, Nicky and Roberta were both eating rolls. He looked back at his dad. "Hear what?"

"We have to keep their wedding a secret for now."

"Okay. I won't tell anybody. Can I wear a tux like I did at our wedding?"

Chase rubbed the top of his head. "I insist on it. We're going to take lots of pictures of you and Roberta."

"Guess what, Nicky?" she piped up. "Daddy says we're going to get a dog."

"What kind?"

"Snoopy."

His eyes widened. "Hey, Dad—"

Vance laughed. "I heard. Maybe we'll all go together and you can pick out yours at the same time."

"What kind do you want?" Roberta asked.

"A mutt like Daddy used to have."

"That's not a breed."

"Actually it's a combination of several kinds of breeds," Annie corrected her daughter so it wouldn't hurt Nicky's feelings.

"Yeah."

"Do you want to watch *The Great Pumpkin*?" Roberta was a quick study.

"I think that's a terrific idea, sweetheart. Come on. Everyone sit down and we'll all watch it." Chase turned off the lights. The next thing Annie knew he'd pulled her onto his lap, her favorite place. He moved her hair to the side. "Almost heaven," he whispered against her neck, sending rivulets of desire through her body.

It took the greatest control to sit through to the end of the film without devouring each other, but somehow Chase managed. Annie had the more difficult time. Rachel's announcement that it was time for Nicky to be in bed didn't come too soon.

Annie got to her feet on rubbery legs and saw everyone to the door. Chase joined her. When she shut it, she found herself trapped by a powerful body. He found her mouth. The kiss they'd been craving went on and on and was quickly turning into something else. "I could eat you alive."

"We can't—even though Roberta's half-asleep on the couch, we're not alone."

He groaned. "I know. We can't be alone until you're my wife. That's three and a half weeks away. I want a real wedding night. We'll pretend it's our first time together."

She bit her lip, knowing it was going to kill her to wait. "I want that, too."

Chase gave her a thorough kiss. "Come on. I'll see you two home."

"The dishes—"

"I'll do them. After I get back from your house I'm going to have so much excess energy, I'll be glad for something, anything to do until I can do what I really want for as long as I want."

Annie knew exactly what he meant.

THREE WEEKS LATER while Roberta looked on, the doctor removed the cast and carefully washed Annie's arm. "There. How does it feel?"

She smiled. "Like my body's a lot lighter on one side."

"The feeling will pass in a day. Your X-ray indicates you've healed beautifully."

"That's a great relief."

"I bet you're glad it's off, Mom."

"You can't imagine." It had been like a wall separating her from Chase, but in retrospect she knew it had been a good thing. Forty-eight hours from now she'd be his bride. She was running a temperature just thinking about it. "How much can I do with it?"

He winked. "Enough to enjoy your honeymoon." Annie blushed. "I'm teasing."

She chuckled. "I know." This doctor was a stranger, but since her parents had driven them to San Francisco to pick up their dresses, Annie had decided to see the orthopedic surgeon her father had said came highly recommended.

"Just ease back into the normal activity of your life and you'll be fine."

The doctor smiled at Roberta. "When's the big event?"

"It's the day after tomorrow."

"I bet you have a beautiful new dress."

She nodded. "It's long and white with a blue sash."

"Are you excited to be getting a new daddy?"

Roberta sent Annie a secret glance. "Yes. I love him."

"Well, I'd say he's the most fortunate man on the planet." His gaze included Annie as he said it.

"Thank you, Doctor. I appreciate you fitting me in so fast."

"It was a pleasure. Congratulations again."

"Thanks." She got up from the chair feeling free as a bird without that deadweight. "Shall we go? Your grandparents are waiting outside the clinic."

"Bye." Roberta waved before they left his examining room.

Her parents beamed when they saw her approach the car unencumbered. Everything had been accomplished so they could head straight back to the park. She'd told Chase they wouldn't arrive until late so she wouldn't see him until the eleven o'clock ceremony the day after tomorrow. It was better that way. She didn't trust herself within a mile of him now.

On her shopping spree she'd bought his wedding ring and a special wedding present. She'd also purchased a gift for Rachel and Vance for being such wonderful friends. Roberta had picked out a unique surprise for Nicky. The car was also loaded with everything her parents would need while they took care of their granddaughter for a week.

Seven days entirely alone with Chase. How would she live till then?

VANCE SPREAD the double-bed air mattress on the floor in front of Chase's fireplace and started to fill it using his old bicycle pump.

"Does that old relic still work?"

"Let's find out."

Who would have guessed? Chase had to admit it still did the job perfectly.

Vance looked up. "You're going to have to tell me how this setup goes over with Annie. After you guys come out of hibernation, I'm thinking Rachel and I will take up where you left off and have a honeymoon at home, too."

Chase had chopped wood all afternoon and was still stacking it on the hearth. "At least your first one was in a hotel with food and maid service."

His friend paused in his task for a minute. "Do you want to know the truth?"

"Always."

"I'd have much rather stayed right here and done what you're doing. The trip to England was for Nicky."

"I know, but think what great memories you made." He set the last load of wood on top of the stack. "One of these days I'll take my family somewhere."

Vance eyed him intently. "Annie was forced to live ten years without you. I'd say she and Roberta are ready to stay put with you. I think it's time for a beer. Our last together while you're still a single man."

"Whatever you say, Chief."

"BY THE AUTHORITY invested in me, I now pronounce Margaret Anne Bower and Chase Jarvis, husband and wife in the bonds of holy matrimony. What God has joined together, let no man put asunder. You may kiss your bride."

Chase's bride stood in two-inch white high heels. No cast in sight. She was a vision in a stunning white lace suit with pearl buttons. A matching strand of pearls encircled her throat. She reminded Chase of a confection too exquisite to touch.

"I don't know if I dare," he whispered in earnest. "I've needed to be your husband for too long."

Her surprised expression was underlined by Nicky's loud whisper. "Isn't Uncle Chase going to kiss her?" His question produced a ripple of stifled laughter that traveled around the room. Their minister laughed out loud.

The comic relief helped Chase give his new wife an appropriate kiss that lasted just the right amount of time, surprising her even more. But he'd done it this way for self-preservation. Otherwise the half-dozen rangers he'd invited would know he was out of control and they'd never let him live it down.

Roberta was the first to break out of line and hug them. Nicky came next in a black tux that matched his father's and Chase's. He kept tugging on her to run into the dining room with him so they'd be the first to get food and wedding cake.

Then came the onslaught of family and well-wishers packed into Vance's living room. Stands of flowers had transformed it. Chase loved the smell of the gardenias pinned to Annie's shoulder.

The small, intimate crowd they'd first envisioned had grown to a considerable size. Besides Annie's parents, Tom Fuller had come with his family. His leg was still in a cast. Ron, Annie's colleague, was also invited and milled around chatting with the guests.

Beth had come with her family. Of course Rachel's parents were here along with the families of the rangers invited. The brotherhood that Chase felt was something to treasure. Only one thing was missing.

His parents would have loved to be here. From the beginning they'd treated Annie like a daughter. They would have adored their granddaughter.

He felt Annie squeeze his hand. "I miss your parents, too. Wherever they are, I'd like to think they're watching."

She was so in tune with his feelings, he drew her into his arms and rocked her for a moment. "How soon do you think we can leave?"

"Right now if you want."

"It wouldn't be rude?"

"Yes, it would be very rude."

He tightened his embrace, relishing the fact that the cast was gone. "We'll stay twenty more minutes."

"In that case we'd better find our daughter and say goodbye."

"Do you think she'll be able to handle it?" he whispered against her neck.

"As long as we're just around the corner, I'm sure of it. The big question is, can you?"

"You know me too well, Annie."

"There's no rule that says you can't phone her."

"How many men do you know phone their children on their honeymoon?"

"Well, I know *one*. The chief ranger of the *whole* park, as Nicky loves to say, took him on their honeymoon. He's grinning at us right now, by the way."

"So are the other guys. We need to get out of here. Let's find our daughter."

Chapter Eleven

Chase lay in front of the crackling fire, his heart pounding unmercifully as he waited for Annie to come. During the hours they'd made love in the bedroom, the afternoon had melted into evening. Now it was night.

After showering together, he'd left her alone long enough to warm up food from their wedding reception. He had everything ready so they wouldn't have to move again for hours.

Outside a wind had sprung up. Snow had been forecast. In the past, a night like this with the advent of winter always made him feel lonely in a way too desolate to describe. Though there weren't any wolves in the park, he'd felt like one who'd been trekking in the forest on a search for his lost mate, an endless lesson in futility. On such a night, he'd wished himself thousands of miles away from Yosemite.

Not tonight. Not ever again.

While the wind moaned around the corners of the house and beat against the windowpanes, he simply crushed Annie against him and let her heat consume him. She filled the empty spaces in his soul. All he had to do was open his eyes and drink in her beauty. He never again wanted to be anyplace other than right here, safe in the arms of the woman who'd cried out her love for him over and over again.

Her body had grown more voluptuous since giving birth. Between her satiny skin and dark, glistening hair, he couldn't stop telling her she was a living miracle.

"Darling? Did you think I was never coming?"

His gaze took in the mold of her body wrapped in the blue robe. "I can't believe you still have it."

She knelt next to him and kissed his mouth before eating several small rolls filled with crab salad. "For one thing, a lovely robe like this never goes out of style. For another, it's the one item saved from our past I can put on and pretend I can feel your arms around me. I remember you bringing it home from the bazaar."

He ran a hand under her sleeve to feel her warmth. "It looked like you, all filmy and silky."

Annie smiled down at him. "I remember thinking it reminded me of you. The material is shot through with silver threads very much like the color of your eyes right now. I'd never received such an intimate gift before. You thrilled me with it. I loved Robert Myers with everything in me. He was exciting and dashing to an impressionable young woman who'd never been in love before. I thought I'd lost him forever." Her voice caught.

"But tonight I see him in the guise of Chase Jarvis, a man whose suffering and heroism have added stature to that other man. I love this new man, now a devoted father, with all the intensity of my soul. Somehow—I don't know how—I'm the blessed woman privileged to be loved by both men. For however long we have together, you're my heart's desire, Chase."

"And you're mine, my love."

They'd already said their vows, but her words just now wrapped right around his soul. He traced the line of her chin with his index finger. "I wish I had something from my past to give you in remembrance, but I'm afraid every possession was confiscated."

Her eyes darkened with emotion. "Since you've come back into my life I've suffered in new ways for you." Tears clogged her voice. "To think your whole identity was just wiped out—everything gone." She took a deep breath. "Wait here for a minute."

She got to her feet and disappeared. The swishing sound he found provocative because the fabric lay next to the lovely mold of her body. While he half lay there in anticipation, he finished off more rolls and a skewer of fruit.

"Close your eyes, darling." He did her bidding and felt her come closer. "Now open them."

He had no idea what to expect, but when he saw the large framed oil painting of his parents as he remembered them weeks before they died, he made a sound in his throat and wept.

"Mom and Dad know an artist who took one of my photos and reproduced it on canvas. Roberta and I made a special scrapbook for you of every picture I brought back from Kabul. She'll give it to you later, but I wanted you to have this now."

Chase pulled on a pair of sweats, then carried the painting to the couch. On the lower part of the frame was a plaque with their first names engraved. He studied their faces. Annie's gift had brought them back to him in living color. Their resurrection was almost painful in its intensity.

Robbed of words, he did the next best thing and reached

for her. They began kissing all over again. Short kisses, long kisses and everything in between until they clung in a wine-dark rapture and found their way to the mattress.

Later, after being temporarily sated, Chase got up to put more wood on the fire. It had burned down to embers. She stared up at him from beneath the quilt. "I'm so happy, I can't believe I've lived as long as I did without you."

He was beyond happy. "I don't want to think about it. All that matters is the here and now."

She reached for him. "Come and get under the covers, darling. I need you within touching distance."

"And I don't?" He growled the question playfully against her tender throat. "How come you never told me your name was Margaret? When Mark said the passenger in the downed helicopter was Margaret Anne Bower, I thought the 'Anne Bower part' had to be an uncanny coincidence, but I didn't believe it was you."

She buried her face in his bronzed neck. "My mom's mother was named Margaret. When I was young I didn't like being called that. It sounded old-fashioned to me, so I only went by Annie."

He pressed a swift kiss to her lips. "I prided myself in knowing everything about you. Until I saw you lying unconscious in the foliage, I couldn't be positive of anything."

She returned his kiss several times. "I heard your voice before I saw you and thought I was back in Kabul. The explosion had just happened and I was trying to find you."

"I know." His voice throbbed. "You called me Robert. I'm still having difficulty realizing it was you lying there too still for my heart to handle."

"Chase?" She cupped his cheeks. "Did you ask to be placed at Yosemite?"

"No. The witness protection program made all the arrangements. I had no say in the matter. I've been thinking about what we should do."

"So have I."

He studied her beautiful features, the singing curve of her red mouth. "What decision have you come to?"

"That we stay here no matter what and brave whatever comes."

"Oh Annie, if you'd said anything else—"

"How could I?" Her eyes filled. "Our life is here. We'll just have to have faith and take every precaution to stay safe. It was all meant to be."

He agreed. In the grand design he believed they'd been reunited for a reason, but to what end? How could anything be more cruel now than to be aware his life was hanging in the balance because of that piece of metal?

Annie smoothed the frown lines between his brows. "What dark thought passed through your mind just then?"

Chase caught her hand and began a nibbling foray up the arm that had been fractured. She was doubly precious to him now. "Do you have any idea how much I love you?"

"Yes," she said emotionally, "but you didn't answer my question."

He rolled her on top of him, tangling her long silken legs with his. "It was nothing, my love. Let's not talk anymore. There are other ways I want to communicate with you and I don't plan to waste a second of them."

Chase needed her with a desperation that put new fear in him. Throughout the rest of the night he found himself loving her with refined savagery, trying to make time stand still while he worshipped this woman with his whole body and soul.

EIGHT DAYS LATER Chase opened the front door to Annie's house. She rushed inside. "Roberta?"

"No," said a voice from the hallway. "It's only me." Her mom chuckled. "She's going to jump for joy to know you're back."

Annie ran toward her mother and hugged her for a long time. "How are we ever going to thank you for what you've done?"

Her mom teared up. "Seeing the two of you looking like a pair of lovesick teenagers is all the thanks I'll ever want."

"We couldn't have had the kind of honeymoon we needed if we hadn't known she was with the two people she adores." So saying, Chase engulfed Annie's mother in his arms.

"Where is she?" Annie could hardly wait to see her.

"She and your dad walked are over to the Rossiters to visit with Rachel's parents. The drove up from Oakhurst this morning to spend the weekend. I just took a pie out of the oven and was about to go over there myself."

"It smelled like heaven when we walked in."

She smiled at Chase. "Roberta told me apple was your favorite. I wanted you to have something to munch on when you got back."

Annie's husband gave her mother another squeeze. "If your daughter didn't make me so happy, we would have come home yesterday as planned. I think I'll grab myself a slice of it right now while it's hot."

He headed for the kitchen ostensibly because he was hungry, but he'd left them alone on purpose for a moment to let them catch up in private. The two women shared a knowing glance.

"You've turned him into a different man."

"I'm married to the most wonderful man alive."

"So am I. Aren't we lucky?"

"Oh, yes—we are!" Annie couldn't resist hugging her mom again. "How did Roberta handle it? Really, I mean."

"Much better than I would have supposed. Chase's decision to stay in his house made all the difference. She and Nicky have drawn close over the last week. I heard her tell your father she wouldn't mind a little brother."

Annie needed to squelch that dream right now. "Chase's injuries have made it impossible for us to conceive, Mom. I'm glad Annie likes Nicky so much because he'll be the closest thing she ever gets to a little brother."

"Oh, honey. I'm sorry."

"I am too. Chase is such a loving father, he deserves to go through the whole experience with me, but we have to be grateful he came back to us at all. And we could adopt."

"Of course." She cocked her head. "You've matured beyond belief, you know that?"

Knowing your husband could die at any time had a way of waking you up to reality, but Annie kept that painful knowledge to herself. "I recognize a miracle has happened. I'll never take it for granted."

Chase walked in on them. He flashed her mom a guilty look. "I think there's a half a pie left. It was ambrosia. I hope you don't mind."

"I'd mind if you didn't eat it."

"Let's all go over to Vance's and pick up our daughter. Where's your parka?"

"In the closet."

"I'll get it for you."

As soon as Chase helped her mom on with it, they left the house. The snowfall of a few days ago still glistened pure white. When they rounded the corner, Annie spotted the kids out in the front yard with Vance and Rachel. They'd made a snowman with a ranger's hat on top.

Wouldn't you know it was Nicky who spotted them first. "Uncle Chase! Hooray!" He jumped up and down like a crazy man and started running toward them.

Roberta just came running and passed him. Chase ran to meet her and scooped her up in his arms. He carried her to Annie and all three of them hugged. Then Nicky joined them and there were four.

Chase kissed her. "I believe you've gotten heavier while we've been gone."

"It's only been eight days, Dad."

Annie smiled to herself. Nothing got past her Roberta. The girl had been marking time.

"Was it that long?" he teased.

"Yes." She hugged him hard around the neck.

Nicky demanded to be heard. "Did you guys have fun?"

"That's what I want to know." Vance had just walked over to them, his blue eyes dancing.

Annie picked up their son and hugged him. "We had so much fun we couldn't believe it." Rachel burst into laughter.

"What did you do?"

Chase lowered Roberta to the ground and took Nicky from Annie's arms. "We played Fish and Monopoly and read books to each other."

"You did? What kind?"

"I'll tell you about them as soon as I look at your snowman." In the distance Annie could see her father with Minnie and Ted, Rachel's parents, coming down the front steps. She gripped her daughter's hand and they all headed toward it.

"Roberta and I made his stomach."

"Good job! Hey—" Chase blurted. "How did he get hold of my hat?"

Nicky burst into laughter. "It's Daddy's old one! You're funny, Uncle Chase."

Roberta smiled up at Annie. What a perfect day.

Don't think anything but perfect thoughts, Annie. Not today.

WHILE ROBERTA WAS in the tub, Annie walked Chase out to the garage. After he climbed in the cab of his truck he leaned out the window to kiss her. He didn't dare engulf her the way he wanted to or he'd never find the strength to leave.

"I'm worse than Roberta. I don't want you to go to work."

"We knew this day had to come."

"I didn't know it was going to be this hard."

"You think I did?" he said in a husky voice before opening the door so he could feel her in his arms once more.

"We're pathetic."

"We're worse than that. I'm an hour late."

"The guys will understand."

"That's the problem. I'm going to be the butt of every newlywed joke for weeks!"

Her eyes glowed. "If I can stand it, you can."

As long as she was here when he got home, he could stand anything. "If there are no emergencies, I'll be back at seven."

"Stay safe, darling." She plied a hot kiss to his mouth before backing down so he could start the engine.

He pressed the remote to the garage door and backed out. She was still standing in place when he closed it.

Through a special arrangement with Mark on the phone last night, Chase was able to wangle another day off. After a certain private discussion with his daughter, he'd decided to consult with his heart doctor in Merced.

Roberta had talked with Ted about his heart condition. She'd learned that his doctor told him his heart would never get better because the technology wasn't there to repair it. Then everything changed and a revolutionary operation had made him a new man.

After hearing that, Roberta urged Chase to have his doctor get in touch with Ted's doctor in Miami. Maybe something could be done. With so many soldiers returning from war carrying injuries like Chase's, Ted said it might be possible new surgical techniques were developing that could help.

Chase had just spent a week in paradise. He wanted it to go on. If something could be done for his heart, he was prepared to go through with it, especially with Roberta urging him. Indebted to his wonderful daughter, he drove as fast as conditions allowed to reach the clinic.

Dr. Winder's staff said they'd find a way to fit him in. He didn't mind waiting. An hour later he was shown into an examining room. When the doctor came in, Chase didn't waste any time explaining why he'd come without an appointment.

The doctor took another X-ray. With his own eyes Chase saw that the shrapnel was still in the same place.

"It's a good sign that nothing has changed, but I understand if you want to consult with another surgeon. Of course, anything's possible. Leave the information with my secretary and she'll fax your records to him today. When he's looked at the film, we'll consult and I'll get back to you."

Chase couldn't ask for more than that. He thanked the doctor and headed back to the park, still able to put in a half-day's work. Around quarter to four Roberta showed up at his office. They had a root beer and talked about his appointment with the doctor.

For the next week he led the life he'd always envied the married rangers. The three of them had decided to live in Chase's house. With everyone's help they'd started moving Annie's things in after work each evening. Before long her home would be freed up to house another ranger.

At this point Chase's house looked like a furniture store, but he'd never been happier. Once everything was accomplished, they'd drive to Oakhurst with Vance and his family. He knew a place where they could pick out dogs for the children. Life didn't get better than this.

He tried to keep his negative thoughts from surfacing. On Tuesday morning while he was in a conference with Vance and a group of rangers, his doctor's office called him. He flashed the chief a message that he had to take it and stepped out of the room to his own office.

"Chase? Dr. Winder here. This is what I've learned."

After he'd explained everything he said, "Think about it and then get back to me."

"Of course. Thank you."

While he sat there shaken by the information, Vance slipped in and shut the door. "What's going on? The look on your face wasn't normal. Is Annie all right? Roberta?"

He expelled a heavy sigh. "They're fine. This has to do with me."

"Go on—"

"Last week Roberta urged me to get another opinion about my heart, so I went for a checkup in Merced."

"*That's* why you weren't around."

Chase nodded. "A new X-ray didn't show any change, but he agreed to consult with Ted's heart surgeon in Miami."

A stillness surrounded Vance. "What was the outcome?"

"He's done half-a-dozen successful surgeries with my particular kind of injury."

Vance let out a low whistle. "What's the ratio of failure?"

"It's still experimental. If mine were to fail, they'd install a pacemaker. Of course there's always the risk of death with any surgery."

"So you have to decide whether you want to live with what you've got and wonder every day if it's going to be your last—"

"Or I can go for the surgery and take my chances. At least with a pacemaker I wouldn't have the same kind of worry unless it malfunctioned."

His friend muttered something unintelligible under his breath. "Does Annie know any of this?"

"No. I'll tell her tonight."

He threw his head back. "Just when I thought things were going to get fun around here…"

Tell me about it.

Later that evening, after they'd kissed Roberta goodnight, Chase led his wife to the living room. "Do you mind if we talk for a little while?"

She grinned. "What's the matter? Do you have a wife who's too eager and wearing you out already?"

"Yes, thank heaven!" He drew her into his arms and they sank down on the couch together.

"All right," she said, moving off his lap. "I know when there's something on your mind besides me."

They smiled at each other, but his slowly faded. "I need to tell you about something I've done." Without wasting time, he related everything. She was so quiet afterward, he picked up her hand and kissed her fingertips. "What do you think?"

An eternity passed before she said, "I think you have to do it for all our sakes. We're a family that has to take every day on faith."

THE WAITING ROOM for heart surgery patients was on the sixth floor of the hospital in Merced. Annie had been sitting there over ten hours, trying to be brave for Roberta, who was watching cartoons with Nicky. Vance and Rachel had come with them yesterday when they'd checked Vance in to get him prepped. They'd been here for her every second and had taken turns entertaining the children.

Though he was heroic himself, Vance was looking more grim with every second that passed. Due to the secrecy involved, Ted's doctor had flown out to do the surgery with Dr. Winder. Early this morning, before they'd begun giving him the anesthetic, she'd kissed her husband one more time.

"Children have God's ear," she whispered. "He's not going to fail us or our daughter now."

His eyes were the color of storm clouds outlined in silver. "You're my life. I believe it if you say it."

She fought the emotions threatening to overwhelm her. "I say it because I believe it, too."

"Annie?" he cried.

"Yes."

"I love you."

"I love you too, darling. See you this afternoon."

Except that it was early evening now. The memory of their conversation kept playing over in her mind until she wanted to scream. Rachel had brought her a sandwich and a drink, but she'd only been able to eat a portion of it.

Convinced something was wrong, she sprang to her feet and hurried out of the room toward the nursing station. She saw Dr. Winder come out of the no admission doors.

He lowered his mask. "Mrs. Jarvis? I was just coming to tell you the shrapnel was removed and Chase is going to live a long life." She almost fainted for joy. "We had a tense moment when he started hemorrhaging, but we were watching for that to happen and stanched it in time."

The tears gushed down her cheeks. "How soon can I see him?"

"He's been closely monitored all day. If everything proceeds on schedule, he'll be transferred to a private room soon. Call the nursing station at nine o'clock. They'll know where he is so you can visit him for a minute."

She nodded. "I don't know how to thank you."

He waved her off before she flew down the hall to the waiting room. Everyone got up when she appeared. "The operation was a success!" Rachel let out a cry of joy. "Chase is going to be fine!"

"Oh Mom!" Roberta launched herself at Annie, sobbing her heart out for happiness.

"Thank God," Vance whispered.

Annie repeated the same prayer in her heart.

"Mr. Jarvis?"

He turned his head toward the nurse who'd just entered his room.

"Do you feel strong enough to have a couple of visitors?"

Chase felt like cursing—he'd been waiting for his family to come for what seemed like hours—but he said simply, "Yes."

"We don't want you getting tired. They can only see you for a minute."

The suspense was killing him until he saw his precious daughter approach the side of the bed. Annie was right behind her.

"You're a sight for sore eyes, sweetheart."

"Hi, Daddy. How do you feel?"

"Wonderful."

"Mommy said your heart is all better now."

"It is, and that's because of you."

"How come?"

"For showing me what I needed to do."

"I can't wait till you come home."

"I'll be there soon."

"The nurse says I have to leave now. I love you."

"I love you more. See you tomorrow."

After the nurse walked her out, Annie drew closer. Their eyes clung, saying all the things they couldn't say aloud.

"I was told not to touch you, darling. Do you have any idea how hard that is for me after learning that you're never going to have to worry about your heart again?"

"They told me I couldn't touch you either or I might get too excited. The problem is, I can't shut off the memories of our honeymoon."

"Chase? You sound tired. I'm going to leave. The nursing station knows where to reach me. We're at a hotel around the corner. I'm only a minute away. Is there anything you need before I go?"

"Besides you?"

She made a sound that could have been a laugh or a cry. "Besides me."

"Tell the chief we're going to start having fun around here. He'll know what I mean."

"I adore you, Chase. Sweet dreams, darling."

Sweet dreams after all these years...

Who would have thought.

THE BILLIONAIRE
IN DISGUISE

BY
SORAYA LANE

Writing for Mills & Boon is truly a dream come true for **Soraya Lane**. An avid book-reader and writer since her childhood, Soraya describes becoming a published author as "the best job in the world", and hopes to be writing heart-warming, emotional romances for many years to come.

Soraya lives with her own real-life hero on a small farm in New Zealand, surrounded by animals and with an office overlooking a field where their horses graze.

For more information about Soraya and her upcoming releases visit her at her website, www.sorayalane.com, her blog, www.sorayalane.blogspot.com, or follow her at www.facebook.com/SorayaLaneAuthor

I am so fortunate to have an amazing support network, and that includes some very special author friends. From daily e-mail chats, text messages and writing sprints, it all means so much to me.
Thank you Natalie Anderson, Nicola Marsh, Yvonne Lindsay and Tessa Radley, for your constant encouragement, support and friendship.

CHAPTER ONE

JESSICA FALLS LEANED against the wooden fence and stared out at the land. She hadn't been home in almost two years, but there was nothing about her surroundings that wasn't familiar to her. The horses grazing in the fields, the smell of the pine trees, the big house behind her—they were all things ingrained in her memory that she would never forget, no matter how long she lived.

But nothing was like it used to be. She wiped away tears that had escaped from the corner of her eye, despite her best efforts to blink them away, and forced herself to turn and go back to the house. She'd only just arrived back, but instead of going straight in she'd walked around outside and done her best to ignore reality. *That she wasn't going to have to live in the house alone, that her grandfather wasn't really gone, that she hadn't just lost everything that mattered to her.*

Jessica moved slowly up the veranda steps, stopping when she reached the door and taking a deep breath. She eventually put her key in the lock and pushed the door open, listening to it creak as she stared into the dark hallway. She picked up one of her suitcases and wheeled it in behind her, moving slowly to the bottom of the stairs. It was quiet, too silent for her liking, but it was something she was going to have to get used to.

"Hello?"

She jumped and turned at the sound of a deep voice, not expecting anyone else to be on the property, let alone at her front door.

"Sorry, I didn't mean to startle you."

Jessica locked eyes with a man leaning against her doorjamb. Who the hell was he? She slipped her hand into her back pocket, feeling for her phone, ready to dial for help if she needed it.

"Ah, can I help you?" She didn't care how handsome the guy was—she didn't want company right now, and definitely not from some stranger.

"I saw you arrive before and I wanted to say hi."

Jessica stood still for a moment, silent, before she realized who he was and felt like a complete idiot. She prized her fingers from her phone and pushed her hands into her pockets instead.

"You're the guy renting the cottage, right?" she asked, wishing she hadn't glared at him like he was some kind of intruder. Her granddad's lawyer had told her all about the guest staying on the grounds, and she'd forgotten about him. "The jet lag must be getting to me."

His smile was genuine when he flashed it, his eyes crinkling ever so at the corners to match the upturn of his mouth.

"Understandable. I only knew Jock a couple of months and I'm already missing him like hell, so I can't imagine how you're feeling right now."

Jessica sighed, not ready to talk about it. She'd just traveled all the way from London without sleeping a wink, left her best horse behind without knowing if she'd ever be able to afford to bring him home, and everything was fast catching up on her. Not to mention the fact that she'd missed the funeral service of the one person in the world she really cared about, because she'd been stuck in a hospital on the other side of the world. Her granddad had been her only family since her mom had died, and she couldn't shake the feeling that she was an orphan now. And the fact she hadn't had the chance to say goodbye to him.

"Is there anything I can do for you? I'm not really sure what your arrangement was with my granddad, but you're welcome to stay for as long as you want."

It wasn't that she particularly wanted anyone hanging around, but from the information she'd received to date, she was going to need the income from the cottage just to keep paying the bills. And from what she'd heard, this guy was paying a small fortune in rent. He wasn't exactly hard to look at, either—brown eyes flecked with gold, dark hair that was a little too long and a smile that made her want to stare at his mouth way longer than she should have.

"I won't get in your way, I just wanted to say hi," he told her. "I'm Nathan."

"Jessica," she replied, holding out her hand and

pressing her palm to his. "But I'm guessing you already knew that."

"Not a day went past that Jock didn't talk about you, so yeah." He pushed his hands into his jean pockets and took a step backward. "I'll see you around, Jessica. Take care."

Jessica smiled and raised one hand in a half wave, wishing he hadn't just surprised her so soon after arriving. Any other day she'd have been better prepared, would have remembered her manners and invited him in for a coffee just like her grandfather would have, but today was tough. Today was about coming to terms with losing everything. Tomorrow she'd try to start rebuilding, and figure out how the hell she was going to save the only place that had ever been home to her. Trouble was, she was used to being a loner, so it was weird having someone she didn't know staying on the property.

She watched him go, the casual way he sauntered off toward the stables, hands still thrust in his pockets, as if he didn't have a worry in the world. Everything felt like it was crashing around her, but she had to stay strong, needed to hold herself together, because that was what her granddad would have expected, and she didn't want to let him down.

Nathan Bell gave the horse a pat and dropped to the ground, nudging his hat down lower over his head, crossing his ankles and shutting his eyes. The sun was warm but not too hot, and he was feeling lazy as hell. He knew Patch wouldn't walk off on him, and he just needed to try to catch up on some sleep. Since Jock had died, his insomnia had come back, and right now he was beat.

He was always worse at night, the memories of finding his wife, the weight of what had happened, always seeking him out in the dark. During the day, he usually managed to keep them at bay, but forgetting what had happened was impossible.

He'd just drifted off, was falling into the sleep he'd been craving, when he received a sharp kick in the leg.

"Ouch!"

"What the hell do you think you're doing?"

Nathan pushed his hat up and found himself staring straight up at Jessica. What the hell was *he* doing? What the hell was *she* doing? Her eyes looked wild, face mad as hell. At least it took his mind off his nightmares.

"I was sleeping, but I'm guessing you already figured that out," he said, drawing one of his legs up and rubbing the spot where she'd kicked him. He had no idea what he'd done to make her so angry between now and when he'd met her.

"I mean what the hell are you doing here? And with my granddad's horse?"

She was seriously pissed with him, that much was obvious, and he doubted he was going to get back to sleep anytime soon. Nathan tried not to smile—she'd looked pretty when he'd met her at the house, even with her tearstained cheeks, but she was gorgeous as sin all fired up and angry.

"Jock used to bring me here, as soon as he'd taught me to ride," Nathan told her, wishing she'd back a step up instead of standing over him and glaring like he'd just stolen something from her. "And the last few weeks before he passed away he wasn't up to riding, so he asked me to take Patch out for him."

"I don't believe you." Her tone was cool as ice.

Nathan wasn't going to engage, not when she was so mad with him. He stood up, reaching for her hand then stopping when she snatched it away before he even came close to connecting with her.

"I know that you're hurting right now, but I'm not the one you should be angry at. I get that this was a special spot for you and Jock, because he told me so, and if he were here right now he'd tell you himself that you're acting crazy. We rode up here almost every day together."

A look passed over her face that he couldn't read, but the anger disappeared from her eyes like a light going out. He understood that the place was special to her—the wooded hill area tucked away from the rest of the property was like a little slice of paradise hidden away from the world. *Somewhere she was obviously used to enjoying in privacy.* But he hadn't done anything wrong, and grieving or not, he wasn't going to let her take it out on him. If there was one thing her granddad had taught him, it was that just because you were grieving you didn't have leave to behave badly.

"He told you that?" Her voice was softer now. "That it was our special place?"

SORAYA LANE   13

"Yeah, he did," Nathan replied. "Now why don't you sit down and we can talk, if you're done being angry with me?"

She didn't apologize but she did look guilty, and he wasn't going to rub salt into open wounds. He knew what it was like to lose someone.

"I didn't think anyone else had been here, which I guess is kind of stupid," Jessica said, wiping the corners of her eyes as she sat down across from him amongst the pine needles. "We started coming here when I was a girl, and it was kind of our thing. He always rode Patch, and I was on my old pony, Whiskers."

Nathan nodded, sitting down beside her and stretching his legs back out. He watched as she grimaced, obviously trying to make herself comfortable, but he didn't say anything.

"I hear you had a pretty good hideout, too. Something about a fort that you thought your mom never knew about up in the trees."

Jessica met his gaze, laughed softly and shook her head. "Now I know you're not lying," she said, "because I still believe that no one else knew about *that* little hideaway."

He held his hand to his chest. "Cross my heart, I won't tell another soul."

She leaned back and stared at the horses, and Nathan did the same.

"Patch must be so old now. He was perfect for my granddad, like they understood exactly what the other was thinking. I've never seen anyone else ride him, not ever." She sighed. "That's why it hit me so bad, seeing you. He's been on the farm since I was a little girl."

Nathan chuckled. "Yeah, which is why he's perfect for me. He's content just to take things slow and teach a newbie the ropes." He paused, watched her, wished he didn't feel so uncomfortable being so close to her. "We came up here a lot, the two of us, just to ride and chat, talk about anything and everything. It was as good for me as it was for the old man."

Jessica groaned when she turned to her side, and he waited a second before saying anything more. It was none of his business, but he'd heard so much about her, knew about what had happened, and she was clearly in pain. Jock had been a good friend to him, a mentor, and he missed him more than she could ever imagine. Which meant that he wanted to help Jessica, if he could get past his own demons long enough to do so.

"Sounds like you were close friends. I shouldn't have reacted so badly. I'm sorry."

Nathan frowned at the grimace she was sporting. "From what Jock said, you're supposed to be resting for the next few months, right? As in no getting back in the saddle?" Maybe he wasn't so good at keeping his thoughts to himself.

Jessica didn't shoot him the dagger-filled look he'd been expecting, but she did meet his gaze. "It's stupid, I know, but I just needed to get out in the fresh air and ride. Take it easy, just not in the way my doctor prescribed."

"It's not stupid to want to ride, but you need to let

your body heal." He paused. "After what you went through…"

"You know all about my fall? What happened?" she asked.

He nodded. There was no point pretending otherwise. "The whole country knows all about it. They played the footage from the Badminton Horse Trials over and over on the news, the headlines were screaming about the downfall of New Zealand's eventing golden girl and the best horse this country has ever produced."

Fresh tears were visible in her eyes now, ready to fall. Maybe a simple yes would have been enough— he knew how much she loved her horse, from what Jock had told him, and the equine's career was most definitely over, forever, even if hers wasn't.

"And now my horse is stuck back in the UK, and I'm all useless and back here on my own." Her voice was barely a whisper. "I wish I'd never taken him over, that I'd just campaigned a European horse. I know it sounds stupid, but he's the most incredible animal and I miss him.'

"Is there anything I can do to help?"

Jessica shrugged and stood up, grimacing as she moved. Nathan jumped to his feet and held out a hand to help her, which she took, taking a moment to steady herself. The warm touch of her palm gliding into place alongside his took him by surprise, even though he was the one to initiate it.

"Just a leg up into the saddle would be great," she told him, stopping to give Patch a pat before reaching for the reins of her own mount. "God only knows if I'll ever be able to get up from the ground again on my own."

Nathan bent and took her knee into his palm, counted to three then hoisted her up in the air. She landed gracefully in the saddle, her back beautiful and straight despite how much pain she must have been in. He knew she'd had a back injury, as well as doing some pretty major damage to one of her legs, but he didn't want to pry.

"Nathan, I'm sorry for the way I acted before. I'm not usually so horrible."

He chuckled. "Good, because otherwise I'd have to think your grandfather was a liar. He made you out to be the perfect granddaughter."

Jessica laughed and he found himself grinning straight back at her. There was something so broken about her, so fragile, but at the same time seeing her sit up there in the saddle showed how strong she was, too. She was torn apart, emotionally and physically, but definitely not broken. *Kind of like him.* Only being around her was forcing him to come out of his shell, to be the stronger one, when recently he'd felt so lost, so weak.

"What's that old saying about rose-tinted glasses?" she asked, still smiling.

Nathan laughed. "Mind if I ride back down with you, or do you want some time alone?"

"Sure thing. It's about time I started saying yes to company instead of pretending like I'm better off on my own."

Nathan tried to mount as gracefully as he could and failed terribly, but thankfully Jessica was either too polite to say anything or she actually hadn't noticed. He might be able to *stay* in the saddle, but that was about the extent of it.

"Not bad getting to ride alongside world eventing's number two rider," he joked.

"Well it's a title I'm fast going to lose, so you'd better take the chance while you can."

She was attempting to make fun of what happened, he got that, but he knew she was heartbroken over the accident. Jock had opened up to him about a lot of things, especially about Jessica, and he knew he had to tread carefully. The only thing her grandfather hadn't made clear was how beautiful she was in real life—the photos in the media didn't do her justice. Every time he'd seen her interviewed she'd either been wearing a helmet or had her hair pulled back into a tight bun, dressed in formal riding attire. But with her long blond hair loose, and wearing jeans and a T-shirt, she looked like a different woman. Only he had to keep reminding himself who she was, that she was Jock's granddaughter. Nathan wasn't ready for anything more than a bit of fun, and that wasn't a category that Jessica Falls belonged in. Not ever. If he hadn't been so close to her grandfather, he would have let that be her decision, but it wasn't. Jock had been too important to him, which meant he wasn't going to even think about Jessica like that.

And the truth was, Nathan didn't know if he'd ever be able to commit to any kind of relationship again after what had happened to his wife, which meant nothing could ever happen between them. But it had been a while since he'd had any female company whatsoever, and Jessica wasn't exactly hard to be around, or to look at, even if she was grieving. And looking was entirely different from letting anything happen.

CHAPTER TWO

"So TELL ME what you're doing in New Zealand."

Jessica slowly rubbed her horse down, paying careful attention to brushing his sweat marks. She would usually have been more vigorous, but her back was starting to ache and she didn't want to push her body too hard, especially since the most strenuous activity she was supposed to be doing was moving from the sofa to the kitchen. The pain was bearable most of the time, unless she overdid it, and then it would hit her like a ton of bricks.

She glanced over at Nathan, watching as he stroked Patch's face. The horse was leaning in to him like they were old friends, and she felt terrible all over again for being so rude to him when she'd found him on the trail. She'd had no right to accuse him of...she didn't even know what.

"I needed some time out from my job and I'd heard how beautiful it was here," he said, looking up but still scratching Patch.

"So you just jumped on a plane and ended up in New Zealand?"

He chuckled. "Yeah, something like that."

She'd been joking, but it seemed she wasn't far off the mark. "So is it everything it's made out to be?"

Nathan put down the brush he'd been holding and walked out of the box stall. "I did the whole touristy thing when I first arrived, but then I found this place a few months ago and I still haven't left."

Jessica untied her horse and nodded to Nathan to do the same with Patch.

"So you've been holed up here with just an old man and some horses for company?" she joked.

Nathan laughed. "Something like that. I've been working my way through a stack of DVD's, staying out of trouble."

"Sounds like exactly what I need to be doing."

"Says the woman who's out riding horses instead of resting up on doctor's orders."

She smiled as they walked through the barn leading the horses out into the open. It was nice to just chat with someone, feel relaxed, even if she did feel guilty for being happy without her granddad around. Her emotions were all over the show right now, and so was her mood, but there was something about Nathan that was drawing her to him.

After letting the horses loose and watching them trot across the field, Jessica and Nathan walked side by side in the direction of the barn again, and Jessica slung her halter and lead rope over her shoulder. At least being home had calmed her, made her feel connected to something again. She was always more settled when she was around horses.

"So it's a different pace of life for you here?" she asked.

"Yeah, you could say that." He looked across at her, his expression more serious, the smile that had braced his lips earlier completely gone. "I had a job I thought I loved, but I was so caught up in working every waking hour that I lost sight of what was important."

Jessica sensed a sadness within him, something that she couldn't quite figure out. There had to be a reason he'd flown halfway across the world, just leaving behind whatever he had in the UK, which meant she was either right about him hurting, or he'd done something he regretted. Or maybe she was just overthinking the whole situation.

"What type of work did you do?" Jessica asked.

"I was a banker," he said. "I managed a private hedge fund, and I was more married to my work than I was to..." His voice trailed off. "To anything else in my life."

She waited for him to continue but he didn't, leaving her wondering exactly what he was referring to.

"Are you expecting anyone?" he asked.

Jessica glanced toward the driveway, saw an unfamiliar black vehicle approaching the house. *Great*.

"I have a feeling that's the lawyer," she said, fighting the urge to get back on a horse and flee in the opposite direction. "Which means I have to face up to reality instead of hiding away for the next few days." She hadn't expected him to turn up on her doorstep quite so promptly—a day to settle in would have been nice.

"Anything I can do?" The concern in Nathan's voice was matched by his gaze, his bright blue eyes telling her that he genuinely cared.

"How about you come over for a drink tonight." The words left her mouth before she'd even had a moment to think.

The worry lines turned into smile wrinkles when he looked at her this time. "Why don't I grab something for us to eat and bring it over? You can't have much in the pantry, and I doubt you'll have time to get groceries. Lawyers take forever to go over wills."

Jessica braved a smile. It wasn't the will she was worried about—she knew her granddad had left her everything—it was the debts she'd inherited that the lawyer would be wanting her to deal with. Debts he'd been more than eager to contact her about even when she'd been in hospital.

But she did kind of want to see Nathan again. "Dinner sounds great." Her stomach was rumbling just at the thought of food, even though she'd hardly been interested in eating since her accident, and then since Jock had died.

Nathan touched her shoulder, tentatively, his touch light, as if he wasn't sure if it was the right thing to do or not. "Don't let him push you around, and if you need a sounding board, I'm right here."

"Thanks," she said, fighting the urge to shrug his hand away and at the same time wishing he'd never take it off her.

"Your granddad and I talked about everything,

so if you need someone, it's not an empty offer." He smiled at her. "You can trust me."

Jessica wanted to know more, wanted to know why and how he'd become so close to her only family member in the months before he'd died, but now wasn't the time. Tonight she'd try to find out everything she needed to know.

"See you around six?" she asked.

Nathan nodded and withdrew his hand, shoving it in his pocket instead and leaving her wishing he was still touching her, that the heat from his palm was still resting on her shoulder. He might be a stranger, but the physical contact had been oddly comforting.

"See you then," he called out.

Jessica walked briskly toward the house, eyes trained on the man now standing at her front door, waiting. She didn't know why, but she had a strange feeling about the lawyer she'd only ever spoken to on the phone. It was an uneasy notion, a niggle of worry in her mind that she couldn't shake, and she needed to forget all about her curiosity about Nathan and focus on her granddad's state of affairs.

The farm meant everything to her, and if it came to it she wasn't going to give up the property without one hell of a fight. It was her last tie to her family—to her mom and now her granddad—and that made it the most important thing in her life.

"So you're telling me that my only option is to sell this place?"

Jessica stared at the lawyer, listening to what he

was saying but finding it almost impossible to process. She was trying hard not to cry, refusing to admit that there was no other option, but from what he was saying it was almost impossible *not* to admit defeat. Her entire body was numb.

"Your granddad didn't make the wisest decisions over the past year, Ms. Falls. I'm sorry to be the bearer of bad news."

His tone was grave, but he hardly met her gaze, wouldn't hold eye contact for more than a moment and she didn't like him at all now. She also didn't believe that Jock would have left her in such a bad financial position, that the man she'd spent her entire life looking up to could have lost so much in such a short time. It just wasn't right, especially given how cautious and successful he'd been in the past.

"And you're certain there hasn't been, I don't know, some sort of mistake? That there isn't other property or money?" She stood, fidgeting too much to stay seated. "There must be something, or at least some sort of explanation."

Jessica turned to look out the window, looking at the land that she was going to be forced to part with. She had nothing—no job, no future doing what she'd trained for her entire life, and now no inheritance. Every horse, every blade of grass, *everything* about the farm meant more to her than she could ever explain to anyone. Except for her granddad. He'd turn in his grave if he knew she was being forced to sell, which was why nothing about this situation seemed right to her.

"Ms. Falls?"

She was about to turn, to focus her attention back on the lawyer, when a movement caught her eye. *Nathan.* Her mysterious guest was crossing the yard, heading for her back door rather than the main front one, and he was carrying two large brown paper bags. She smiled for the first time since she'd stepped inside. If anyone could help her understand what had happened in the weeks and months before her granddad had passed, it was Nathan. She knew they'd been close, and from what she'd learned today, they'd spent a lot of time together.

"I need a few days to process all this," Jessica said as she turned, squaring her shoulders and staring the lawyer straight in the eyes. She could have been imagining it, but she was certain he looked uncomfortable.

"My advice would be to list the property for sale immediately and consider how to mitigate your losses."

She gave a curt nod and planted her hands on the desk, the coolness of the oak beneath her palms helping to calm her, taking strength from the piece of furniture she'd so often seen her grandfather sit behind.

"Once again, I appreciate your advice, but I'll be taking a few days to consider my options."

The more she could find out from Nathan, the better. But that wasn't the only reason she wanted to see him. There was something about the man that intrigued her, something unassuming about the stranger who'd befriended her granddad that made her want to know more. He was hiding something behind his quiet smile, she just knew it, and she wanted to know what it was.

"I'll see myself out," she heard the lawyer mutter, clearly frustrated with her. He'd probably expected her to admit defeat and sign anything he waved in front of her.

Jessica squared her shoulders, even though her back ached from simply standing so straight after she'd been on her feet all day. Men like this lawyer might think she was weak, that she'd been through so much recently that she'd lost her strength, but mentally she was more determined than ever. To get back in the saddle—which she'd already done—to compete again one day, and most of all to make her grandfather proud and continue his legacy. So she wasn't going to let this lawyer, or any other man, walk all over her. She'd made her mind up years ago that she was in charge of her own destiny, and she needed to hold on to that belief no matter what life threw her way.

"How long did you say you'd been working for Jock?" she asked, her tone cool.

He stopped, briefcase clasped in one hand, the other fisted at his side. She didn't trust him at all. Her grandfather hadn't acquired this farm and a handful of commercial investments without being smart.

"Ah, for some time now. I'd have to consult my records to be absolutely certain."

She nodded and watched him leave. If her intuition was right, she shouldn't trust this man or anyone else until she'd figured out what her grandfather's state of mind had been before he died. If there was one thing he'd taught her, it was to trust only herself in life.

Nathan had seen Jessica in the office when he'd walked past, but he hadn't acknowledged her, instead letting himself in and sitting in the kitchen so he wasn't disturbing her. The oversize wooden table was bathed in sunlight, and he was nursing a beer when Jessica finally walked in to join him. He'd thought about not turning up, or leaving a note with the take-out food and leaving, but he'd made himself stay. It was time to start facing up to reality and stop hiding away, even if that did seem like mission impossible to him right now.

"I hope you don't mind," he said, raising the glass bottle.

Her smile reminded him of a look his wife had once given him, years ago, when they'd first met, and it surprised him by making him smile straight back at her. She looked a combination of exhausted and determined, but she also looked happy to see him.

"You can drink the lot," she told him, opening and shutting the fridge, then disappearing from sight. She reemerged with a bottle of wine. "This is more my taste."

He watched as she searched a few drawers for an opener.

"I think you'll find it's a screw top," he said in a low voice, grimacing when she glared at him.

"You've got to be kidding me." Jessica frowned then shook her head. "I can't even open a bottle of wine. This is definitely not my day. Un-freaking-be-lievable."

Nathan jumped up, leaving his beer on the table, and leaned over the counter to take the bottle from her. Her determined look had been replaced with one that verged on defeated, and he didn't like it. Whatever the lawyer had said had really taken it out of her. He knew what defeated felt like, and it wasn't an emotion he wanted her to experience.

"Bad meeting?" he asked.

"The worst," she admitted, turning away only to reach for a glass. She set it on the counter. "I've basically spent the last couple of hours listening to some idiot lawyer try to tell me that the one person I admired most in the world, who's looked after me my entire life, had lost his marbles. Either that or he wasn't the astute investor I believed him to be—only I don't buy that theory for a second."

"That's rubbish," Nathan shot straight back, anger flaring within him. "I might have only known Jock a short time, but he was as sharp as a tack right to the end. That makes both theories impossible."

"Really?" Jessica asked, taking the glass of wine he'd poured and taking a long, slow sip. "Do you honestly believe that? You're not just saying it to make me feel better?"

Nathan shook his head and moved back to the table, motioning for her to join him. Her gold-flecked eyes were wide again, locked on his as she crossed the room and sat across from him. She tucked her long hair behind her ears, one hand on the glass, the other palm down on the table. He forced himself to glance away, out the window, to stop from staring. There was no denying she was beautiful, even if he was trying not to think about her like that—she was strikingly feminine yet at the same time fiercely strong. And something about that drew him to her as much as it made him want to walk straight out the door.

"Jock was old, but his memory never wavered. We must have spent hours talking every day, and if we weren't just shooting the breeze talking, he was teaching me about horses," he told her.

She sighed and took another sip. "So you're telling me I shouldn't believe the lawyer? That I could be right?"

"I'm telling you that you need to trust yourself." Nathan leaned forward and nudged the bags of food in Jessica's direction. "So how about we eat and you tell me what this so-called lawyer's been saying." He was pleased they had something to focus on while they ate—it took some of the pressure off.

Her gaze shifted, moving to the takeout he'd brought. "How many dishes did you order?"

Nathan grinned straight back at her. "I had no idea what you liked, so I went for Chinese and chose a little of everything."

Jessica was still smiling when she started poking around, taking cartons out and looking inside. "I'm thinking we'll both have enough leftovers to keep us in food for a week."

He liked her easy smile, the way she'd gone from not trusting him to confiding in him, and it was as if he already knew her. After hearing so much about her from Jock, he'd been wanting to meet her, and that was before he'd realized how gorgeous she would be. Not to mention he'd been expecting someone a little more...broken. Jessica might be in pain, might have almost died and ended her career, but she didn't look anything close to broken to Nathan. The fiery blonde was all bent out of shape over whatever the lawyer had said to her, and he wanted to know more. Because if he could help, there was nothing he wouldn't do, not when it meant helping the granddaughter of the man who'd brought him back from the brink and made him believe he at least had a future ahead of him. He had a long way to go, but life wasn't as dark as it had seemed when he'd first arrived.

She held up the throwaway chopsticks and broke them apart then pulled a lid off one dish, expertly helping herself to noodles like she was as used to using them as he was a knife and fork.

"So what do you think of this place?"

Her question took him by surprise. "I wouldn't have stayed so long if I didn't love it."

Her sigh made him look up, forgetting what he'd been about to eat.

"Why?" he asked.

She met his gaze, eyes dull as she opened her mouth to answer him. He tried not to stare at her lips, at the way they moved when she blew out a breath.

"Because from what the lawyer's telling me, it'll

be on the market before the end of the month, so I might need a buyer. You interested?"

He put down his chopsticks. "You're serious?" He'd realized things were bad, that Jock's affairs obviously hadn't been left in order, but to sell the place?

"Deadly," she answered straight back.

He had no idea what to say. "You're sure that's something you have to consider?"

"Honestly?" She shook her head, tears making her big brown eyes look like they were swimming. "I hope not, but from what I heard tonight I don't know what else I'll be able to do."

Nathan picked up a spring roll between his fingers and dipped it in sauce, slowly eating it as he digested her words.

"If it comes to selling, if it's what you have to do, I'll buy the place myself."

She laughed. "Yeah, right."

Nathan cleared his throat and looked up, not wanting to sound arrogant but needing her to know it wasn't an empty offer. That he could buy it tomorrow and come up with the cash immediately if he had to. "I'm serious."

Her laughter died, the uneasy smile wiped from her face. She studied him, eyes no longer full of tears—her gaze was serious now. "You could actually buy this place, just like that?" she asked.

He shrugged, not wanting to make a big deal out of it. A year ago, hell, a few months ago, he'd have had no problem letting anyone know what he could afford, but since coming here…he just didn't want to be that guy anymore. Staying on the farm had given him the break he'd needed, and it had also given him a fresh start, even if he was going to have to face reality and head home one day soon.

"Yeah, I could. But if I did I'd need a manager, so there's no chance I'd evict you."

Jessica smiled, but he knew she wasn't sure what to say or how to take his words.

"But it won't come to that, so don't even worry," he assured her.

She took another mouthful of noodles and nodded, but he sensed the change in her, as if she was suddenly viewing him as a stranger when before she'd treated him like an ally. Money attracted a lot of women—the wrong women—but he doubted Jessica fell into that category, even if she was desperate for an injection of cash to save her assets. If she did, her eyes would have lit up, her smile would have become wider—he knew all the signs—and yet she'd looked more alarmed than anything else. She could just be good at hiding her emotions, but she'd been so honest about her grief that he doubted it.

"So you said you're a banker, when you're not traveling?"

"I was, back in London," he said, taking the lid off another dish. "I managed a private hedge fund."

"Ahh, I see," she said, like finding out what he did told her everything she needed to know.

It felt like a lifetime ago to him, and in some ways it was. The guy he was here was nothing like the man he'd been for most of his adult life.

"So will you go back? To being a banker?"

It was something he'd thought about a lot lately, and he still wasn't sure. "That life took everything from me," he said, pushing the memories away that were trying to claw their way back in, the memories that so often took hold of him and refused to give him any relief. "I need to go back at some point, but right now I'm happy pretending to be someone else."

The smile she gave him this time lit her eyes again, as if she was happy with his answer. "So does the person you are here have time to help me figure out what the hell happened to my inheritance?"

Nathan grinned. It had been a long time since he'd hung out and chatted to a beautiful woman—he couldn't even recall the last time he'd chilled out and eaten take-out food with his wife. This was the type of evening he'd missed out on over the past decade, what he'd thought was overrated. Now he knew otherwise. And it had also been a while since he'd been able to really use his brain, and if he was honest with himself he kind of missed that part of his old life.

"It just so happens that I'm great with numbers, so if you need me to look at any transactions, bank accounts, anything, I'm your guy."

At times like this, he knew his old lifestyle hadn't been worth what he'd lost, the memories he'd have to live with for the rest of his life. He'd tried so hard to have everything, and all he'd done was lose what he'd spent years striving for. Jessica was like a breath of fresh air, even if she was in need of his help. So long as he kept reminding himself that she could be only a friend, he'd be just fine. Because not only was she Jock's granddaughter, she was also an attractive woman, and part of being away from home was about keeping his life complication free.

Jessica was vulnerable right now, and he wasn't going to take advantage of that. Although if there was something he could do to help her, he would. "So tell me what the lawyer said."

She rolled her eyes and took another mouthful before leaning back in her chair, anger taking over her face again.

"You know, when I met you earlier, I told myself to be nice to you because you were a paying guest."

He chuckled, curious. "And now?"

Her dark eyes locked on his. "Now?" she shrugged. "Now I think that I was a little harsh. I can't be an island forever."

"An island?" He had no idea what she was talking about, but she had a great knack of taking his mind from his thoughts.

"Let's just say that I usually keep to myself. I've always been a loner."

Nathan didn't know if she was just being friendly or if she was flirting with him. He'd been married for half of his twenties and part of his thirties, and even if he hadn't been he'd worked almost every waking hour since he'd graduated, which meant he'd been out of the game for way too long. So darn long that he couldn't even figure out if Jessica was interested or just being friendly.

"For the record, I'm pleased you've given up the whole island thing."

She laughed. "Yeah?"

So much for not flirting. He'd even managed to throw a dumb joke in there, or at least his pitiful attempt at a joke.

"So tell me what it's like being a banker," she asked between mouthfuls.

Nathan refused to be drawn back into the past, to let himself think too much about what she'd just asked him. But Jessica knew nothing about what had happened; she was just asking an innocent question. It wasn't her fault that just the mention of his past brought back memories so vivid, a gut-wrenching pain so deep, that it seemed like he could choke just trying to breath.

"In my first year one of the other interns died from staying awake almost 24/7 and working insane hours," he told her, watching as her jaw physically dropped, mouth gaping open. "The poor guy was so fatigued, had worked a few days straight, and he had a heart attack."

"You're kidding me. Please tell me you're kidding."

"I wish I was," he said with a grimace. "The kind of industry I was in, it took a lot from plenty of us, but the game of what we do is so addictive that sometimes it takes something pretty major to jolt us out."

Her eyebrows bunched together as she stared at him. "And a young guy dying didn't alert you to the kind of job you were getting yourself into *before* you'd committed?"

Nathan shrugged. It was something he'd asked himself so many times after he'd lost his wife, but he knew the answer. The truth was that nothing could have made him give up his job back then—the money had been too good and he'd loved what he did each day—until he'd found his wife. He blinked a few times in fast succession, as if it would make the memories magically disappear. And the way his family were, their expectations; they had almost made his career decision for him. But he wasn't about to talk to her about his family, because that would be going back in time to something else he was only too happy to forget.

"That's why I'm here," he told her. "It took me a while, years, but I finally realized that there was a life for me away from Mayfair. I just had to leave London to figure that out." *If only it hadn't taken him so long.* "I lost someone I loved, and it made me rethink—" he paused "—everything. But I know that if I was twenty-one all over again, nothing anyone could have said to me would have made a difference."

Jessica's face was soft, her expression kind as she watched him. "Sometimes it takes losing what we love to show us how much that person or thing meant to us in the first place," she said, her voice low, almost husky. "I've spent my entire life looking up to the world's best riders, and then when I finally achieved my dreams I lost everything."

He didn't know what to tell her, because nothing he could say would change how she felt. He still hadn't come to terms with what had happened to him, which meant there was no way in hell she would in the near future, either.

"I bet every second person tells you that it'll get better. That you'll learn to deal with what's happened."

Jessica slowly nodded, running her fingertips across the wooden surface of the table. "The only way I'll come to terms with what happened to me is when I'm out competing again."

He sensed there was something else, that she was holding something back. Jessica was staring past him; he guessed she was looking through the window even though the light was fading fast and it was almost dark. She was keeping secrets, just like he was.

"And then there's Teddy."

Nathan knew instantly who she was talking about, because he'd read all the news stories about her when it had happened. She hadn't mentioned her horse, so he hadn't asked, but from the way she was biting down on her bottom lip, tears glinting in her eyes, he was guessing the outcome wasn't good.

"Did he, ah, recover from his injuries in the end?" He tried not to grimace, worried he'd said the wrong thing and not wanting to upset her.

Jessica poured herself another glass of wine, sighing and taking a large sip before looking back up. "I'll never be able to compete him again, but he means the world to me, Nathan. He deserves a retirement here on the farm, going for a ride every now and again if he's not too stiff, or even just being in the field with a few of the youngsters to keep them company." Her voice was shaky. "I just want him with me."

"So where is he?"

Her eyebrows pulled together, frustration clear on her face. "He's still stuck in the UK. I don't know if I'll ever be able to raise the money to bring him back now, which means I'll—" she closed her eyes for a moment, taking a visibly deep breath "—have to have him put down. He's worthless to anyone else, and I won't be able to afford the livery for long, if at all."

Nathan could feel her pain, could see how upset she was talking about an animal she so clearly loved. He reached for her across the table, covered her hand with his before even thinking about what he was doing. Nathan squeezed her fingers, wondering what the hell he was doing as he looked into her eyes. It was almost painful just touching her, connecting with another human being, but he forced himself not to pull away.

"How much do you need to fly him home?" he asked.

She shifted her hand beneath his but didn't remove it. "Too much," she replied, voice soft.

Nathan slowly took his fingers from hers, sliding them away and reaching for his beer. But that wasn't why he'd withdrawn—her skin, so soft and warm, was making him think how much he wanted to keep touching her. How much he'd missed being with a woman, or even just being close to any other person.

"Find out how much and I'll take care of it."

Her eyes went wide, round like saucers. "No." She shook her head like she was trying to convince herself otherwise. "Absolutely not."

"Why not?" If it meant that much to her, he'd pay the bill without a second thought. "Your granddad meant a lot to me, so just think of it as my way of repaying him."

"No matter how much he did for you, he wouldn't let you spend thirty grand on bringing a retired horse home."

Nathan chuckled and raised an eyebrow. "I thought you didn't know how much it cost."

She shrugged. "That's the rough price, but honestly? There's no way I could ever afford it, not now, and I'm not taking handouts from anyone." Jessica sighed. "Besides, this place won't even be here then. I'm going to have to sell, which means I won't even have somewhere to keep him or any of the others. I have to face the cold, hard facts."

Nathan stared long and hard at the grim set of her mouth and the sad look in her eyes. It was almost like looking at a reflection of himself, of the way he felt so often. "Look, if you want him back I'll pay, no strings attached. And I want to make it clear that I'll buy Patch if it comes to that, and I'll pay for somewhere nice to stable him if I need to, for as long as he needs it."

Jessica's expression changed, her eyes soft, the faintest lines appearing at the corners as she smiled at him. "Thank you," she said. "That old horse means a lot to me, too."

Nathan resisted the urge to reach for her again, but the way she was looking at him made it almost impossible. There was something about being in New

Zealand that had changed his outlook, made him appreciate the more simple things he'd taken for granted most of his life, but until now he'd also appreciated the time on his own. Or maybe he'd just been terrified of ever letting anyone close again. Now? He knew he'd been traveling solo for long enough, but even the thought of Jessica's beautiful smile didn't make it easier for him to think about…what? He didn't even know what. He only knew that he liked her, and that she made him want to push past what had been holding him back for so long.

"So you'd let me buy him?"

"If it comes to that, yes." This time her smile was determined instead of kind when she flashed it. "But I like to win my own battles, Nathan, and that means I don't want to be anyone's charity case."

From the look on her face she'd been offended by his offer when all he'd been trying to do was help. "So I can help you with one horse, but not the other?" He should have kept his mouth shut but the words just slipped out before he could help it.

"The difference is that you genuinely like Patch. He means a lot to you and you're attached to him. But if I let you help me with Teddy then I'd owe you a debt I could never repay." She laughed, but it was more of a nervous chuckle. "Besides, I've never wanted to be some rich man's bought-and-paid-for mistress."

This time he should have said something, but he only stared at her. All his life he'd been surrounded by people impressed by wealth, seen women flock to

rich men, and here Jessica was rebuffing him immediately *because* of his money. *Money she desperately
needed.* It shouldn't have mattered to him, but something about her words only made him more intrigued.
Made him want to help her all the more, a challenge
that he couldn't ignore. And a challenge that made
him forget all about his demons, at least for the moment. Or maybe it was the comment about being his
mistress that had shocked him into forgetting.

"You know, I think we kind of got off track," he
finally said, breaking the silence.

She only raised her eyebrows in response.

"Tonight was supposed to be about cheap and
cheerful food and a few drinks," he continued.

"And you helping me solve the mystery of my
grandfather's demise," she added, smile back on her
face.

"Let me look through all Jock's paperwork in the
morning," Nathan suggested, wanting an excuse to
see her again as much as he wanted to help. "If there's
one thing I can do, it's figure out if anyone's swin-
dled the old man."

Jessica held up her now half-empty wine glass.
"I'll drink to that."

Nathan raised his beer bottle and met her stare,
surprised that she held his gaze instead of looking
away. Earlier in the day she'd hardly been able to
look at him, had seemed more annoyed than anything
that he'd stopped by to introduce himself, and now
her smile alone was warming a part of him that had

been cold for the better part of the last year. A part of him that he'd thought would never heal.

"So tell me about this gorgeous old horse of yours," he said.

"Hey, who're you calling old?"

Jessica stood at the door and watched as Nathan walked slowly backward. She raised her hand in a wave, before crossing both arms over her chest, more for comfort than for the cold. It was weird spending time with someone who knew so much about her, but who was essentially still a stranger. Weird but nice at the same time.

"Thanks for coming over," she said, leaning against the doorjamb

Nathan stopped, hands pushed into his pockets. "So tomorrow we start investigating?" he asked.

"Maybe we should go for a ride," she suggested, liking the idea of anything that meant she got to spend extra time with him.

"Sounds good. I'll see you tomorrow."

She stared after him, watching as he went part way down the drive before crossing over the lawn and heading for the cottage. So much for wishing she didn't have a guest to deal with. Spending time with Nathan had pulled her from her own miserable thoughts, stopped her from wallowing in what had happened and what could happen in the near future. And it had made her more determined.

Jessica shut the door and headed for the kitchen, sighing as she looked at the table where they'd been sitting. There wasn't much to clean up, just a couple of beer bottles, the take-out containers and her wineglass, and then she needed to head to bed. Although no matter how tired she was, the jet lag making her entire body fatigued, she knew sleep wouldn't come easily. Not tonight.

As she collected the bottles and put them in her recycling container, she thought of Nathan, and then her granddad. One man was making her body tingle, making her wish she'd never been so snappy with him earlier in the day, and the other...he was making her worry. Worry about losing the last thing in her life that truly meant something to her. She'd grown up without her dad, but Jock had been the only male role model she'd ever needed. Her mom had been amazing one moment and downbeat the next, and she tried so hard not to think about her sometimes, because it only brought back memories of losing her. Of what had happened. How traumatic her death had been.

Jessica pushed the thoughts away and left the kitchen, deciding to finish cleaning up in the morning, and headed for the stairs. She looked up, ready to collapse into bed when a sliver of light caught her eye. She'd left the light on in the office by mistake, but she took it as a sign.

Jessica looked up the stairs one last time, groaned then padded barefoot to the office, stretching her back as she walked. She might be tired, but she was also on the cusp of losing the farm. She had the rest of her life to sleep and only a short time to save what she loved. She just had to remember to make time for her exercises, because if she let her back seize up and not heal, she'd become too stiff to ever get back in the saddle again. And a life without riding would be a life not worth living.

CHAPTER THREE

JESSICA GRIMACED AS SHE stretched her body out, holding the yoga pose even though it was killing her. She pushed out a big breath then inhaled again as she slowly released, before forcing her body to comply again. What she needed was a hot yoga class to go to, but she doubted there was anything local—she'd have to travel at least an hour and she didn't have the time. Same with acupuncture—she would have loved a session, but she wasn't keen on letting just anyone stick needles into her.

"That looks painful."

She froze, shutting her eyes for a second. *Nathan.* She hadn't expected him to be about so early, let alone to be dropping in to see her. When she relaxed out of her pose and opened her eyes, she looked up at him and saw that he was dressed in workout gear, too.

"Painful would be an understatement," she replied, slowly stretching out and standing. "But if I ever want my old body back, I'm prepared to deal with the consequences."

His low laugh made her smile. "That's how I felt

when I started back running. It's been ten years since I pounded the pavements around London, and I'm finally getting fit again."

"Another perk of quitting your job?" she asked, reaching for her water and taking a long sip.

"Something like that."

They stood and stared at one another for a moment, until Jessica put down her bottle. There was something awkward about having Nathan so close, about him staying on the property—awkward but nice at the same time. And she could tell that even though he was friendly, that he wanted to be around her, too, he was finding the whole thing as awkward as she was.

"I'd ask you in for breakfast but I don't really have anything to offer." It was the truth—some bread in the freezer was all she had to eat, which meant she was going to have to do a trip to the supermarket if she didn't want to starve. "You could join me for yoga, but that's about as good as it gets."

Nathan stared at her as if he was deep in thought before he said anything. "How about you give me five minutes for a shower and come over to the cottage? I'm on a serious health kick right now, so my refrigerator is jam-packed with food."

She glanced down at her workout gear and touched her ponytail, running her fingers through it. It was a beautiful morning: the sun was already shining bright across the lawn and filtering onto the porch, and there was nothing she'd rather do than sit with Nathan and eat something other than toast. If she could shower first, that was—it had been a long night and she felt terrible.

"Give me half an hour," she said, smiling at him. "Breakfast would be lovely."

As he turned to walk away, she called out to him. "Hey, if you're on a health kick, how did we end up eating greasy noodles and spring rolls last night?"

The grin he gave her made her wish she didn't have so much other crap going on that she had to deal with. That she could just enjoy flirting with a handsome guy instead of stressing about every other aspect of her life. Although given what she was going through, maybe he was the perfect distraction.

"I'm allowed the odd treat day," he told her. "And besides, you looked like you needed comfort food."

She rolled up her yoga mat instead of staring after him as he disappeared, but she couldn't wipe the smile from her face. A morning of not dealing with reality wasn't going to kill her, and besides, she was starving. Now she just had to move at lightening speed to shower and get ready.

After what felt like the fastest half hour of her life, Jessica wandered across the grass toward the cottage, trying not to hurry and telling herself he wasn't going to notice if she was five minutes late. It had been a long time since she'd seen the little house, and a smile came to her face as she looked at the climbing rose that still covered one side of the wooden structure. It was almost like an oversize kid's playhouse, and it had been the place she'd lived in when she was younger, before her granddad had managed to convince her mom that she was crazy for insisting on being so independent. Then they'd moved into the main house, and this had been used for friends and family, or for guests when Jock had felt like some company over the past few years. She'd always guessed he'd rented the place when he was lonely, as he liked having younger people around him, but now she wondered if he'd needed the extra money. It was all just so frustrating not being able to ask him what the hell had happened.

Jessica inhaled deeply, convinced she could smell coffee but certain she must be imagining it. She ran her fingers through her hair, a nervous habit that she was always prone to whenever she wore it loose. Most of her life she'd worn a ponytail or plait, having worn a helmet almost every day and needing to be practical, but lately she'd liked blow-drying it and leaving it out, one of the only things she'd enjoyed about not training.

"Hey."

She looked up and saw Nathan standing barefoot in the doorway, wearing faded jeans and a white T-shirt. He looked like he was born to live on the farm, relaxed and sporting a smile as casual as his clothing, which made it hard to match him with the banker he'd described. In fact, there was almost nothing about him that would ever have hinted at what his usual life was, except maybe his posh English accent. And that hint of sadness that reflected in his gaze—something she doubted he was even aware that he did—that told her he wasn't as carefree and relaxed as he looked sometimes.

He'd disappeared almost the moment he'd called out, so she just walked slowly to the low porch where the old table was set. She ran her hand along the chair, smiling as she thought about the times she'd sat there in the past. First it had been with her mom, then as somewhere fun to play and have pretend tea parties as a girl, and later it had been a place to sit and think when she'd been a teenager. And when her mom had died, it had been oddly comforting to sit and remember her, sometimes on her own and other times with her granddad silently sitting beside her. Although remembering had always been a lot tougher than trying to forget.

Jessica brushed aside the tears that were pricking her eyes, blinking as she heard Nathan coming out. She didn't need to go back to that night, to the sirens wailing and the lights flashing in the dead of night, the police car arriving to tell her and her granddad what had happened. She'd been so numb from news of the crash that it had passed as a blur, in the beginning anyway. And it just made her more determined not to let anyone too close, so she didn't have to experience that kind of loss again.

"I hope you're not expecting anything too exciting," Nathan said, putting two bowls on the table and standing back. "I've started eating kind of simple food since I've been here."

Jessica looked from him to the table. "Are you serious? What about this is simple?"

The bowls were filled with gourmet muesli, then piled high with every kind of berry. It was exactly what she needed after not looking after herself properly while she'd been overseas, usually too busy riding and making sure her horses got the best of everything, then forgetting about herself. Her go-to food had been grilled cheese and frozen meals—or anything fast when she'd been short on time.

"The farmer's market here is amazing," Nathan said, ignoring her compliment and disappearing inside as he called over his shoulder. "You should come with me tomorrow."

Jessica sat down, using a fork to nudge aside the berries and steal a few blueberries from the bottom. She hadn't eaten them in years, and the sweet tartness made her taste buds explode, flooding her mouth and making her crave more.

She watched Nathan make his way from the door to the table again, holding another bowl. There was no denying how handsome he was—hair tousled and slightly messy, skin tanned no doubt from the hours he'd been spending outside. It was a weird feeling, but there was something nice about knowing that the hours he'd spent on horseback had been with her granddad. That he'd been the person her grandfather had seen everyday.

"This," he said, "is coconut yogurt. Believe me when I tell you it's the best thing you'll ever eat."

Jessica couldn't help but burst out laughing. "Coconut yogurt? Next you're going to tell me that you meditate all day."

"*Well,*" he began, a serious look on his face. Then he grinned straight back at her with a playful expression that masked any hint of sadness. "I'm just trying to stay healthy, that's all. Eating clean food, cooking and exercising, doing the things I neglected for too long." He chuckled. "But I haven't taken up meditation and pilates just yet."

Nathan nudged the yogurt in her direction and she dipped her spoon in, taking his word for how delicious it was going to be. She licked her spoon and then ate the lot, eyes opening wide at the flavor.

"Oh my god, it *is* incredible."

"Told you so," he said, a smug look on his face. "That's the passion fruit one, my favorite. Although it has nothing on the chocolate coconut ice cream."

She took a mouthful of everything together, nodding, as he raised an eyebrow at her. "I think you're on to something with this health kick."

Nathan made a noise in his throat that she couldn't decipher before answering. "A heart attack will do that to a guy."

She almost dropped her spoon. Did he mean him? Surely not. "You mean your father or someone else close to you?"

He shook his head, looking at her from across the table. "Nope. Me."

No way. "But you're like, what? Thirty-something?"

This time he nodded. "Thirty-two. Way too young for a heart attack, but it happened."

Jessica concentrated on her next few mouthfuls,

but she couldn't even remember what they'd been talking about before the whole heart attack thing.

"So what do you say to the market?"

"Market?" she mumbled back, still trying to process what he'd said.

"The farmer's market. Tomorrow."

She sighed. "Sorry, I'm still kind of stuck on the whole heart failure thing."

His eyes met hers, a blend of chocolate warmth and strength that she couldn't look away from. "Now you get why I'm trying to be healthy, though, right? I'm not just trying to stick to some crazy New Year's resolution, I've changed everything. My lifestyle, my attitude, *everything*."

She finished her mouthful, wanting to know more but not game enough to ask. "The market sounds great. Maybe while we're there you can tell me what I need to shop for. And how to put it all together."

"Just think what cavemen would have eaten, and you'll figure it out pretty quick," he joked.

Jessica fought the urge to stare at Nathan, to study his face. There was something else, something beneath the surface that she couldn't quite figure out. The heart attack was…unbelievable, but she knew there was more to what had happened to him, more than he was telling her. His eyes told of sadness, although when he looked at her like he was now and smiled, that look almost disappeared. *Almost.*

The closer she got to thirty, the more she started to question the fact that it had been so long since she'd been in a relationship. There were only so many times she could blame her distrust in the opposite sex on her deadbeat father, even if deep down she did believe that her trust issues were his fault. Not every man was her ex either—after two years she had to start telling herself that. *And believing it.*

And being with Nathan…maybe it was just that she hadn't met a man she was attracted to in a long time, but being around him it was kind of hard *not* to think about how her body was reacting to his.

When he'd touched her the night before, when his hand had closed over hers, it was as if her skin had come alive, tingling with desire. Now she wanted to reach out to him, to run her fingers down his arm, feel his skin. But she'd missed the moment. She could have done it, could have gotten away with touching him when he'd confessed about his heart attack. Now it would just seem plain weird, and she wasn't even sure about how she felt, what she wanted.

"So are you going to look through any of your granddad's paperwork today? Try to figure out where everything started to go wrong?"

Jessica yawned, though she tried hard to suppress it. "Would you believe me if I said I sat up until almost four a.m. rifling through everything I could find?"

His smile was warm. "Absolutely. I would have done the same."

She put down her spoon, no longer hungry, although she hadn't finished. "I'm starting to think I'm crazy, that the jet lag is doing weird things to my brain, but…" She let her sentence trail off, not wanting to sound like a madwoman. She was doubting herself that she could be right, that her stupid conspiracy theory was exactly that.

"Tell me," he said, setting his spoon down and leaning forward slightly, elbows on the table, like he was waiting for her to divulge some big secret. "I promise I won't laugh."

She fiddled with the edge of her top, picking at the hem absentmindedly. "From the correspondence I could find, it seems that Granddad sold a lot of investment properties over the last year. He didn't use a computer, but he wrote everything in his diary, and he was meeting with his lawyer around the same time as each property was sold. His notes are meticulous."

Nathan's eyebrows shot up before pulling together, causing a crease to appear between them. She tightened her fingers into a fist, resisting the urge to reach out and smooth his skin, to touch his frown away. Part of her wanted to connect with him, and the other part was terrified. And she didn't know whether he might run a mile if she did touch him out of the blue like that.

"He wasn't losing his mind, Jessica, and the notes he made prove it. I think you need to trust your instincts."

"So you don't think I'm crazy for thinking that his lawyer could have—" she paused, considering her words "—taken advantage of him?"

"No, not crazy at all." Nathan stood up, taking both their bowls and nodding toward the kitchen. "There's plenty of things he could have done fraudulently, but the tricky part is figuring out what and then trying to prove it."

She stood too, following him inside and momentarily forgetting what they were talking about when she saw a shiny, state-of-the-art coffee machine taking pride of place in the tiny kitchen.

"I take it caffeine is allowed on your new healthy regime?"

Nathan turned around faster than she expected, almost knocking her over. She took a step back at the same time as he reached for her arm, his hand closing over her elbow to steady her, the look on his face almost alarmed when he realized how close they were, that his skin was covering hers.

"Thanks," she managed, staring up into his coffee-bean-dark eyes. Now that he was standing so close he seemed so tall, so…masculine. Everything about him was making the room seem smaller, making her acutely aware of the fact that she was up close and personal with a man she was most definitely attracted to. She only had to move an inch, push up onto her tiptoes and tilt her head back, and she'd be so close to kissing him, to touching her mouth to his.

"There's nothing wrong with a good, strong coffee," he finally said, staring down at her for what felt like an eternity before letting her go and stepping back.

And there would be nothing wrong with a kiss, either. Jessica shoved her hands in her pockets and looked around the kitchen and small living room.

"How do you like it?"

She spun back around. *How did she like it?* "What?" she asked.

He smiled, the awkwardness disappearing as he laughed. "Your coffee. How do you like it?"

Jessica felt her cheeks burn just enough to make her embarrassed. "Cappuccino. Thanks," she managed, turning her back so he couldn't see her face. "With sugar."

"So back to your sleuthing. Do you think there's any chance your granddad signed a power of attorney over to his lawyer?"

She shut her eyes, trying to recall the conversations she'd had with her granddad in the months before he'd passed. If anything it made her stop thinking about how she felt being around Mr. Tall Dark and Handsome. He had mentioned something about making provision in case something happened to him, but...*yes*. It was all starting to come back to her. "He did."

Nathan fired the coffee machine into life, the hiss of frothing milk making her turn around to watch, curious.

"Then that's where you need to start," he said.

"You think he's blatantly ripped Granddad off? Sold my inheritance out from under me?" Her heart was beating faster just considering the possibility, her body felt as if it was on fire just from her thinking about it. Surely he couldn't have, could he?

Nathan put one coffee cup down before starting on the next, glancing at her as he worked. "It wouldn't be the first time a lawyer did this kind of thing. Honestly?" he said over the noise of the machine. "I think it's a more plausible theory than Jock losing his marbles and selling the investments he'd worked so hard to acquire. I flat out believe that didn't happen."

Jessica took the coffee Nathan offered her, bending to inhale the aroma. "Smells heavenly," she told him.

"There's no decent coffee close by, except for Sundays when the market opens, so I decided to teach myself. It beats driving twenty minutes for one."

She laughed. "And spend a small fortune on a machine."

"There is that. But it's not like I'm spending a lot of money living here."

Jessica already knew her guest wasn't exactly strapped for cash. In fact, if she had to guess, she would bank on him being wealthy even by London standards, and she'd met a lot of people when she was living there with enough money to make her eyes pop. He'd been so quick to insist that he could buy the farm, not to mention offering to write the check to bring Teddy home for her. But she couldn't accept, it just wasn't right, and she didn't want to be that much in debt to anyone.

"You'll get to the bottom of all this. We'll figure it out together, because he's bound to have left a trail, and we just have to follow the crumbs."

"So the saga begins," she muttered, wincing when she touched the side of the hot coffee cup. If her hunch was correct then she was up for one hell of a battle, but it was oddly comforting knowing Nathan was helping her, that she wasn't alone.

* * *

"So tell me what it was like to compete at the World Equestrian Games."

Jessica looked across at Nathan as they walked, tucking her thumbs through the belt loops of her jeans. Part of her didn't want to go back in time, didn't want to remember what it was like, but the other part of her was so determined to get back there one day that she was terrified of losing the memories. Like with her mom—she'd spent so long trying to forget, and then even longer worrying that she wouldn't be able to remember her face if she kept pushing the memories away.

She slowed her walk and went back to gazing across the fields. "It was amazing," she told him. "Experience-of-a-lifetime kind of stuff, and riding alongside some of my childhood idols was incredible."

They strolled along in silence until they reached the yards, large pens that ran alongside the barn. They were empty—she had left all the horses out to graze the night before—but she still hitched one foot up on the wooden rail.

"Will you ever get back there?" Nathan asked, his voice soft and low.

Jessica shut her eyes. Behind her lids she could see herself cantering around the cross-country course, feel the steady beat of Teddy's hooves as they traveled fast toward a jump, soaring through the air and landing clear on the other side. *Yes.* In her heart she couldn't stand the thought of a lifetime without competing, and she wasn't the sort of person to take no for an answer. Screw the doctors and what they had to say. So long as someone would let her campaign their horse, since she wouldn't ever be able to afford her own, she believed she would.

"One day I'll be back there," she said, angling her body so she was facing him. "And even if it is unlikely, I'm not ready to take no for an answer. Not for a long time yet."

Nathan's eyes were fixed on hers, and she would have known he was smiling even if she hadn't been able to see his mouth. His whole face crinkled slightly, his expression warm all the way to his eyes, all awkwardness between them long disappeared, for the moment anyhow.

"You'll get there."

She swallowed hard, goose pimples spreading across her skin as he continued to stare at her, not breaking contact for even a second. She felt her breathing become shallow, anticipation making her body hum; waiting for him to move closer, for something to happen between them. She might be confused about a lot of things, but Nathan kissing her, *touching* her, wasn't one of them. It was the kind of distraction she was craving.

"Jessica…" he started, shuffling forward a little, his gaze moving from her eyes to her mouth then slowly back again.

Her lips parted, staring back at him, waiting. He hovered, seemed to somehow rock forward then back away again. And that was when she noticed it, as his hand moved up slowly, reaching for her face, about to cup her cheek.

Her heart started to beat fast for another reason entirely, her blood feeling as if it were on fire in her veins as it pumped through her body. *He was married?* How had she not noticed the fact that he wore a fine gold band before now?

"You're married," she managed, her voice catching in her throat and sounding all husky when she wanted to sound mad.

Desire was replaced by anger. She had no idea what was going on, but she wanted to know—now. Not that she had any right to demand him share his life story, but if he'd kissed her and then she'd found out he was married? The idea of it made her physically sick. She would never do anything even remotely intimate with a married man, not when she'd seen firsthand the emotional impact of infidelity. It had crippled her mom and she would never let another man close to her, not ever. And then when she'd found out her ex had another partner, was engaged to another woman and had been lying to her for months... Jessica's body shook. *How dare he.*

Nathan took a step away from her, leaning against the rails. "I'm not married, Jessica," he said.

She wanted to scoff at him, to accuse him of lying when she could so blatantly see his ring, but before she could react he held his left hand out and shrugged, rolling the ring around his finger before slipping it off and holding it up to the light, inspecting it. She kept her mouth shut, waiting for him to explain himself.

"Old habits die hard," he muttered, shoving it into his pocket. "I'm a widower, actually. I just don't like to think about it if I can help it."

Jessica wished the ground would open up and swallow her. *A widower?* Now she felt awful. The thought hadn't even crossed her mind. It was the second time she'd jumped to conclusions where Nathan was concerned, and she felt like a fool.

"I, um," she stuttered, not able to take her eyes off him or manage to say anything coherent. "I'm sorry."

He shrugged again, but she could tell she'd hit a raw nerve. Was that another reason why he'd traveled halfway around the world to escape his normal life? It sure explained the sadness she'd kept glimpsing.

"It's been a while, but I guess I'm just so used to wearing it. I should have taken it off months ago."

Jessica nodded, not sure whether to ask him more or just wait for him share if he wanted to. At least now she understood why he'd been so caring, so genuine when she'd been talking about her grandfather. Nathan knew loss like she had, or maybe even more so if he'd lost his wife. Which was no doubt why they'd connected so quickly, why he'd been comfortable talking with her about moving on and things getting better, something most people shied away from.

She wished they could rewind, go back to that moment when something had been so close to happening between them, but it was long gone. Now Nathan was staring into the distance, his mind no doubt a million miles away, and she was feeling numb.

"I might, ah, head back and start sorting through

some more paperwork. Try to figure everything out."
And stop thinking about the fact they'd almost kissed.

Nathan turned, slowly, his expression soft again,
dark eyes suddenly as inviting as warm hot chocolate
on a freezing cold winter's night. When he reached
for her hand, she didn't pull away, instead letting him
hold it as she looked at his golden skin against hers.

"We'll figure all this out, Jessica." He looked as
unsure about touching her as she did about receiving the affection, but they both stayed still. Stayed
connected.

She smiled, because she trusted what he was saying. "Thank you." Although part of her wondered if
he was talking about her money issues or the attraction simmering between them.

"I'm just going to stay here awhile," he told her.
"See you tomorrow for the market?"

"Sure."

Jessica refused to feel disappointed when he let
go of her hand, when nothing else happened between
them. If something was supposed to happen, if she
was supposed to feel those full lips of his pressed
to hers, she just had to believe it would. *Sometime
when she wasn't accusing him of almost committing
adultery.*

She made her way back toward the house, groaning
at the thought of the papers she had to look through.
But one breath of clean country air, one look at her
surroundings, only made her more determined to get
to the bottom of whatever was going on. And then
once she'd figured all of that out, she needed to fig-

ure out how to get her horse on a plane. Somehow she'd figure it all out. *Somehow*.

Nathan wished he could find a way to start over, but every time he thought he was moving forward, that he was dealing with what had happened, something slapped him right back to where he'd started. And if he was honest with himself, it was Jessica who'd affected him this time, who'd made his memories come tumbling back. Not that he was ever going to forget them, but still—she'd made them worse, but only because of the way he was thinking about her. He'd had a wonderful woman in his life, a woman who'd deserved so much better than him, and he would never forget lifting her body down and holding her, lifeless, wishing he'd been there for her when she'd needed him most. That he hadn't found her with the noose around her neck. That the mental image of her in his office wasn't burned into his memory to haunt him forever.

Just now, when Jessica had been standing with him, and back at the house when he'd touched her hand, both times there was a pull so great that he'd almost given in to it. *Almost.* She wasn't only Jock's granddaughter, she was a woman with her own set of problems, her own web of issues that she needed to work through, and she deserved better than him, too. And he hadn't told her the truth about his ring. He'd purposely worn it all this time to avoid women, so he could pretend he was married and avoid the reality of being single. Of having to explain anything.

What he needed was to stay on track, deal with everything, before even thinking of letting someone else close. Even if he was in the company of a woman who was so tempting she was...*forbidden*. He needed to think of her as forbidden, and then he wouldn't be tempted. He could help her with finding the rat who'd stolen her inheritance, enjoy her company for a while, but that was it. Before long he'd be on a plane back to London to pick up the pieces of his old life and somehow try to redefine that particular puzzle so he didn't get sucked straight back into his former existence.

He dropped his forearms onto the rail of the yard and watched the horses walk slowly across the field. He picked out Patch straightaway, standing tall and surrounded by a group of mares. Seeing the old gelding made him smile. If someone had told him a few years ago he'd have learned to horseback-ride and be living on a farm in New Zealand, he'd have laughed himself stupid, but now? Now he couldn't think of anything worse than leaving it all behind, especially the old horse he'd become so attached to.

Nathan shut his eyes and breathed deep, listening to the native birdsong that had once sounded so foreign to him. It was so familiar now that he could whistle the tunes straight back to the bellbirds—they woke him just after day break with their peaceful melody. Or more often than not he was already awake, unable to sleep, preferring to be conscious so he could keep pushing the memories to the back of his mind.

He pushed back off the railing and unhitched his boot, taking one last look at the horse before walking away. Sometimes he thought about never going back, just staying here and remaining an anonymous foreigner living in the country. There was nothing he couldn't replace about his old life, even if there was a lot he felt guilty about, but he couldn't hide forever.

Nathan kept whistling back to the bellbirds as he headed for home—it was the only way he could stop himself from thinking about Jessica. And how much he wished he'd just pushed past whatever was holding him back and crushed that pouty mouth of hers against his.

CHAPTER FOUR

THE ROOM WAS starting to fill with light and Jessica shut her eyes, trying to block it out. She'd been awake since early morning, had listened to the birds slowly start to sing, and she was exhausted. Her eyes felt as if they were on fire, burning when she opened them, but it was infuriating trying to keep them shut because she knew she'd never find sleep, not after she'd been awake so long. What she needed was another five hours of shut-eye, or an entire day, even.

She kicked the covers off and stretched her legs, then sat up on the edge of her bed. If the birds hadn't been chirping, the house would have been painfully silent, just like it had been every night since she'd been home.

Jessica stood, pushed the blinds back and stared down over the fields. There were horses on the land that had been there for years, broodmares her grandfather had loved, his old horse, and a handful of young sport horses he'd been excited about finding riders for. One he'd even thought was special enough for her to campaign in Europe. But that was all over now. Even if she sold the youngster, it still wouldn't cover the full cost of bringing Teddy back.

She balled both of her hands into fists, nails digging into her palms so hard it hurt. The only consolation was that it stopped her thinking about the pain in her back that had niggled her every time she'd turned in the night—punishment for riding when she was supposed to be resting.

Jessica took a deep breath, blew it out and did it again. Her physiotherapist had told her that looking after her body was as much about looking after her entire well-being than just her physical strength, but dealing with so much loss was making it impossible for her to cope with what had happened. If she'd still been in the saddle, still been competing, then maybe she could have dealt with losing her granddad and the possible fraud with the lawyer, but right now she had nothing. *Except the farm.* And that was about to be taken from her, too.

A movement caught her eye, and she looked across toward the cottage. She smiled when she saw a little black cat, making a mental note to add cat food to her shopping list. There was always the odd wild cat around, and since she'd been a girl she'd made sure to put food out for any animal she thought might not have a home.

And then she saw Nathan. Her breathing slowed and she touched her forehead to the cool of the glass as she watched him. There was something wrong about staring at another human being without their knowledge, as if she was spying on him, but she couldn't look away. His chest was bare, his skin a lighter shade on his torso and belly as he stretched his arms above his head and stood on the porch. He was wearing shorts and nothing else, and she wondered if he'd slept in them or if he was about to go out for a run. Either way, she liked the view. His body was trim, his arms muscled, and the way he ran his hand through his hair…she gulped. She could just imagine him running his fingers through her hair, down her back, his hands firm on *her* skin.

Jessica stepped back from the window and shook her head. *Enough.* The last thing she needed was to complicate her life with a relationship, especially with everything else that she was dealing with, but it was impossible to look at Nathan and not think about him in that way. About what it would be like to be in his bed, at his side, this time of the morning.

Her phone rang, the shrill noise piercing the air and jolting her from her daydream. Jessica walked quickly down the hall and picked it up.

"Hello."

"Morning. All set for the market?"

Nathan. She hoped he hadn't seen her watching, that he didn't know she'd been admiring his half-naked body when he'd thought he was stretching in private.

"We never did decide what time we were going," she managed, shutting her eyes then popping them straight open again to get rid of the image of his chest in her mind.

"I was thinking soon. Get there before all the good produce goes."

"They have real coffee, right? You weren't just saying that the other day to get me to go?"

He laughed, a deep, throaty rumble down the line. "Yeah, but how about I make you one for the ride there? I have a stash of take-out cups handy."

"Sounds perfect," she replied. And so did he. She just had to keep reminding herself that she wasn't available for a relationship. Although if he just wanted some no-strings-attached fun...

"I'll come by in half an hour," he told her.

She hung up, dropped the phone on the bed and sprinted for the shower—she could eat breakfast there. She might not be able to ride, she might not have her granddad, but she could make an effort to make Nathan notice her. At least being around him was one thing that made her smile right now. And if he attempted to kiss her again... A slow shiver ran down her spine. Then so be it.

Nathan was pleased he had to concentrate on driving, because if he'd found Jessica distracting before, now it was virtually impossible to keep his eyes off her. She was staring out the window, oblivious to the effect she was having on him—he couldn't stop glancing at her bare thighs so close to where his hand was resting, her skin lightly tanned, her legs long and toned.

He swallowed and gripped the steering wheel tighter with the one hand he had on it. *Seriously.* It was as if he were a teenage boy lusting after a girl for the first time. He usually had way better self-control, although usually he had work to focus almost every hour of his life on. Here, there wasn't much else he could throw himself into, which was making it very hard to ignore how attracted he was to Jessica.

"Is that it there?"

Her question jolted him from his thoughts. "Yeah, that's it. I can't believe you've never been."

She turned in her seat, her body facing his now. "I was gone way longer than I expected."

"I think the market's been running for a few years, but they've become the trendy thing to do, so it's pretty popular."

She laughed. "I didn't realize so many people around here would go."

"Not from around here," he said, glancing across and catching her eye. He looked back at the road just as fast, not wanting to stray into dangerous territory. "Most of these cars only come near a country road for market day. Town people buying their organic vegies and free-range eggs, letting the kids take a ride on a pony for an exorbitant amount of money, that type of thing."

He grinned when she started to laugh even harder. "Are you serious?"

"Deadly."

"Then what the hell are *we* doing going there?" she asked.

He winked at her then inwardly cringed, wishing he hadn't done something so cheesy. "Because those town folk are on to something," he said in a stupidly executed hick accent.

Nathan noticed Jessica sink back a little into the

seat, her body language relaxed as she went back to staring out the window. He was certain she had no idea how beautiful she was. There was nothing fake or over the top about her beauty—she was just a genuinely attractive girl with big brown eyes, thick blond hair and a smile that could make a guy do anything she asked. *Or at least it could make him do anything.* And up until he'd met her, that wasn't something he thought he'd ever feel about a woman again.

"You know, it's been a long time since I've laughed like this," she said.

It had been a long time since he'd laughed and relaxed with a woman, too. If he was true with himself, it seemed like a lifetime ago; and he felt like a different man to the person he was back in London, no matter how much he might miss that life sometimes.

"Jock always said that I had to meet his amazing granddaughter," Nathan told her. "But I didn't expect the old man to go and die just so we could have dinner together."

She made a weird noise like laughter, but it quickly turned into a short sob that had her wiping at her eyes with the back of her hand. She was smiling but she was still looking out the window, clearly not wanting to meet his gaze.

"Too soon for jokes about him," he said, wishing he could kick himself for being such an idiot. He had no idea how the hell he'd gone from all messed up to trying to make stupid jokes so quickly. "I'm sorry, that was—"

"—good," she said, interrupting him. "Joking is good. It just kind of took me by surprise, that's all."

Nathan nodded at her. The last thing he'd meant to do was upset her—he knew better than anyone how hard it was to deal with loss, to move on. He took a deep, shaky breath and gripped the wheel a little harder with his right hand. He seriously needed to get a grip.

"When I lost my wife, I didn't think I'd ever…" He grimaced, the words almost impossible to expel; his chest was tightening, constricting, from his trying to talk about what had happened. He wanted to let her in so she would know that he wasn't lying when he said he understood, but it was harder than tough. It was almost impossible.

Jessica was still staring out the window, unable to face him or maybe finding it too hard to accept what they'd been talking about, trying to keep her emotions in check. But she did reach for his hand, her fingers searching out his and squeezing.

The contact gave him the prompt he needed to continue, wanting to reach out to her. Nathan fought the choke in his throat—he'd tried to talk to friends, then a therapist, and yet the closest he'd ever come to opening up was with Jock during the hours they'd spent talking. Now he was almost ready to confide in the old man's granddaughter. *Almost.*

"Jessica, my wife, she…" He shook his head, hating what he was about to say, changing his mind at the last minute, not wanting to see the look on her face if she knew the truth. Because it was his fault—he blamed himself and he always would. And since he'd been in New Zealand he hadn't spoken about it once, hadn't told anyone, because he was ashamed and it was easier hiding from the truth.

Now Jessica's fingers were interlocked with his and she'd finally angled her body more toward him. He was glad he was driving, because it meant he didn't have to look at her as he spoke.

"The way she died was pretty traumatic," he finally said, stopping short of telling her that she'd committed suicide in their own home. He just couldn't get the words out. What would Jessica think of him if she knew the truth? "So when I tell you I understand what you're going through, that you can talk to me and I'll get it, I'm telling the truth." It was a cop-out and he was angry with himself, but he was also scared of losing whatever connection he had with Jessica. Of talking about what happened with someone who didn't already know. "I know what it's like to have no one to open up to."

The car was silent, the only noise the rumble as they turned off the main road onto a gravel one, slowly heading into the entrance of the property where the market was held.

"So that's why you're here," she said, her voice soft, almost a whisper, as if she were thinking out loud. "It wasn't just the heart attack that sent you packing."

He didn't say anything. There was nothing to say, not when he didn't want to tell her any more of the story.

"You needed to get away from everything, including the wife you'd lost."

She moved her fingers across his, loosening her grasp on them as she touched him. It was an unfamiliar sensation to him now, the soft, gentle touch of a woman—the way his wife used to touch him, before they'd slowly, painfully become like strangers.

"She was an artist, well known," he told her, "and I didn't handle being in the public eye so well. She thrived on it, in the beginning, anyway."

Jessica's touch was firmer now, as if she was trying to comfort him rather than fire the flames of whatever attraction existed between them. "So you needed some time. Understandable."

He pulled over when they were close to the market. "I have to go back soon, but right now this is where I want to be."

Their eyes locked, her expression impossible to read. Was it stupid to think that where he wanted to be was right here with her? A woman he hadn't even truly known a few days ago? Maybe he'd just become lonely here without people around him, especially since Jock had passed away, although the way he was feeling about Jessica seemed a whole lot more about being attracted to her than just loneliness.

Jessica patted his hand one last time, before unclipping her seat belt as he pulled over behind a line of other cars. He watched as she tucked her long hair behind her ears and smiled across at him; his eyes were drawn to her lips, her full mouth as the corners tipped up. It was so easy to forget everything else when he was with her, at least for the moments when she was looking back at him.

"Sounds like we both need to be distracted from reality," she said. "What do you say we drink coffee and forget about everything for a morning?"

He pushed open his door, needing to get out of the car and away from being so closely confined with Jessica. He didn't trust himself not to just lean over and kiss the words from her mouth.

"How about we make it coffee and pastry?" he suggested, locking the car once she'd stepped out and being careful not to walk too close to her. "The pain au chocolat is seriously good."

"So much for healthy food, huh?" she said jokingly, nudging him in the side with her elbow and moving way too close for comfort.

He resisted the unfamiliar urge to loop his arm around her waist and draw her closer. It was weird how comfortable he already felt with her—comfortable in some ways and completely out of his depth in others. "A guy has to have a treat every once in a while."

Jessica cast a quick glance sideways at him before her eyes darted away again. She was as hesitant as he was, which meant they were doing a kind of dance around one another, waiting for something to happen that might not if he didn't just…what?

Man up and bloody well kiss her, that was what. Only right now it was a hell of a lot easier to say than do.

Jessica stopped at the stall selling pastries, her nose filling with the delicious aroma of pastry, fruit and chocolate. The only thing that came close to making her taste buds so happy was the cappuccino she was already sipping.

"So this is breakfast, huh?" she asked.

Nathan leaned over her shoulder, so close she could smell his aftershave. If she moved a tiny bit to the right she'd be able to touch her cheek to his, feel if he had a hint of stubble already on his jaw, but instead she stayed dead still and stared at the food in front of them.

"Morning!"

A friendly voice sung out at the same time as a woman appeared.

"Good morning," Nathan replied, pointing to the pains au chocolat they had been salivating over. "Make it four this morning."

Jessica laughed. "Four? They're massive."

His mouth was dangerously close to hers when he turned, grinning. "Yeah, but they're so good that I usually get a second coffee and eat another on the drive home."

The woman beamed at them as she handed over two paper bags. "You two make such a gorgeous couple. I can't believe you've never brought your wife here with you before."

It took Jessica a moment to process what the woman had just said, and when she did she looked at Nathan, wide-eyed. She was sure he'd be as surprised as her.

"Oh no, we're not—" Nathan tried to say.

"I mean, he's always wearing a ring, so I knew he had a wife, but you're even more gorgeous than I expected."

Nathan cleared his throat, loudly, and Jessica just made some kind of a grunt in her throat before taking the bags and numbly nodding.

"Thank you," she mumbled.

"You're welcome. Come anytime!"

Jessica nudged Nathan with her elbow, hating the awkward silence between them and not knowing what else to do. She hardly knew what to say!

"Well that was weird."

He shot her a funny sideways look that turned into a smile. "Sorry. The one day I don't wear my ring and someone goes and thinks you're—"

"—your wife," she finished for him. "At least she thought we looked *gorgeous together.*"

Nathan gestured for her to sit on the grass, then bent down himself, put his coffee cup on the ground and opened his brown paper bag.

"I think she said *you* were gorgeous," he mumbled. "And it was worth it for how good these will taste."

Jessica followed his lead and took a bite, raising her eyebrows as she did so. *Wow.* "Okay, so for the second time in as many days you've managed to give me something incredible to eat. Amazing."

Nathan's eyes left hers and dropped to her mouth. She watched him, held her breath as he silently stared.

"You have a little something…" He put down his bag and leaned forward, brushing his thumb against the side of her mouth.

She started to reply, to wipe it away herself, but when Nathan's skin met hers everything else stopped. Jessica stayed impossibly still, her breathing becoming shallow when he tipped even further toward her. She licked her coffee-and-pastry-sweet lips, and when Nathan's gaze drifted to her eyes again, made it clear what he was thinking, she decided not to hold back.

Suddenly it was as if there was no one else in the world except them, as if the crowd gathered at the market had disappeared. Nathan closed the distance between them before she had time to overthink what was happening, his mouth barely touching hers for a split second, giving her the chance to pull away then tentatively touching hers. Jessica was still holding her coffee in one hand, the other propping up the weight of her body; the only part of her moving was her lips. She matched the gentleness of Nathan's kiss, a little sigh escaping her lips when he pulled back, pausing before kissing her again. Only this time it was less gentle, his mouth firmer against hers as their tongues collided.

Nathan stroked her shoulder as they kissed, his thumb moving back and forward in a gentle massage. And it wasn't until he slowly took his lips off hers that she came back to reality—heard the squeals of children and noticed how many other people were bustling around them.

She looked up at him, into his rich brown eyes that now seemed even darker, more intense, than she'd ever seen them. But what she saw took her by surprise; there was conflict in his gaze. A flicker from happiness to concern, maybe regret, and right then in that moment she wanted to do whatever it took to wipe that edge of uncertainty away.

"Hey," she said, leaning in closer again, never breaking their eye contact.

"Hey back," he replied, propping his arm behind hers so he was leaning closer to her as he supported his weight, his expression more relaxed instead of looking as if he was about to bolt.

Even though she'd fantasized about him all morning after she'd seen him half naked, the kiss had still been unexpected. *Unexpected but definitely not unwanted.* And his hesitation had been kind of unexpected, too, although given that he'd lost a wife she didn't know why she should have expected anything different.

"So, ah, I hope that's not going to make things awkward between us," he finally said.

Jessica laughed at the husky tone of his voice. He was so close to her, her head tilted back to look up at him, that she could have kissed him without having to do anymore than lean a little. *And she decided to do exactly that, to show him how she felt.*

She raised her chin and looked up at Nathan, stretching up and catching his lips against hers. She abandoned her coffee cup and draped her arm around Nathan's neck instead, her hand cupping just under the base of his skull. When she let her mouth slide off his, she stared straight into his eyes again as she spoke.

"Definitely not awkward," she murmured. "But a whole lot more interesting."

His laugh was soft, as was the kiss he dropped to

her lips before closing his arm around her shoulder and drawing her close.

"How have I managed to stay out of trouble this entire trip, and now here I am kissing a girl at a market?" His tone was relaxed now, the worry lines that had bracketed his eyes as good as gone.

Jessica shook her head. "No idea. I'm supposed to be miserable, mourning and convalescing, so this definitely wasn't part of my plan."

"Oh, so this is all my fault?" he asked, leaning dangerously close to her again. His morning stubble tickled her cheek, brushing just hard enough against her to make her feel it.

"Definitely your fault. You're the one who suggested the pastries, so you can take all the blame."

Jess reached for her coffee again and took a sip, as much to avoid the full intensity of Nathan's stare as anything else. She might have sounded confident sparring with him like that, but her stomach was starting to flip like a pancake now that he was slowly coming out of his shell. Nathan was gorgeous and charming, so there wasn't a part of her that didn't want to be in his arms. Her problem with men was in the long term, even though logically she knew that wasn't going to be an issue with Nathan. He'd already told her that he wouldn't even be in the country much longer, so what harm was there in having a little fun?

"Want to take a look around the rest of the market?" he asked, sitting up straighter and finishing the last of his coffee.

"Sure. Maybe we could buy some food to stop my pantry from looking like no one lives in the house."

"And maybe we could buy some ingredients so we can cook dinner together tonight?"

Jessica took his hand when he held it out and stood, unable to stop smiling when they walked off hand in hand. There'd been a spark between them before, but now there was a pull so strong, sending flushes through her entire body, that she knew there was no way she could say no to him even if she wanted to. Something had changed between them, and she liked it.

He shouldn't have done it. No matter how incredible it had been kissing Jessica, after thinking of doing little else for the past two days, it had been stupid. He should have gone with his instincts and kept his hands and his mind off her—or maybe it had been his instincts that were getting him in trouble.

He was renting her guest house. She was Jock's granddaughter. She was...he ran his hands through his hair, pleased they were walking so she didn't notice his agitation. *She was a beautiful woman.* That was the truth of it, and nothing about that was going to change anytime soon. And he was in no shape to enter any kind of relationship.

"Look at these," he heard Jessica say.

He stopped when she tugged him back to a stall.

"Gourmet meals to take home," she said, glancing at him as she spoke. "The chicken lasagna looks amazing."

Nathan ran a hand down her back, fighting the feelings of guilt at touching her, her body warm to the touch even through her T-shirt. It had been a long time since he'd felt like this, not since he'd first met his wife—the thrill of every bump and touch of another human being—and it was so foreign to him that it was intoxicating. Was worth being outside of his comfort zone.

"Sounds like a much better way to impress you than trying to cook something from scratch."

Her smile caught him like an animal in the glare of a headlight. There was something about Jessica that changed his mood when he was around her.

"Let's not stop there, then," she said with an easy laugh. "How about we go back to the cupcake stand and take a few of those home for dessert, too?"

Right now he would have said yes to anything she wanted if it meant keeping that beautiful smile beaming in his direction and his mind off everything else.

"Anything you want," he said, nodding to the stall owner who was hovering over the lasagna.

"Anything?" she asked.

He raised an eyebrow and took a quick survey of the market. "Anything," he affirmed. "The worst you can do is go crazy on food, right?"

So much for his vow to stay single after his wife had died, to never let himself get close to another woman again. Everything had been going so perfectly to plan, and then Jessica had appeared and crushed all his best intentions as if they'd never even existed. He should have told her about Marie when he'd had

the chance before, but the truth was he wasn't even
going to be in the country for much longer. Why tell
her something that could change the way she thought
about him when he could just keep it to himself and
enjoy Jessica's company? So long as she knew he was
here for only a short time, that was all that mattered.
He couldn't commit to anything more than a fling at
best, no matter how he felt about her.

*And the less he thought about his past, the better
he was starting to feel about his future.*

CHAPTER FIVE

EVEN IF SHE'D wanted to, Jessica couldn't stop smiling. There were plenty of things that should have stopped her—the pain shooting intermittently through her back and the prospect of losing her farm for starters —but a certain someone was making her body hum like it hadn't in a long time. *And that certain someone had arrived.*

As the sound of his knock at the back door echoed through the living room, she took a sip of wine for confidence, then spun around to find Nathan less than twenty feet away.

"Sorry, should I have waited?"

She shook her head. "No."

"Jock always had the door open, and I was used to wandering on in whenever I was passing."

She opened the fridge and retrieved a beer for him. "I still find it hard to comprehend that you knew him so well. I mean, it's kind of weird but also kind of amazing at the same time."

Nathan took the beer bottle and clinked it against hers before taking a sip. There was still a flicker of something, a hint that he wasn't quite as relaxed in her company as he appeared. The nervous way he picked at the label of the bottle, the way he glanced away if they held eye contact for too long.

"Talking about Jock," he said, taking a few steps back and sitting on the edge of the table, his concern obvious. "Do you think he'd be okay with what happened today? Between us?"

Jessica liked the fact that he thought so highly of her granddad. "The one guy he warned me about turned out to be a jackass, but I'm guessing he wouldn't have steered me away from you. Not if he liked you enough to spend so much time with you."

She watched as he swilled back a whole lot more beer. Something was definitely on his mind.

"Want to talk about him?" he asked.

Jessica sighed. "Not really. All you need to know is that he was engaged to another woman, and I had no idea."

Nathan almost choked on his beer. "You're kidding me?"

She shook her head. "'fraid not."

"I really like you, and I would never lie to you like that," he said, face serious as he spoke and making her almost drop her wineglass. "But I need to be honest before—"

"—we eat our amazing lasagna?" she attempted to joke.

He smiled but his expression was still serious. "Jess, I have to head back to London sooner than I thought. Probably in a week's time," he said with a grimace. "I've had this rule that I only turn on my phone once a week, clear my messages and let my assistant run through anything urgent with me, and it's kind of backfired. I just checked them before I came over—that's why I'm late."

She laughed, but it didn't sound natural. How could he need to leave when she'd only just met him? She'd known it wasn't going to turn into anything serious between them, but a week?

"I'm not sure whether I'm more shocked that you're leaving so soon, or that you only turn your phone on once a week."

He pushed off the table and reached for her hand—it was an unexpected gesture that made her wish she had longer with him.

"I've been here for months, and suddenly I meet you and have to leave," he said. "Ironic, but true."

There was something so easy between them, but at the same time the attraction was enough to make her blood feel like it was on fire, bubbling through her veins at his touch.

"So it's just me and you for a week, huh?" she asked, letting go of his hand and touching his jawline. The stubble was gone, replaced with skin that was impossibly soft.

"A week," he replied.

They stared at each other, neither moving for what seemed like a lifetime. Jessica could hear the exhale of her breath, every one of her senses aware—the aroma of Nathan's cologne, the cool of the glass against her hand, the thud of her own heart as she waited... *for what?*

Nathan reached for her glass, his eyes never leaving hers even as he took it from her and set it down on the counter behind her. Jessica stayed immobile, becoming breathless as he slid his hand down her back, stopping when he reached the curve just above her bottom to pull her body hard against his.

"What do you say we make the most of this week?"

The husky, lethal tone of his voice would have melted her to a puddle at his feet if he hadn't been holding on to her. Gone was any uncertainty, replaced with a desire she could see shining from his eyes.

"I say…" she began, but she didn't bother finishing her sentence, standing on tiptoe to show him with her mouth instead.

His mouth was hot and wet as he kissed her back; his arms were still around her as he pulled her forward and against himself again. All thoughts disappeared from her mind as she let her tongue explore Nathan's mouth, running her fingers through his hair, her other hand sliding across his broad, muscular shoulders. She wanted Nathan, there was no hint of a doubt in her mind, and the fact that he was only here for another week…*it was perfect*. Long-term relationships terrified her, and so did one-night stands usually, but this was different.

"Jessica." Nathan's voice was a whisper across her lips.

"Mmm," she managed back, tugging at his hair to try to get him to kiss her again, and nipping at his lower lip when he didn't comply.

"I don't want you to get the wrong idea," he mumbled, as she tried to distract him with her mouth. "This can only be—"

This time she managed to silence him, and he didn't bother trying to finish his sentence. Jessica sighed against his mouth, and for the first time in what seemed like forever, she forgot about everything else going on in her life and just enjoyed the moment.

So much for staying out of trouble. There was something about Jessica that had made him forget everything except for how much he wanted her in his arms. And there was also something about her that was helping him put his painful past in a compartment of his mind.

"You," he whispered in her ear, "are so beautiful."

She turned her face slightly so he was looking straight at her, her long lashes hiding her eyes when she glanced down. He didn't give her the chance to change her mind or become shy, dropping his mouth to hers in a kiss that had him fighting to hold himself back. Jessica's fingers dug into his shoulder, fisting a handful of his T-shirt as their lips moved back and forth, holding on to him like she didn't want him to escape.

Nathan tried to keep things slow, wanting to enjoy every second of Jessica against him, but he couldn't hold back. When she slipped a hand under the front of his top, her smooth palm exploring his torso and then running up his chest, he was a goner. He scooped her up, both hands on her bottom to support her weight, groaning when she locked her legs around his waist.

Nathan walked forward a few steps until her back was against the wall, taking her weight in one hand, the other palm pushing flat against the wall above her head. He dipped his mouth to her neck as she moaned for more, lips quickly finding hers again, his hand dropping almost as fast as it had risen to push up the hem of her top, sliding across her smooth skin. He wanted to touch every part of her, to lose himself in her arms, and he wanted it now.

"The bedroom," she gasped against his cheek when she pushed him back.

Nathan didn't need to be asked twice, and he didn't give a hoot about where they were, so long as she didn't want to stop. He kept her in his arms, easily carrying her, walking through the living room and trying to kiss her at the same time.

"This way?"

She nodded, nuzzling his neck and pressing such soft kisses there he could hardly stand it. "Uh-huh." Her tongue traced a line almost to his ear before trailing back down again, then she sucked, laughing when he protested.

"You," he said, stopping at the stairs and bending forward to drop her on one of them, "are wicked."

She laughed and arched her back. "Ahhh." Her smile turned into a frown filled with pain as her body twisted to the side.

"What happened? Your back?" Nathan didn't know what to do other than hover over her.

"It'll be fine," she said, but he could tell she was still sore. "One minute it can be fine, just a noticeable ache, and the next I get a shooting pain that sends me through the roof."

"Would a massage help?" he asked, leaning over her and kissing the frown away.

"Maybe," she replied, the pain starting to disappear from her face, eyes softening again.

"Then how about I carry you to your room and rub the pain away?" he suggested, carefully scooping her back up in his arms and carrying her up the stairs.

Instead of her legs wrapped around him, this time she had her head against his chest while he carried her. "Sounds heavenly," she murmured.

What was heavenly were the soft tendrils of her hair brushing his face, the faint scent of perfume, the weight of her in his arms. And if he had to go slow and massage her, then that was exactly what he'd do.

"In there," she said when they got to the top, her arms locked around his neck.

Nathan kicked open the door so they could enter, stopping only when he got to her bed. He lowered her onto her side, not wanting to put her on her back again in case he hurt her.

"I'm not going to break," she said, looking up at him.

He smiled. "So you'd rather I was rough?"

Her grin made him laugh. "Just forget about my back," she ordered. "I'll tell you if it hurts."

Nathan shrugged, kicking off his boots and pushing her over so she was on her stomach. "Once I've massaged you," he said, "then I'll forget about your back."

He brushed aside her long hair and gently started to massage her shoulders.

"Mmmm."

Her moan was encouraging. Nathan ran his fingers down her back a little further, spreading out his palms so he could knead with his thumbs, fingers edging out toward her sides. He kept going, inching down her back, listening to the soft noises she was making. When she stiffened a little he stopped, not wanting to put pressure on somewhere that hurt her, but as soon as he did she mumbled to keep going. So he did exactly that.

Only the longer he had his hands on her the faster his resolve to take things slow started to disappear.

Jessica turned, pushing Nathan back slightly as she did so. His gaze held a question that she was only too happy to answer. She cupped the back of his head and brought his face down to hers, kissing him slowly at first. He complied—it was she who wanted more, who couldn't keep the painfully slow pace.

"You liked that?" he asked in a husky voice. "Because there's plenty more where that came from."

CHAPTER SIX

It HAD BEEN a long time since Jessica had woken with a smile on her face. Usually the second she opened her eyes everything came crashing back to her—the accident, the pain and her granddad. This morning was different. Sunlight warmed her bare arm, and the rest of her was heated by Nathan's warm body pressed against hers. The weight was comforting, even though she was used to having her bed to herself, and when she turned slowly to make sure she stayed in his arms, she was able to indulge in surveying his face. His nose was straight, dark eyebrows and lashes the perfect outline for his chocolate eyes when they were open. There were faint lines around his eyes and a light laugh line bracketing his mouth, but otherwise his strong face was flawless.

"Good morning," he mumbled, eyes opening slowly after he spoke.

"Morning," she replied, leaning in to brush a kiss across his lips.

Nathan kissed her back, but it was a lazy kind of kiss—nothing like the night before but every bit as enjoyable.

"I've been thinking," he said, breaking contact only to speak, his mouth searching out hers again.

"While you were sleeping?" she murmured.

He chuckled and stroked her cheek, brushing hair from her face as it fell across her eye. "Before I fell asleep actually, and then again the moment I woke up and saw your face. Which is unusual for me, because usually I lie awake half the night and do nothing but think because I can't sleep."

She liked that he'd slept well with her beside him, and it had been the same for her. Being asleep in Nathan's arms had been so comforting, made her feel so safe, that she'd slept peacefully right through the night, too.

"There's something about being with you," he said, "something that's made me, hell, I don't know."

"What?" she asked, even though she felt the same. That there was something about being with him that had made her relax, made her believe that she would get past everything that had happened.

"I guess I just feel like I can talk to you," he said, his fingers twirling a strand of her hair. "Like I can just be me, and I haven't felt like that in a long time."

She relaxed against him. "I know what you mean." It was as if they were two lost souls, the losses they'd both suffered drawing them together, and each somehow understood a little of what the other had been through.

"This is going to sound crazy, but that thinking I was doing overnight? Well, there's something I want to ask you."

Her heart started to beat a little too fast, just as it had the night before when he'd first kissed her. *He'd been thinking about something to do with her?* "What is it?"

"Come with me."

His words were a simple statement but they held as much power as if he'd just delivered a presidential speech.

"Come with you?" She wasn't sure exactly what he meant, what he was asking her.

"To London," he said, stroking down her arm and catching her hand, linking their fingers. "You can fly back with me, see Teddy, have a holiday."

She took a shaky breath, forcing herself to stay still. Her instincts when it came to men were to flee, because she knew how easy words were to say and how easier promises were to break. *He actually wanted her to go with him to London?*

"I don't know what to say." It was the truth—she had no idea what she even wanted to tell him.

"Then just say yes," he said, leaning in to kiss her jaw before making a trail down her neck and to her collarbone. "I'm not ready to say goodbye to you yet. It's a win-win situation."

"For who?"

His throaty laugh sent a shiver through her body.

"Both of us. I want to see more of you, and this is the only way that's going to happen," he said.

"So we'd extend our fun for another week or so?" Jessica asked.

"Uh-huh. What do you say?" He looked at her,

waiting for an answer. "I have to book my flights later today."

What she really wanted was for him to go back to kissing her, to lie in his arms and think about nothing else for the rest of the day. Or the week.

"Yes," she said, not sure if it was the right thing to say when she'd only just got back and had so much going on. Then again, the distraction would be kind of nice, so long as she had enough money in the bank to keep someone on to feed the horses and keep an eye on everything for her.

"Great," Nathan said, taking her mind off her worries again as he stroked her shoulder. "I'll get my assistant to book us first-class tickets today."

Jessica sighed as he kept up the stroking, his fingers like silk as they drifted across her skin. There was something dangerous about spending time with Nathan—she didn't want to get used to luxuries like first class, not when she couldn't even afford to send her horse back via ship, and having a man like Nathan around...he was kind, gorgeous and fun, and that wasn't something she wanted to become accustomed to, either.

He brushed his mouth over hers, his hand to the small of her back. She might not want to get used to this, but it sure was fun for now.

"So what are we going to do today?" Nathan asked Jessica as he came up behind her and looped his arms around her waist, nudging aside her hair so he could nuzzle her neck.

She twisted in his embrace and kissed him, casually dropping her arms over his shoulders. It was weird to be so relaxed with him, to be touching him so openly after they'd danced around their attraction in the beginning.

"Maybe we could take the horses out?" she said.

"Or maybe I could go over some of your granddad's paperwork with you? Take a look with fresh eyes in case you've missed something?"

She groaned. "Or maybe we could just go back to bed?"

He dropped a kiss to her forehead. "I'm tempted, but I also want to help you get to the bottom of this before we go."

This time her groan was even louder, but she pushed off him and leaned back against the counter. "How about I show you where to look and leave you to it for half an hour?" she asked. "I've gone just about cross-eyed trying to sift through everything, but I'd love you to take a look."

Nathan followed her, planting his hands on the counter on either side of her and leaning in for one last kiss, moving his lips slowly back and forth across hers.

"I'm going to call in a favor from an old friend, see if he can help," Nathan said, knowing that she'd probably protest if he told her he was going to spend money on a private investigator to get to the bottom of the issue. "There's no way anyone's going to force you into selling this place, not if I have anything to do with it."

Jessica's smile told him he was doing the right thing. He took her hand when she offered it, and she led him to Jock's office. The room was immaculate, just like it had been when the old man was alive, and he followed her to the desk at the far end of the library-like space. There were a few piles of paper and Post-it notes stuck over everything.

"I have this sneaking suspicion that some of the properties have been sold either without my grandfather knowing somehow, or at a huge loss. I can't figure it out completely, but I feel like I'm on the right trail."

Nathan let go of her hand and moved behind the desk, scanning the piles and nodding as he listened to her. "We need to find the deeds, make a list of who else he used for business. His accountant, any other professional advisors."

"Sounds like a plan. You take a look over everything, I'll take a shower, then we can sit down and work through it all."

Nathan dropped into the big chair and ran his hand across one of the paper piles, then reached for a pen. It had been a long time since he'd sat down to work in this type of environment, and he felt an almost forgotten type of buzz at actually taking on a task. He'd had a great time doing nothing for a while, but there was a part of him desperate for a purpose again, for a challenge that only work could bring, and he knew he was doing the right thing heading home.

"Nathan?"

He looked up.

"Thank you," she said. "I don't find it easy to trust sometimes, but I feel like, I don't know, that we've kind of told each other everything. That we can count on each other."

He refused to let his smile fade until she'd left the room, and then it dropped into a frown. *He'd told her a lot, but he hadn't told her everything.*

Jessica stretched and tried to ignore the twinge in her back. She needed to head outside for a walk and do her exercises, but she had this feeling they were about to figure something out. That they were so close to realizing what had gone wrong with Jock's affairs, that the answer was right under their noses and they were missing it each time they came close.

"Do you know what I think?"

She dropped the time line she'd been studying and drew her knees up to her chin, sitting on the floor. "What?" Her eyes were stinging from staring at the tiny words from all the legal documents she'd gone over, and her back was seriously starting to ache.

"I think your grandfather agreed to sell the individual properties, but what he signed or agreed to aren't the transactions we see in front of us."

Jessica crossed her arms, listening carefully to Nathan. "I don't know that I'm following you."

He stood and walked slowly over to the window. She watched as he stared out, as if he was still processing the whole thing in his mind.

"Let's say that he believed there was a willing buyer at a certain price." Nathan turned around and ran a hand through his hair, a gesture she'd started to notice that he did a lot. "Jock signed the sale and purchase agreement, in front of his lawyer, who has then fraudulently forged the rest of the paperwork at a different price to a completely different buyer, because there was no genuine one to start with."

She shook her head. "You don't think that's too far-fetched?" It wasn't that she didn't think it could have happened, but for it to have happened to her granddad was kind of hard to get her head around.

"I just don't see how else it could have happened, because from what I see here Jock intended on making the sales. Maybe he wanted to free up some money because he knew he was..."

Jessica froze, the tone of Nathan's voice and the way he'd just stopped talking sending alarm bells off in her head. "He knew he was what?"

His face remained impassive, not even a flicker of change, as if he was trying to pretend he hadn't just said what he had. But she knew he was keeping something back, something she needed to know.

"Nathan?" She said again. "He knew he was what?"

He blew out an audible breath, leaning back against the windowsill. "Because he knew he was dying," he said in a soft voice.

Jessica's hands started to tremble and she folded them on her lap, trying to stay calm. "You're telling me that he knew something was wrong? That he was sick?" *Surely her granddad would have told her, would have given her the chance to come home and seen him before he passed.*

Nathan nodded, crossed the room and dropped to the carpet beside her. "Yes."

He took both of her hands in his and stared into her eyes, his expression so full of concern that it made it hard for her to hold back her emotion. She didn't want to believe him, but she knew deep down that he was telling the truth. This man who had been so kind to her, who had helped her heal in a way she could hardly comprehend, would never lie to her. They'd shared a lot and she trusted him so much it scared her.

She sat up straighter, even though it hurt. The easy thing to do would be to yell at Nathan, take her anger and sadness out on him, but she knew it wasn't his fault. If she wanted someone to blame for not telling her the truth, it wasn't him.

"Jess?" Nathan's eyes sought out hers, his dark gaze stormy.

"How about you finish telling me your conspiracy theory?" she replied in a quiet voice. "Then we can go for a ride and you can tell me what I need to know."

Nathan nodded and let go of her hands. He stayed close, but even though his body was near she'd never felt so alone. Emotion threatened to choke her but she blocked it, tried to push the thoughts out of her head and just concentrate on what Nathan was saying.

"I don't think he could have acted alone," he told her. "For this to have worked, the lawyer must have had a buyer lined up, perhaps even a company he's involved with, and then they would have purchased it well below valuation and resold it soon after for a big profit. Or he planning to sell each property soon."

It all made sense, she had to give him that. "And because my grandfather was sick, he never realized what was going on."

"Not to mention a power of attorney putting his lawyer in a genuine position of power."

Jessica shut her eyes, taking it all in, processing what Nathan was saying. If he was right, she *had* to fight to get to the bottom of it, to save what was rightfully hers.

"So what do I do now?" she asked, standing and carefully stretching her body to limber up her back before she moved too far.

"Now you let me appoint an investigator, and we have a fun week before we pack up and head for the airport. If he's guilty he'll be prevented from ever practicing law again, and you'll be able to sue him."

She still couldn't believe she'd said yes to traveling back to London with Nathan—there was so much in her head she could hardly process it all at once.

"I can't afford an investigator," she said.

"But I can," Nathan told her, rising and standing behind her. His hands closed over her shoulders and rubbed gently. "And don't go telling me that you won't take charity," he said when she started to protest. "You can pay me back someday if you like, once it's all sorted out, but I'm doing this as much for Jock as I am for you."

As heavenly as the massage was, she forced herself to step away and turned around to face him.

"Speaking of my grandfather," she said, "how about we go for a walk and you can start on that telling-me-everything promise."

Nathan walked alongside Jessica, glancing at her every few seconds. She was beautiful. From the way her golden hair tumbled over her shoulders, the way her eyes always locked on his when she smiled, and the glimpses of skin he kept getting when she stretched—it was impossible not to think about the night they'd spent together. Just the flash of her bare stomach when she held her arms above her head before had reminded him of his mouth on that particular stretch of skin, how she'd felt in his arms.

He clamped his jaw and tried to push the memories away long enough to talk to her about her grandfather. The words had slipped out earlier, which meant he was about to break a promise to a man who'd meant so much to him. Not to mention the fact that he was shaking in his boots over the way he was behaving with Jessica, how natural it seemed to be with her.

"So tell me," Jessica said, not letting him stay silent any longer.

Nathan knew she'd be hurt that he knew something about Jock that she didn't. He reached for her, touching his hand to her lower back as they walked.

"We talked a lot, every day, and there are things I told your granddad that I'll probably never tell another soul."

Jessica glanced at him before looking straight ahead again, arms folded across her chest now.

"And he opened up to you, too?"

"Yeah," Nathan replied, not wanting to betray the old man's confidences but needing to tell her some of it. "He knew he was sick, but only for a short time, and he didn't want you to give up on your dreams when you were so close. He said it would have meant you not competing at Badminton."

She stopped moving and Nathan put his arms around her, drawing her close when he saw tears in her eyes. He wanted to comfort her, wanted to help break the pain that he knew was taking hold of her.

"The old bugger knew I'd come straight home, didn't he? And then he probably felt even worse when I had the fall."

Nathan nodded, holding her tight in his arms, his chin touching the top of her head. "He said there was nothing you could do for him, and he'd rather know you were doing what you loved. But then he regretted it, because if he had told you…"

Her body shuddered and he kissed her forehead, wrapping his arms even more firmly around her.

"I might not have had the accident."

"He was an incredible man, and he didn't want you to see him dying," Nathan told her, keeping his voice low. "But in the end it was the heart attack that killed him, not the cancer."

Jessica's arms were around him now, her head pressed to his chest like she wasn't ever going to let go or step away.

"At least he had you during those months," she mumbled, sniffing as she spoke. "At least he had you."

Yeah, he had. But the truth was that Jock had done a lot more for him than vice versa. When he'd arrived he'd been in a hell of a state—a dark vacuum that he had never thought he would be able to emerge from. And Jock had patiently waited him out, let him talk in his own time, then given him advice from the heart.

And then along had come Jessica. And for the first time in months, he'd almost found peace. Almost. Her granddad had been there for him, but it was being with Jessica that had slowly started to make him heal.

Jessica stared up at the sky, one hand held high above her head to shield her face from the bright sunshine. Today had been…*interesting*. She'd woken up in bed with Nathan, they'd talked about what might have happened to her inheritance, and she'd found out just what lengths her grandfather had been willing to go to for her. Always putting her ambitions ahead of his own.

"You never did say why, after all this time, you're having to leave in such a hurry," she said, thinking out aloud as they lay side by side.

Nathan reached for her hand, the one that was absently plucking grass, tucking his fingers over hers.

"I'm not just a banker."

The man was full of surprises. "You're not?"

"I saw an opportunity to buy into a small company

that was trying to launch a new energy drink a couple of years ago," he said, propping himself up on one elbow and looking down at her as he spoke. "I purchased the majority share, invested a crazy amount of money into the company, and we've not long ago started to distribute through North America as well as Europe. I need to go back to finalize the deal to float the company on the public stock exchange. All in all, it's been a pretty amazing investment."

She laughed. "Sorry, I don't think it's funny, I'm just kind of amazed that you're so…"

Nathan grinned. "What?"

"I don't know, you just seem so normal. But you're also this crazy successful business person."

"I am normal," he insisted, dropping a kiss to her mouth that was casual yet so unexpected that it had her pulse racing way too fast in less than a second. "Although I think I'm still hanging on to part of my childhood. I still want to prove to my father that I can do anything I want and be successful in my own right, so aside from that, yeah, I'm pretty normal."

"But you're also insanely wealthy, right?" she asked, wondering if she should have just kept that particular comment to herself. "I guess that's a good reminder to your dad."

Nathan shrugged, but she knew what that meant. He just wasn't going to brag about it even if he was proud of what he'd achieved.

"So when I'm in London, would you be offended if I head to the Cotswolds to see Teddy the day after we arrive?" she asked.

Nathan bent down low over her, his mouth barely an inch from hers. "It's the only reason you said yes to coming, isn't it?"

She tried to shake her head but he caught her mouth, his lips punishing hers. He then moved her hands above her head and pinned them there.

"It's not the only reason," she whispered back to him.

His laugh was husky. "Then how about you show me what the other reasons are?"

Jessica fought a giggle as he nipped her ear, before taking her mouth against his again, his lips impossibly soft as he grazed them back and forth over hers. There were so many things she should be doing, so many things that needed her attention. Although faced with a decision between reality and Nathan, it was impossible not to choose the latter.

A warning signal in her brain was trying to alert her again, she knew it was, but she chose to ignore it. Nathan was here for less than a week, and she was only going away with him for a short time. Which meant she couldn't get attached to him, didn't expect anything from him other than what they were doing right now. Just because her mom had pined for a man who'd broken her heart when he left didn't mean Jessica was ever going to make the same mistake. She was in charge of her own destiny, and nothing was going to change that. Not a riding accident, not a fraudulent lawyer, and certainly not a man. One bad ex didn't mean she needed to avoid all men for eternity, either.

Nathan could distract her all he wanted in the short term. That wasn't something she was ever going to say no to. Not with his mouth grazing her lips and his hands skimming against her skin. This was the kind of distraction she was only too happy to surrender to.

CHAPTER SEVEN

"I CAN'T BELIEVE we're actually boarding this plane."

Nathan slung an arm around Jessica's shoulders. He could hardly believe it, either. After so long in New Zealand there had been times he'd thought he might never leave. Going home was something he'd dreaded, although now he was getting excited about work again. Banking, not so much. But the company was something he was passionate about, and if he left it for much longer…well, there was only so many meetings that his poor assistant could defer on his behalf. It was one part of his career that he definitely wanted to salvage.

"You know everything's going to work out while you're gone, right?" he asked.

Jessica leaned into him, her arm finding his waist. "Yeah, but even if you're right about everything, what's the best that can happen?"

"The fraud is exposed and you sue them," he said, frowning at the worried look on her face.

"And that'll take how long?" she asked with a groan. "And if they've got no accessible money, I might never get anything back and I'll lose the farm anyway."

"You won't."

"I could."

He held her closer, their bodies skimming as they walked side by side. "I won't let that happen." She might not be comfortable with him spending his money to help her, but he was, and that was what mattered. The fact that neither she nor her grandfather would have ever expected his help was what made him so determined to offer it.

"Mr. Bell, right this way, sir."

He nudged Jessica with his shoulder when she glanced at him, shook her head and rolled her eyes.

"Perks of the rich and famous, huh? The VIP lounge and then first to board the plane."

"Hey, you can always ride in coach if you'd prefer."

She pretended to be horrified and clung to his side, laughing. "No way! I'm already tasting my first glass of champagne. And besides, if I'm about to be poor as a church mouse, I might as well enjoy my one chance at luxury."

Nathan nodded to the attendant as she ushered them down the air bridge. *He was about to board a plane and head home.* Funny, but it felt as if he was leaving home rather than returning to it.

He slipped his arm from around Jessica and reached for her hand instead. She glanced across at him, her smile infectious. It was also hard to believe that this gorgeous woman was going to be in his life for such a short time, because it felt as if he'd known her his entire life. Letting her go was going to be one of the hardest things he ever did, especially now he finally felt like himself again. Or at least a version of himself.

Although facing his house, the office that he hadn't set foot in since he'd found his wife there, was going to be bloody hard, too.

"You okay?"

He squeezed her hand. "Fine. Just hard to get my head around going back, that's all."

Her smile was full of warmth when she shone it in his direction. "You could always stay. I happen to know of a little guesthouse that might like you to take up permanent residency."

They both laughed as they walked, but the truth was, Nathan was sorely tempted. "I'm just glad you're coming with me." *Even if it was just delaying the inevitable.* "My assistant's going to freak out when she sees you, though."

"Why?"

"Because Natalie micromanages every part of my life. Before I left there wasn't anything she didn't know about me."

They passed their tickets to the attendant and were ushered to their seats. The wide-eyed look on Jessica's face made him chuckle—he'd become so used to traveling first class that he'd forgotten how exciting it was the first time.

"You do realize you've ruined flying for me forever," Jessica said as she sat down in the large seat and stretched out. "The flight home's going to be tough."

He didn't say anything, because he knew he'd give himself away by smiling if he so much as looked at her—he'd already paid for her first-class return ticket, so she wasn't coming home coach class on his watch.

"So you and Natalie…" she started, taking the glass of champagne as it was passed to her by their flight attendant.

"We'll call for you if we need anything," Nathan said, nodding at the attendant after taking his champagne.

"Yes, Mr. Bell. Please do."

"This is insane." Jessica was sipping her champagne, surveying where they were sitting.

"Just don't drink too many glasses," he told her, settling down beside her and resting his hand over hers, knees bumping. "Otherwise you'll go to stand up and you'll be legless. It goes to your head a lot faster in the air."

"So back to you and Natalie?" she asked tentatively.

"Strictly professional," he said, before grimacing and changing his answer. "No, we're actually great friends, too, but professional in the sense that nothing would ever happen between us."

"So how long will we be flying?"

He shrugged and settled back, pleased that line of questioning was over. Natalie was his right hand woman, but she was with a great guy and he was happy for her. "Almost a day, including the stop over."

"Well I'm not complaining. This is amazing." She sighed. "We can watch movies, drink champagne and eat—"

"—pretty much anything we want," he interrupted. "She'll bring the menu over soon."

Jessica sat forward and leaned across him, eyes flitting over his before dropping to look at his mouth. Her grin was wicked.

"Or we could do this," she suggested, brushing her lips across his.

Nathan kept hold of his glass in one hand and reached for her with the other, stroking through her hair. "Oh yes, we can definitely do this," he murmured against her mouth.

He might be about to hit reality when their plane touched down, but for now he could distract himself with Jessica. And if he was completely honest with himself, his reasons for bringing her along for a couple of weeks had been completely selfish. He didn't want to deal with returning on his own when being with her took his mind off everything. Until he had to let her go, and then it would be hell all over again.

Jessica stood in the open door to Nathan's house and tried to stop her jaw from hitting the polished timber floor beneath her feet. Before they'd arrived she'd been exhausted, and now she was wide awake, looking around in awe.

"How was it you managed to put up with the cottage for so long?" she asked.

Nathan walked past her, flicking on lights and putting their bags down. "This place might look great, but your place has a soul," he said. "And besides, all the cottage was missing was a great coffee machine. Once she had that she was perfect."

Jessica kept moving through, taking in the white walls and the stainless steel kitchen, the huge pieces of contemporary art, the immaculately clean spaces full of what she was certain was designer furniture. It was amazing.

"Your house is gorgeous," she said. "Absolutely gorgeous."

"Wait till you see the bedroom," he growled in her ear, looping his arms around her from behind and kissing her cheek.

Jessica turned in his arms and let him kiss her. "So are we going to test the bed out now?"

She groaned as he pulled back, the last press of his lips to her cheek far too brief for her liking.

"I need to head into the office," he said, spinning her around so she was in his arms. His lips were soft to hers, warm and familiar, and she wanted them there all day. "But I'll be back in time to take you out for dinner, I promise."

"Sounds good," she replied, not about to be the kind of woman to moan about being left. Besides, what they had was only supposed to be a causal fling—it wasn't like they were in a relationship. "I'll explore this gorgeous house some more then catch up on some sleep while you're gone."

He grinned. "I know the minute I walk out that

door you'll be on the phone finding out when you can head out to see Teddy."

She tried not to smile back and failed miserably. "You got me."

"Go see him today," he said, "unless you'd rather sleep?"

Jessica shook her head. She'd love to go see Teddy, but...

He reached into a drawer and threw her a pair of keys. She caught them and looked from them to Nathan.

"Take my car, then you can drive yourself there and be back in time for dinner. It has GPS, so just jump in and go. It'll only take just over an hour if you really put your foot down."

Jessica pushed them into her pocket and put her arms around Nathan's neck, gazing up into his eyes.

"Thank you," she said. "For everything."

They stared at one another for what felt like forever, before Nathan kissed her and stepped back.

"I'm going to shower and change then head straight out," he said.

Jessica watched him walk away, eyes following his every move. She crossed the room into the kitchen and opened the fridge, surprised to find it fully stocked. No doubt his assistant could take credit for making the house ready. She took out a carton of juice, found a glass to pour it into, then leaned on the counter. There was no part of her that wasn't exhausted, but she did want to go see Teddy. She missed him like crazy, and she had a feeling he'd be fretting without her, no matter what the stable hand told her every time she called.

Nathan appeared what seemed like only a few minutes later, his hair still wet and dressed in a pair of suit pants and an open-neck shirt, gold cuff links glinting when he ran his fingers through his hair. His cologne wafted toward her, making her smile, and he raised his hand before he raced out the door. She could tell he was anxious to go, that he had other things on his mind, which was kind of strange because she'd never seen him like this. At home everything about him had been relaxed, whereas here he was the same person but different, focused on something other than...*her*.

"Have fun," he said.

"You too."

Jessica watched him go and fought the crazy feeling that the man she'd known these past couple of weeks had disappeared. It was one thing telling herself that they weren't in a real relationship, that it was only *for now,* but the thought of walking away from him soon was tough. She didn't want to rely on a man, to put all her trust in any man and have him turn around and hurt her. That was what her mom had done, and Jessica had ended up with a mother full of regrets and pining for the man who'd left her, and a childhood without a father. Her granddad had been all the father she'd needed, but it had still been tough, especially when she knew what her mom had had to give up to raise her. And she'd never stopped wondering what it would have been like if she'd had a dad, and her mom had had a husband.

Jessica rinsed out her glass and stretched out her back. Her mom was the reason she'd been able to ride and compete, because she'd sacrificed everything for her, and she was going to salvage her career and the farm in honor of her family—no matter how hard it was going to be to walk away from Nathan when the time came. In her heart she knew he was the kind of man she could fall in love with, if she let herself. *Only she wasn't going to.*

She kicked off her shoes, scooped them up and then collected her suitcase on her way to the bedroom, walking slow to enjoy the thickness of the carpet beneath her toes. He lived an amazing lifestyle here, but from the way he'd talked he could have easily left it all behind forever. Part of her had wondered if he might do exactly that, although now she'd seen his house and the type of life he was used to living, she knew it was a fantasy that would never happen. Which only made her all the more certain that she had to enjoy their time together, knowing that when she left, she was leaving him behind forever.

Tears threatened, brushing against her lashes, but she blinked them away. There was no use getting all sad now. She was about to go and see her horse, and Nathan had lived up to everything he'd ever promised her and more. Which meant she had everything to be grateful for and nothing whatsoever to be sad about.

Nathan closed the door behind him as quietly as he could, trying not to make a sound as he crossed the room and flicked on the light. The house was silent except for the faint hum of his refrigerator. He poured a glass of water, drank it down then headed for his bedroom, surprised to see the faint glow of a lamp spilling out into the hallway. He found Jessica asleep on his bed, wearing one of his sweaters that she must have found, curled up with a book still in her hand. Nathan carefully took the book and placed it on the bedside table, then pulled the duvet up to cover her.

He undressed and flicked the lamp off, bathing the room in blackness as he crawled in beside her. *Bloody hell.* He'd been back only one day and already he'd let Jessica down and left her waiting for him. After telling himself that he'd changed, promising that he wouldn't be the same man all over again, he was turning into that same guy he'd thought he'd left behind. It went against his nature not to throw every part of himself into his work, but if he did that again he'd end up in an early grave, alone in the world, or both.

He turned in bed to face Jessica, not touching her to make sure he didn't wake her, but letting his eyes adjust to the darkness so he could see her silhouette beside him. Telling himself he'd made her no promises about their future didn't help, because he didn't want her to go, didn't want to face the reality of her leaving for good. His problem was that his work took so much from him, and finding balance wasn't something he'd ever succeeded in achieving. He was either full on working or relaxing—neither seemed to go hand in hand with the other.

But while Jessica was here, he didn't want to disappoint her. That look on his wife's face still haunted him, the one he'd seen countless times but never so sad as the last morning he'd seen her. The disappointment shining from her eyes, the dullness in the way she looked at him—he didn't ever want to see that kind of look again, and especially not on Jessica's face. Not after she'd been the one to help him find his way back to being himself again.

Nathan shut his eyes, jet-lagged and tired from the papers he'd had to sift through. He could make it up to Jess in the morning—right now he needed to sleep.

His phone buzzed and he reached for it, checking his emails.

Or not. Because already Natalie had scheduled an eight a.m. meeting for him, which meant he'd have to be out the door before Jessica probably even woke.

Jessica woke to the crunch of paper beneath her cheek. It was the third time she'd woken like that in as many days. She groaned and pushed up, blinking in the bright light and squinting as she read the note. Nathan was beginning to make a habit of arriving once she'd fallen asleep and leaving before she was awake, and she was starting to get grumpy. She was about to flop back down again when she heard a noise. Jessica glanced at her watch and saw it wasn't even seven yet, which meant…she jumped out of bed, grabbing her robe and slipping it on as she ran down the hall.

"Nathan!"

The heavy footsteps stopped and she saw him, hand poised on the door handle, about to leave.

"Hey," he said, opening his arms as she walked into them.

Nathan dropped a kiss into her hair, rubbing a hand up and down her back. She inhaled his cologne, relaxed into his big body, cheek against the lapel of his jacket.

"You sure you don't want to come back to bed with me?" she murmured against him.

"Believe me, every time I leave you in there alone, it's torture."

"Then don't leave me," she said, pushing back to look up at him.

She could see the conflict in his gaze, knew he was being truthful, but she still wanted to make him feel at least a little bit guilty about going. She'd started to crave his touch, his company, and she wanted to see more of him.

"I wish I didn't have to, but..."

"It's okay." She pressed a kiss to his cheek, hands on his arms. "I get that you have to work. You've been away for months, it wasn't like you were ever going to be able to act like a tourist with me."

He looked away, over her head, then focused on her again, eyes locked on hers. The look on his face reminded her of the Nathan she'd fallen for on the farm. "You know what?"

She raised her eyebrows, waiting, still holding on to his arms.

"How long will it take you to get ready?"

"Ready for what?" she asked.

He grabbed her bottom, making her wriggle out of his way, laughing, all thoughts about being annoyed with him for leaving her long gone.

"Breakfast. Let's go grab something to eat before I head in to the office."

Jessica watched his face to make sure he wasn't kidding, and all she saw was a smile that told her he meant every word of it.

"Give me ten minutes."

He folded his arms and nodded, glancing at his watch. "Go."

"Just don't walk out that door," she said, moving backward. "You can't get my hopes up and then bail on me."

"I wouldn't think of it."

Jessica hurried back to the bedroom, grabbed some clothes and went into the bathroom. She felt as if she'd hardly seen Nathan since they'd arrived, and she needed a reminder that this whole thing between them wasn't something she'd somehow fabricated. Because right now she was starting to feel like a neglected mistress, and deep down she knew that Nathan cared about her as much as she cared about him. No matter what she tried to tell herself, no matter what she'd promised, there was no part of her that was okay with having less than a week left with the one man in her life who'd told her he couldn't commit to anything more than fun, yet somehow managed to make her care about him more than any other man she'd ever met.

So much for keeping her distance.

* * *

"I want you to know that I never meant to just leave you to your own devices."

She forked a piece of waffle covered in syrup before answering. "Is that the British way of telling me you're sorry for ignoring me all week?" The expression on Nathan's face made her reach for him, squeezing his hand and knowing she'd overstepped. "Sorry, that came out all wrong."

"No, it came out all right," he said with a loud sigh. "I'm a workaholic, and the minute I arrived back in this city I was sucked straight back into my old life. I tried to make it different and it just didn't happen."

"You never made me any promises, Nathan. It's okay."

He pushed his plate away. "No, but I was selfish asking you to join me and then spending every waking hour at the office."

"Is it worth it?" she asked, still eating her waffles and trying not to think about the first time they'd shared breakfast together on the porch of the cottage, wishing they were still there, that things could have been different.

He paused as he was about to take a sip of his coffee. "Financially? Yes." He shrugged. "But that doesn't mean that I shouldn't be spending more time with you instead. I just can't seem to find that balance, which sounds like a complete cop-out, I know."

"Nathan, I don't have long here, but…"

"I'm going to make it up to you," he said.

What she should have been doing was taking the

chance to distance herself from him, reminding herself why she didn't want to get close to Nathan, how much it would hurt to leave him, and instead...

"What do you have in mind?"

Instead she was lapping up his attention. Deep down she was lying to herself, hoping that somehow they didn't have only days or weeks left together. That he would stop spending all his time at work and turn back into the easygoing, relaxed guy she'd known when she'd first met him. That they would somehow find a way to be together.

"How about lunch?" he asked, checking his watch for what seemed like the hundredth time since they'd sat down.

"Today?" Jessica asked.

He frowned, reaching for his phone. He scrolled through quickly before looking up. "Tomorrow?"

Jessica smiled, but inside she felt like a flower wilting in the hot sunshine. Slowly dying but trying to stay bright. Lucky she was good at hiding her feelings—a childhood of trying to stay bright for her mom's sake, to keep her happy, was to thank for that.

"I might head out to see Teddy today," she said, even though seeing him again would only remind her that she was going to be heading home soon without him for the second time. That despite distracting herself with Nathan she was still on the brink of losing everything. "Tomorrow sounds great."

He opened his wallet and dropped his credit card on the table, then waved their waitress over. Nathan leaned across the table and kissed her, but unlike the usual spark she felt, the tingle that had run through her body every single time he'd kissed her in the past, this one was somehow tinged with…*sadness*. There was a finality to it that she wanted to stamp away, that made her want to kiss him until it disappeared, only she wasn't sure if there was anything she could do to take them back to what had been, when they were living in a little bubble outside of reality.

"Don't wait up," he said, slipping into his suit jacket. "You take the car and I'll take a cab."

Jessica watched him go and forced a smile when the waitress returned with Nathan's card. She was alone, just like she had been when her dad had left. Just like she had been when her mom had been killed, when she'd had to cope with the police arriving to tell her her mom hadn't made it. *Just like she'd been when her granddad had died.*

And she hated it.

CHAPTER EIGHT

"You must be the famous Jessica."

Jessica turned around to find a beautiful brunette standing behind her, an earpiece in one air and a pen in her hand. "And you must be Natalie, aka assistant extraordinaire."

She shook the other woman's hand and smiled, knowing straightaway that she liked her. Nathan had talked a lot about the "other woman" in his life, and she knew from what he'd said that he'd spent more time with Natalie than virtually any other person in the past decade.

"I hope he's told you nice things about me," Natalie said.

Jessica frowned. "Well…"

Natalie looked anxious and Jessica quickly shook her head.

"I'm kidding! Honestly, he's told me that you're one of the most important people in his life. That he couldn't do what he does without you running things behind the scenes."

She looked relieved. "Honestly? Nathan is the

best employer I've ever had. He makes me work long hours, but he's done so much for me. I'd die if I thought he *didn't* say good things about me!"

Jessica was curious what she meant. Part of her had been worried that there might be more to their relationship since they were obviously so close, especially now she'd seen firsthand how beautiful Natalie was, but something told her there was more to the story. That there was nothing like that going on. It was her nature to expect the worst when it came to men—but she needed to let that go. Nathan wasn't her ex, and there was no other woman.

"Nathan said you've had a well-deserved break while he's been away?"

Natalie touched her arm and gestured for her to follow, holding up her hand for a moment as she answered a call and transferred it through to Nathan.

"I've had a seven-month vacation on full pay," she said, keeping her voice low as they talked and walked at the same time. "Not to mention the fact that when my husband walked out on me a few years back, Nathan paid my daughter's school fees and made sure I didn't lose my house." Natalie laughed. "And he paid for a terrific divorce lawyer, too, so my ex never even knew what was coming until it hit him."

Jessica was starting to get a picture of what Nathan was like in his usual world. He might blame himself for being a workaholic who didn't spend enough time with his wife, but he was generous to a fault in so many other ways. When he cared about someone he obviously had his heart in the right place, which was why he'd been so quick to offer to help her with Teddy and the farm. Maybe she shouldn't have gotten her back up and turned him down so fast—she'd been offended when all he was trying to do was help.

"So is it worth the long hours you have to work?" Jessica asked.

"Absolutely. I work hard, but I haven't had to miss one school sports day or prize giving. Nathan works himself to the bone, but he more than respects the fact that I have a daughter to look after."

It shouldn't have mattered to her so much—she was only here for a few weeks before heading home, which meant that what Nathan did wasn't really any of her business. But the fact that there was nothing going on between him and Natalie, and hearing how kind he was, did make her happy. It also told her that there was no chance of him ever leaving London for good, though, no matter how much she might have secretly fantasized about it. His work was too important to him. *But it was what she wanted, no matter how hard it was to convince herself sometimes.* She'd made her mind up years ago that she wasn't a relationship type of girl. She just had to convince herself that what she'd already had with Nathan was better than something long-term.

"So his office is through here?"

"Yes. Go on in. Do you take chocolate or cinnamon on your cappuccino?"

Jessica paused and looked back at Natalie. "How did you know I like a cappuccino?"

Natalie shrugged, the phone ringing at the same

time. "It's the little things that make me good at what I do. And besides, I don't have that many coffee orders to remember."

She watched Natalie go then knocked on Nathan's glass door, unable to see in without standing on tiptoe. There was a frosting across all the glass for privacy, meaning the office was no doubt full of light but Nathan and anyone else inside were kept away from prying eyes.

"Come in."

Jessica would have recognized Nathan's deep voice anywhere. She pushed the door open and stepped into his office, taking a moment to look around and survey the place where he spent all his working hours. There was a massive glass desk in the center of the room with a backdrop of the city below, two chairs placed in front of it. A modern sofa with chrome legs sat off to the side. It was more contemporary than she'd imagined, right down to the abstract artwork adorning the far wall, but then she wasn't sure what she'd expected. Maybe worn leather, a bottle of scotch and an old antique desk—like she'd seen in movies.

"Hey beautiful." Nathan dropped his pen and pushed some papers aside before standing and moving around his desk to greet her.

"Your office is gorgeous," she said, smiling up at him as he bent forward to kiss her.

His lips were warm, even more inviting because they were so familiar to her, and she sighed into his mouth. She could spend every hour of every day in his arms and never tire. When he finally pulled away

Nathan took her hand and led her to the sofa, dropping down onto it and waiting for her to do the same. "I had Natalie organize an office makeover while I was gone," he said, brushing her long hair back and over her shoulder. "She did a great job."

Jessica leaned back and crossed her legs, half-facing him. "Natalie's lovely. I had a chat with her before I came in."

A buzzing noise caught her attention. Nathan jumped up, reached for his iPhone and frowned as he stared at the screen. He started to tap away and she uncrossed her legs and leaned forward.

"Everything okay?"

He nodded but didn't look up. "Yeah. I just have a lot to…" He didn't finish his sentence, but reached around for his office phone and pressed a button. "Natalie, I need you to contact Leigh, tell him I'll have a revised portfolio to him by the end of the day."

Jessica stood, not sure whether she should stay put or leave and let Nathan get back to whatever he was working on. Instead she just fidgeted on the spot.

"I'm guessing we're going to have to reschedule lunch?" she asked, trying not to sound too disappointed. He had work to do, she got that, but she'd been looking forward to spending time with him.

"Oh, honey I'm sorry." He put his phone down and suddenly directed all of his attention toward her. "Is that okay?"

She nodded, planting a smile on her face. It wasn't as if she expected him to put his life on hold for her, but after spending so much time together it was hard seeing him like this, back in work mode and focused so completely on something else. And she hadn't even seen him before he'd left this morning.

"It's fine. I'll just…" She shrugged. "I don't know, but I'm sure I can find something else to occupy my time."

His phone started to vibrate again, and she could see how hard he found it to ignore the message or call that was coming through.

"Jess, I know we were going to stay home tonight, but I've been invited to a cocktail party. Tell me you'll come with me to make it bearable?"

"Sure." Except she had nothing even remotely suitable to wear in her suitcase. "I might have to ask Natalie where to go to find a dress." She also didn't have money to spend on clothes that she'd never wear again, not when she needed to save every penny she had to keep the farm going while she still could.

Nathan's smile could have melted her heart, but that warm fuzzy feeling started to fade when he pulled out his wallet from his pocket. "Take this," he said, slipping his credit card out and putting it in her hand. "Buy yourself whatever you want. New dress, shoes, beauty treatments, whatever. I'll have Natalie organize anything you need."

She closed her fingers around the card and looked up at Nathan, knowing that he genuinely thought he was just being generous to her and nothing else. To her, it made her feel like an expensive mistress, but that was only because she wasn't used to the kind of money he had. Nathan was just trying to do something nice, to pamper her, and it wasn't something she wanted to start a fight over. It was the same as him offering to help with Teddy, and she had to keep reminding herself of that.

"Thanks," she managed. "So I'll meet you at home later?"

He'd already turned away, phone back in his hand and a frown fixed on his face again. His eyebrows were drawn together, his full lips downturned in a way she'd never seen on him before. He glanced up to answer her, staring at her for a second like he was trying to remember her question.

"Ah, no. I'll have to stay here until later, so I'll send a car for you."

Jessica nodded and turned to go, feeling numb. She had no idea what was happening, what had changed between them, but all the spontaneity and fun they'd had, the closeness between them, seemed to be trickling away from them like a slow running current in a stream.

"Jessica," Nathan said, his hand suddenly on her arm.

She turned, feeling like an idiot for being so hard on him when she looked up into his eyes.

"I'm sorry about lunch. I'll make it up to you tonight, I promise."

Jessica pressed a kiss to his cheek. "See you tonight."

As she listened to him cross the room again as she left, she also heard him pick up his phone.

"Natalie, anything Jess wants, make it happen. Can you make sure she has what she needs?"

That sad feeling swept through her body again. When he'd said that in the past he'd been married to his job more than his wife, she'd wondered if he was exaggerating, that maybe his wife had been too precious for her own good. But now she was starting to see a pattern emerge that she would struggle with should she be in Nathan's life long-term. She'd probably end up speaking to his assistant more than the man himself, and anything they arranged would either be canceled at the last minute or rescheduled so they could go somewhere or meet with someone who was good for business. *Which meant she'd turn into his wife, into someone who resented the hours he spent away from home.*

And it shouldn't have bothered her, but the idea of going out and spending his money like some trophy wife just didn't seem right to her. A new dress, pretty shoes and an afternoon of being pampered was a dream come true…if she'd been paying for it herself.

Lucky she was only in this for the short term. *Or at least that was the lie she needed to sell herself, pretending that she'd rather be independent than dependent on anyone.* All her life she'd been a loner of sorts, when all she'd really wanted, deep down, was someone to care for her. Aside from her grandfather, no one had ever truly taken care of her, not ever.

Nathan ran a hand through his hair, leaning back in his chair and then spinning it around to look out at the city. When he'd been away, he hadn't missed anything about London. To start with, it had been unusual being in a different country, but he'd settled in as soon as he'd found the place he wanted to stay. Now that he was back, it was as if he'd never been gone. He didn't have as many clients to deal with, but he was busy with his other business and it was a struggle to keep on top of everything. Or maybe it was a struggle because he was trying to stick to more civilized work hours for Jessica's sake—and failing terribly.

He'd seen the look on her face today, the all-too-familiar cloud of disappointment and hurt that he'd seen countless times on his wife's face. Near the end, he'd thought his wife simply no longer cared, but now he knew that she'd just become an expert at hiding her feelings. Feelings he should have thought about instead of pretending that everything about his home life was okay.

He was at a crossroads, and he needed to figure out what the hell he was going to do to find some balance in his life. He couldn't punish himself with ninety-hour weeks again, but he also couldn't spend the rest of his life doing nothing.

A soft knock echoed on his office door, and he swung around to see Natalie standing there.

"I thought you were long gone," he said, rubbing his knuckles into his eyes and wishing he wasn't so tired.

Natalie's smile put him at ease, as it always did. He had no idea what he'd do without her.

"Ellie's with a babysitter, and Steve's going to meet me downstairs," she told him, holding up his bottle of whisky and pouring small amounts into two glasses when he nodded. "I'm going to get ready here."

It had been such a crazy day that he'd almost forgotten about the cocktail party. The last thing he wanted was to network at a social function disguised as a party, but it was the first time he'd been able to accept an invitation in months. Plus it meant he could spend the entire evening with Jessica by his side.

He took the glass she offered and finished the whisky in two big gulps as Natalie took tiny sips of hers.

"Did your dress arrive?" he asked, pulling at his tie and discarding it before bending to take off his shoes.

"For the hundredth time, you did *not* need to buy me a dress or anything else for this evening."

He laughed. "Yeah, but if I hadn't you'd have had to leave work early to get something from home. It was a win-win situation." He inwardly cringed. Only a short time ago he'd used the same terminology when he'd been trying to convince Jessica to travel back to London with him.

Natalie went to leave, glass still in hand, then stopped. Nathan watched her, knowing she was waiting to tell him something, that she had something on her mind.

"Can I ask what's happening between you and Jessica?" she asked. "I know it's none of my business, but you seem so happy with her, happier than I've ever seen you, and I don't—"

"What?" he asked, eyebrows raised. "You don't

want me to stuff up this relationship by giving all of myself to my work again?"

Her eyes were sadder than a puppy without its mother. "I love you, Nathan, you know that. I just want you to be happy, and she seems great."

Nathan forced a smile and watched Natalie leave. He wasn't angry with her for speaking her mind, because at the end of the day she'd just said what he'd been thinking anyway, and she was right. Jessica was the best thing that had happened to him in a long time, and he needed to figure out what he was going to do to somehow keep her in his life. They'd both agreed it was no strings attached, that they were just enjoying one another's company for however long they could, but he didn't want to let her go.

He took his tuxedo and white shirt from his office closet and got dressed, tying his bowtie and then reaching for his Tiffany cuff links. He would have preferred a night at home eating something great and with Jessica tucked by his side on the sofa, just the two of them. Instead he was going to have to wow her with a night out on the town, and try to convince her that they could make whatever it was between them work...*somehow.*

Jessica stepped from the car when the driver opened the door, a shiver running through her body when the frigid air hit her cheeks. Thank goodness she'd decided to buy the jacket the sales assistant had been so pushy about—without it she'd have frozen before reaching the entrance to Nathan's building.

She thanked the driver and hurried, moving as fast as she could without slipping on her four-inch heels. It wasn't as if she was used to wearing such high shoes, and it was starting to snow as she walked.

"I think we might be heading to the same place."

Jessica clutched her purse tighter, trying to give just a quick glance at whomever it was who'd spoken to her. A man dressed in a black suit, bow tie and heavy overcoat ran a few steps ahead of her and held open the door—he didn't look like he was about to rob her, so she let go of the fierce hold she had. The warm blast of air from inside the building hit her the moment she stepped in, and her cheeks burned from the sudden, shocking change in temperature.

"Thank you," she said to him, as he moved through the door behind her. They walked side by side to the elevator.

"You must be with Nathan?"

She nodded, realizing who the man must be. "Yes. And I'm guessing you're with Natalie?"

He smiled. "They're the only two working this late, so it's not hard to guess, is it?"

Jessica let him select the correct floor, and they stood side by side in the elevator. He waited for her to step out.

"The best thing about these dos is they have plenty to drink," he said with a chuckle. "After a couple of bourbons the whole thing becomes kind of bearable. So if you want my advice, head straight for the bar."

She laughed with him. "It can't be that bad." If anything, she was looking forward to a night out, especially if it meant spending time with Nathan. "I'm Jessica, by the way."

He stopped for a moment and held out his hand, shaking hers when she offered it. "Steve. If you're dating Nathan, we might end up seeing a whole lot of each other."

She raised her eyebrows and was about to ask exactly what he meant, when he touched her back and they started walking again, across the thick carpet toward Nathan's desk.

"I don't know how many times Natalie has ended up staying late, traveling for work or attending things with Nathan. She's always telling me what a great employer he is, but they work long hours, and you kind of get used to being let down at the last minute." His grin made her smile, even though what he was saying wasn't what she wanted to hear. "All I'm saying is we could end up having dinner together a lot, because it would sure beat getting stood up."

Nathan appeared just as Steve finished talking. His eyes met hers before slowly traveling all the way down her body and up again. The way he smiled at her reminded her exactly why she was so attracted to him. The corner of his mouth kicked up into a smile as he stepped forward to greet her. If a man had ever looked sexy in a tux it was Nathan—the sharp lines of his black suit, the immaculately tied black tie, the white shirt against his tanned skin. The man was like a walking advertisement for a designer menswear store.

"You look amazing," he said as he took her hand

and kissed her cheek, his lips lingering long enough to make her melt. With Nathan, it was as if every kiss was their first, and that thrill of his mouth on her skin still lingered every single time. *Making her forget all her concerns all over again.*

She smoothed one hand down the satin-and-sequined fabric of her dress, still not sure she'd made the right decision with her purchase, even if Nathan did think she looked good.

"Did you have fun shopping?" he asked, taking her hand and rubbing his thumb across her skin. "I wasn't lying—you do look incredible."

"You don't look so bad yourself," she murmured, as he kissed the inside of her wrist.

"And I see you've met Steve," Nathan said, finally acknowledging there was someone else in the room.

Steve was now sitting in an oversize leather chair in the waiting area, flicking through a magazine, although he dropped it and looked up when Nathan spoke.

"Yes we—" Steve jumped up. "Hey, beautiful girl."

Jessica turned at the same time as Nathan did, to find a very glammed-up Natalie doing a twirl for her man.

"So who's going to be at the party tonight?" Jessica asked, as Nathan tucked an arm around her and they headed back toward the elevator. "A whole lot of stuffy old guys you need to network with?"

He made a face like he was horribly offended. "Are you calling me old and stuffy?"

Jessica pushed her shoulder into his as they walked. "Definitely not." She ran her fingers down his lapel while they waited for the elevator, pressing her body to his and tilting her head back for a kiss, refusing to think about anything other than just enjoying Nathan's company. "As long as you wear that tux I'd go anywhere with you."

He pressed his mouth so softly to hers he hardly had any of her red lipstick on his lips. "How about we skip the party?" he murmured. "Because that dress looks good, but it would look even better off."

"Always the charmer," she said with a laugh, slipping her hand under his jacket. His chest felt warm even through his shirt. All thoughts about doubting him or what she was doing with him vanished from her mind. He was an amazing man who had to work a lot—it didn't mean he wasn't the same person she'd first met. She needed to give him a break.

He groaned when she pressed a kiss to the underside of his jaw. "Maybe we could just stay for a little while, to make an appearance. Then I'm going to take you home and strip you down to—"

"Get a room, you two."

Jessica's face flushed at being caught out by Natalie and her partner, but Nathan hardly even blinked at Steve's comment.

"As soon as I've made an appearance and a few hefty donations to whatever charity they're raising money for, that's exactly what we'll be doing."

Jessica swatted at his shoulder, cheeks burning as she laughed along with the others. Maybe tonight wasn't going to be so bad, after all. So he'd brought her a beautiful outfit and paid for an indulgent afternoon of beauty treatments—he had a ton of money and he wanted to do something nice for her. She needed to loosen up and stop worrying so much. He had a demanding job, and she understood only too well what that was like—she'd put her career first all her life, too. Only now she was drifting without a purpose, no longer focused on achieving her own goals.

She reached for Nathan's hand and linked her fingers with his, looking up at him as he smiled down at her. If only they didn't live so far apart. Because this was the first time in her life that she'd ever met a man she could imagine a future with. And that was why her emotions were leaping all over the place— she was certain of it.

CHAPTER NINE

THE ROOM, FULL OF elegantly dressed people, was like nothing Jessica had ever seen before. Immaculately dressed waiters passed around food on shiny silver trays held high in the air, a string quartet played just loud enough not to hinder conversation, and all the women were dripping in expensive jewels. Add to that the posh English accents, and Jessica felt as if she'd walked into a party fit for royalty. She spotted a few younger women, but the crowd was a lot older than she'd expected.

"I'm taking it these are more your clients than your peers?" she asked as she stayed snug to Nathan's side.

His lips skimmed her cheek before he spoke directly into her ear.

"The older men are the ones investing money with me, hence the need to schmooze."

It was on the tip of her tongue to ask why he didn't solely focus on his other business instead of banking, when it was something that he could do without working such long hours or at the same level of stress, but she didn't. The last thing she wanted to do was argue with him when they were finally spending some time together. *She needed to let it go.*

"Once we've finished here I have something to tell you." His voice was still low, husky and just for her ears.

She tugged his hand, making him pause. "What is it?"

"It wouldn't be a surprise then, would it?"

His smirk made her place the hand he wasn't holding on her hip, giving him a cheeky glare, but before she could protest someone called his name and he turned away from her.

"Jess, come meet some of my clients," he said, grinning as he raised a hand at a group of men standing only a few feet away.

"How about I go find us some champagne first?" she suggested, spotting Natalie and Steve standing near the bar. "I'll be back in a moment."

Nathan gave her a quick smile but she could tell from the look on his face he was back in work mode. *So much for just the two of them.* No matter how much she tried to convince herself otherwise, Nathan simply had a different role to play here, and she needed to stop expecting him to change. This was his world, and she needed to suck it up and deal with it if she wanted to enjoy her time with him before she had to head home. *If she had a home to return to.*

Jessica pushed the thoughts aside. There was nothing she could do about that part of her life until she heard back from the investigator. At least she'd have something to focus on when she boarded the plane, because leaving Nathan was going to be one of the hardest things she ever did.

"Jessica," he said, his hand over her forearm making her pause instead of walking away.

"Yes?"

"It means a lot to me that you came tonight. I know I let you down today."

She shrugged, even though he was right. Half her problem was that she'd never been one to wait around for a guy or to rely on one, which made Nathan choosing work over spending time with her all the harder to deal with.

"We're together tonight," she said. "That's what counts."

He gave her another kiss, this time on her forehead, lips lingering for long enough to make her want to melt against him.

"I don't want to make the same mistakes again," he murmured. "You mean too much to me."

She let him kiss her, this time on the lips, before she finally made her way to the bar. When she glanced over her shoulder she saw Nathan patting a few other men on the back, laughing and joking as if he didn't have a care in the world. She smiled to herself. She'd had the very same thought the first day she'd met him, when he walked away from her across the farm. How incredibly wrong she'd been then.

Jessica sipped on her champagne, wishing she'd taken a few more of the blinis when they were being passed around. Her stomach was starting to growl.

"So did you have a nice afternoon?" Natalie asked as they stood side by side, surveying the room.

"It was lovely," she said, not wanting to sound ungrateful. "But to be honest, I'd have happily traded it for a few hours with Nathan." It was the truth and she doubted Natalie was going to judge her for being honest.

"Believe me, I know what you mean," Natalie said, her gaze warm. "And if it makes a difference, he's trying. He still beats himself up for what happened to Marie, and if he could change anything it would have been spending more hours with her."

Jessica was about to take a sip of her champagne but instead paused midair and held it down lower. "It must have been hard on him, losing her."

Natalie let out a big sigh. "Impossible. Especially when he blamed himself for what happened. I mean, the way he found her, the things they'd argued about the night before…"

A cold shiver shimmied like a trail of ice down Jessica's back. "I don't know what you're talking about."

Jessica smoothed her hands down her black dress, cringing as she connected with her bare thigh. She should never have worn something so short. It had seemed like a good idea at the time, but now she just wished she was back in her jeans, her hair pulled up in a ponytail and a tub of ice cream resting in her lap. Or better still, back home and riding a horse. And she sure as hell wished she wasn't standing in the corner of a crowded room, holding a glass of champagne she no longer wanted and feeling like an idiot making small talk with Nathan's assistant about a woman she hadn't even known. At one point she'd thought he was making his way over to her, but instead he'd stopped and talked to what seemed like every person in the room, and she'd left his side to get another drink and not returned. She was starting to wonder if he'd even noticed she was gone. And now she wasn't even sure what Natalie was saying, or trying to say to her.

"I guess I just thought, well, that after spending so much time with you that he would have…"

Natalie never finished her sentence and Jessica was left waiting, annoyed at what she didn't know. There was something weird going on, something that had been hidden from her, that Natalie was on the brink of telling her, and she wanted to know.

"He told me his wife's death was…" Jessica paused, trying to remember the exact word. "He said it was traumatic."

Jessica had imagined a car crash, the same way her mother had died, or a fast illness. But from the look on Natalie's face it was something that was hard for her to talk about.

"I hate that I'm the one to tell you, but it's not like it's a secret," Natalie said in a low voice, her eyes darting across the room. "If you stay much longer, it would be impossible for you to not find out."

Jessica looked in the same direction and saw Nathan, watched as he spoke to another man, his big frame standing out in the sea of black tuxedos and bow ties. Looking at him now, as at ease among this crowd as he had been mucking around with horses on her farm, she wasn't even sure she knew the man she'd started to fall for.

"Please," Jessica said, putting her glass down and staring at Natalie. "Just tell me or I'll walk over and ask him myself." She didn't want to be the fool, not in on something that Natalie had obviously expected her to know. *That she should have known.*

Natalie cleared her throat and raised her glass to her lips, before leaning in closer toward her even though there was no one near enough to hear them over the string quartet playing.

"Nathan's wife hanged herself in the office in his house," Natalie said, her voice barely louder than a whisper, her tone somber. "He arrived home late from work, on the night of their wedding anniversary, and there was nothing he could do."

Oh my god. Jessica closed her eyes for a beat and took a deep breath, her hands trembling as she tried to comprehend what she'd just been told. *His wife had committed suicide? How could he not have told her when they'd talked about everything? When they'd confessed so much to one another?*

"And everyone here tonight, except me, knows what happened?" Jessica asked, feeling as betrayed as she was sad. She'd thought they were so close, had shared everything about her own past with Nathan. *Everything.*

"One of the reasons he took off and went traveling was to get away from the media. It was front-page news that the art world's darling had taken her own life, and Nathan blamed himself for what happened. I think he still does in a lot of ways."

Had he lied about anything else to her or just omitted the truth about his wife? Betrayal stung her body, making her feel like such a fool. After vowing never to let a man lie to her, to hurt or betray her, now here she was finding out secondhand the truth about Nathan, just like her mom had found out about her cheating husband. Just like she'd found out the truth about her ex. It wasn't infidelity, but it was a lie that struck her right to the bone.

"Did he have a heart attack?" She needed to know that was at least true.

Natalie nodded. "He's always worked such long hours, and when she died he started to work around the clock without leaving the office at all. That's when he ended up in cardiac arrest and was rushed to the hospital. I thought I was never going to see him again."

Jessica picked her glass back up and took one long sip, then another. At least she knew now. Surely Nathan had known he wouldn't be able to keep something like that a secret from her. She could have heard it from anyone, read about it in the paper, even—and he'd just decided to keep it from her like she would never find out?

"I think I'll head home," Jessica said, trying to sound strong even though she was shattered inside. "Would you mind telling Nathan I've left?"

Natalie shook her head, eyes wide. "Jessica, please don't go. I didn't mean to upset you. If I'd even for a minute thought he hadn't told you I would never have—"

"I know," Jessica said, touching the other woman's arm before stepping away. "You were telling me something that you thought I knew. That I should have known. It's not your fault."

"But I've upset you." She grabbed Jessica's hand and held tight. "I've never seen Nathan so happy, Jessica. Please don't go, not yet. Give him a chance to explain himself to you."

Jessica fought the tears pricking her eyes and braved a smile. She thought she'd been happy, too, but the truth was that nothing had been the same since Nathan had gone back to work, since he'd fallen straight back into the lifestyle he'd told her so many times he'd wanted to distance himself from. She could only guess that he was addicted to what he did, to the life he had here, to ever walk away for good, even if he claimed that was what he wanted.

"I'm sorry," Natalie said.

"Me too," Jessica replied, her voice barely louder than a whisper.

It was over. Deep down, she'd known there was something pulling them apart, as if the bubble they'd been tucked safe within back in New Zealand couldn't keep them safe forever. She looked over at Nathan one last time, before saying goodbye to Natalie, squaring her shoulders and heading for the door. She'd collect her coat, find a cab, and let herself into Nathan's place. If she was lucky, she'd be able to pack up and leave before he was even home from the party.

* * *

Nathan stood still and scanned the room. She was gone. He'd looked everywhere for her, with the exception of the ladies' powder room, but no one had seen Jessica, and he was starting to worry. She wasn't exactly easy to miss in her short, black, sequin-and-satin cocktail dress, her long blond hair loose and tumbling down her back, especially amid a roomful of brunettes, and he was certain she wasn't in the room.

"Nathan."

He turned to find Natalie standing behind him. When she closed her hand over his forearm, her eyebrows drawn together, he knew he was in for bad news.

"Where's Jessica?" he asked, staring at her like he could compel an answer from her by glare alone.

"She's gone, Nathan. I'm so, so sorry."

He had no idea what had happened, why she'd left, but he did know that things had been strained between them the past few days. *Idiot*. He never should have come back, stepped back into the life he'd worked so hard to distance himself from since…

"You've got nothing to be sorry about," he told Natalie.

Her wide-eyed, guilty gaze said otherwise.

"It's my fault. I didn't know you'd kept Marie a secret from her," Natalie managed, her voice breaking like she was about to cry. "About how she died, what had happened."

Nathan groaned, but he wasn't about to blame his assistant. He should have told Jessica, had wanted to so many times, but after everything they'd discussed it had never seemed like the right time, and he'd left it wait too long. And now she'd gone, no doubt feeling like an idiot for being the only one not to know.

"Did she say where she was going?" he asked.

She shook her head. "No. But she was pretty upset."

He squeezed Natalie's hand and did his best to smile, even though he had absolutely nothing to be happy about. "Don't beat yourself up about this. Her not knowing was my mistake, not yours."

Nathan turned to go, but Natalie's grasp on his arm again stopped him.

"Don't lose her, Nathan. When you're with her, you're the happiest I've ever seen you."

He didn't answer her because he didn't know what to say. Natalie was right—when he was with Jessica everything fell into place. What had started out as something fun, a connection that was only supposed to be a holiday fling, had turned into something a whole lot more important.

Nathan stopped to collect his jacket and scarf and ran through the lobby, slowing only when he reached the pavement so he didn't slip on the ice. Snow was starting to fall, white flakes that would otherwise have been beautiful, but right now all he could think about was getting home. He needed to make things right with Jessica, because...

He jumped into a cab and gave the driver directions before leaning back in the leather seat, eyes shut as his fingertips started to defrost, painful heat spreading through his bones.

He loved her. Pure and simple. The reason she couldn't just jump on a plane and leave him was because he loved her. Which was why he was so embarrassed that he'd kept something so important from her.

His problem now was convincing her how he felt, and making her forgive him. He'd already lost one woman he loved, a wife who'd deserved so much more of him, and he wasn't going to make the same mistake twice. Meeting Jessica had been an amazing stroke of fate, but stopping her from walking out of his life wasn't something he was going to leave to the gods to decide.

"You having a good night?"

The cabdriver's question made him look up. He wasn't about to start sharing his life's worries with a stranger, so he just smiled and nodded.

"Good, thanks. Shame about the snow."

He also wasn't about to engage in small talk about the weather for the next twenty minutes, so he pulled out the paper folded in the pocket of the seat in front of him and pretended to read the front page.

Jessica swiped at the tears spilling down her cheeks, furious that she'd started crying. Her stupid emotions were getting the better of her, and she hated crying like some girls hated getting dirt beneath their fingernails. She'd fought the tears after her accident, refused to sob when she'd hugged her horse and left for the airport to go home, and now she was choking on tears that just would not stop. It was like a river flowing with no chance of slowing.

The sound of the front door opening and then being shut with a bang made her jump. *Please no.* She didn't want to see Nathan, had thought she'd be able to pack up her suitcase and leave for a hotel before he'd even left the party, but it seemed she'd underestimated him.

"Jessica!"

His deep, loud voice seemed to echo through the house, but she didn't answer him. Instead she leaned into the door for a second, eyes shut, breathing deep. She wiped under her eyes with the back of her fingers and patted her wet cheeks, opening her eyes only to look down at her dress. She'd kicked off her heels, but she was still wearing the satin-and-sequin number Nathan had bought for her.

"Jessica!"

This time she didn't have to answer, because he stepped into the room almost the moment her name left his lips. She folded her arms across her chest, the air around her seeming cool all of a sudden even though she knew it was warm.

"Jessica." He said her name softly this time, his eyes traveling from her to the almost full suitcase on his bed, then back to her again.

She had no idea what to say to him, where to even start, but at least what she was doing, or attempting to do, was obvious. Instead of talking, of looking at him, she crossed the room to take down the last things from the closet to fold in her bag.

"I know what Natalie told you," he said, standing as still as a statue. She could feel his eyes on her, knew he was watching her every move, but she still couldn't look at him.

"It shouldn't have been Natalie telling me," she managed, snatching her hand away when he reached for her. Then she stood away from him, anger replacing her tears.

"I'm sorry, Jess. You have to believe me."

She shook her head, fists clenched at her sides. "Your wife died in this house, the room down the hall," she said, "and you never thought to be honest with me when every other person in your life—every stranger, too, probably—knew what had happened?"

He dropped his gaze, shoulders slumping. She'd expected a fight, or anger when he saw her packing, but instead what she saw was defeat. Nathan knew how much he'd hurt her, and she hoped it hurt him like hell.

"You deserved better, Jess. I'm sorry."

"Sorry that I found out, or sorry that I ended up looking like such a bloody fool?"

He straightened and looked into her eyes, the defeated look replaced with something a whole lot stronger, more determined. She wanted to walk away, but she also wanted to slap him hard, to leave a red mark on his cheek that would sting and make him realize just how deeply he'd hurt her. But instead she dug her fingernails into her palms and stared back at him, refusing to look away. She might be angry with him, but she wanted him to know how strong she could be, even if she was crumbling on the inside.

Jessica didn't move when Nathan stepped forward, his hand reaching for her face, but she did flinch—she couldn't help it. She'd gone from craving his touch, loving his hands on any part of her body, to cringing at the thought of it. He'd betrayed her trust and she didn't want him so close, not now.

"I'm sorry because I love you, Jessica," he finally said, his hand falling to rest at his side. "I should have told you days ago, about Marie, and about how I feel about you, but I'm telling you now."

He loved her? Jessica took a deep, shaky breath and hugged her arms around herself. A few days ago, even this morning, those words would have meant so much to her, but now they just sent a fresh jolt of pain through her body, making the tears almost impossible to fight.

"Jess, say something," he said, holding out his hand and waiting for her to take it, the pain in his gaze reflecting hers.

She shook her head. "No," she managed. "How do I know you're not just saying that to stop me from leaving?"

His expression turned to anger—she could see the change in him. But when he spoke his voice was still calm, still even. "I know there's nothing I can say that will stop you if you want to go, but I'm not lying about how I feel."

She knew he was telling the truth, that he wouldn't, *couldn't,* lie about his feelings to her face. But she also didn't want to believe him, because walking away from the man already felt as if a knife had been thrust through her heart.

"Jess?"

"I just need some time to myself, Nathan," she murmured, turning away from him so he couldn't see the tears spill from her eyes and trickle down her cheeks.

"No," he said, his voice low before booming, *"no."*

She finished filling her suitcase even as she felt the change of energy in the room, could sense how furious he was. The next thing she knew, his hand had closed around her wrist and was holding her motionless.

"Let go of me," she whispered, wishing she wasn't so torn between wanting to hate him and wanting to throw herself into his arms so he could hold her and tell her again that he loved her.

"The weeks I've spent with you has been the best time of my life," he said, standing so close behind her, still with his fingers tucked around her wrist, breathing so hard that she could feel every exhale against her bare skin. "I tried to tell you, Jess, I did, but I just couldn't get the words out and then it seemed too late."

"Well you obviously didn't try hard enough," she snapped, hating the sound of her own voice.

The last few weeks had been amazing, but she needed to come to terms with what had happened, what she'd learned. And deep down she knew they were from different worlds, that if he had wanted to open up and be honest with her, he could have.

"I need some space," she said, refusing to turn back around. "Just let me go, Nathan. You need to let me go."

He slowly released her hand, and she sensed him step back, knew he wasn't standing so close to her anymore.

"I'll call a cab and have one waiting," he said.

She took a shaky breath. "Thank you."

Just when she'd thought he had gone, when she was ready to collapse onto the bed and sob, his deep voice echoed out.

"I was going to surprise you tonight, but…" He paused and she held her breath, waiting to hear what he was going to say. "Teddy's flight and quarantine have all been organized. He'll be back on the farm before the end of the month."

Jessica shut her eyes, fresh tears wetting her lashes for an entirely different reason this time. She turned, bravely facing him, pleased that he was standing in the hall instead of in the bedroom. *So this was what he'd been waiting to tell her.* With everything that had happened she'd forgotten all about the surprise he'd promised.

"Thank you." She'd told him not to do it when he'd offered weeks ago, but he'd gone ahead and done it anyway. She wanted to reprimand him, but the truth was that having Teddy home would be a dream come true, and she didn't want to argue anymore—she just wanted to go.

Nathan nodded, but before he turned to go she told him a lie, almost as much to convince him as herself. It was a barb that she wanted to sting when she told him, even though it hurt her just as much.

"It was only supposed to be a holiday fling. Just some fun, right?" It was what she'd told herself from the very beginning, even when she didn't truly believe it.

"It was *supposed* to have been, but you know and I know it turned into something a whole lot more than that."

He was right and they both knew it. The only difference was that he was ready to admit it and she wasn't.

Nathan stood silent and still in his kitchen, clutching the tumbler full of whisky that he'd just poured. He'd already downed one—his throat was still burning from drinking it in a single swallow—and he was almost ready to gulp the next when Jessica appeared. She was standing in the doorway, her suitcase at her side, her eyes red and puffy. Her usual spark was gone, replaced with a look that would haunt him forever, because once again he was responsible for making a woman he cared about deeply feel as if he didn't care one iota. And the reality couldn't have been further from the truth.

But there was nothing left to say. He'd told her how he felt, and now he was just waiting in case she changed her mind, in case she had something to tell him. What he'd done had hurt her, he knew that, and he should never have kept his feelings from her, especially not after she'd been so honest about why she'd never let men close. She'd been let down in the past and lied to by her father and a boyfriend, and that alone meant she deserved better. He'd known that, and still he'd hurt her.

Jessica walked across the room toward him, stopping at the table while he stood still at the kitchen counter. She glanced up at him, sadness like a veil over her face, and placed a key silently on the table.

It was over. He knew it was. And the worst part about it was that it was his own fault. Just as when his wife had died, he only had himself to blame.

"I'm sorry, Jess. I'm so, so sorry." His voice echoed out between them, seeming to boom off the walls. "If I could start over again I'd tell you, but I sure as hell wouldn't change what happened between us."

"Me neither," she murmured, folding her arms across her chest then seeming to change her mind and coming toward him.

She stood on tiptoe, painfully close to him as he stood with his fingers wrapped around the glass, trying not to squeeze it so hard that it smashed. When her lips touched his cheek, the soft press of her mouth against his skin, he shut his eyes, knowing it would be the last time she was this close to him. She was about to walk out of his life forever.

"Goodbye Nathan," she said in a low voice, walking backward then away from him as quickly as she'd come toward him.

He should have told her not to leave; he should

have told her one last time that he loved her; he should have done anything physically possible to stop her from walking out that door. Instead he stood as still and silent as a statue until he heard the bang of the front door.

Nathan shut his eyes against the fury building within him, threw back the double shot of whisky then hurled the glass across the room. His only relief was hearing it smash into a dozen pieces as it hit the wall and fell onto the floor.

Jessica was gone, and he only had his stupid self to blame. He shouldn't have been such a coward the day they'd gone to the market, because if he'd have told her then when he'd meant to, none of this would have happened.

He left the mess behind him and walked down the hall and into his office, staring at the place where he'd found Marie. It was a room he avoided like the plague these days, but the way he felt right now... he wanted to punish himself. Nathan dropped to his haunches, body suddenly fatigued, and then slumped to the ground with his back against the wall, head hanging between his knees.

It was then that the tears started to well, emotion catching in his throat so deep that it choked him. Everything he'd been through: the trauma of finding his wife, his heart attack, burying her...he'd never cried, until now. After everything, it was losing Jessica that tipped him over the edge, that pushed him to the brink.

A sob escaped from his mouth as the tears started

to fall and he surrendered to them, gave in to the overwhelming sensation that he'd lost absolutely everything he'd ever cared about.

Nathan sucked back a big lungful of air, trying to regulate his breathing and force the emotion away, focusing on replacing his despair with determination.

Jessica might need space, she might think this was over, that they couldn't ever go back in time and start over, but he disagreed. He'd spent his entire life never taking no for an answer, so why the hell should he walk away without a fight from someone he loved? Some people believed in letting someone go if you loved them, but not him. There was no way Jessica was flying away from him that easily.

He swiped the tears away and pushed himself up on his feet. All the money in the world couldn't make him happy if he wasn't with Jessica, and that meant he needed to face the facts about the life he was leading. *Starting now.*

CHAPTER TEN

JESSICA RAN HER HAND down Teddy's neck and across his back. His coat was like silk, dapples shining through his dark bay coloring as he stood patiently in the sun for her to fuss over. She still couldn't believe he was back home, and she made a mental note to phone her friends back in the UK to thank them again for taking such good care of him.

But it wasn't just Teddy putting a smile on her face.

Jessica wished she could tell someone, that she had someone to share her news with. *Or a particular someone.* Not a day went past that she didn't miss Nathan like crazy, no matter how much she tried to forget about him, tried to hate him for the way things had ended between them. Because every time something happened, her first thought was telling him— she could imagine the broad smile on his handsome face when she told her granddad's lawyer was going to be in court on fraud charges, and that she'd found a way to save her farm.

"I take it this is Teddy."

The deep, husky voice from behind jolted her from

her thoughts. *It couldn't be.* She waited for a beat, told herself she hadn't just imagined it and swung around...to find Nathan staring back at her. *Nathan.*

"You do realize this is the second time you've surprised me like this." She should have been angry with him still, but after not seeing him for almost a month, there was a part of her that was just so pleased to have him standing so close again. Especially now that she'd had time to think everything through over and over, when she'd truly believed she'd never, ever see him again.

He took a step closer and the smile that slowly crossed his face was cautious. "You can tell me to get lost, Jess, but I'd prefer if you'd hear me out."

She sighed and shook her head. "You've flown halfway around the world to get here, Nathan. I'm not just going to tell you to get lost." Even if she'd wanted to, she couldn't.

Now his smile reached his eyes, that familiar eye crinkle telling her how happy her words had made him. When he was happy there was no way to avoid noticing it.

"Will you hear me out?"

"How about we go for a walk down to see your old friend?" she suggested. "I have a feeling he'll be pleased to see you." And she could do with the distraction of walking.

Nathan went to move closer then obviously thought better of it, shoving his hands into his pockets and walking alongside her.

"Jess, what happened the night you left..." He

didn't finish his sentence straightaway, but he did look at her. "I haven't stopped thinking about it since. We were so honest about everything else, and I never lied to you about how I felt. Nothing I ever said to you was a lie, and I need you to know that."

Ditto. She chose not to reply, because she'd said what she needed to say the night she'd left, and even though she'd missed him like hell, she didn't regret being honest. He'd hurt her, there was no getting around that, even if she was prepared to hear his side of the story this time around. To understand why he'd kept something so important from her.

"What I came here to say is that I was an idiot for not being honest with you, and I can only imagine how stupid you felt being my partner at that party yet being the only person in the room not to know what had happened."

"I just thought I meant more to you," she told him, pleased she'd had so much time to think through what she could say. The night she'd left him, the only emotions she'd been capable of were hurt, anger and humiliation—the feeling that their friendship had been built on lies when she'd thought they'd shared everything with one another. Now she wanted to understand.

"But that's the thing, Jess," Nathan said, taking a few long strides to walk ahead of her then blocking her path with his big body.

He stared down at her, not letting her look away for a second, as if his eyes were able to hold hers in place forever. She stared into eyes as dark as the richest chocolate and resolved to stay firm, to not just give in because she still cared for him so much.

"You mean more to me than any other human being ever has," Nathan told her, his eyes never leaving hers, never even blinking as he stared at her. "I love you, Jess. I wasn't just saying it that night. I meant every word, and if I have to spend the rest of my life proving it to you, then I'm prepared to do exactly that."

Her heart started to beat a little too fast as hope built within her.

"What are you saying?" she managed to whisper. He was standing in front of her, all the way from London, and surely he wouldn't have come this far if he didn't mean it.

Nathan lifted one hand and reached out for her, taking hold of her fingers and gently holding them against his. His touch made her tremble, sent licks of shivers down her spine. In the month they'd been apart, she'd gone to sleep at night and dreamed of Nathan's hands on her, of being in his arms again with his mouth against hers. And then she'd wake and be so angry with herself for the way she felt, but now... now Nathan was standing before her, and she wanted to hear him out.

"I'm saying that I want to be with you, Jess. I will do whatever it takes, because the only thing I do know about my life right now is that I want you in it."

She took a shaky breath to give herself a moment to think, to consider what she was about to say instead of responding with her first thought.

"We have completely different lives, Nathan. I can't move to London."

He smiled. "I don't expect you to. It's why I'm standing right here."

She almost choked on her words. "You want to move here? To New Zealand? What about your job, your home, your..." Jessica was sure she was dreaming. There was no other explanation for what she was hearing. *And she wasn't even sure what she wanted, if she could open up to him again and truly trust him.*

"There's a lot we need to talk about, but I'm standing here because I want to be with you, no matter what." Nathan's other hand cupped her face, fingers gently stroking her cheek. "There's nothing in this world I want more than you."

Jessica pushed into his touch, indulging in having him close again, unable to resist. "Why don't we go see Patch, and you can tell me everything," she said, prepared to hear him out. After everything they'd shared, what they'd been through, she wasn't going to say no to listening.

Nathan knew this was his last chance with Jessica— if he even had a chance at all—and he was going to say everything to her that he should have said before she'd left London. He'd never given up on a fight in the boardroom, and he wasn't going to give up on Jessica until there was no hope left.

"I really don't know why I didn't tell you about Marie," he said, as they slowly walked across the grass. "If I'm completely honest with myself, I've been ashamed from the day I found her, and I guess I just didn't want you—" he forced himself to get the words out "—to think less of me. We had this connection, and I was scared of losing it if you knew it was my fault that my wife had died. That she'd taken her own life."

Jessica made a noise that he couldn't decipher, and he wasn't sure what it meant. Then she reached for his hand as they wandered slowly, her fingers tangling with his.

"I wouldn't have judged you."

He knew she thought she was telling the truth, but he wasn't so sure. "It's easy to say that now, because you've had time to think about it. You know me now," he said. "But what if I'd told you that first day when you found me with Patch? Or that first night we had takeout?"

She let go of his hand and folded her arms, and when he glanced at her she looked uncomfortable.

"No matter what you did, or think you did, you can't blame yourself for her suicide." Jessica's voice was quiet but he was relieved that she didn't sound upset or angry. "Your wife took her own life, Nathan, and I can't imagine what that was like for you, but if you blame yourself for it you'll spend your entire life torturing yourself by trying to figure out what you should or shouldn't have done."

He braved a smile. "You kind of sound like my therapist. *And* your granddad, if I'm completely honest."

"She must have been a very wise woman, huh?"

Jessica replied with a chuckle. "And I know that everything Jock said was always worth listening to."

Nathan laughed. "I didn't think so at the time, but she was the one who suggested I leave my job and travel to some faraway country, and here I am. Then I met Jock, and then I met you." He looked into her eyes. "And you were better for me than any therapist, Jess. You're the one who made me heal, who made me whole again."

Jessica didn't reply. The smile that had been hovering over her mouth disappeared as fast as it had appeared. He knew he had to talk fast, needed to convince her that things had changed. Maybe she was surprised that he'd confided in her grandfather, but if she was he couldn't tell.

"Talking about my job," he said, moving to walk slightly closer to her so her shoulder was almost brushing against his arm, "I've been tying up some loose ends these last few weeks, and I'm officially retired. From banking, anyway."

She stopped walking and spun around to face him, her eyes wide. "You're what?"

He put one hand on her arm, stroking her shoulder then tracing his fingers down her bare skin. When she looked away he touched her chin and tilted her head up so her eyes met his. "When I lived here, I was a different man. It wasn't just you who liked that guy a whole lot more. I did, too."

"You did?" she asked. "You'd honestly rather be here than in a posh house in Mayfair?"

It might have sounded crazy, but that was exactly

what he wanted. "There's nowhere in the world I'd rather be than right here, Jess. I want to move on, and I don't want to be some jerk more interested in work and money than people."

"And how do I fit into this puzzle? Are you looking for my approval so you can move on with your life?"

Her question hurt—like a knife being jabbed into his heart. "I want to be here with you, Jess, here in New Zealand. I know it's a little country, but I'm sure there's plenty of investments to be made to make it worth my while."

He'd said it as a joke but he could tell from the crease between her brows that she wasn't sure.

"I'm kidding," he said, still cupping her cheek and rubbing his thumb gently across the lower part of her cheek. "I'm moving here because I want to be with you. In case I haven't made myself clear, I love you."

Her eyes were still fixed on his, but she hadn't said anything.

"Jess?"

"You know, all these weeks, since I arrived home, I've done everything within my power to forget you."

He baulked when she paused. "And?"

She sighed. "And I failed miserably."

Nathan tried not to smile. "So does that mean you'll give me a second chance?"

She shook her head and then threw her arms around his neck, engulfing him in a hug that was so out of the blue it almost sent him tumbling.

"It means I love you back," she mumbled against

his chest, face pressed to him as she held him tight. "I've tried so hard not to, but I love you so much."

Tears filled his eyes followed by a choke that he only just managed to swallow. He'd put everything on the line, risked walking away from the only life he'd ever really know in London to move halfway around the world to be with this woman in his arms, and it had all been worth it.

"So can I pay the cabdriver waiting in your driveway and bring my bags in?" he asked, his lips against her silky hair.

Jessica burst out laughing and stared up at him, her mouth wide open. "What? You're telling me some poor driver has been waiting all this time?"

He shrugged. "Hey, the exchange rate was pretty good for me, so it's only cost me half of what you're thinking."

She rolled her eyes and grabbed his hand before standing on tiptoe and pressing an impromptu kiss to his lips. Nathan wrapped a hand around her back, the other cupping her head, not letting her pull away. Instead he gently kissed her again, loving the soft moan Jessica made when he dipped her back slightly, teasing her tongue with his and stroking his fingers through her hair.

"I think you should go pay that driver," she murmured when he finally let her go.

"Oh yeah?" he whispered, his voice sounding gruffer than usual.

"Yeah," she said with a laugh. "Then you can grab your things and come inside."

"Really?" he said, grabbing her again with both hands and tugging her tight against him.

"Uh-huh."

He crushed her mouth to his this time, no longer content with being gentle when he'd fantasized about this moment for weeks—what it would be like if she heard him out and actually gave him a second chance.

"So no more guesthouse?" he asked, his lips less than an inch from hers as she breathed heavily against him.

Jessica shook her head. "I think you've made it to the master bedroom."

Nathan dropped a quick kiss to her forehead as she laughed, then jogged backward for a few steps before turning to run. "You don't have to tell me twice!"

He slowed to a walk, listened to the sound of Jessica's laughter and took a moment to look around, to just breathe in the fresh country air and appreciate how lucky he was to be alive. A year ago he'd just lost his wife and had a heart attack—there was no imagining how different his life could have turned out if fate hadn't intervened and let Jessica cross paths with him.

He owed a lot to her granddad, but he owed even more to her. And he was going to show her just how much every single day for the rest of his life if she'd let him. Because without her, he had no idea what kind of life he'd been facing right now.

Nathan whistled a tune as he walked past the house and out onto the driveway, pulling his wallet from his back pocket and nodding to the driver, who was leaning against the cab waiting for him.

"So what did she say?" the older man asked him.

Nathan grinned. "I'm bringing the bags in."

They both laughed, and Nathan passed him a wad of cash.

"That's too much," the driver told him, shaking his head.

"Then call this your lucky day," he said with a wink. "You listened to me talk all the way from the airport and you've waited here all this time. Just promise me you'll do something nice with your wife tonight. Take her for dinner."

The driver shook Nathan's hand and thanked him, but Nathan wasn't going to hang around to chat. He already had a mental picture of Jessica lying on her bed, and had no intention of keeping her waiting.

CHAPTER ELEVEN

JESSICA STRETCHED OUT one arm above her head, the other draped over Nathan's bare chest. So much had happened in the weeks since she'd seen him, and not once during that time had she thought that she'd ever be in the same room as him again, let alone in bed with him.

"I can't believe you're here," she said against his chest, her lips brushing the soft skin just below his collarbone as she lay on him.

He made a grunting noise that she guessed was a laugh. It sounded like a loud rumble. Nathan's fingertips were playing across her skin, stroking in long movements up and down her arm. The sensation sent tingles through her entire body.

"I've been wanting to call you," he said, dropping a kiss to her forehead and holding her even tighter. "But every time I picked up the phone, I'd start to dial your number and then realize I had no idea what to say."

"A lot has happened since I came back."

He went still, waiting for her to continue.

"I hope you weren't coming here expecting a damsel in distress."

He pushed her back slightly so he could look down at her and into her eyes. Jessica tried not to laugh at the confused look on his face.

"You're talking about the farm?"

She laughed. "I know you probably thought you'd have to write a big check to save my home, but I've spoken to the bank and everything's safe." Jessica had only finalized the details with her new bank manager the day before and was still buzzing from the news herself. "I'm not going to lose the farm."

"So you don't need my millions then?" He kept his face straight for a second before grinning, kissing the smile off her face before letting her continue.

"I don't need so much as a penny from you, I'll have you know," she told him. "In fact, I'll even be able to pay you back for bringing Teddy home."

He shook his head. "Not a chance. That was as much a gesture for your granddad as it was for you."

She sat up, bursting to tell him her news. "You were right about the lawyer," she said. "The investigator you hired uncovered everything, and I've already pressed charges. The serious fraud office is investigating his practice and the business manager's firm."

"That's great news."

Jessica was smiling so hard her cheeks were starting to hurt. "I've got a long battle to get any money out of him, but one thing Granddad did retain was a property in Australia."

Nathan's eyebrows were drawn together and she grabbed his hand, trying not to babble in her excitement.

"He owned a property there that his lawyer must have thought was worthless, out in the middle of nowhere in Western Australia, and I've already had an offer in the tens of millions. They've found iron ore there, and I'm selling out to the highest bidder."

"You're screwing with me," Nathan said, laughing as he spoke. "You've got to be."

Jessica shook her head, nearly bouncing on the spot like she would have as a little girl when she was hyped about something.

"You're serious. You're freaking serious?" Nathan's eyes were wide, shining bright.

"Tenders close next week, and suddenly my bank thinks I'm a pretty important client."

Nathan held his hands on either side of her face, and her long hair tangled around them as they kissed.

"You deserve this, Jess. I'm so proud of you for figuring it all out."

She kissed him again, closing her eyes and savoring the taste and smell of the man, looking into his dark brown eyes and letting herself imagine that she'd be waking up looking into those very same irises for so many mornings to come.

"I knew Granddad wasn't losing his marbles, but with everything stacked against him I was starting to doubt myself," she admitted. "And I couldn't have done it without you."

"I believed in him. And in you." Nathan said. "I knew it would all work out, but a windfall like that?" He blew out a low whistle. "Now that shows the old man was sharp as a tack."

Jessica didn't want to cry, but just talking about Jock after everything she'd been through lately upset her. "He would have loved us being together."

Nathan's lips making a warm trail across her forehead made her smile, his mouth then caressing the few stray tears that she hadn't been able to blink away as they trickled to her cheek.

"We've both lost a lot, Jess," Nathan said softly, "but we're strong together. I promise I won't keep any secrets from you, not ever again."

She tucked her body even closer to his, tiredness like an ache in her bones as she shut her eyes. Sleep hadn't come easy to her when she'd first come home. Then, with everything going on, she'd had so much on her mind that it had been almost impossible to avoid the insomnia that had plagued her. With Nathan beside her, she had a feeling that was all about to change.

"So what are you going to do? I mean, for work?" she asked as she listened to the steady beat of his heart.

He chuckled. "You're worried I'm using you for your millions now?"

She swatted playfully at him, laughing when he grabbed hold of her wrist.

"I just don't want you to be bored, that's all." It was true; a little voice in her head was telling her that this gorgeous, successful man couldn't be happy just pottering around a farm all day every day.

"I'm still the majority shareholder in the energy drink company, and I just signed off on a deal to expand into Australia and New Zealand." He held her wrist more gently now and pressed a kiss to the soft skin below her pulse. "I'll find the new sites, do the startup, actually get more involved in the grassroots part of the business. It'll be a challenge, but it'll be a change of pace. I'll be home cooking you dinner by five each night, I promise."

Jessica gave in again to her sleep-deprived eyes, listening to Nathan's voice and smiling at his words. "So you're going to be my househusband?"

This time his laugh was a loud rumble against her ear.

"You'll be training again soon, and a star needs someone at home looking after her, doesn't she?"

Her smile was even wider this time. "You really believe in me, don't you?"

"Yeah, it just so happens that I do," he murmured against her hair. "I'll do everything I can to help you get there, Jess, and I'll be with you every step of the way."

Jessica drifted into sleep, the sensation of being lost to her unconscious leaving her in a dreamy state. She could hear Nathan's heart, could feel every inhale and exhale of breath from his lungs, and the gentle touch of his fingers against her skin.

"I love you, sweetheart. I think I have from that very first night we sat and talked."

She managed a little nod. "Me too," she whispered.

Something cool touched her hand, sliding over her finger. The sensation jolted her awake, eyes popping open.

"What…"

She looked from her hand to Nathan's face, unable to believe what she was seeing. A massive diamond adorned her ring finger on her right hand, sparkling even in the low light. The small ones that made up the entire platinum band were equally as bright, twinkling back up at her.

"This," he said, raising her hand and inspecting the ring, "is my way of saying that I want to be with you forever. When you're ready to tell me the same, I'll put a bigger one on your left hand."

She almost burst out laughing then stopped herself, realizing he was serious.

"Bigger than this?" she asked. "I'm not sure that's even possible."

His smile told her that he wasn't kidding, and she was kind of terrified by his bank balance, but right now all she wanted was to lie in his arms and stare at her ring.

"Thank you," she managed to tell him.

"For the ring? You're welcome."

She stretched her arm out as far as she could above her head so she could gaze at it. "Not just for the ring. For coming back here, for loving me, for…" She paused and turned so she was facing him. "For everything."

Now it was tears shining in Nathan's eyes. "You're

worth anything and everything," he told her in a deep, gruff voice. "One day soon you'll realize I'm the lucky one and you'll feel completely duped."

She doubted it. "When you say anything…"

He pushed up on his elbow and looked down at her, bending slightly to kiss her mouth, lips barely touching hers. "Anything."

"I think you could start by making me waffles."

"Waffles?"

"Yes, waffles," she said, wriggling against him and moving her lips to his neck, teasing him with wet kisses along his most ticklish spot.

Nathan groaned and she moved back to his mouth, playfully nipping his lower lip between her teeth. He let her away with it for only a second before grabbing her around the waist and flipping her, making sure she was pinned beneath him, holding her wrists down so she couldn't move.

"You asked for it," he growled.

Jessica squealed as he nipped her lower lip, then her earlobe.

"Nathan!"

He laughed as he slowly released her wrists, his big frame still keeping her locked in place.

"Jumping on a plane and coming here was the best thing I've ever done," he said, suddenly serious as he stared down at her.

Jessica reached for him, cradling his head in her hands as she met his gaze. He was right—arriving on her doorstep was the best thing he could have done. She'd saved her property and her horses, and she had her man.

"The only thing that would make life more perfect right now would be a career back in the saddle," she admitted, stroking his cheek. "I just need to keep reminding myself how lucky I am that I can walk, right? I could easily have ended up a paraplegic the way I landed."

Nathan's cheeky smile made her push him back a little so she could study his face more carefully. He was up to something, she could tell.

"What? Why are you smiling like that?"

"I can't just smile at the woman I love?" he asked, far too innocently for her liking.

"That's your up-to-no-good smile," she said. "Tell me."

He chuckled. "Let's just say that I might have organized for London's best sports physiotherapist to take an extended vacation in New Zealand sometime soon."

"Nathan!" She couldn't believe it—or maybe she should where Nathan was concerned.

"Hey, I had to have something up my sleeve in case you wouldn't hear me out."

Jessica sighed as he lowered himself further down over her, hands on either side of her head supporting his heavy frame. She might never get used to the amount of money the man was prepared to spend, but she wasn't exactly going to say no to anything that could help her get back competing again.

"I don't know how I'm ever going to repay you. Or thank you enough," she muttered.

His kiss stopped her from saying another word, although Nathan did pull back for a second.

"Believe me, sweetheart, I'll think of something."

Oh, she bet he would. And funnily enough, she didn't mind one bit.

EPILOGUE

JESSICA GLANCED UP as the first raindrop fell on her bare arm. The clouds were starting to swirl, closing in fast, and the sky was turning from light gray to black. She sighed and nudged her horse on, out of the arena and back toward the stables. Their training session was over.

"You did well today," she praised, patting her horse and smiling at the way his ears pricked up at her voice. "Good boy."

"How did he do?"

Jessica looked up at the sound of Nathan's call and saw him standing just outside the barn, protected from the now big plops of rain and watching her. She stifled her laugh at how at home he seemed on the farm—his jeans were worn, his stock boots were scuffed and he was wearing a checked shirt with the sleeves rolled up, showing off his tanned forearms. Completely different to the corporate, Hugo Boss–suit-wearing man she'd glimpsed in London.

"He's amazing. You wouldn't believe how hard he was trying for me," she called back.

She halted her new mount when she reached Nathan, rolling her ankles when she took them out of the stirrups before swinging one leg over the saddle and landing with a soft thud.

Nathan's hands were on her waist the moment her boots hit the ground, and he spun her around to kiss her. She kept hold of the reins in one hand, and the other snaked around his neck.

"Ugh," Jessica moaned as the rain started to soak her T-shirt. She ran the short distance to the stables; her horse trotted alongside her and Nathan jogged with them.

"You looked great out there."

She grinned at him. "Great enough to qualify for the World Equestrian Games?"

His smile matched hers. "Absolutely. You'll get there."

Jessica finished taking the gear off her horse, gave him a quick brush then threw his cover on, aware that Nathan was leaning on the stable door and watching her every move.

"I still can't believe I'm so close," she confessed. "It wasn't so long ago that I was told I might not ever be able to ride, let alone try this."

"Jess, if anyone was ever going to do it, you were."

She touched her back more from habit than because she needed to, still half-expecting the dull throb of pain that had niggled her for so long. Even though she'd stayed so positive, she'd still wondered if it was a pipe dream to even think about making a career of riding again. And yet here she was, on an amazing new horse and already selected to try out for the top team. The team she'd known all her life she was born to be a part of.

Nathan reached for her hand when she walked out of the stable, a look on his face that she hadn't seen before, almost as if he was...*nervous*. Her thoughts flipped from riding to him, wondering what he was thinking, why he was looking at her like that.

"Why do you look like you're about to tell me bad news?"

She took a step closer to him, about to reach for him when an even stranger look crossed Nathan's face. Jessica stopped and planted her hands on her hips—he was definitely up to something.

"Take a look in your brush box."

She went from worried to nervous, her heart launching into a fast beat, pulse racing. Why did he want her to look in her brush box?

Nathan tried to keep a straight face and failed when Jessica moved her hands from her hips and folded them across her chest, fixing her gaze on him. Her expression made him burst out laughing—she expected some terrible practical joke to be played on her.

"I promise it's not a dead rat, if that's what you're worried about."

She pressed her lips together in a look he was certain was supposed to be angry but was sexy as hell to him. He'd seen her truly mad only a few times, and each time he'd struggled to take her seriously because of *that* look.

"Nathan," she demanded, "why are you looking at me like that?"

He shrugged, resisting the urge to kiss the pout from her mouth. Or, better still, he could have scooped her up and carried her over to the hay so he could tease her out of that look.

"Stop asking questions," he said, deciding to just stand still and watch her.

Jessica moved slowly and Nathan leaned against the door of the opposite stable as she bent to look. He'd expected her to find it as soon as she finished her ride, but instead she already had a brush perched on the door and she just used that on Sammy. His plan had been all about surprise, until she'd gone and changed her usual modus operandi. He'd watched her for days and never seen her bypass the box full of brushes and hoof picks when she brought her horse in after a ride.

"Oh my god." Her words were barely a whisper the first time. "Oh my god!"

The second time she was squealing, frightening the life out of her new horse as she spun around, eyes wide with excitement. She stood there, a little box in her hands, not moving.

"Nathan, I..." She looked from him to the blue Tiffany box in her hands, cupping it like he imagined she would a baby bird. "Is this what I think it is?"

He took a step forward and touched under her chin,

tilting her face up just enough so he could kiss her, stroking his fingers down her cheek.

"Open it," he said in a low voice.

Jessica swallowed, visibly, before tugging the thick white ribbon and letting it flutter to the ground. She looked up once before carefully taking the lid from the box.

"I'm getting it all dirty and it's so pretty." Her voice was so soft he hardly recognized it.

"We can get you another box." He didn't care at all about the box—what he wanted was to see her reaction to the surprise he had inside of it for her, and then the answer to his question.

As she opened the box, her mouth parting as her jaw dropped, Nathan lowered himself to one knee, reaching for one of her hands as he did so. Now he couldn't have wiped the smile from his mouth if he'd wanted to. He stared up at Jessica's beautiful face as she looked from him to the ring. It was a five-carat pink diamond surrounded by smaller diamonds, set on a platinum diamond band—he'd had Natalie help him choose it and arrange to have it sent over. From the way she was looking at it, they'd chosen right.

"When you said you'd buy me a bigger ring one day…" She laughed. "Nathan, you're crazy! This is insane. Amazing, but still insane."

He ignored her, not about to start discussing why he'd spent so much on a ring when he was waiting to ask her something a whole lot more important.

"Jessica, every day I spend with you is the best day of my life," he said, running his thumb over the back of her hand as he held it. "There's nothing I wouldn't do for you."

The tears shining in her eyes made it hard for him to continue. All he wanted to do was wipe them away and cradle her in his arms, even though he knew they were happy tears, but he needed to finish what he had to say. If everything went his way, he'd have a lifetime of holding her when she needed him.

"Jessica, will you do me the honor of becoming my wife?"

Instead of the yes he'd been hoping for, she gasped out what sounded like a sob, tears now falling freely down her cheeks. This time he did jump up to fold her in his arms, holding her until she pulled back and looked up at him, her tear-stained face brightening with a wide smile.

"Yes," she told him, arms looping around his neck. "Yes, I'll be your wife."

Nathan scooped her up into his arms and kissed her as if they had only moments together instead of a lifetime. He moved his lips slowly against hers, then with more intensity, smiling down at her when she put her hand to his chest and pushed back a little.

"Nathan," she whispered.

He kissed her again then gently put her to her feet.

"This ring, it's too much," she told him, letting him take the box from her when he reached for it.

"Nothing is too much for you, Jess. Don't you get that? I'll spend the rest of my life trying to prove that to you."

She shook her head like she disagreed, but her smile gave away her true thoughts.

"It's beautiful," she said. "Probably the most beautiful thing I've ever seen."

Nathan carefully slipped it over her finger, admiring the way it sparkled when she turned it toward the light.

"If I can't spend my money on you then it's not worth having."

The eyes that met his, the love in Jessica's gaze as she looked from him to the diamond then back again, told him that she was worth anything and everything.

"I love you, Nathan. I love you so much."

"Will you still love me if I tell you that I want a wedding with just the two of us? No fuss, no guests, just—" he paused to consider her face, relieved she didn't look disappointed "—us?"

"Just you and me," she murmured back as she stood on tiptoe to kiss him.

Nathan held her tight as they kissed, walking her backward until her back was against the stable. He was about to pin her arms above her head, show her exactly what he wanted to do to her now she was his fiancée, when a head appeared over the stable door, and her horse nudged them apart with his nose.

"Sammy!" Jessica laughed as she tried to push him away, but he only became more interested in what they were doing, nibbling the edge of Nathan's shirt.

Nathan looked down at Jessica and shrugged. "So maybe it'll be you, me and the horse."

They both laughed and gave Sammy some attention. Nathan scratched him behind the ear, and Jessica blew on his nose before tickling him. Nathan might have to wait to have her all to himself, but he wouldn't have had it any other way.

* * * * *

MILLS & BOON®
By Request

RELIVE THE ROMANCE WITH THE BEST OF THE BEST

0917/05